THE BUTTERFLY'S WING

by the same author:

A Sense of Loss
Weekend

MARTIN FOREMAN

THE BUTTERFLY'S WING

THE GAY MEN'S PRESS

First published 1996 by GMP Publishers Ltd,
P O Box 247, Swaffham, Norfolk PE37 8PA, England

World Copyright © 1996 Martin Foreman

A CIP catalogue record for this book is available
from the British Library

ISBN 0 85449 223 2

Distributed in Europe by Central Books,
99 Wallis Rd, London E9 5LN

Distributed in North America by InBook/LPC Group,
1436 West Randolph Street, Chicago, IL 60607

Distributed in Australia by Bulldog Books,
P O Box 300, Beaconsfield, NSW 2014

Printed and bound in the EU by The Cromwell Press,
Melksham, Wilts, England

I.	Tom: Berkshire	9
II.	Andy: Near Cuzco	125
III.	Tom: Lima and Cuzco	235
IV.	Tom: Berkshire	249

This book is dedicated to the memory of
Francesco Silbano (1962–1993)

I
Tom: Berkshire

It's Tuesday, 2nd March; eleven months and fourteen days after you left here and eleven months and ten days after I last heard your voice. It's five o'clock in the afternoon.

I don't know where to start. I've spent half an hour looking out of the window and the other half writing rubbish and deleting it. It makes me nervous, this machine. Everything on the screen looks so real, so solemn. You'd laugh if you saw me tapping out the keys one by one. The number of mistakes I make! Next time I go into town I'm going to get one of those typing manuals that tells you where to put your fingers. Well, they didn't have computers when I was at school and I never saw the need for one. Remember you offered to teach me how to use it? For all the letters I never write? Maybe I should have paid attention.

Anyway, it's here as always on your desk, with that picture of us in Rio beside it, the one where we're sitting on a wall leaning against a tree. You're smiling and I'm screwing up my eyes against the sun. I dust them both every week or so and talk to them as if they were you. Telling you all the things that I would if you were here. And one day I thought I should write it all down, as a diary for when you come back, but when I took a pen and paper it didn't look right, especially with all the scoring out. So I started learning how to use the machine, feeling I shouldn't at first, because it's yours. Except I know you wouldn't mind.

So here goes. Tom Dayton's diary. For Andrew McIllray.

I got up at eight this morning, the same routine. Let Sheba out, made a cup of tea, fed the birds. Then I took a walk round the perimeter. Sheba rushed around as usual, but didn't find anything. It was quite warm — fourteen degrees on the thermometer and nine the night before.

Anne called when I was having coffee. I see her and George about once a week and she calls every couple of days. I don't see many other people — the shopkeepers of course and Doris if I'm walking past her cottage — but that's all. Eric and Dave call a lot. Then there's friends of yours like Guy and Kathy who ring up every month or so, but that's about it.

Most days there's something to do just to keep the place ticking over. I weeded the vegetable patch and went up to the copse after lunch for kindling. I cut up the old fir last year; it lasted most of the winter. I brought back bundles of smaller branches I'd left earlier. I thought about you as I was doing it; it was the one job you always enjoyed. I stopped about four, made myself a cup of tea and sat down here.

Things haven't changed much. The only difference is we've got no money. I lost my job last year. Fewer pupils means fewer school dinners, so they cut back on staff — me. I got some redundancy, but not enough. I had a hard fight to get Brian to pay enough of your salary to cover the mortgage. All I've got to live off is Income Support. There's still £1,000 in the building society, but I'm keeping that for an emergency. I'm trying to save money and live off the land — you'd be really proud.

That's it. Me, Sheba, the cats and an empty house. Like every time you went away. Only this time I don't know when you're coming back.

* * *

Wednesday 3rd March. The third day of sun today. Sheba and I walked down to the stream. It really felt like spring. The sun on my back and the stream high. Some birds singing, but apart from the woodpigeon I still can't tell which is which. The primroses you planted are about to come out. There were rabbits dotted all over the field opposite. I haven't seen any on our land recently, but I swear Sheba smells them; she was snuffling every hole in the ground.

I miss you, Andy. I miss waking up with you each morning and seeing you grumpy until you've had your tea. I miss your coming in and kissing me and pretending you're going to make supper.

I miss your calling from the other side of the world, that official voice you always use away from home. I miss everything about you.

* * *

Thursday 4th March. You were on the radio again this morning. BBC, part of a report on South America. Nothing has changed since the first day I heard. You hadn't called for a week, but that wasn't unusual. Then Brian phoned up one afternoon when I'd been out with Sheba and told me you'd been kidnapped by guerrillas. Shining Path. I'd never heard of them before.

My mind went blank for a moment, then I remembered the hostages in Lebanon and that made me think *Thank God you're still alive.* And Demotica's an international organisation, grass-roots, close to the people, as you kept telling me. They must be able to do something. They'll have contacts. They'll get you out. But Brian said it didn't work like that. They had to wait for the kidnappers to get in touch again. "You can't do nothing," I said, but you know how Brian is. He gave me a little talk about how it was a very tricky situation and no one could do anything until they had more information.

I put the phone down and sat staring at the wall. I didn't know what to think. I rang Anne at work and the way she said "Oh my God," when she's always so calm and quiet, worried me more than anything Brian had said. It hit me then that you were in danger and there was nothing I could do to help. She said she'd come right over. I didn't see the point, but after I put the phone down I was in some kind of shock and I was really grateful to see her. Not because she could do anything; just to be there. I spent the night at their place and the next day I went up to London to meet Brian and your parents and go over to the Foreign Office.

I got to Demotica about eleven. Everyone was very sympathetic and tried to tell me everything would be all right, even people I hadn't met before. Kathy said I could come and stay any time I wanted a break, which was nice, although I've never taken her up on it. Your Mum and Dad had come down overnight and were already there. It was a bit strange meeting them. I'd only met them once before, with you, and you remember the strain that was. Everyone trying to be polite, and all the time they were wondering what this was that you'd found under the woodwork.

Brian, your Mum and Dad and I took a taxi to the Foreign Office. There was a stone courtyard and a big wide staircase leading to a grey room at the back somewhere. There was nothing in it but an old desk, a filing cabinet and some papers on the mantelpiece. I thought Richardson was going to be stuffy and middle-aged, but he's younger than me. Brian introduced me as your "partner" and from the way Richardson looked at me I was sure he was gay. We all sat down and a girl brought us in some tea.

Brian told us everything he knew. This trip was no different from all the others. You were to meet a few people and attend a conference of community leaders. You'd been driving from Cuzco to some other town to see the local mayor and you, the car and driver had all disappeared. The next thing anyone knew was when the embassy got the letter saying you'd been kidnapped. Richardson showed us a copy. It was in Spanish, one sheet of typewriting. I looked at it and thought, there's a mistake; this has got nothing to do with Andy. Then I saw your name, Andrew Cameron McIllray, in the middle of all these meaningless words and it hit me again. You'd really gone, been taken by people I'd never met, never heard of, for no reason at all and there was nothing I could do.

Richardson said Shining Path were a group of Maoists who were trying to overthrow the government. They'd been strong in the 1980s, but now most of them were in prison and there were very few still active. Brian said he thought you'd been in touch with some of them. Then everything'll be okay, I said, but I was wrong. Brian said that it was probably because you knew them that you were being held. Then Richardson said he wasn't sure about the letter. He thought that Shining Path were more likely to kill you than kidnap you. Perhaps some other group were holding you. Your mother went on about how she was sure you were alive and once whoever was holding you realised there was no point in keeping you, they'd let you go. Richardson nodded and I knew she was barking up the wrong tree.

Your Dad asked what was being done to find you. Richardson said it was difficult for the government to do anything. Demotica wasn't a charity handing out food and clothing but a political organisation which had put quite a few backs up. Some governments didn't like your going around promoting democracy. The Peruvian government was one of them. It wasn't easy to put pressure on them and even if we could, they couldn't put pressure on the guerrillas. We would just have to wait and see.

That wasn't good enough for me or your parents. Your Mum asked if someone had gone out there to look for you and your Dad thought maybe some other government could do something. Richardson said that some enquiries were being made, but we probably had to wait to hear from the guerrillas. I thought Demotica could send someone out, but Brian said it might not work. Look what had happened to Terry Waite.

"What about publicity?" your Dad asked. "If we get it in all the papers, it'll put pressure on the guerrillas." Richardson said he doubted it. Brian said there was good publicity and bad publicity and once it had started, there was no way of controlling it. Of course the press would be told, but they would be asked to keep it low key. No mention of the fact you were gay. I started to argue; it was the 1990s and there were gay MPs and rock stars and everything. But your parents weren't happy about it and Brian and Richardson said there'd be a lot less sympathy from the public if they knew you lived with another man. I didn't like it, but I shut up. Everyone agreed to say you lived in London, so no one would come snooping around the village.

That was it. You were in the newspapers for a day or two. British aid worker — they got that wrong — kidnapped in Peru. They soon forgot you. It's like when some girl gets arrested in Thailand for drug smuggling. For a couple of days it's all over the front pages, then everyone forgets about her. Apparently there have been other kidnap victims that get even less publicity. Richardson told us of a whole family who'd been held somewhere in Africa for over a year. No one had ever written about them.

He showed us on a map where you'd gone missing, although they could have taken you hundreds of miles away. They could keep moving you around, although that would be dangerous; you're too obviously a foreigner, so you're probably near where they took you.

The next day I went to the library and borrowed a book on Peru. You know something? Where you were looks beautiful. There's this picture of Lake Titicaca and it's smooth and calm and the mountains on the other side are reflected in the water. They're tall and sharp and grey and covered in snow. There's an island in the middle with some trees. Everything is so blue; the lake, the sky. It was so calm and peaceful, like some kind of paradise. It seemed all right for you to be there, because if you were stuck there you could always look out and see that view.

Then I realised you might not be anywhere near the lake and even if you were, there could be all sorts of problems. You could be blindfolded or in a room with no window. Maybe you can't get to a toilet and maybe you're still wearing the same clothes they took you in. Then I read that even in summer it gets freezing at night and I worried if you'd be warm enough or catch pneumonia.

And if that wasn't enough, I began thinking they might torture you. Sometimes I still think that. I'm working outside or watching television and suddenly I see you screaming in pain. They're pulling out your fingernails or electrocuting you or beating you with sticks and they don't stop. I don't know who they are or what they're doing or why. I can't stop these pictures going through my head. I want to hit those people who are hurting you. I want to hurt them, kill them, shoot them, stab them, do to them what they're doing to you. And then I want to hold you and comfort you and kiss you and tell you everything's all right. If only I could.

I want so much for you to be all right. I want so much to be with you.

* * *

Sunday 7th March. I wrote so much the other day that my fingers and arms hurt. I was up half the night. I've got the manual now and I try to make myself use the right fingers for the keys. It takes longer than before, because now I've not just got to look for each letter but decide which finger I'm going to hit it with. Yesterday I swept out the henhouse and put in new straw. Then I decided to give the walls a coat of distemper. So this morning I had all the hens and Billy Joe locked up in the barn kicking up a row and Sheba prancing around in the yard.

It was while I was painting that it hit me that a year had gone by and nothing had changed. All the things we'd talked about — getting some animals, making it a real market garden — I'd just left, waiting for you to return. But I realised I couldn't go on doing nothing for another year. I can't afford to. I can't just let everything slip by. So after I'd finished and put the hens back and had dinner, I sat at the kitchen table with a piece of paper writing down all the things I thought I could do. I felt bad at first, because even though I'm the one that does the work, I never do anything without agreeing it with you. But you aren't here, and I've got to make my own mind up, so I sat up after midnight until I had a clear idea of what

I'm going to do. I'll make the vegetable patch about six times bigger. I can sell the produce to a wholesaler or to some of the shops in Newbury or Reading; I might even run a stall at the gate. And there's room for a pigpen to the right of the barn. I can fatten a couple up and sell them or keep the meat in one of the freezers. I might even get a couple of cows. It'll all be a lot of work, but I haven't been exactly busy for the last year. And it'll be something for you to return to, so you won't think I've been sitting on my backside all the time you were away.

* * *

Monday 8th March. George and Anne came over yesterday. Anne had her baby six months ago. Her name's Ada. Anne keeps asking me, don't I think she's beautiful. I pretend she is, but to be honest, I think she's as ugly as any other baby. What's surprising is to see George. You know how quiet he is. But he really loves that kid. He dangles her and plays with her and makes her laugh. You and I both thought Anne was the one who wanted the baby because she was almost forty. And now George turns out to be a natural dad; he's even thinking they should have another one.

They gave me Ada to hold. I hadn't wanted to before. I always thought she was going to piss on me or dribble. But yesterday she smiled at me and giggled and held my finger. I liked it. I suddenly realised, hey, this is someone, a real person, not a badly trained pet. Anne was watching and said she'd always believed I'd be good with kids and I got embarrassed and handed her back.

After they'd gone, the house was quiet and empty. I was alone again. I started thinking that maybe we should have had a kid; it might have made it easier for me with you gone. There's Sheba, of course, but she's just a dog and she'll always stay the same. She'll run around and wag her tail and slobber all her life, but a kid takes on its own personality. It's part of you and yet it isn't. And I wanted that. I wanted a son to tell things to, to teach, a son that was yours and mine, that looked a little like you, with fair hair and a frown and an occasional smile no one could forget. It was a strange feeling.

I started thinking that this diary was for that kid, so that he can know all about me — and you. Except he doesn't exist. But you do exist, Andy, and I miss and I love you.

* * *

Wednesday 10th March. I spent all day sorting out wood in the barn and drawing up plans for the sty. I haven't been so busy for months. I spent a year doing nothing, just waiting for you to come home. Day after day moochi ng about the house and the garden, keeping them tidy, but that was about all. Going into work until I got sacked. You know none of them asked about you? They didn't put two and two together. They knew I lived with a guy called Andy, but they didn't connect you with the guy in the newspapers. Mary — the short Irish one — asked how you were doing a couple of times and I just said you were okay. They must have thought I'd gone a bit strange, because I talked a lot less than I used to. I'd just go in, get the ovens going and see what was on the day's menu. Maybe that's why I lost the job. I was the only man and the others didn't want me any more.

I didn't do much over the summer either. Eric and Dave came down a couple of times. I think they kept me sane. You can't stop laughing when Eric's around. He doesn't stop talking from morning till night. We just sunbathed or drove down to the coast. They paid for everything; I had to fight to buy a round of drinks. We'd talk about you sometimes — still do when they phone; not like anything had happened to you, just like you were out of the room or off on a trip and would be back in a couple of days.

When autumn came round, I just curled up in front of the television. Like I told you, George and Anne came over, but I hardly saw anyone else. I spent Christmas with Eric and Dave — just the three of us, just what I wanted — and they came down for New Year. Dave's been promoted, runs the whole personnel section now. Eric's afraid he's going to be made redundant; there's another health authority reshuffle and he doesn't know if his department is going to go.

All year I kept thinking there was something I should do for you, but didn't know what it was. The first week I spent hours on the phone every day trying to find out what was happening, what was being done to get you out. Richardson kept saying that they were doing all they could and Brian said he'd asked a contact of his in Cuzco to make enquiries. But I soon saw that nothing was going to happen quickly. There would just be rumours and more rumours. And I couldn't afford the phone bill, so I stopped calling, except to your parents every couple of weeks.

Living without you wasn't difficult; it was just a permanent pain, like a headache or a missing limb. Even when I wasn't thinking of you, I'd be aware of you, the fact you weren't there, you weren't anywhere I could get hold of you or talk to you. Now it's a bit different. Maybe because it's spring and everyone feels better when the days get longer. Or maybe because I've got used to you not being here. But it doesn't mean that I don't miss you or don't want you. You're the most important thing in my life, Andy. You always have been; you always will be.

* * *

Friday 12th March. I couldn't sleep last night. I'd driven over to the garden centre in Reading and bought a new spade and hoe and a few other things. I looked at a mini-plough, but it cost over a thousand, so, surprise, surprise, I'll just have to use my own sweat and blood. Half the night I was lying in bed eyes open thinking about where I'd start and what I'd plant and that led on to what the hell was I doing living on my own in the country, with a lover kidnapped thousands of miles away.

When I was a kid in Runcorn, I never dreamed I'd live on a farm — if you can call a dog, three cats, two geese, half a dozen hens, a rooster and a vegetable garden a farm. I never really thought about what I'd do when I grew up. I suppose I thought I'd get a job in some garage or factory, get married, have a couple of kids and spend my holidays in Majorca. Instead of which, I ended up here.

I remember when I was about six years old I wanted to be a footballer. Not because I fancied football, but because Jeff and his mates were always going on about it and if your older brother's into football then you should be too. So like him I was an Everton supporter and knew all the players, but only because I felt I ought to, like learning the times table at school. If Everton were on television, I'd watch because everyone else did. Jeff and his mates would be there commenting on every pass while I hardly knew what they were talking about. It wasn't surprising; he was twice my age, but I sort of felt I was failing him by not knowing what was going on. When I was about eight or nine I lost interest in football, especially when Jeff didn't want me hanging around and wouldn't take me to any games. He would get pissed off with me following him around all the time and tell me to get lost and I didn't know what to do except sit down and cry.

I'd forgotten that. It would be a hot day in the middle of summer and Dad would be out somewhere and Mum would be at one of the neighbours' gossiping and Jeff would be off up the canal with his friends from school or hopping on the bus to go into town. When he was walking out the door I'd sort of leave with him, hoping he wouldn't notice. And he'd ask "Where do you think you're going?" and I'd say I wanted to go with him. He'd tell me no way and he'd drag me over to wherever Mum was and tell her to keep me out of his way. Mum would be annoyed and she'd tell me to go and play with the other kids my age. Which was the last thing I wanted to do. Most of them were girls and all they ever did was play dolls while Jeff was going to do something exciting like go into shops or have a fag or do things I couldn't even imagine. Sometimes Mum would hold me while Jeff ran off. I'd burst into tears because it seemed as if he hated me and Mum hated me too or she would have made him take me and it was hot and I was tired and unhappy and no one loved me in the world.

I never got over that feeling. Being alone. I just got used to it. I still feel it these days. It's only when you're here that it goes, that I feel all right with the world.

* * *

Sunday 14th. I've been busy. On Friday morning I borrowed a book from the library on market gardening. In the afternoon I started digging up the new bit. It's about a hundred feet by thirty. I almost gave up after a couple of hours. Even with a pick and the new spade it was hell on my back. I've been back at it since and it's much easier. I just need the exercise. I thought about buying that mini-plough again, but muscles are cheaper and look so much better. At least they will do when I get them.

On Friday night I sat down with a piece of paper and drew a diagram of what I was going to plant where. There'll be more potatoes, cabbages and onions and I'm going to try a whole lot of new things, like broccoli, asparagus and parsnips. It's not going to be easy. I'm sure it'll be different growing a load of decent vegetables to sell rather than a few greens for you and me to eat. If I'm to do it properly, there's a lot of things to learn and the book will take me ages to read. There are tools like aerators that I don't have and can't afford and things like the quality of the soil that I know nothing about. I'll just have to play it by ear. I'll get there, in the end. Just wish me luck, lover, and sun during the day and rain at night.

* * *

Monday 15th. It poured all day. I couldn't work in the garden, but I'd already decided that any free time I had I'd spring-clean. The whole house, top to bottom. I started with the attic. I went in thinking, right, I'll throw out half this junk, we never use it, but of course I didn't. I just tidied it up. I stacked the furniture and sorted out the stuff in the drawers. There were some old clothes of mine that I've brought down for one of the charity shops and some spare bedclothes I'd forgotten about. Mostly it was box after box of stuff of yours. Newspapers and books from university and documents from World Aid and Demotica and all sorts of papers. More personal stuff as well, like job applications and a whole bundle of diaries.

Then there were all your souvenirs. African statues, wooden fruit, cloth from God knows where and guidebooks from all over the place. I tried to sort it out some way, into size or different countries, but I soon gave up. I couldn't remember where half of it came from. A lot was from before we met, but even the stuff you got recently I couldn't remember where you'd bought. It was always the same; you'd come back from India or Kenya, show me things that were nice enough but nothing special, like a block of wood that someone had carved or an oil-can that had been made into a child's toy. You'd give it pride of place on the mantelpiece or on your desk. Until a couple of months later you'd be off to Thailand or Japan and come back with something else. Everything got shifted round and bit by bit it all ended up in the attic. Where it's now sitting neatly gathering dust.

All kinds of thoughts went through my head while I was looking at your souvenirs. Like the fact that we're so different. You collect junk; I throw it away. I'm a drama queen — five minutes' anger and it's over. You hardly lose your temper, but when you do, you sulk for hours. I talk rubbish; you talk sense. You've got lots of friends and I hardly know anyone. You like to travel and I hate to go anywhere. Then I got to thinking that if you didn't have itchy feet, if you had the kind of job where you came home every night, where you didn't spend half the year on the other side of the world telling people how to run their lives, this wouldn't have happened. You'd still be here and I wouldn't have spent the past year alone.

I got so angry with you that I wanted to hit something. I wanted to throw all your souvenirs out the window — except there's only the skylight. So I punched the floor and not only hurt my hand but got a splinter in it. That calmed me down. I came downstairs and got the splinter out and cleaned it. And once I'd done that I was hungry so I made an omelette and just sat there thinking of you. I remembered that I loved you for all the reasons that had made me so angry. I love you because of who you are. I love you because you care, because you help people. I love you because you make a difference, because there are people alive because you got food to them and there are people with jobs because you helped train them. And I love you because you come home to me. I love you because you're handsome and your body smells good. I love you because you make me laugh and I love you when you're determined and angry. I love you because you bought this house and land for both of us. I love you because you love me, because you want to spend your life with me.

And I hate the fact that you're not here and I'm alone night after night after night and I can't hold you and tell you I love you. And I hate you and I love you and I hate you and I love you and I love you and I love you so much.

* * *

Wednesday 17th. Anne came over in the morning. We sat in the kitchen for an hour over coffee and talked. Or she talked. Ada was at someone else's house. Anne was wondering whether she should go back to work. It was partly the hassle of finding someone to look after Ada full-time and partly that she's fed up with being a social worker. She's getting old, she says. She wants to be a stay-at-home mother, but she feels guilty living off George. She said it wasn't fair to make him earn a living for both of them. I said I didn't think he was the type who preferred changing nappies to making serious money. She laughed and said she knew he would be quite happy; it was more a problem in her head than in his. Anyway, I told her I was hardly the person to give her advice since I've more or less lived off you since we met.

Eric phoned this evening. Upset because Dave has just announced he wants a non-monogamous relationship and Eric's not sure whether it's the first step towards a divorce. We talked a bit and he admitted what you and I always knew — that both of them always had an eye out for others, even though they'd never done anything about it. Dave just wanted to take advantage of it before he grew too old and both of them are sensible enough always to take precautions.

It felt odd reassuring Eric for a change. I told him not to worry, although I'm not sure what it means either. I know that if I ever wanted anyone but you, something would be wrong. But I seem to be different; lots of gay men stay together while having bits on the side.

* * *

Thursday 18th. I can't keep away from this machine. I just want to write down whatever comes into my head.

When I first saw you I thought you were a prick. Standing there in the Brief with a glass in your hand laughing too much. I was there on my own, pissed off with the world. It had been a hard day at the cafe and I was tired but didn't want to go home. The Brief was full of the usual trendy young types whom I'd seen before but never talked to. I was half-drunk squashed in a corner because the bar was filling up and you were a Hooray Henry six feet away. You looked at me a couple of times and I stared back. We both agreed afterwards that I had a fuck-you expression, except I meant fuck off and you meant let's fuck.

And when you came over to speak I was just about to say fuck off. All I saw was a guy a few years older than me, my height, not particularly handsome, wearing a collar and tie, about to give me some boring pick-up line. Which it was. "Can I buy you a drink?" I said yes just to spite you. So you brought it over and asked if I wanted to join you and your friends. I did, because I had nothing better to do. And, although I wouldn't admit it, because I was lonely and at the back of my mind I fancied you. And you and your friends turned out to be all right. You introduced me to everyone and made me feel part of the group and no one stared at me as though as I was just a pick-up.

When the others walked off at closing time there was just me and you. I looked at you and thought, he's not bad-looking. But I wasn't in the mood to go home with you. Another time, perhaps. You told me afterwards you weren't sure what to do. You didn't know if I was the type who wanted to have sex on a first date. If I was and you didn't ask, you might not see me again. If I wasn't and you did ask, the same thing might happen. So you said you were tired but could we meet again? I gave you my phone number, although I wasn't sure you were going to call. Still, on the tube home I kept thinking about you. I was in a better mood than I'd been for months, simply because someone half-decent had come up and spoken to me.

You know all that, of course. You know everything about me and you still love me. That's why I can't stop loving you.

* * *

Sunday again. Time goes by so quickly. But I've sown half the new garden and covered it with netting. I probably haven't done it right. By digging up the earth I've probably just resown the grass, so when shoots come through I won't know which is vegetable and which is weed. We'll see.

I've also cleared out the junk in the barn so I can store the vegetables when they're grown. All the stuff the previous owners left that we'll never use I've dragged to the gate, like the bed and the mangle. I'll phone the council tomorrow to get them to come and pick it up. I finally chopped up the chest-of-no-drawers for firewood. The next stage is to work out storage. What kind of shelves do I put up? How deep are they? Do I make or buy them? You think it's easy to make a simple decision like growing spuds or sprouts and don't realise all the work you're getting into.

Today I'm resting. I thought of going to see Eric and Dave, but they said they'd be out for most of the day. I called Peter and John but only got their answering machine. Then I called Anne to invite myself over but her sister and kids are visiting and I wasn't in the mood to play Uncle. I watched television for a while, but there's nothing on now except football and a Disney film.

Actually, I was thinking about kids again, wondering if I'd really like to be a father. Probably not. It sounds like a great idea at first, but it's not something you can do for a while and walk away from. You've got to be there every day for twenty years. And at the end of it, there's no guarantee you're going to like your kid or he's going to like you. But whatever happens, whatever he does, you've got to like him, you've got to love him. Otherwise there's no point in having kids at all.

Not that that stops people having kids and getting tired of them. That's what happened to Dad; he just got up and walked away. I was ten years old and came home one day — late, because it was summer and I'd been up by the canal — and found Mum in a foul mood in the kitchen. She'd been drinking. "Your Dad's gone," she said. I didn't know what she meant at first. "He's bloody left me. He won't be coming back." I just stood there, not as surprised as I might have been. "Is it a woman?" I asked, but she didn't know. It didn't matter anyway, she said; he always was a selfish bastard.

I think Dad left because he didn't want the responsibility of a family. The only thing he cared about was karate and his mates. He had this big macho thing about keeping fit and being able to defend himself. He was in the Territorials and always going off training somewhere. He'd never been around much. "Y'all right, son?" he'd ask when he saw me and that was it. If he wasn't going to be there any more, I felt something was missing, but didn't know what. When Jeff came home that night and heard that Dad had gone, he just shrugged his shoulders.

Mum was always there, but she wasn't happy. She'd had Jeff too young and thought once he'd grown up she could do all the things she missed out on looking after him. But then I came along and she had to bring me up too. So she spent her days just smoking and drinking and gossiping. She wasn't a bad mother — she always made sure we had enough to eat and were wearing enough clothes and she taught us good from bad — but she wasn't perfect either. By the time I left home it was too late for her to do the things she wanted and she was too old to find a man that didn't have a wife and kids of his own. So she just carried on smoking and drinking until one day I got a letter from Jeff saying she was in hospital with lung cancer and before I had time to go up and see her she'd died.

When you're a kid, you don't realise you're unhappy. You think everyone's family is the same. Your brother doesn't want you around, you're not sure if your Dad's going to be home tonight or what mood your Mum's going to be in when you get back from school. Things weren't much different for the other kids I knew. Some of them had more money and things like expensive bikes, but those were the ones I didn't like so I didn't care. The only place where life seemed perfect, where all the kids had parents who loved them and lots of adventures where everything turned out all right in the end was on television, so it didn't count; it was unreal, just a dream.

So the part of me that says I'd like a kid is just like my Mum and Dad. When it happens, it's too much trouble. You've got better things to do than look after it twenty-four hours a day. And think about the kid you and me would have. It's bad enough growing up with gay parents, but with you where you are and me with no money and no children nearby, it'd be hell for him. Company for me, but hell for him. If it was a girl, it would be worse. I wouldn't know how to look after a girl; I wouldn't know what to say.

* * *

Wednesday 24th. Yesterday was the anniversary of your disappearance. When I woke up and remembered, I felt angry and depressed. For a year I'd done nothing but sit at home. I'd let you down. If I really loved you, what I should do was get on a plane, fly out to Peru and look for you. Then I thought about all the problems about being in a strange country. If there was no one to help me and translate for me I wouldn't have the foggiest what to do. I could hardly stop passers-by and ask where Andy McIllray was being held. If Demotica and the government can't get you out, there's nothing I can do, except wait and keep the farm going until you come home. But it's not enough.

You were in a lot of the papers. I've cut out all the articles and pasted them into a scrapbook I've started, along with this diary. None of them said anything new. They still think you live in London and there are a couple who've got your age wrong. There were some quotes from your parents and Kathy and Brian. The *Mirror* calls Kathy an old girl-friend; is there something you haven't told me? The Foreign Office claims that strenuous efforts are being made for your release. If only it were true.

When I'd been through all the papers, I sat for a while in the front room trying to remember as much as I could of you — the way you stand, the way you talk, the way you hold a glass or move about. It was difficult. I had to look at your photo, the one I had blown up of you on your birthday. You're standing with your back to the sink in the kitchen. White shirt, jeans, hands in pockets. You're looking straight at the camera and laughing. You've got everything you need to be a pop star — short blond hair, blue eyes and an expression that looks straight into you — but you're just a bit too old. Then I tried to remember the last time we talked, when you were in Lima and you told me there'd been a power cut. You told me who you'd been meeting and where you were going that afternoon. And that was it.

I didn't work very much; every so often I'd stop and find myself thinking of you. In the evening Brian and your parents were on tv. Your Mum looks worried and old. Your Dad's so British, stiff upper lip. He's sure you're coping, keeping your spirits up. "Andrew knows the language, he's lived rough before." That kind of thing. All the heavy questions were for Brian. He couldn't give any details but both governments were doing all they could to get you freed. "Bullshit!" I shouted at the screen. "No one's doing a fucking thing." There was a statement from the Foreign Office. No interview; not even Richardson. They should have had the Foreign Secretary, or even the Prime Minister. But you're not important; Peru's not important. You can rot as far as the government's concerned.

That was it. The newsreader moved on to some factory in Yorkshire that's going to close and you didn't exist any more. The BBC have done their bit. Now everyone can forget you for another year.

I got angry because it should have been me on that screen telling the world what had happened and what needed to be done. They need to send someone undercover or send in the army. Look at all that money spent on Salman Rushdie. He's worth protecting; why aren't you? Because he's famous and you're not. Maybe if they saw there was someone who loved you, someone who cared, who needed you, they'd get off their arses and do something. But nobody knows I exist and so not one fucking thing is being done to get you free.

Anne called. She wanted to know if there was anything they hadn't reported. I said there wasn't. I must have sounded down because she asked if I was all right and if I wanted them to come over. I said no, because although I was feeling lonely, the only person I wanted was you. With other people around, even Anne and George, it's too much effort. It's easier to be in a bad mood on your own.

Then Guy phoned, the first time in a couple of months. He was really apologetic that he hadn't kept in touch, but he'd had problems with his lodger and been changing jobs. He wanted to know if there was anything he could do. "Get Andy out," I said. I shouldn't have been so rude, but he wasn't offended. He offered to come down and visit for a couple of days if I wanted company. I was a bit surprised. He's your friend and I've never been sure whether I liked him. But I was sick of being on my own, so I said okay. He'll be down the weekend after next. In case things don't work out I warned him that I spend all day working and wouldn't have much free time. He said he'd give me a hand. Well, we'll see.

When I went to bed I had dreams about seeing you on television. I reached out for you, but my hand hit the screen and I woke up half angry, half crying.

* * *

Thursday 25th. The second time Richardson invited me and your parents up to London, in May, I thought there must be some news. He wouldn't get us to make the journey if there wasn't. His office looked just the same, kind of lost and meaningless. He told us what they'd learnt so far. Almost nothing. There was a thick report that we could read but couldn't take away. We had to sign the Official Secrets Act and not tell anyone about it. It was all in official language and said absolutely nothing. People were unwilling to talk because they were Shining Path sympathisers or because they were afraid of Shining Path. Or because they didn't know anything or didn't care.

Brian told us that a Peruvian representative from Demotica had finally got in touch with someone from Shining Path, or what's left of them. He'd apparently admitted that they were holding you, but he didn't know where. Brian had sent a message saying Demotica wanted to negotiate, but nothing had come of it. We just had to wait and hope you'd be released soon. Richardson tried to reassure us that we'd get more news soon, but I didn't believe him. And that's the way it's stayed ever since.

After we left and Brian had gone back to Demotica, your Mum and Dad took me for a meal in one of these steak houses in Shaftesbury Avenue where they charge the earth. All pink tablecloths and waitresses who can't speak English. I felt really sorry for them. There they were — an old couple whose only child was being held prisoner on the other side of the world. They might never see you again. And all they had to remember you by was me — not even a wife and kids, just a Merseyside queer. Your Mum apologised if they'd been rude when we first met. She'd never really understood your being gay, she said. It had hurt both of them, but they'd accepted it was your life to do what you wanted and they couldn't stand in your way. I think she'd rehearsed the speech on the way down to London, but she meant it and I tried to think of something suitable to say.

The whole meal was about you, nothing but you. Mostly your Mum talking, but sometimes your Dad. What you were like as a kid, the school you'd been to, when you'd first started travelling, how they worried about you. It made me realise how much they loved you. I'd never known. You hardly ever talked about them much and you never told me that you loved them.

I found myself talking about you in the same way. Not the intimate stuff, like the way you smell and the way we have sex, but things like your mood in the mornings and the tv programmes you like to watch. I told them how we'd met and what we used to do when we lived in London. How we chose Sheba and where we bought the chickens and geese.

It was the middle of the afternoon when they went back to King's Cross and I got the tube to the bus station. Now that I'd got to know them, I was almost sorry to see them go. I haven't seen them since then, but we talk every so often on the phone. We don't have much to say, but I'm glad they call. Sometimes I think I'm reassuring them, although I don't do anything. It's your Mum who finds it difficult to cope. I wish I could help her, I really do.

* * *

Saturday 27th. You can see how much I write on this machine. It's becoming much easier. I'll never get all the fingers right, but at least I try. I've even started experimenting with other programmes. The spreadsheet's fun, but I don't know enough maths to use it. I started working out how much money I'd make if I sold a cabbage a day and the programme told me I'd end up earning £25,436.79 by the end of the year!

I meant to write down every day what I was doing, but you can see I haven't. It's boring. The weather's been good, but it's too early for any of the seeds to show, and at the end of the day I don't want to sit down and put down every little thing I'm doing, like I've finished digging up the new patch of garden or I've been reading about pig-keeping and trying to find out whether or not we need a licence to sell eggs. If anything important happens, I promise I'll write it down.

I miss you, but you know that. I'm going to bed. Wish me — and you — pleasant dreams.

* * *

Sunday 28th. I've been thinking about you and when we met. After that first time. You'd called a couple of times and I wasn't in. I'd meant to phone back but kept putting it off. Then one evening you rang while I was in and we talked for half an hour. Mostly you asking questions. Where I worked, what pubs I went to, did I go to the cinema? I thought you were a nosy bugger, but I didn't mind. I didn't want you to hang up. You had this quiet, calm voice and you really wanted to talk to me. You told me afterwards you had to keep asking questions because otherwise I wouldn't say anything. I did ask you what you did for a living, but it didn't mean anything to me. Project Development for World Aid, you said. I'd never heard of it. When you said it was a charity, I thought it meant you sent out medicines and sacks of rice and flour, but you said it was more like organising teachers and community workers.

There was a kind of pause and I thought you'd decided you didn't want to meet me after all. Then you asked if you could meet me at the cafe the next Saturday afternoon, at the end of my shift. I didn't realise how nervous I was that day until I looked at the time and saw you'd be there in quarter of an hour. It had been one of these days when time flies past and I hadn't had time to think about you. I squeezed into the toilet and sniffed under my arms and tried to wipe away the sweat with toilet paper. I'd brought a spare t-shirt to put on and I was in the middle of changing when Mark knocked on the door and said a handsome stranger was asking for me.

You stood there on the other side of the counter in a check shirt and old leather jacket. Had no one told you the clone look had been out of date for years? To tell the truth, I was a bit disappointed. You looked better than you had in the pub, but not as good as I'd imagined on the phone. You had this cold expression, standoffish. I think like me you were shy. We both kind of smiled stiffly and I said goodbye to the others and we stood in the middle of Soho wondering where to go.

Soho hadn't yet gone gay, so the only place we could have a drink was at the Brief. Then we went to the cinema and saw that film about the useless lawyer. I was laughing away when I felt your hand on my knee; I turned and saw your face in the darkness. You weren't a pin-up, but you weren't bad looking; you were just quiet and strong and serious and masculine. Almost without thinking, I put my hand on yours. And in a way I forgot about you for the rest of the film; it was just enough that we were touching each other.

We drove back to your place to eat. I sat at the kitchen table watching you boil pasta and make a salad. I offered to help, but you said I'd had enough serving food all day. We talked about this and that and you told me about university and work and living in Brazil.

I didn't understand a lot you were saying. There were things that were obvious to you that I knew nothing about. I knew there was famine in various places, but I couldn't point to a map and say where each country was and I had no idea whether it had mountains and monsoons or deserts and diarrhoea. I'd never even known that diarrhoea was such a problem. But I was interested because I wanted to know about you, what made you tick. I could see how important it was to you to do things for other people. You went on about how World Aid wasn't enough. You wanted to change your job to do something bigger and better, but you weren't sure what.

All through dinner I was half eating, half listening to you and half wanting to push everything aside and reach out and kiss you. It wasn't just your eyes but your lips and the fact that your shirt was open, just waiting for me to reach inside and feel your warmth. I didn't even think about what would happen next; it was enough just fantasising holding you. Of course we ended up in bed together, although I don't remember the details — just waking up late in the morning from the deepest sleep I'd had in months. I looked round the room, saw all the books, the pile of dirty clothes on the floor and loved it; it was welcoming, like home. We got up and had breakfast and there we were in the kitchen sitting stark naked when Keith came in, after you'd sworn he'd gone away for the weekend. You were cool, I was embarrassed and he just laughed.

It was stupid, but right from the start I was in love. I hadn't learnt anything from John or Alex. Not true; I'd learnt a little. I was afraid you might not be in love with me, but I trusted you not to hurt me, not to lie to me. I could have been wrong. You could have been a bastard but I suppose it was third time lucky. That first morning I didn't say what I felt; I didn't want to frighten you off. I just left about two o'clock saying I had a whole lot of housework to do. It was bollocks, of course; I'd done my share the day before.

You don't know how much that first evening meant to me. I was twenty-six years old, everything had gone wrong in my life. I'd wanted to end it all and suddenly you appeared. To think I'd almost told you to fuck off! It would have been the stupidest thing I'd ever done. The last five years have been the best in my life. Well, not the last year, but it's been better knowing you were there than being totally alone. It hasn't always been easy but it's always been good. It's always been wonderful just being in love with you.

* * *

Tuesday evening. I told you; once I get started, I can't stop. It all wants to come out. Sometimes I'm in the house in the middle of the day and I see the machine and there's something I want to write down and I think it'll just take a moment. I have to stop myself because I know it won't.

I've done some more spring-cleaning in the last couple of days. I've been right through the spare bedroom. The same thing — I wanted to throw out a lot of stuff and couldn't because it was yours. That chest of drawers, for instance; we could easily keep the sheets in the cupboard in the hall. Then there's your collection of posters; you're never going to put them up and they just sit there under the bed gathering dust. Anyway, I hoovered and dusted everywhere and moved some of the pictures around. The one of the fishermen that your grandmother gave you is now in the living-room, above the fireplace. I never liked it before, but now it reminds me of you. Not because it's yours, but because it's men in danger fighting to come home. The abstract that always irritated me, all those red and yellow stripes, is now in the spare room at the back. I'm sure Guy'll love it when he comes to stay.

That's my life. Not very interesting, is it? I wonder what you're doing, whether you're thinking of me. I've told you: sometimes I imagine you tied up and tortured. At other times I see you in this bright room, looking out over Lake Titicaca. Maybe you've got some books or newspapers to read. You might even have a radio. If you're lucky, you're just sitting there, relaxed, because everything's so calm and peaceful. At least that's what I hope.

* * *

Thursday 1st April. Eric phoned yesterday. He's a bit more relaxed about Dave. He thinks everything's going to work out. Dave's away on business next week and Eric's already planning which clubs he's going to go to. He wanted me to come up and join him. I said I couldn't leave the livestock. I made him promise to come down, the two of them, one weekend soon.

It seems so long ago now, living with them. Three years in Leytonstone, getting the Central Line into town every day. I was lucky to find them, although I didn't know it at the time. They looked after me; they made me welcome. I wasn't just a lodger. Talking to Eric last night made me realise how good they'd been to me.

Today's been dull. Clouds, wind and showers. I didn't do much. Weeded, worked out how much wood I'd need for the pigpen. I've already marked out the ground. I wanted to get back to this diary. It's becoming like a drug, writing about you and me. It's all I've got of you at the moment. I've been trying to remember what we did the first few times we met, but I've forgotten most of it. I know I was desperate to call you after that first night but I was afraid to. I didn't want to sound too eager. And I didn't want to be disappointed. I could have called and you would have been polite and I would have kidded myself that you really fancied me and it would hurt all the more when I realised it wasn't true. If you called me, it would mean that you really wanted to see me again. But you didn't call; you came into the cafe again, which I hated. I couldn't talk to you because I was serving. I looked a mess and because I was busy and nervous I probably sounded like an idiot. At the same time, I was pleased you were there, even if you'd timed it wrong, because I was just starting a shift, not finishing. So we arranged to meet the following evening. After you'd gone the staff who hadn't seen you before were going nudge, nudge, wink, wink, where had I picked you up and did you have a brother. I was both embarrassed and pleased. If they thought you were good-looking, I must be doing something right.

I don't remember what we did that time, or the next or the next. It was usually going to the cinema or eating out, ending up at your place afterwards. We had a few drinks, of course. I wanted to take you to all the gay bars in London, so everyone could see what kind of guy I was with. You used to drink that awful low-alcohol beer. There always were things about you that were naff!

Each time I met you it got better and better. It was funny how you changed. You'd started off as this snooty prick with a big nose and sour expression and you'd become this handsome, down-to-earth guy with a wicked sense of humour. And for some reason I couldn't understand, you wanted me. Everything was perfect. The only problem was I couldn't keep my hands off you. I wanted to have sex all the time, but at the same time I wanted just to talk to you, just to be with you. Have these deep, meaningful conversations about Third World debt and the purpose of life while fucking you stupid.

I remember a Sunday morning after we'd been to Heaven. The curtain was half-open and the light had woken me up. You were sprawled on my side of the bed as usual, head on the pillow, mouth open. I looked around. There was the usual mess on the floor, a spare amplifier and speakers you'd dug up from somewhere and were meaning to sell, and my bag open on the chair. But the thing I really noticed was that your breath stank. And that made me love you. It was a symbol of something, God knows what. It brought you down to my level, made you more human, made me realise that in some ways you were just like me. And because you were just like me, you really could love me as I was. I didn't have to pretend to be someone special. I could just be me. It was wonderful, that feeling.

The other day I tried to describe you in words, but deleted it. All I get is a series of measurements. You're a little taller than me — six foot. You've got fair hair, blue eyes. You're clean-shaven, with quite a thin face. You weigh about twelve stone. You've got a good body, but not too many muscles. You've got some hair on your chest and a lot on your legs. I love your armpits and your arse. Your cock is brown and stubby when soft and just the right size when erect. But whatever I write doesn't say how attractive or handsome you are. It doesn't explain why I want to hold you and be held by you. It doesn't explain why I love you, how happy you make me feel.

Before that Sunday morning I hadn't been sure how much I meant to you. I thought you might just see me as an easy lay. I was afraid that if you saw what I was really like you'd lose interest. That was why I took so long to invite you back to my place. I mean, you had this nice flat of your own in Hampstead and all I had was a room in Leytonstone. I had some tacky pictures on the walls, a few fashion magazines and that was it. And I wasn't sure about Eric and Dave. They were my closest friends, but Eric was as camp as Christmas and I thought if you met him, you might think I was like that too. Dave was all right but a bit too intellectual; if you came over, you might spend more time talking to him than to me.

But you made me invite you over and that kind of set a seal on it — on the two of us. I spent hours that morning making soup and roasting a chicken for dinner and the four of us sat in the kitchen all afternoon getting roaring drunk. We all got on like a house on fire. God knows what we talked about; I remember Eric and me slagging off some drag act we'd seen and you and Dave saying she was the best on the scene. There were a whole lot of other things, but what mattered was the fact that you kept looking at me and smiling and I realised that you really did want me. That made me happier than I'd ever been. That night we went to bed and talked and talked and talked. I told you a lot of things about me that I hadn't mentioned before — about Mum and Dad and John and Alex and everything else. And finally we made love and it really was love and for the first time I told you that I loved you.

* * *

Tuesday 6th. I'm sorry. I got caught up in so many other things. Richardson phoned on Friday to tell me another meeting had been scheduled in Lima. It was the first I'd heard from him in over a month. He feels things are improving and it may become easier to get hold of whoever's holding you. But he's said that kind of thing before and nothing has happened.

Guy came down on Saturday morning. He's older now, got much less hair and is putting on weight. He arrived about eleven with bags full of stuff from Tesco. I'd told him he'd have to bring some food down, but I hadn't expected him to bring as much as he did. There were piles of things I can't afford to buy: salmon and expensive cheeses and even champagne. He brought a whole load of packets and tins and frozen food that'll keep for ages. I wanted to pay him for it, but he refused. Well, he can afford it more than I can and I need every penny I can save.

I never really liked him before. Partly I was jealous; you'd known each other so long. In Hampstead, every time he came round for dinner, the two of you would drink a bottle of wine each and start talking about all sorts of things that I wasn't interested in. Politics and philosophy and religion, him cleaning his glasses and you leaning back on your chair. Half the time the two of you'd be making sense, half the time you'd be spouting rubbish and all through it you'd be name-dropping. I'd get pissed off, especially if there were other guests there. We all had to listen to it.

But on his own, he was quite different. He was quiet and considerate. He asked how I was getting on; he said he was as worried about me as he was about you. He made lunch while I finished tidying up the garden. Over lunch he told me about his new job as head of some AIDS charity. He gets to meet MPs and different Royalty, not just Di. In the afternoon he helped me put up shelves in the barn and then we walked round the perimeter. He kept throwing sticks for Sheba, but she just looked at him and wagged her tail with a big grin on her face. She wouldn't fetch them even for me. It was just before sunset and there was no wind. We stopped at the copse and looked over the fields. They were just bare earth with trees at the far side, but it was so calm and peaceful I felt somehow different. Like whatever was going to happen, it would be okay, we'd get through. It had something to do with Guy being there, not so much him but the fact there was someone beside me, someone who cared.

On Sunday I thought he'd lie in, but he got up with me to feed the birds and we finished the shelving in the barn. In the afternoon we whitewashed the north wall. We talked about the two of you at university. I'd heard most of it before, but I liked hearing it again. I'd always had the impression that you were the same in Edinburgh as you've always been, only younger, but Guy says you weren't. He says you were a mixture of shy and pompous. He admires you a lot, says your work is very valuable; it makes me proud to be your lover.

In the evening I got out all the old photos and we looked at them together. You as a kid in your school uniform. In some park, nineteen, twenty years old, baby-faced with ridiculous long hair and baggy jeans. I wouldn't have fancied you then: you were too young and naff. But you have the same smile and the same body and I can imagine you pompous all right, trying to put the world to rights. I kept the photo out and stuck it on the mantelpiece. I'll find a frame for it sometime.

On Monday we went for a drive and ended up in Portsmouth. It was a bit cold but we went for a walk along the front. It was strange. It was the kind of thing I would have done with you or with a whole group of friends. Doing it with Guy was almost like we were a couple. On the one hand we weren't but on the other hand we were, because we'd spent the weekend together and I was feeling close to him and less lonely.

He wanted to know everything being done for you. He thought all sorts of things were going on that the press didn't report, like villagers being bribed to talk or the army putting up road blocks or a reward being offered. Well, if all that's happening, I said, I don't know about it.

He wanted to know why there wasn't a national campaign, like there'd been with the Lebanese hostages. Because Brian and Richardson don't think it's a good idea, I told him. "But it's been over a year!" he said, and I began to feel bad again because he made me feel that there were lots of things I could be doing for you and I wasn't doing any of them. Then he apologised and said he just felt frustrated and he was sure I felt even more frustrated than him. And he felt guilty because he'd been so busy in the last year that he hadn't done anything for you.

I was sorry to see him go. Before he left, he asked if he could come back and I said sure, any time. Odd, isn't it, how people change, or maybe it's only the way you think about them.

* * *

Wednesday 7th. New resolution — to keep it short and keep you up to date.

I spent the morning in the garden. In the afternoon I finished whitewashing the barn. Same weather — clouds, a bit milder.

I've started clearing out the bedroom. Your clothes are gathering dust. I thought about packing them away but I couldn't bear to do that. I've been wearing some of them. That dark blue shirt, for instance. The right sleeve got torn when I was out with Sheba — it got caught on a bush by the road. Forgive me?

I've started using your weights. Outside at the back of the house where no one can see me. It feels like I'm really putting on muscle. You won't recognise me when you come back.

* * *

Thursday 8th. Cooler today, lots of rain. Slugs in the cabbage patch.

Richardson called. The meeting in Lima he'd told me about has been postponed. He was really apologetic about it. I found myself telling him how much I missed you and he said he'd feel the same if Craig — his "partner" — was in the same position. It was the first time he'd said he was gay.

It's almost midnight. I can't keep away from this machine. I can't stop thinking about you. I can't stop wanting you, worrying about you. I don't know where you are or what's happening to you. You're lost in the middle of nowhere and I can't help you. I'm useless. You're all alone and I'm doing nothing to get you freed.

One day I'll go over there and find the bastards who are holding you and hurt every one of them. Torture them, kick them in the balls, punch them till they bleed and scream and beg for mercy. Except I won't show them any mercy. I'll just keep hitting and hitting and hitting till they're bloody and sobbing and crying. How can they do it? How can the bastards do it? How can they keep you for so long? How can they fucking do it?

I love you, Andy. Whatever happens, I love you, I love you, I love you.

* * *

Friday evening. I got almost nothing done today. I had a surprise visit from Jack Burns. He arrived about quarter to twelve, while I was working on the sty. I heard a car on the drive and saw this red Ford come in.

He's not like your other friends. He's got a loud voice and thinks he knows everything. He had a couple of days free before he started his new job and he'd come down here on the spur of the moment. I took him in and we had some coffee and then I made lunch while he sat and talked. He said he hadn't seen you for years. He wasn't sure how much you or he had changed. He's given up working for charities — he thinks they do good work but he's become too selfish, looking after number one. His new job's in recruitment.

We talked all afternoon. He wanted to know the whole story — what happened, how I had heard, what was being done to help you. He wondered why there hadn't been more publicity and I had to go into the whole gay bit again. It was obvious he wasn't gay and he was trying hard not to be prejudiced, but he still said some stupid things, like he expected me to be bed-hopping every night. Then he wanted to know if you slept around when you were on a trip. I said it was none of my business. I should have said no; he probably thinks you fuck like a bunny and I'm too polite to say so. I was getting a bit fed up with his questions so I asked about him about his private life. He's living with a girl called Eleanor. You wouldn't know her; he only met her a couple of years ago. She runs a record store in the West End.

I showed him round the farm. He left about six o'clock. I was getting tired so I was glad he went. He gave me his phone number, asked me to call if I was ever in London. By the time I'd given the birds their evening feed, the light had almost gone. I left the sty for tomorrow. I just brought in the tools and made dinner, watched television for a bit — *Roseanne* and *The Word* — then sat down at the computer here. Another day gone by. Another day I miss you.

* * *

Sunday afternoon. My day off. I finished the sty yesterday! Congratulate me. I don't think it'll fall down. I'll give it the first coat of creosote tomorrow. By the end of the week I'll have the fence up and then it's pig-buying time.

Anne called, in a bad mood with George, something to do with him working late instead of looking after Ada. Guy called to say hello. The weather was a bit warmer. Now that the clocks have changed the evenings are lighter. I take Sheba out to watch the sun go down. She's curious about the sty. I don't know what she'll think when these strange animals come in. Do dogs and pigs fight?

You know what's been on my mind for the last few days? You having sex when you're away. I think you do, but I'm not sure. I don't ask and you don't tell me. But you did say right at the beginning that you'd never promise to be faithful and sometimes when you were on one of your trips I'd be sitting at home watching television and I'd suddenly wonder what you were up to. It wasn't the sex itself that bothered me. I was more afraid you might catch AIDS or get mugged. Sometimes I thought you might meet someone more attractive than me. You'd always gone for foreigners before and I thought it could easily happen again. Then I told myself that if you fell for someone, you wouldn't be with him for more than a couple of weeks before you had to leave him and come home.

Some people say that you can be turned on by someone without being in love with them — that's why some guys fuck around so much — but I can't. The only person that turns me on is you. There are lots of attractive guys that I don't fancy because they're not you — they may have the same looks or the same body, but they don't have your mind, the way you think and talk, the way you care for people and for me. There hasn't been anyone since I met you; there never could be.

Making love with you was telling you how much you meant to me. Fucking you and being fucked by you were different ways of giving you pleasure, trying to turn you on so much you would never, ever want anyone else. It wasn't all for you, of course. I was turned on too. Sometimes I hated to be a man and have only one orgasm at a time; I wanted to come inside you and have you come in my mouth and have you fuck me, all at the same time, all without stopping, long into the night. We did our best, but it never quite happened that way.

By the time we moved here sex had changed. It had become quiet, unhurried, comfortable. We did it less as well, two or three times a week, maybe, instead of every night. I suppose it's the same for every married couple. But if you came home now, it would be like the first time we met; I'd be desperate for you, desperate not to let you go, desperate for it to go on forever.

Maybe I should delete this; it's too personal. It says too much, and yet it doesn't say half of what I feel.

* * *

Monday 12th. Dull, showery. I couldn't creosote the sty, so I started the foundations for the fence. I've marked where they'll go and dug the first half dozen.

At lunch I went over to the market in Reading to look at piglets. Not to buy, just to get a feel of the place and check prices. I thought it would be full of farmers saying "Ooh, arrh," but of course it wasn't. They're just businessmen. It shouldn't be difficult choosing. I'll go back next week to look again and the week after I should be ready to buy.

* * *

Thursday 15th April. It's getting better now, but the last three days have been the worst in my life and I'm worried what it means for you. Guy says everything may be all right. It may blow over and nobody'll hear a word of it in Peru. I should just write it down so you can read it when you come back. If you ever come back. I might as well. I can't sleep and I'm not going to take any more pills. I'd be out in the garden now trying to put it to rights if it weren't cold and if I had a proper light. I hate them. I hate every fucking one of them.

It was your "friend" Jack Burns. Only I should have known from the start he wasn't a friend. I should have known from the way he talked that he'd never met you, that he'd never worked for World Aid or any charity, that he didn't give a damn about you or me. He was simply a bastard out to make money by stirring up as much shit as possible.

The first I knew was when Guy rang on Tuesday morning. I was out creoseting the sty and I was pissed off because he'd dragged me in and I was getting creosote on the phone. He asked if I'd seen the *Sun*; there was an article about you and me. There were a lot of things in it that weren't true, but I shouldn't worry too much. I should get a copy and call him back when I'd read it.

I didn't know what to think, driving into the village. So there was an article about you; that was nothing new. It was about time the *Sun* printed something. The woman in the shop didn't react when I walked in. I got back into the car and opened the paper. There it was on page seven — colour photos of you, me and the house and a big headline: "SECRET LIFE OF BRITISH HOSTAGE: GAY LOVER TELLS ALL. A SUN EXCLUSIVE by John Bretherton." Underneath there were smaller headlines like "McIllray plotted coups by day and seduced boys by night" and "Tom sits at home wondering if he'll ever see his globe-trotting lover again".

It didn't seem to make any sense. There was your name and mine, but I couldn't make head or tail of the words in between. I took a deep breath and started again, reading each sentence very slowly. It was really difficult to concentrate. I felt I was walking against a really strong wind or I was trying to do something simple like boil an egg while being slapped around the head.

It went on about how the *Sun* had discovered you were gay and lived with me in the country. You travelled first class round the world and had wild parties everywhere you went. You're particularly fond of Japanese but you'll sleep with any man. I'm just a pathetic queen who sits at home all day. I'm in love with you because I have a thing for strong men who abuse me. It had all sorts of quotes from me that I didn't say, like we'd moved here because I didn't want you spending all your time in the gay bars in London, or you'd given me half the house on condition that I did all the housework.

There was more. Demotica is really a left-wing pressure group. You're unstable and reckless: you knew that you might get kidnapped when you went out to Peru and you did nothing to protect yourself. Some Peruvian says you just wanted to meddle in his country's affairs. The British government's spent hundreds of thousands of pounds trying to get you back.

Then there's a photo of you I hadn't seen before, at your desk at Demotica; it makes you look like a supercilious git. There's a photo of me working on the sty that must have been taken from the road with a long-distance lens. I look like an idiot with my mouth hanging open and my eyes blank. There's a caption under the photo of the house saying "Lonely Tom waits and waits".

I sat in the car going slowly out of my mind over all the things that were lies or not quite true. I tried to think where they got all the information from until I realised "John Bretherton" was Jack Burns. I didn't know what to do next — sit there, go home, phone Brian or drive to London to the *Sun*'s offices to make a scene. Then I remembered Guy had said to call him after I'd read it. So, very carefully, because my hands were shaking and I couldn't think clearly, I drove home.

The phone was ringing as I walked in the door. A woman from some news agency, calling about the article in the *Sun*. Could I answer a few questions? I sat there, not quite understanding but saying "yes", "no" and "uh-huh". Then it clicked that she was just another journalist and I said I didn't want to talk and put the phone down. It rang again, this time a man from Radio Oxford asking if I was free for an interview that afternoon and I panicked and told him to fuck off and slammed the phone down. It rang again and I didn't even listen to whoever it was but picked it up and left it off the hook.

My mind cleared a bit. I had to ring Guy, but thought I should look at the article one more time. I sat there reading every word. It's here along with all the other articles, in a special box. It didn't hurt so much now that I knew what it said; it just made me angry that people could write such things that weren't true. Then I remembered what everyone had said about not wanting the guerrillas to know you were gay. I know they don't read the *Sun* in Lima, but it only needed one Peruvian in London to read a copy and somehow tell the people who were holding you that you were gay. I remember reading somewhere that they kill gay men in Peru. And I thought if they didn't kill you, they'd could do all sorts of things. I once heard that the Nazis tortured gay men by raping them with broomsticks.

By then I was really in a state. I called Guy and he was really good. He asked whether I'd been bothered by phone calls or visitors. I told him about the phone calls but I hadn't thought about visitors. He said he'd be surprised if at least a couple of reporters didn't turn up. He was more than right, it turned out. He thought

I should come up to London for a few days and stay in his flat where no one would know where to find me. But I couldn't leave the animals. It wouldn't have been fair to ask Anne and George to look after them if there were going to be reporters bothering them. So Guy said he'd come down. I didn't see the point at first, but he said I needed someone to deal with the press. I couldn't just call the police to send them away. Then I heard a car outside and told Guy. He told me not to let them in. That made me realise I needed him; I couldn't handle this alone.

There was a hammering at the door and I saw a face peering in through the front window. It was a woman in a dark jacket with nasty little eyes. Sheba started barking. I put the phone down, suddenly really uptight. The hammering didn't stop. The woman was staring at me from the window. She smiled and beckoned me towards the door. I wanted to kick her teeth in. I thought about ignoring the knocking or opening the door and getting Sheba to bite her or whoever was out there. But Sheba's too friendly and if she did bite someone, she'd get put down. I wondered where the geese were, why they weren't making a noise, then I remembered I'd locked them in the barn while I was creosoting. So I shut Sheba in the front room and went to the door. There was the woman and a man in a leather jacket. The phone started ringing and Sheba kept on barking. The woman said she was from the *Mail* and could she come in and ask a few questions. The phone kept ringing and Sheba kept barking and the man stood back and started taking photographs of me and the house. I was about to blow my top when I remembered how calm Guy had been and that he would be here in a couple of hours. So I said I had nothing to say and would they please leave and slammed the door.

Sheba shut up when I let her out again. I picked up the phone and it was the BBC. I told them I wasn't speaking to any reporters and put the phone down. Outside, I saw the people from the *Mail* looking around. The photographer was about to trample on the cauliflowers. I went to the door to shout at him but the woman was nearer. "We just want to get the facts from you," she said. "We'd be willing to pay for an exclusive story." "What's so exclusive about it?" I asked, "the whole world seems to know." She came back over to the door but the man had wandered off behind the barn. "Tell him to come back," I said, "he's got no right to walk on our land." She said he was just getting the feel of the place. I said I had nothing to say, if she really wanted to get you out of Peru the best thing she could do was go back to London and leave me alone.

I went back and the phone was ringing again. I ran upstairs and lay down on the bed, staring at the ceiling and wishing the whole world would just go away. It was like the day I'd heard you'd been captured except now you were being held hostage by guerrillas and I was being held hostage by journalists. It got worse and worse. More reporters turned up. I watched them gather outside. They walked round the house, all over the land. From time to time one of them knocked on the door but I didn't answer it. The telephone never stopped ringing. I picked it up, because that way I felt more in control. There was the BBC again, the *Times*, the *Independent*, some foreign news agency. *Sky* said they'd send down a camera crew to ask me some questions. I said I wouldn't speak to them, but they sent one anyway. I didn't answer the phone while I made myself some coffee. It was a stupid idea; it just made me more jittery. And because I hadn't eaten, I had to go and piss. Standing there, I imagined all the reporters could see what I was doing. It was like being in prison, with warders watching your every move.

Brian called. He'd been trying to get through all morning. He was a bit uptight, but knew it wasn't my fault. Bretherton had called him a couple of days before, pretending to be a friend of yours. He was annoyed with what they said about Demotica, but people were always trying to discredit them. I don't give a fuck about Demotica, I almost said; all I cared about was you. He tried to reassure me. He said it was your politics Shining Path were interested in, not your sex life. I hoped he was right.

Guy turned up around half past twelve. There were about a dozen people outside and half a dozen cars parked on the driveway and in the road, but they'd left the space in front of the door clear and Guy just drove up and got out. As I opened the door to him they all came rushing up. He turned and said something like: "Mr Dayton will have a statement for you shortly. Please leave the premises until then." That didn't stop them shouting questions, but it meant that once he was inside they left us alone.

I was so glad to see him. He'd brought some sandwiches and fruit for lunch, and we ate in the front room with the curtains closed while he worked out what to put in the statement he'd promised. He said we had two choices. We could hope the whole thing would die down or use it as an opportunity to launch a campaign to get you freed. He wasn't sure that the kidnappers knowing about your being gay was a serious problem. Anyway, now it was out, nothing could be done about it.

It was good having him there. He knew just what to do. He sat at the computer and typed out a statement from me saying the *Sun*'s article was an invasion of privacy, but now the story was out, I was happy to confirm that you and I had lived together for five years. No other details of our private lives would be available. I was grateful to the British and Peruvian governments for the efforts they were making on your behalf, but considered there was an opportunity for a broader-based campaign for your release. I would welcome some privacy and Guy Spesson, a friend of yours for many years, would answer any questions on my behalf.

The phone wasn't ringing so much and Guy called Brian and Richardson and read them the statement. They didn't have any objections. By ten to three we'd printed out twenty copies. I put on better clothes and we went to hand them out.

I was really nervous and at the same time quite calm. We opened the door and all these people gathered round. There were two television cameras, as well as photographers and journalists with tape recorders and notepads. It was kind of strange going outside after being stuck in all day. Guy read the statement and I stood with my hands at my sides trying not to fidget. Then everyone started shouting questions. Guy took control, letting first one, then another speak. Some of the questions were quite serious but others, like "when did Tom first realise he was gay?", were so pointless that Guy just refused to answer. Finally he said, "That's enough, no further questions."

* * *

It's Saturday. It's taken me two days — nights, really — to write it all down. I thought everything would sort itself out after we gave them the statement, but it didn't. Only a couple of cars drove off. I could see the rest standing around in little groups. Two men were sitting on the sty. I hoped it was the bit I'd creosoted, because I wanted them to get tar all over their clothes. Guy said they were working out how much they could offer for an exclusive story, and he was wondering whether it would help. On the one hand it could mean publicity and money to start a proper campaign for your release. On the other hand, we couldn't guarantee the right message would get across and people might think we were just being mercenary. In the end we decided to go ahead; we needed the money and we would just have to do our best to get our message across.

The phone had been ringing off and on and Guy finally answered it; it was one of the reporters outside using his mobile phone. I could see him in the yard. He was from the *Express*, offering £5,000 if I'd agree not to speak to any other paper or tv station. Guy said I'd think about it. The phone rang again and there was someone at the door and Guy dealt with them all while I went back upstairs with a splitting headache, wondering how long it would go on. Then there was a call from your father, who was very upset because reporters had been on to him and your mother asking what they felt about having a gay son. Guy told him everything that had been happening here and he calmed down.

Guy and I sat and talked about the different offers. Or he talked and I listened. Finally we agreed that I'd speak to the *Mail*, on condition that I could also appear on the BBC and could talk to any other newspaper in a week's time. For that we'd get £40,000 to start a campaign fund for you. So the couple that had turned up first came in and I spent three hours talking to her while he took photos. We sat in the front room and she set up a tape recorder and opened her laptop. It got sent to London by modem and half the story appeared the next day, with the sequel on Thursday. Wednesday's paper has a big picture of you on the front page — the one of you at the party that I like — and on the double page spread inside there's one of the house and one of me sitting on the sofa. I don't look bad — I'm wearing that green sweater of yours and a pair of jeans and look like a young farmer. You'd even fancy me. On Thursday, you're on the front page again and on the inside there's a photo of you as a kid and the one of the two of us together in Brazil.

The story isn't bad. Instead of making us out to be perverts, it treats us like any other married couple. Guy said there was no point in the paper emphasising the gay aspect because we were so obviously "normal"; the real story was you being held hostage. There were a couple of things I wish I hadn't said, like how unhappy I was before I met you and the fact that I didn't really understand your work, but they don't matter. There are quotes from your parents and even some minister at the Foreign Office. There's even a short interview with Brian about Demotica and how you important it was to promote European-style democracy worldwide.

The BBC wasn't too difficult. I was on the lunchtime news on Wednesday morning. Guy had stayed the night and drove me up to London. I was feeling slightly dopey because he'd given me some pills to help me sleep, but by the time I got there I was feeling much better. They put make-up on and took me into the studio and sat

44

me down opposite Moira Stuart. Guy had told me just to relax and keep my answers short. It was quite easy, actually. She was efficient and friendly, like Kathy but not so fierce. She asked when had I last heard from you and what was being done for you. That let me say the bit I'd rehearsed, about it being time for a broader campaign to bring you home. I saw myself on video and decided I looked a bit stiff but hadn't done badly.

It wasn't all good. There were articles about you and me in other papers even though I hadn't spoken to them. The *Sun* did a story on all the countries you'd worked in for World Aid or Demotica. It said that in every country you'd been to there were still dictatorships and starvation and so on. Guy said it was sour grapes, but it still made it seem as if you weren't worth rescuing. And the *Times* had an article about Demotica which Guy said wasn't very helpful either. One or two of the other papers had quotes from people in the village about how we kept ourselves to ourselves and how it was a nice quiet place and they didn't want us bringing lots of gay people down from London. But there were some good things as well; the woman writing in the *Telegraph* said I was a friendly, good-looking young man.

On the way back from the BBC I thought it was all over. I could get back to the garden and the sty and everything else. But of course I couldn't, because Guy started talking about the campaign to get you out. He was saying there would be things like meetings and conferences and press releases and I'd have to spend a lot more time in London and travelling around the country. I felt guilty because I didn't want to do it and yet I knew I had to if it was the only thing that would get you free.

There were three cars sitting in the drive when we got home. As we got out all the journalists came up asking questions. There was one with a Scottish accent who kept shouting questions like "Has Andy got AIDS, Tom? Mr Spesson, this is the second night you're spending here; can you comment on the relationship between yourself and Tom?" Guy had warned me not to say anything, but I couldn't stop myself telling him to fuck off. "That's not very nice, Tom," he said as we got in and closed the door. I can still hear him.

The telephone was ringing and I just about screamed. I hadn't realised how tense I was. Guy told me to relax and have a drink, and he answered the phone and went to the door when the knocking started again. I just sat in the front room with the curtains closed, my mind a mess, thinking about you, those bastards outside and how unhappy and angry I was.

I don't know what Guy said or did, but after an hour the journalists went away and the phone calls stopped. I heard him talking to Brian and your parents and finally he came in to the front room. "Are you all right?" he asked. "No. I'm not," I said and I burst into tears. I had some kind of fit where I was crying and shouting and hitting things. I cursed the guerrillas for holding you and you for letting yourself get caught and the journalists for the lies they printed and me for being so stupid and helpless, sitting at home day after day not doing a thing. The *Sun* was right, I was a pathetic queen.

Guy put his arm around me until I calmed down. He told me he knew how I felt but it wasn't my fault. I felt stupid for letting go like that, but now that I'd done it, it was a relief and I felt much better. We went through to the kitchen and made something to eat and there I was on television again, a clip from the lunchtime interview. Then Sheba barked to get out and I realised it was almost dark and I hadn't given the birds their evening feed. So we went out and I saw the mess the journalists had made of the garden. The sty was crooked where they sat on it; I've had to take the whole thing down and start again. Then I fed the animals and walked down to the stream with Guy and Sheba and thought about you.

* * *

It's Monday evening. I've tried to get back into a routine. All the articles of the past week are in the box with this diary. I've read them so often they don't mean anything any more. Except I'll suddenly read something that makes me mad, like the letter in the *Telegraph* from an ex-ambassador to Peru saying that everything was all right until you went out there. Or the article in the *Star* by someone called Peter Gilbert who claims to be one of your former lovers; I thought it was all invented, but he knows about Yuki. What I hate is the fact that reporters think they ask you anything, print what they like, when it's all private and nothing to do with anyone else. The only thing they should write about is that you're being held hostage and you should be freed. Nothing else matters; whether you're gay or straight or what kind of relationship we have. I don't want them to know what you were like as a little boy or what we do in bed or what colour underwear you wear. There's no privacy at all.

I've rebuilt the sty; it wasn't difficult. I hope their clothes were ruined. We only lost a few vegetables in the garden, mostly cabbages. Sheba's a bit quiet. I think she was upset by having so many people around. A lot of friends have been calling. Eric and Dave were impressed by my tv appearance. So was George. He's donated £500 to the campaign. Guy calls every evening to see if I'm okay. I even had a phone call from Keith, your old lodger, the first time we'd heard from him since we moved; he's also given money for the campaign.

I ought to feel upbeat but I don't. I'm just tired. Then I think of you and how I have nothing to complain about.

* * *

Thursday 22nd. Sheba's at the vet's. She wasn't eating and didn't have any energy. I almost had to drag her outside to do her business. The vet's keeping her in overnight. It'll cost, but the money in the building society will pay.

There's now an Andrew McIllray Committee. It was set up yesterday with four members — me, Guy, Brian and your father. There's a plan of action to make publicity, develop contacts in Peru and raise money. Brian's responsible for Peru, Guy for publicity and raising money. Your father will keep the accounts. Me? I have to speak to the press — do any interviews and press conferences that Guy arranges. I'm not very happy about it. What do I say apart from you're a hostage and they should let you go? If people start asking about your work, I can't tell them anything. And does it help if I stand up in front of a hundred people and say "I want Andy home"? It makes me sound like a wimp. I shouldn't need to say anything at all. It's wrong that they're holding you in the first place.

Life on the farm continues. I've decided to buy the piglets on Monday, which means I have to get the fence finished by the weekend. It shouldn't be too difficult.

Nothing else has been happening. I still love you.

* * *

Friday 23rd. Sheba's back. Something's wrong with her liver. She's got pills and a special diet. I have to take her back to the vet's in a week. It's cost £120 so far.

The weather was better today. It really felt like spring. I spent most of the day weeding the vegetables and putting up the rest of the fence. Guy's coming down tonight.

I love you.

* * *

Sunday evening. Guy has just gone. It was a beautiful weekend. Sunny, warm. We went for a drive this afternoon to the Cotswolds. Got stuck in traffic and came home.

It was the first Sunday after the *Mail* embargo and Guy spent a fortune buying every paper to see if you were in it, but there was almost nothing.

At least we're in all the gay papers. *The Gay Gazette*'s used the photo of us in Rio and it's given the Committee address for contributions. The *Pink Paper* printed an editorial saying the government doesn't give a damn because you're gay. I'm sitting here feeling quiet and peaceful. It's so different from a week ago. There's no more reason to hide and things are beginning to move. All that's missing is you.

* * *

Monday 26th April. They're here! They're sleeping on the straw in the sty. I've even given them names — Willy and Wally. Wally's the one with the dark patch on his back. I tried to check they were healthy by looking for cracks in their skin, like the book tells you to. The man I bought them from seemed honest enough — typical farmer, overweight, about forty-five, red-faced. He helped me load them into the car. He thought I was mad and wondered why I didn't have a van. Of course one of them pissed and it went through all the newspapers onto the seat. You should have seen the fun I had trying to get them into the pen. Squealing piglets are heavy. When I let Sheba out I kept her on a leash in case she leapt over the fence to attack them, but though she sniffed a bit, she didn't pay them any attention. She's better, but doesn't run around so much; she just sits there wagging her tail as if she's begging me not to take her for a walk. Anyway, I put them in the pen and watched them run around. They found the water soon enough but didn't seem hungry — they only ate later. Anne came over in the afternoon. She's impressed, but Ada was a bit frightened. It must have been the smell or the noise. I'm not sure if I'll sleep tonight. I'll be too worried that they'll escape or a fox will get in. Are piglets too big for foxes to attack?

* * *

Thursday 29th April. I've been reading over this diary. There're lots of things I never tell you — like the fact I finished the spring cleaning. Guy says all the best diaries are just people talking to themselves. It's a kind of therapy. It helps you think. I find it relaxing, sitting here, typing away. Sometimes I delete it, usually I just leave it. I'm using all the right fingers; you'd be very impressed. Thank God for the spell-check programme or it would be a right mess.

I know you're not supposed to, but I've been wondering lately what made me gay. There are all these theories we talked about: hormones, genes and things. The *Mail* said I'd had an unhappy childhood and realised I was gay when I was fourteen, as if the two were connected. I thought that was ridiculous. I'm sure it's not upbringing. Look at your parents and mine; they were quite different but we're both gay. I had an absent father, but yours was always there. Even our mums are quite different. I can't imagine yours with a fag in her mouth and a gin in her hand in the middle of the afternoon.

Anyway, it's not true that I realised I was gay when I was fourteen; that was just the first time I did something about it. When I was really young — seven or eight — boys Jeff's age fascinated me. There was one who lived almost opposite. He must have been about fifteen. I'd sometimes see him in running kit. He had long fair hair and a thickset body; he looked handsome and confident and clean. I don't think I wanted to have sex with him — I was about nine and still didn't have a clear idea what sex was. I just wanted to get to know him.

There were other boys at school. Not the ones who smoked and swore — they just wanted to act like adults and adults were people like Mum and Dad. The boys I fancied were different somehow. The ones who weren't lads but weren't cissies either. Like a friend of Jeff's called Frank who played the electric guitar. I wanted to play the guitar too so he would notice me. I asked Mum for one but she just laughed at me. There was another boy, the brother of one of the boys in my class. I don't know what it was about him, but I tried to get friendly with his brother so I could get to meet him, but I never did.

Like I said, I was fourteen when I first had sex — that time in the cottage I told you about. It's probably closed now, with all the council cutbacks, but everyone in our area knew it was the place where queers went. I didn't think I was queer, because all queers did was play with each other's cocks in public toilets and I didn't want to do anything like that. I wanted a guy a little older than me, eighteen or nineteen; I wanted to hold him and feel him holding me. I wasn't sure what would happen next; I wasn't sure whether we'd be wearing clothes or not. Maybe just holding would be enough. But I couldn't see how it was going to happen; I was old enough to realise there was no way I could hug the guys I fancied.

That day I went into the cottage on my way home from school because I was desperate to piss. I didn't even notice there was anyone else in there until I'd shaken myself dry. Then I saw this guy at the far end, watching me. He was about eighteen, good-looking, like a footballer. And I knew right away, not just that he wanted me but I wanted him. That made me so nervous. I couldn't put my cock away, because it was already getting hard. I looked away in embarrassment and just stood still, red as a beetroot, half-hoping my cock would go soft and half-hoping it wouldn't. "Hey, you," I heard. There was no one else in there so I looked round. His hand was on his cock and it looked enormous — I'd never seen another guy's cock properly stiff before. He gave me this smile that was half friendly, half something else. "Do you want to go somewhere?" he asked. And suddenly everything was all right; I'd found the guy who wanted to hold me. I sort of stammered yes, though I had no idea where we would go or what we would do when we got there.

I told you about the van — an old Morris Minor that he'd borrowed from his dad. We drove out of town, parked in this lane and got in the back. At first I just wanted to put my arms around him, but I soon forgot about that. Without a word he'd unzipped my trousers and pulled out my cock and started sucking. It was so amazing that I forgot about anything else. Then he pulled my hand onto his cock and made me start rubbing. We came pretty quickly — me in his mouth and him all over my hand. It was mind-blowing. I'd played with myself before, but it was nothing like that. It was like the most incredible drug, like stereo after mono, colour tv after black and white. I couldn't speak for a bit afterwards. He gave me an old towel to wipe my hand with and asked if I was all right. "Yes," I said, "I'd just never done it before." He looked a bit worried at that, but didn't say anything. We got back in the front and drove back into town. I asked him his name was and where he lived, but I could tell he wasn't telling the truth. I wanted to see him again but didn't know how to ask. He didn't offer, either. He just dropped me off at the end of the road and I walked home over an hour late. Mum said something but she didn't really care; she'd long decided I was old enough to look after myself. I had something to eat and went upstairs and my cock was hard again and I made myself come thinking of him.

* * *

Monday 3rd May. Guy's been here for the long weekend. We've extended the garden and planted several more rows of strawberries which he bought. I think it's too late and they're not going to fruit this year, but he said we should try them anyway. We talked about fencing off the dozen acres furthest away from the house and renting it out. He thinks the grazing would be good enough for sheep. Because he's a vegetarian he's not happy about the pigs. I told him it was none of his business. Then I remembered you going on about that you could feed more people if we didn't recycle grass through animals. So he has a point, but I've got them and I'm going to keep them.

Brian came down yesterday. We have these fortnightly Committee meetings and Guy suggested having one here. Brian's sorting out the legal requirements to make us a registered charity. Thinking about that was depressing, because it seems so permanent, like you're going to be there for years, and what I want is for us to do something spectacular that gets you out in a couple of weeks.

Guy's put together a media pack to send out to the press. It's got a biography of you and a description of Demotica. He's tried to be sympathetic to Shining Path; he says there's no point making things worse for you. There's a couple of lines about me and at the foot it says that we're all available for interview. It goes out next week and there'll be a press conference in London the week after that. Guy's spoken to your Dad and he thinks that the two of us should speak.

We talked about other things as well — balloon races and getting you adopted by Amnesty and things like that. I asked why we didn't go to Peru and do the same kind of things there. Guy half agreed with me but Brian didn't. He said the embassy and his contacts were doing all they could; we would just interfere. I said that when the hostages were being held in Beirut, some of their wives and girlfriends had gone out and appeared on tv. They both said Peru was different and maybe your father could do it, but I couldn't because it would just remind everyone that you were gay.

Your dad didn't come down for the meeting. Guy had sent him all the papers and we talked to him a couple of times on the phone. I spoke to your mum as well. She sounded tired. I think she's beginning to think that she'll never see you again. Then she said why didn't I go up and visit them and that was a bit of a surprise. I can't, because of the animals, but to be polite I said I'd think about it.

Today we did some odd jobs. I feel in control again, not like when all the journalists were here. We chatted a bit about having a stall by the road. I'm not sure how it'll work. If there's just me, how can I spend all day on the road trying to sell things while I've got the land and animals to look after, not to mention the Committee? Guy said I was worrying too much and it would all work out.

Now Guy's gone and I'm on my own again. Part of me likes it and part of me doesn't. When he's here, he's someone to help, someone to talk to. Everything becomes much easier. But you become more distant. Even when we're talking about you, somehow you're not here. I feel closer to you when I'm on my own, when I'm just sitting here writing or looking at you. I've changed the photo — it's the one of you in Budapest with your hands in your jeans and your crotch sticking out. You thought it was ugly but I think it's sexy.

Andy, Andy, Andy. Will you ever come back and put your arms around me and stay with me like that forever?

* * *

Tuesday. Willy has a long gash in his side. Some of the fencing had worked loose and cut him. I spent all morning rewiring it. I washed the dirt out; the cut isn't too deep, but I don't know if it'll leave a scar. And Sheba's still got no energy. She lies there and looks at me and gets up to eat and drink, but when I call her she moves very slowly. She's only seven years old, but it's like she's twice that age.

Guy's arranged a long article about you in the *Guardian*. It'll appear the day after the press conference. Anne came over with Ada. Then I was in the shop looking through the papers to see if there's anything about you, when this old guy comes up and tells me it's a shame about you and he hopes I'm keeping my chin up. It's the second time a complete stranger has come up to me to wish me well and it's really good. Guy was right. We needed a campaign. We should have done this right at the start. Will you ever forgive me?

* * *

Thursday 6th. Sheba's ill again. She stopped eating a couple of days ago and I took her back to the vet today. He says her liver's stopped functioning and he doesn't know why. There could be all sorts of causes, like a virus or cancer or poison or an injury. He's taken her to the animal hospital in Reading where they'll give her some pills to see if they work. I asked if they could operate to find out what was wrong, but he didn't seem to think that would help. He tried to be optimistic, but he didn't look too hopeful. The last I saw of her, she was lying on the table in his surgery. There was just this furry face and dark eyes looking at me and her tongue panting. And though she's quite big she looked so vulnerable. I cried on the way home.

* * *

Friday. Sheba's still in hospital. They don't know how long she'll have to stay. It could cost hundreds to keep her there. It means there'll be no emergency money left. I hate to think of her there, not knowing what's going on, not knowing where I am. First you leave, then I desert her. That's no life for a dog.

When you read this, Andy, everything will be back to the way it was. You'll be home and Sheba'll be running around all right again. Everything'll be fine and all of the last year will just have been a horrible nightmare.

* * *

Saturday. The end of the week. It really is spring. I was out in the garden with no shirt for most of the day. I've got quite a tan. The pigs are fine — Willy's cut has healed and you can hardly see the scar. I killed a hen and plucked it — much easier than the first time. Remember how I flustered and you refused to help me because I had insisted that I would be the one to do it? I called the hospital; Sheba's the same. If she doesn't get any better, I have to decide on Monday what to do. Guy called about the press conference. Your mother called to chat. Kathy and Frank are coming over tomorrow. Never a moment's peace...

I was remembering the first time we argued. It was about six weeks after we met. One morning you got it into your head that I should get another job. I didn't see why. I was doing all right at the cafe. I wasn't making a fortune, but I was making ends meet. And it was fun. I'd spent my life working in cafes and restaurants where the pay was poor or the shifts were too long or the manager was a pain. I liked the Wensley and I liked the people I was working with. But you thought I ought to be a manager or go on some course or do something completely different, like work in travel. I didn't want to do any of these things. I just wanted to stay where I was. But you insisted and we started shouting at each other. Not really shouting, but angry. I would have walked out if you hadn't finally got it into your head that I didn't want to change.

I know now that you going on about my getting a better job meant that you cared about me. The problem was, you weren't seeing it from my point of view. If you'd been in my position, you would have wanted to run your own restaurant or learn a new trade, and because that was right for you, you thought it was right for me as well. But it wasn't. All I ever wanted was peace and quiet and someone to come home to. And that's what you gave me.

It worried me for a few days, that argument. I thought it meant you'd lose interest in me if I didn't change my life in some way. So I did think about doing something different. I went into a catering agency and talked about a better job, but they said I had to have a City and Guilds and I knew I'd never stick out the course. So I left it and hoped things would be all right with you and in the end they were.

We get on pretty well together. We could argue a lot more than we do. There are things you do that I don't like, like leaving doors open and leaving stains on the washing up, but I don't mention them because it's not worth it. There are probably some things about me that get your back up. I haven't the foggiest what they might be...

Ever since I was a kid, I hated arguments. Sometimes I'd shout back and sometimes I'd say nothing until it all blew over. At home, the older I got the more I argued with Jeff and Mum. And there was always someone in London I didn't get on with. Like Roger in Archway; he kept hogging the bathroom and tv and he'd get mad if you said it was your turn to get in or watch the programme you wanted. Then there was the chef at the first place I worked at when I came to London. All chefs are bad-tempered, but this one was a bastard. He'd get an order and only do it if he was in a good mood. Otherwise he'd make the waiter wait and that would upset the customers. I was just the busboy and had nothing to do with him, but he was always shouting at me for getting in his way when I wasn't. I even argued sometimes with Dave and Eric. The worst was John, but you know about him. After the first few weeks it was nothing but arguing — or him shouting and me not knowing what to say.

But it's never happened with you, and I'm really grateful.

To the man I love, I love you so much.

* * *

Sunday 9th. Kathy and Frank were here. I'd only met him once before; he's a nice guy, quite good-looking. I like his deep Jamaican voice. It was kind of strange watching them the two of them together. Kathy talks most of the time. Frank either nods his head or doesn't seem to be listening. When he did say something, it was direct, no nonsense. How was I managing without you? How much did I pay for the pigs, how much weight did they put on each week? Kathy's more like you and Guy; she talks theory half the time and I'm not quite sure what she's saying.

They picked me up about eleven and we drove to that village full of bookshops you keep wanting to go to. We must have gone into at least a dozen. Compared to all the nice middle-class ladies and couples they get, we must have looked strange — this well-dressed black couple with the poshest of accents and me in jeans and an anorak straight out of *Brookside*. Frank is into science fiction; Kathy was looking for English literature. I was looking for books about smallholdings. There wasn't much. Plenty of Miss Smith the vicar's daughter writing about village gossip, but very little on keeping cows and shovelling shit. There were a couple of books on livestock that I might have bought, but they were years old and the regulations have probably changed. George says you need to know more about the law than the land to be a farmer.

Frank and Kathy must have spent about fifty quid. I didn't buy anything, although Kathy offered to get me what I wanted. We got back about seven. It was strange coming back to a house with no Sheba. It was a nice day. I realised I missed the kind of life we had in London before we moved down here, when we visited friends or had them over for dinner. It's civilised just sitting over a long meal, even if I do sometimes complain about your conversation.

Now I'm on my own again. Three cats and me. No Sheba; I called the hospital, but whoever answered was useless. She had no idea what kind of day Sheba had had. She just told me not to worry. What, me worry? It's all I ever do.

* * *

Monday 10th May. Sheba's gone. The hospital said it was cancer and there was nothing they could do. She would just get weaker and weaker. I asked about an operation but the vet said it wouldn't help. I said she was only seven years old, but she said that dogs can get cancer at any age, just like humans, and there was nothing they could do. I had to go and sign the authorisation to put her to sleep. So I drove over and Sheba was lying in a large cage, all thin and unhappy. She recognised me and got up and came over, but she moved so slowly. I could see she wasn't going to get better. The nurse said that the best thing to do was let her go. So I sat in this waiting room while they did it and kept staring at all the adverts for worming pills and vaccinations showing all these healthy, happy dogs and cats.

Then the vet came out with Sheba in this plastic bag and helped me put her in the boot, carefully as if she was just asleep. I drove home very slowly, partly because I was trying hard not to cry and partly because the sooner I got home the sooner I would have to bury her. I remembered the day you and me went to the Dogs' Home. There were two or three dogs we liked, but we chose Sheba because she had this beautiful thick fur. A cross between a collie, a labrador and something else, the woman said. I was so happy to get her, because she was proof that we were staying together. She's always been here whenever you were away, keeping me company, running around, barking at nothing in particular or sitting half on my lap and half on the arm of the chair. And now she's no longer here.

I buried her at the foot of the hillock, near where the daffodils bloom. It took me ages to dig the hole and while I was doing it she just lay there in that black bag. Finally it was deep enough and I put her in gently and started covering her with earth. I wanted to make some kind of ceremony, but I couldn't think of anything, so I just kept on saying, "Goodbye, Sheba, goodbye," and when I'd finished I just broke down and cried and cried.

It's because she's part of you and she's gone and won't ever come back. And I sometimes wonder if you'll ever come back. When you do, things will be different. Sheba will have gone and there'll be a huge market garden and pigs and perhaps a cow and we'll both be different people and we'll have to start all over again. And maybe you won't want to start again.

Come home, Andy, please come home. I need you, desperately.

* * *

Sunday 16th. Almost a week. On Wednesday and Thursday I was up in London for the press conference. It went off okay. Guy had hired a room near Trafalgar Square and about twenty journalists turned up, including three camera crews. He gave a short speech saying it was the four hundred and sixteenth day of your disappearance. You represented not just one individual held hostage but the hopes for democracy throughout the world. Then your father spoke, then a woman from Amnesty, then me. Your father sounded good — a gentleman of the old school saying you were an honourable man being held for his ideals. I was nervous, but Guy had helped me write my speech. I said that I knew that many people considered that being gay was somehow wrong, but being gay was no different from being black or being red-haired. As your partner, I was affected as much as you were by your imprisonment and I had every right to demand your freedom.

Most of the questions were serious, but there were some really stupid ones. Afterwards, Guy said he thought it had gone well. Both ITV and the BBC had clips of me and your dad on the evening news and there was a lot of coverage in the papers. Quite a few gave the address to send donations. The *Pink Paper*'s even got a photo of you on the front page and "416 DAYS" in big type.

Guy was here for the weekend. We worked yesterday and got up late today. It was sunny again and we sunbathed. I kept looking for Sheba, but she wasn't there. I've definitely decided to get another dog. I'm going to call the RSPCA tomorrow and see what they've got.

* * *

Monday 17th. I lead a double life. Half the time I'm in the present — working in the garden, doing the dishes, talking to Guy on the phone — and half the time I'm in the past, thinking about you and things like my life before you. I remember much more than I did when I was with you, probably because I've got nothing else to do but think. And I want to write it down so I don't forget it again.

After that first time I went back to the cottage a lot to see if I could meet the same guy but he was never there. There were usually two or three older men who'd stare at me as I came in. I hated that — it was like walking into the middle of a conspiracy and you thought they might attack you. Sometimes there were guys I fancied, but I didn't want all the others to see. What I wanted was private and I didn't want anyone else to know. So though I went in there a lot, I didn't pick anyone up.

By the time I was sixteen I was old enough to know I really was gay, although I wasn't too happy about the idea. Partly because of what Jeff and Mum would say and partly because I didn't like the gay men I saw. They were either camp as Christmas or dirty old men — I mean, hanging around public toilets is no role model for gay teenagers; it just makes all gays look like perverts.

I didn't know what to do. All the boys my age were talking about what they did with their girlfriends and some of it was true. I wanted to have sex too, but didn't know how to go about it. When I was fifteen I actually had sex with a girl once, at a Christmas party where everyone was drunk. I think because some of the boys saw me getting off with her, that stopped them thinking I was gay. But I knew I was and I hadn't a clue what to do about it.

After I left school I went on a training scheme to become a chef but never completed the course. I just fried hamburgers at the Wimpy bar and went into Liverpool on my days off, to the gay bar I'd discovered near Lime Street station. I'd stand in the corner listening to Donna Summer and Gloria Gaynor, waiting for some handsome guy to sweep me off my feet. The trouble was, the place was a dump and most of the men were old and ugly. Sometimes I'd see guys I fancied, but they never looked at me. Some guys did chat me up and I'd go back with one or two, but it never meant anything. The one who fancied me most was a lorry-driver in his thirties called Eddie, a lonely guy who lived in a small flat full of photos and statues of naked boys.

Then Mum discovered the gay magazines I'd hidden under the mattress. She must have had a fit. I walked into the house after a day at work and there were my copies of *Quorum* and *Gay News* on the kitchen table. Mum sat there with a cigarette and a glass of gin, probably her third or fourth, asking me what I was doing with stuff like that. I had enough sense not to tell her that I wanked over them. I just said I was gay but didn't want to talk about it. She said no son of hers was queer and that was an end to it. Of course she told Jeff and Jeff threw a wobbly. "If you're queer, you can get out of this house," he told me. I said it was Mum's house and it had nothing to do with him. He just looked at me as if I was filth and walked out.

It didn't get any better. I don't think it upset Mum as much as it might have done, but Jeff was mad at me. He told all his friends his brother was queer and soon the whole street knew. I was walking home one night when a group of girls saw me. One of them shouted out, "Here comes the bender!" and they all started giggling. I got redder and redder as I got nearer and tried to ignore them but I couldn't. One called out "Do you fancy my bra? It would look good on you." I wanted to say the one clever thing that would make them shut up and leave me alone, but I didn't know what it was. So they just carried on shouting comments like "Look at those hips."

That was it. I knew I couldn't stay. It might not get worse, but it wouldn't get any better. I hated being at home with Jeff around. I didn't have any friends. I thought about moving to Liverpool or Manchester, but I thought I'd just end up like Eddie and all the other men in the bar. So at the end of the week I packed a bag and hitched down to London. Like thousands of others in search of happiness. Which I found, in the end.

* * *

Tuesday 18th. We've got a new dog — James. He's about two years old, a lab mongrel but very different from Sheba; he's got short black hair and smaller ears. He belonged to a woman in Thatcham who was killed in a car crash last week. I chose him because he came running up to poke his tongue through the cage at me. The girl who worked there said that she would have taken him straight away if she'd had room. He was a bit excited when I drove him back in the car. I was afraid he was going to piss on the seat but he didn't. I took him into the house and gave him some water and food out of Sheba's bowls, then took him into each room. He followed me everywhere and seemed to recognise his name. The cats took one look at him and jumped up on the sideboard; he hardly seemed to notice them. Then I took him for a walk, on a lead in case he ran away. The geese made him jump and he didn't want to go near the sty, but other than that he sniffed around and shat and seemed quite happy. It was funny seeing him cock his leg; I'd forgotten that males do that. I kept the lead on when I took him out last night, but I think tomorrow I'll let him free.

I hope you like him. He's bound to love you.

* * *

Wednesday. I've started building a trestle for the stall. It comes to bits to make it easy to carry and it'll have a canopy to keep the produce in the shade. When I sit out there I'll have a chair, an ice bucket and the portable phone too. A radio and a book to read as well — there are all these novels of yours just sitting there. There's bound to be one or two I would enjoy.

Like the computer, the books are a part of you. Just looking at them makes me feel closer to you. Sometimes in Hampstead, when you'd gone off to work and I wasn't on till the afternoon, I'd wander around your flat. There was so much to look at. All your souvenirs and books. I'd look at the titles of some of them, things like *Banking the Unbankable* and *War Wounds* and I'd wonder who ever read them and why. They were a kind of mystery and I felt that if I could understand them I would understand you. So I'd take one or two off the shelf and start reading and it would be gobbledegook. Or dead boring. It would all be about Africa or ecology or the International Monetary Fund, and while I could listen to you talking about such things, I couldn't stand to read about them. At least you had some things I liked, like gay novels and cartoon books.

The bathroom was very plain and ordinary — you wouldn't have thought of painting it if I hadn't insisted. The kitchen needed a coat of paint as well. More than that really, but I couldn't start spending your money on a food-processor and all the utensils you didn't have. The bedroom was always a mess, but at least I cleared up the clothing and put some of the books away so that there was room to walk around and when we made love there was more than just the bed....

The whole flat was you — it smelt of you, it looked like you, it felt like you, a warm welcoming presence which put its arm round me the moment I walked in. What I loved best was the fact that I was there at all. That you trusted me enough to leave me alone in your home and give me a key even though I wasn't living there. And you didn't mind when I started clearing everything up. You didn't take advantage, in fact you tried to stop me. That made me love you more.

Then you asked me to move in with you. I didn't want to. We were getting on okay as we were. I was spending almost all my time in Hampstead anyway, but that didn't mean I wanted to move in permanently. You might turn out to be John all over again. It would be your flat and your furniture and your belongings and you'd start telling me what I could or couldn't do and when to have dinner ready and things like that. That's what I told myself, even though by then we'd known each other long enough for me to know it wasn't true. I really did want to move in with you, but not to your flat, to somewhere new, to a place that belonged to both of us, not somewhere you could kick me out from if you got tired of me. So I kept my room in Leytonstone. I needed somewhere to go home to and Dave and Eric would always be there when things went wrong. But Hampstead became my second home; when Keith left I started using his room for my clothes and left a spare toothbrush and razor in the bathroom. And more and more I'd wake up in the morning and feel I wasn't in a stranger's flat but one that was mine, ours.

It went on like that for months until we started talking about living in the country. I wanted somewhere to call my own, a house with a garden all the way round. You wanted a bigger home, for all your stuff as well as mine. And I think you liked the idea of being a country squire, although it hasn't worked out anything like that. My next worry was money. You'd got the deposit from your flat and your grandad's legacy, but I didn't have anything. For a time I thought it would end up just the way I didn't want — me living in your house, so you could kick me out at any time. Instead of which you said you'd put our joint names on the mortgage and the title deeds. I know it was partly for tax reasons, but you didn't have to do it. But you did, and it was like a wedding ring — something binding that couldn't be broken. It proved to me how much you loved me. As I have always loved you.

* * *

Thursday 20th. Another day. The pigs get fatter, the vegetables get taller. James sniffs around but comes when I call. I went over to Anne's — Ada tries to walk, she totters and falls. Anne was hinting I might babysit. I ought to, but I don't want to. Eric called; no news, just gossip. He had a fling with someone he met at the LA, said he hadn't had such fun for years. Suggested I should try it, but it doesn't appeal.

* * *

Friday. Another day. I should be writing about the Committee and everything Guy is doing, but I can't be bothered. If it works, you'll get out and we'll tell you all about it — the balloon races and the letter-writing campaign and all the lunches Guy's been having with MPs and reporters. And if it doesn't work... Well, it will. It will.

Each day you become more remote. No, that's not true. I never stop thinking of you, but, like I wrote before, sometimes I find it difficult to remember details about you. Is it the same for you? Do you remember everything about me? My hair and the spots on my skin? Can you hear my voice? Do you remember holding me? Where your arm fits into my waist and your hand holds my head? And my nose and mouth in your neck, kissing you? Do you remember all that? Or are there too many things in the way? Do they leave you alone hour after hour, day after day, so that all you can do is think of me? Or do they never stop talking to you, shouting at you, trying to break you down? Hitting you, hurting you? Is all you can think of staying alive?

Another day passes where you're there and I'm here and I haven't done a single thing to get you out of there. What are you going to think of me when you come home?

* * *

Monday 24th. Dayton-McIllray Enterprises has begun to make money. £10.40. Guy and I set up the stall yesterday to sell broccoli and the last of the sprouts. There wasn't much, because it was all from the old garden. Seven cars stopped, five bought something. It was sunny and warm and there was a lot of traffic. The stall's just by the gate, so cars can see it as they come over the hill. I put a sign saying "Broccoli and Sprouts for Sale" about a hundred yards back. The cars have to pull onto the verge, but it's not dangerous. If it gets really successful, I'm thinking of moving the fence back so cars can pull properly off the road.

It wasn't so good today. There weren't so many cars and most of them were locals. I only made three pounds in five hours. Guy wasn't here and I was bored rigid. I had the portable radio but the batteries went flat. I started reading one of your detective stories — *The Boy Who Followed Ripley* — because there's a cute boy on the cover, but it doesn't seem to be as gay as I thought it was.

At least I can make some money at weekends. The next problem is do I declare it or not? Guy says not to bother unless it gets to be a lot — sixty or eighty quid a week or so. Otherwise there'll be a whole lot of paperwork and I might lose the social security. I don't know. I'll have to think about it. In the meantime I'm putting all the money we've earned in its own box at the back of the henhouse. No one would think of looking there. We're going to be rich, lover. Well, maybe a little less poor. I'll take you on that holiday to the Canaries or Ibiza we promised ourselves.

* * *

Tuesday 25th. Brian called a couple of hours ago. He said not to get my hopes up, but he thinks one of his contacts in Peru has met one of the people who are holding you. He's thinking of going out to try and negotiate your release. It might take some time, he said, but he sounded more confident than I'd heard him before. I said that if they knew where you were, the Peruvian government could go in and free you, but he said they didn't know where you were, just that it was somewhere south of Cuzco. Even if they did know, the army couldn't get anywhere near you. Or if they did, there's a risk you'd be killed in the fighting. He still thinks the best way to get you out is have some Peruvian that the guerrillas respect persuade them to release you. He has the names of one or two people who may be able to do it.

I called Guy and your parents, but Brian had spoken to them first. Everyone was pleased, but still thinks there's a long way to go. Only your mother sounded uncertain; I think she thinks she'll never see you again. She sounded very tired, as if she'd aged a lot. I don't know how old she is; nearly eighty now?

Then I just sat here for a while. It was getting dark, but I didn't put the light on. Outside I could see the barn in moonlight and it looked somehow different. You seemed to be suddenly very real, very close. I knew you were thousands of miles away but I could almost see you from the corner of my eye, sitting in your armchair, a foot over the arm as usual. It was the same you, but older, different. I was different too. We were in love, but a deeper love than before, because we didn't need to tell each other so much. I started talking to you, quietly, about how much I missed you, what had happened to Sheba, how Guy had helped. I wanted to reach out and touch you, but I knew I couldn't. Finally I turned the light on and as I knew, I was alone.

Maybe Brian's wrong. Maybe someone in Peru is lying and nobody knows where you are. But I feel stronger today; I really feel that you're alive and you'll come back to me, some day, perhaps soon. Then I can really tell you how much you mean to me.

* * *

Monday 31st. Another long weekend. Guy has just gone. We made thirty-five pounds! Rich, rich, mad cackle, we're rich!

We were out yesterday and today. It's been sunny and a lot of people stopped to buy. Including two gay couples who stopped because I wasn't wearing a shirt. Not only does the farmwork give me a tan, but the weightlifting has begun to pay off. The Tom you're coming back to is definitely hunkier than the Tom you left.

Everything seems to be going better these days. There's the farm — it really does feel like a farm, now that we're selling food. There's the weather — it's getting warmer. There's Guy and other friends who visit or call. But mostly I'm feeling good because I'm managing on my own. Guy helps, but I'm the one who holds it all together. I'm the one who gets up early every morning and feeds the livestock. I'm the one who's digging the holes and putting in the fence to separate the field we're going to rent. I'm the one who waters the plants, checks the leaves and does most of the weeding. I'll be the one to take the pigs to get slaughtered. I'm the one that does it all.

It's a strange feeling, this new me. Most of my life things seem to have gone wrong. I never found the right job or the right flat or the right lover. I didn't even have the right family. It's working out now, but it's taken so long. When I left Runcorn I thought it would be easy; I just had to get to London and I'd find my feet. It's what all teenagers think and they're always wrong. The moment I arrived in the city I was lost. The guy who was giving me a lift dropped me off in Hendon at six o'clock at night, pointed me to the tube station and said I could get into the West End from there. I didn't even know what the West End was. I looked at the map, saw Piccadilly Circus and thought if I get there, I'll meet someone who can help me. But I got lost changing trains and by the time I got to Piccadilly it was almost eight o'clock and I was tired and hungry. I didn't know where to go or what to do, just stood there in the middle of all the flashing lights and crowds and wondered what the hell I was going to do.

I knew there were gay hotels in London, but didn't have a clue how to find them. Finally I stopped a guy who was obviously gay. He told me to go to Earls Court, so I got back on the Underground and when I got there I saw all these hotels. I knew they couldn't all be gay, so I just went into the first one and got a room. It charged a fortune, so I could only stay a couple of nights. The next day I got hold of a copy of *Gay News* and started phoning up people offering rooms, but I couldn't afford the deposit for any of them. In the end I found one of these really cheap hotels where you share a room with four other people. I hated it. It was full of Australians and Americans going on about how much beer they drank and how many women they were screwing. The bathroom was always busy and before I bought a padlock for my locker some of my clothes got stolen.

It took me ages to get a job. I didn't have the right experience or references and I had to buy black and whites, which left me with almost no money. I just walked into one cafe or restaurant after another until I got that first job as a bus-boy. It paid just enough to get by. I tried to look for a second job but I couldn't get the shifts right. It went on like that for two months. I got really depressed sometimes, sitting on that bed in the evening with no friends and no money to go out. I'd go down to the tv room, but it was worse there. There were always people coming in and out, shouting down the corridor and cracking stupid jokes. I was the only English person in the place, all the rest were foreigners travelling round the world, staying for a few days before moving on. I'd go back up and try to get to sleep but someone would always come in late and drunk and switch on the lights and wake me up.

Then I met John and moved in with him and for a while everything seemed to be okay. He was twenty-five, good-looking and a tube driver, which really impressed me, and he lived in this nice two-roomed flat on the top floor in Clapham overlooking the Common. I should have realised from the beginning it wouldn't work out. Things like his locking away his cheque books and valuables, even after I'd moved in and he'd given me the key of the flat. At the time it didn't seem odd; he was older than me and his affairs were none of my business. But after a few weeks he started to change. He started telling me how to comb my hair and what clothes to put on. When we met his friends, he kept putting me down and calling me Thomasina. He'd get angry if I didn't do things just right. He kept shouting at me, telling me I was no good at anything. I didn't understand what I was doing wrong. I was getting more and more miserable. I was in love with him and he was in love with me, otherwise why would he keep me? At the same time I was afraid of losing him. If he kicked me out I had nowhere to go. Whatever happened, I was determined no way was I going back to living in that hotel.

It's late. You've heard it all before. I know now that however bad it was, at least I was free. I could have walked out on John any time. It took me a long time, but I did in the end. It's different for you. You're not free. You can't walk out. You can't come home. I'll never complain again. Never.

* * *

1st June. Summertime. Cold in the Andes. I hope you're warm. Nothing new here. I love you.

* * *

Wednesday 2nd. Life goes on. James runs around. He's different from Sheba; he's got more energy but he's much more timid. I suppose it comes from living with a little old lady.

No news of you. Guy's working hard; I don't know how he has time for his real job. Money for the AMC keeps coming in. There's a secretary who comes in to deal with the correspondence twice a week. There's talk of Brian going to Peru, once we hear back from his contact in Cuzco. I'm doing my bit. I'm speaking to some gay group in London next week.

No other news. I love you.

* * *

Thursday 3rd. No news, no news. I saw Doris today, the first time in weeks. It's my fault, I haven't been to see her for months, since she no longer wanted the eggs. She hasn't been well. "My insides," she tells me, whatever that means. She asked about you and said it must be lonely for me in the evenings. I told her I was writing my diary for you to come back to. "Tell him I was asking for him," she said. Maybe she thinks you somehow get to read this every day. So, Andy, Doris is asking for you. So am I.

* * *

Sunday evening. It's quiet. The sky's beautiful, all pink clouds. You don't want it to change but you realise the light's dying and suddenly it's dark. What are the sunsets like with you, lover? Do you get to see them at all?

We made over £40. I give a quarter of all the takings to the Committee, put a quarter in the henhouse and spend the rest on things we need, like paint and feed. I'm going to have to declare it soon. Eric says why bother — I need all the money I can get. Guy says it's up to me, although I think he'd prefer me to declare it. I don't know. I need the money but I don't like cheating people. I'm like Mum that way. She had this thing about not depending on anyone — not even Dad. And part of not depending on anyone was not taking things that weren't yours. And deep down, that always seemed to me right. Even when I was with John or Alex I didn't want to take anything from them without asking first. I don't mind claiming social security when it's my right, but I don't want to if it isn't.

I don't know what you'd think. You've never been on the dole. And though you talked a lot about social justice and the welfare state, it was all theoretical. Or you were always going on about how the West was rich and other countries were poor, but you never talked much about poor people in this country and what they should do. I suppose even poor people in this country are richer than those in the Third World. So, if I'm earning money I should stop claiming social security. It can go to someone else who needs it. Like the Chancellor of the Exchequer.

Guy says hello. I say hello and I love you. Goodnight.

* * *

Monday 7th. It rained all day. I stayed in and cleaned out the kitchen. Defrosted the fridge and washed down the cupboards. All your teas are still sitting there, including the Dragon tea and that orange stuff from Turkey. I had some of the Dragon tea and realised why I never drink it. How the Chinese can, I don't know. I'm not even sure it's fresh. I thought about throwing it out, but you'd never forgive me.

I'm off to London in the morning. Meeting Brian and Guy in the afternoon and speaking to the Kingston and Richmond Area Gay Society in the evening. I've prepared a little speech like the one I gave to the first press conference. I'm nervous, though I suppose I shouldn't be.

Anne's coming in to feed the animals. I haven't seen much of her or George lately. A year ago we were always popping in and out of each other's houses. I wasn't so busy and she didn't have Ada. Funny how people drift apart. Before, I'd drop in any time; now I call before I go over. In a way I miss her. She was like an elder sister

I sometimes wonder what it would be like to be married — to a woman. I look at Anne and George and Kathy and Frank and it seems very different from what you and I have got. More secure. There's nothing to hold us together. That's not true — there's the house — but it feels that way. Sometimes I think you and I might just fall out of love one day and we'd just walk away from each other. It could be as easy and sudden as that.

I write rubbish late at night, I know. It's time I went to bed. I love you.

* * *

Sunday 13th. It's been a busy week. We had a Committee meeting in London. Your dad was there. To be honest, I was bored. Guy was going on about the people he'd talked to and Brian was telling us about Peru. There was still no response from his contact in Cuzco but he felt it was worth going out just the same. What if you get kidnapped too, your dad asked. Brian didn't have an answer to that. He just said he'd be very careful. He gave us the names of the people he hoped would negotiate on our behalf. I don't know who they are. I said I wanted to go out to Peru too, but no one else agreed. I know they're right — I'm a foreigner, I don't speak the language, I'm gay, I wouldn't know where to start, what to do — but it still feels wrong. I want to go.

Guy went with me to the gay meeting. It was in a room upstairs at a community centre. It was mostly men in their thirties and forties, two or three women as well. I was going to read the speech I'd prepared, but Guy thought it was better if I spoke off the top of my head. I was very nervous, felt my face going red and rambled all over the place. It was easier after I'd stopped and they all asked questions. Guy answered some, much better than I did. Afterwards a lot of them came up and thanked me for coming. One or two were really sympathetic. Next time, Guy says, I should put in a bit more personal stuff. Start off with when you and I met, our life together, that sort of thing.

The rest of the week was catching up on the farm. The pigs are getting bigger, but I've no idea how much they weigh. We didn't sell so much on the stall. It was a dull weekend and not many cars. Life carries on.

* * *

Tuesday afternoon. It's been raining a lot the last few days and I'm beginning to worry about the soil getting waterlogged. I didn't think about drainage properly when I dug it up.

Remember the houses we looked at? That one near Guildford with the sixteenth-century hall and the outside toilet? The one in Wales — all that land and the beautiful view. Too much money or too far from London. We were lucky getting this place, I suppose, although neither of us realised how much work it was going to be. Or you realised, you bastard, and knew that I was going to be the one doing it. I was months with all that paint in my clothes and my hair. Maybe it's a fetish that turns you on.

I wonder if every couple makes love the moment they move in. It was such a wonderful feeling being here — the house empty and the furniture stacked up in front room. All the land outside, no curtains and no one to look in. You standing there in ripped jeans, with filthy hands and dust in your hair; it made you look different, sexier, more alive. I can't imagine what I looked like. I probably stank of sweat. I was so happy because it was our house and I was with you and that was all I ever wanted from life. Making love was part of it — it brought us together and kept us together, like we were exchanging wedding rings.

Two weeks later you started with Demotica. After a year of studying in London, you were travelling again. I knew it was coming, but I didn't like it. All the weeks added up, that first year you were away for over four months. I complained and you tried to explain why it was so important for you. All this guff about helping and advising people. In the end I just accepted it's one of the things about you that'll never change; you want to go to all these countries and meet all these people and attend these conferences, when all I want to do is stay at home.

That's one of the great differences between us — I want to settle and you don't. I used to think about going with you, although God knows where I would have got the money from. It wouldn't have worked out. Brazil proved it. I hated every minute of Rio. It was too hot and I couldn't go to the beach or anywhere else, because I couldn't speak the language and there were muggers everywhere. You were at the conference all day. At night we'd go out for a meal and to a bar for a disco, but you kept on bumping into people you knew and speaking Portuguese with them while I stood there like a wallflower. The time we spent travelling around was better, although I still got fed up with not being able to speak to anyone except other tourists. The good thing was that we didn't argue. You knew I wasn't enjoying myself and you did what you could do to make me feel better; I didn't want to upset you because you'd spent all that money on taking me there. But it was so good to come home.

I stopped to make some tea and look at the photos from that holiday. You on the Sugar Loaf, me at Iguazu, the harbour in Salvador. Salvador was weirdest — all the gold in the churches and everyone so poor. That restaurant in the catering college, where the waiters were young and nervous and we could eat as much food as liked. I'd never tasted that kind of food before, things like lobster in crab shells and sweet potatoes and spicy sauces. It didn't taste nearly as good when I tried it at home. Then there was that cheap hotel overlooking the harbour. I never told you about the morning I got up early to piss while you were still asleep. There was this beautiful boy, about twenty-one, in the hall. Brown skin, beautiful dark hair, wide eyes, my height, slim. I passed him on my way to the toilet. He came in after me and just stood there, not saying a word, just watching me. I looked at him. I could have had him if I wanted. For the first time since we'd been together, I thought about it, seriously. He was so good-looking and we were far from home and everything was different because we were on holiday. But nothing happened. I didn't say anything; I just walked out. Not because you might find out, but because I would know that I had betrayed you. And I didn't want to do that. So I walked back to our room and got back into bed. It was so warm we just had a sheet. You were half-awake and put your arm around me and I lay there looking at you and thinking about the boy, but glad that I'd come back to you.

He wasn't the first guy to cruise me in Brazil — it never seemed to stop — but there was something about him, the time and the place, that I've never forgotten. It was like he was offering something completely different, but I didn't know what it was. Sort of if I'd had sex with him I'd have become Brazilian, I would have been able to speak Portuguese, I would have been able to walk out into the streets and become part of them. I wouldn't have felt as lost and uncomfortable as I did. But if I'd had sex with him, I would have lost you and it was better to be alone with you than to be with all those people.

The only other time we went abroad was to Mykonos. That was okay. Everyone spoke English. It was easy to chat to people and I liked lying around all day. Maybe we'll go back when you return. Lie in the sun all day and drink ouzo all evening and fuck all night. That's what life should be.

* * *

Wednesday 16th. It's still raining. There's a large puddle outside the barn which flows round and into the sty, soaking the straw. It's because there's a slight slope there. I'll even it out some time, but today I dug a channel either side of the sty to drain the water away.

I'm worried about the garden. The soil isn't flooded, but the plants haven't had sunshine for days. I was wondering — not seriously — about plugging in an ultra-violet lamp and holding it over them. I suppose all it would do is give me an electric shock in the rain.

James caught a rat in the barn last night. I didn't think he had it in him. And I thought the cats kept rats away. Now I wonder if the rats can get at the pigs and hens. What about all the diseases they carry? I heard him growl but wasn't sure what he was doing. When I went in to look he'd caught it and had it between his teeth. It was quite dead. I took a shovel and dug it in a hole by the gate.

I called Brian, but there's still no news. Then I called Anne and George, Eric and Dave, Kathy and Frank just to say hello. I need all the money from the stall just to pay the telephone bill.

Sleep tight, lover. Sleep as well as you can.

* * *

Thursday. It's stopped raining. I got on with digging in the fence for the new field. It's going to be a long process. God knows when I'll be finished. It's a good thing I haven't yet tried to find someone to rent it. If I don't find anyone, I suppose I could always hire a lion and call it a safari park. Make a fortune selling ice-creams and tickets to our ancestral home.

Good night, Lord McIllray. Your humble servant greets you.

* * *

Friday. Guy called. He isn't coming down this weekend. He's going to a party tomorrow night in Camden. He wanted to know if I wanted to go up. I thought about it; I could see Eric and Dave, but it was too late to see if Anne would feed the animals. I'm feeling guilty about it anyway, because she does it every time I go up for Committee meetings. So I said no. I've been watching *Roseanne* and there's a horror film coming on. I'm not sure if I'll watch it — it's the kind of thing I'd prefer to watch lying on the sofa with my head in your lap. Instead of which all I'll have is James on my lap. His breath smells as bad as Sheba's used to.

Pwsch. How do you write the sound of a kiss? Llllmmlll.

* * *

Saturday 19th. Sun at last, but we didn't sell much. Only £17 to add to the kitty.

I called your parents. They sounded the same. Your mum asked how things were on the farm but you could tell it was an effort to talk to me. Your Dad surprised me by repeating the invitation to go up and visit them. He said if it was a question of money, then he'd pay. I think it must be to see your Mum, to cheer her up.

Don't the kidnappers know you've got a family? Even if they don't care about me, they must know you've got a mother and father. You could have brothers and sisters and really old grandparents for all they know. How can they hurt all these people like this? What if it was their family suffering? I suppose if I knew the answer to that I would know everything. I would know why they were holding you and what would make them set you free. Instead of which I don't know anything. I don't even know if you're still alive, for all Brian's talk of contacts and promises to go out to Cuzco. I don't know what's going through their head, or your head, or anyone's head, come to that. I'm not even sure about mine.

* * *

Sunday 20th. Two more days and it will be Midsummer. I'm going round to George and Anne's to celebrate.

£25 today. The last of the broccoli, beans, lettuce and onions. The weather's been dull and there haven't been many cars. It's not much fun sitting out there on my own. I get tired of reading. Then I listen to the radio and when I get bored with the commercials and Tracey from Devon going on about her boyfriend, I listen to the news, which is always depressing, or classical music. I play a few tapes but the battery soon runs down.

No more rats in the barn. The new fence is almost complete. James is panting beside me. When you come back, he'll wonder who this stranger is walking through the door. He may even try to bite you. I hope you don't give him rabies. Sorry, that wasn't funny.

I love you.

* * *

Thursday. Life goes on. I finally finished the fence. It looks good, though I say it myself.

On Tuesday I went over to Anne and George. I hadn't realised they'd invited four other people and I turned up in my oldest jeans and without shaving. At least I'd showered and had on a clean shirt. Two of them were from the village. Jack and Silvana Robertson. He runs a delivery company and she teaches. I'd never met them before. The other two were friends of Anne and George's from London, come down for a couple of days. Everyone was very friendly and I relaxed after I'd had a couple of glasses of wine, but I didn't really enjoy myself. I mean there were three couples and me and no matter how friendly everyone was I still felt uncomfortable. But the food was good and Ada played with me and I drove home carefully and came to bed.

* * *

Friday 25th June. Nothing new. Guy's coming down tomorrow. There's nothing on tv. I thought I'd carry on with my life story. I left it with John — not the best place to be.

When he started hitting me, I didn't know what to do. Sometimes I'd hit back, but never as hard as he hit me, because I was afraid if I hurt him, he'd throw me out. So I hit him just hard enough to push him away. It didn't happen too often, but I couldn't predict it. It didn't matter whether he was drunk or sober. He'd be in a bad mood, I'd do something he didn't like and he'd just lash out, slap my face mostly, sometimes punch me in the stomach, call me a fucking idiot. Not hard enough to do any permanent damage, although once I had a bruise right across my cheek.

I shouldn't have let it happen. He wasn't any bigger than me. I wasn't a child any more. Other eighteen-year-olds would've stuck a knife in him as soon as look at him. I should just have hit him back hard, once, the first time. That would have stopped him. Even better, I should have walked out. But I couldn't; I had nowhere to go. He must have seen that I was trapped and felt he could do what he liked with me. Whatever we did, he had to be in control. Everything had to be just right, just the way he wanted: the flat, the food, me. He must have loved driving that train, all these people, all that metal and only him in charge.

It got worse and worse and I didn't know what to do. Then one night, after I'd been there almost a year, he came back half-drunk and in a really foul mood. Usually if he wanted a meal at the end of a late shift he'd phone. That night he hadn't called and I'd gone to bed. I was sound asleep when he stormed in, switching on the light and shouting why had I left the phone off the hook. "What are you talking about?" I asked. "The phone in the front room." I got up and went through; the receiver was on the floor. I must have knocked it off when I was tidying up. "You're fucking useless," he said and started slapping me around the head. It was giving me a headache and I wasn't thinking clearly enough to protect myself. Then something snapped and I shouted "Get off." He stopped for a second and said, "Don't you tell me what to do," and started hitting me again. This time it was really nasty. He was like a boxer, punching my ears and jabbing me in the stomach. I tried to get away and fell back against the sofa. "Get up," he said. He was going to hit me again and that was the moment when I knew I had to get out. "Get up!" he shouted and pulled me up by the hair. "Get off!" I screamed and we both stopped for a second, surprised at the way I'd reacted.

I ran into the bedroom, yanked open every drawer and started pulling out shirts and underwear. He came in after me. "What are you doing?" he asked. I said I was going out. He punched me in the stomach and slapped me so hard across the face that I fell on the bed in some kind of shock, not sure what he happened. Then I felt him pulling the clothes out of my hand. "You're not going anywhere," he said, "you're staying right here." "No I'm not," I said, getting up and feeling my whole body shake. I thought I was going to be sick and I was scared of what he was going to do next, but I knew I had to get out of there if it was the last thing I did. He watched me stagger up like I was some kind of animal and just as I got to my feet, he pushed me back onto the bed again. Something in me snapped and I screamed "GET OFF!" and before either of us knew it, I'd pulled the clothes out of his hand and rushed into the bathroom and locked the door.

He was knocking on the door shouting at me to come out and my head was ringing and I still thought I was going to be sick and the light was too bright and I couldn't think straight. I was looking at the clothes in my hand wondering which ones I should wear and I pulled on just anything and realised I didn't have any socks or shoes. When I opened the door he was just standing there. "Don't you touch me," I said. "Why not?" he asked, kind of laughing. "What are you going to do about it?" and he slapped me across the face again, not hard this time, like he was playing with me. I just went berserk. I pushed him so hard that he hit the wall and fell against the table by the door. He must have been as dazed as I was, but I didn't stop to check. I just ran into the bedroom, grabbed the first pair of shoes and the first jacket I could lay my hands on. Then I picked up my wallet and went to walk out. He was standing by the door.

"If you leave," he said, "you're never coming back." "Fine," I said. I thought he was going to hit me, but he let me edge past him and onto the landing. "You cunt," he said. "You stupid fucking cunt. You don't know what you're giving up," and he kicked at me so hard that if I hadn't seen it coming it would have knocked me halfway down the stairs and I'd probably have broken my neck. Instead of which I just jumped down as fast as I could, wondering what the neighbours were thinking about all the noise. Down in the street I must have run a couple of hundred yards before I stopped and turned and realised he wasn't following me. Then I collapsed and puked up everything I had in my stomach and sat there shivering until I calmed down and realised I was freezing cold and had nowhere to go.

Half of me was glad to be out of the flat and half of me was shit scared. It was the middle of the night, November, and freezing cold. I wasn't wearing enough clothes and I had no money on me and I didn't know where to go. The only people I knew were John's friends and the people I worked with at the restaurant. There was no one I could call to ask if I could come over. Then I remembered there was a shelter for the homeless somewhere in Soho, so I thought if I got a tube there I could look for it. But it was the middle of the night and the last train had gone, so I had to walk into town. It must have been about two in the morning when I was wandering around Soho looking for that shelter. There was no one around, not like now, when you're always tripping over people sleeping in the streets. I saw a couple of policemen but there was no way I was going to ask them. I was shivering with cold and since I couldn't find the shelter, the only place I thought of going was Waterloo.

Finally I found the dossers along the South Bank. There were all these bodies and cardboard boxes and nobody moving. Then I heard an old Scots guy calling "What do you want, son?" I said I didn't have anywhere to sleep. "Is that all you're wearing?" he said. "Nothing to keep you warm? Come over here." I went over and he said I could doss down with him. "First night out?" he asked. "Here, have a drop of this." It was whisky, the real stuff. "Now if you've any sense, you'll lie down and go to sleep." So I lay down next to him and he covered me with his blanket and I just lay there on the pavement, cold and sore and thought about John. I knew I wasn't going back, but I had no idea what I was going to do next. I thought maybe I'd have to sleep in the streets for the rest of my life.

But here I am twelve years later going upstairs in my own house to a warm comfortable bed with a duvet. In the morning I'll wake up and have a decent breakfast watching tv. And there's you, brought up in a nice big house and never had to sleep rough in your life and God knows where you're sleeping now. Life is weird, the way it always changes. God knows what'll happen next.

* * *

Saturday, 7am. I can't sleep. I kept having nightmares about you. Everything was confused. I was in Peru and John kept hitting me, but it was really you he was hitting. Then it wasn't John but the guerrillas and they were hitting you with rifle butts and you were lying on the floor all curled up. And I was there but I couldn't do anything to help you. You just lay there and didn't move. I woke up but when I went back to sleep it all started again. This man or these men went on hitting you again, only sometimes it was you and sometimes it was me and sometimes it was the guerrillas doing the hitting and sometimes it was John. And it was cold and dark and I kept waking up and every time I went to sleep again the whole thing started again.

It's the first nightmare I've had about you for months. I used to dream of you falling away from me. It was dark and I could hear you but I couldn't see you. I reached out and tried to catch you, but there was no one there. Another time we were fighting each other; you'd turned into this monster that was attacking me. I had to fight you off and change you back into Andy, but didn't know how.

Now I'm just sitting here exhausted looking out of the window. It's a beautiful morning and it's too late to go back to sleep. If I did, I don't think I'd have another nightmare. But for you I suppose it's always a nightmare.

* * *

Sunday evening. £60! The weather did it. All these cars dawdling past. Mr & Mrs Average and their kids, Kevin and Sharon. All types and accents. Yuppies trying to beat us down in price. Spoilt brats picking up onions and pretending to steal them. Married couples who don't talk to each other. There was one gay couple — the one who looked like Tom Cruise flirted with me. Don't worry, I wasn't tempted.

When there are no customers Guy and I chat about this and that. You and the Committee. Life in general. The farm. He's much better on his own than with you. He's been telling me about his past, the fact he didn't know he was gay until he was thirty. He had a couple of girlfriends, but nothing serious. I thought maybe it was knowing you that had made him come out, but it wasn't. He said it was a kind of feeling that grew on him and he realised he looked at men in a different way than he looked at women. But he's never had a boyfriend. He says he's never wanted one, always been too busy. It would be nice, he said, but he thinks he's too old and not attractive enough and no one would be interested. I told him he had to make a bit of an effort. Get trendier clothes, wear contact lenses instead of glasses, go to pubs and clubs. Afterwards I thought about it; me, give advice on finding a lover? It makes as much sense as the royal family offering marriage counselling.

He came down yesterday morning and reminded me it was Gay Pride. They'd asked me to speak and I'd turned them down. He asked if I wanted to go up anyway. I didn't; I just wanted a lazy weekend. There were odd jobs I should have done while Guy was looking after the stall, but I couldn't be bothered. They'll keep.

* * *

Monday 28th. I love these long warm summer evenings. When I've finished work I come back in and watch the news with a cup of tea. There's never anything about you or Peru. Then I take the weights outside for three-quarters of an hour. Where no one can see me from the road. After that I cook dinner and have a beer. Then I watch tv or make some phone calls or write to you. Sometimes I go over to George and Anne's. Ada recognises me now. She says "Um" a lot. I don't know if she means "Tom" or she's just babbling.

It should always be summer and long sunny evenings.

It's stupid saying that. You should always be here. There shouldn't be war or hunger or unhappiness in the world. That was about the only thing we used to disagree about. Although I was really proud of the work you did, sometimes I didn't see the point in giving money to charities or running around the world trying to put things right, because it didn't seem that anything would ever change. There would always be wars and people starving. The place might change from year to year but people would never stop dying. Whatever you did, whether it was for World Aid or Demotica, was only a drop in the ocean. You'd tell me it was more than a drop; things did get better in a lot of countries, like China and India. Even if they didn't, that was no reason to do nothing; you couldn't just let people die. I'd say why give money to buy food for places like Somalia when it just gets stolen and you'd say some of it gets through and even the stuff that does get stolen gets eaten by someone. Maybe we'd got it wrong in Africa but one day we'd get it right.

I didn't know enough to argue with you. Besides, I was never sure I understood the work you do; I could never imagine what you talked about in your meetings or what they achieved.

It was easier with World Aid. You were raising money for projects like education and family planning all over the world. That made sense. But Demotica? Where you just talked about alternative voting systems? I couldn't see how that made people's lives better. You said that strong democracies meant less corruption and stronger economies. "Like Britain?" I asked. That was about the only time I could almost get you mad. I suppose the real reason we disagreed was because I didn't want you to go away. It wasn't so bad at World Aid; you didn't travel so much. And the first couple of times you went off for Demotica I didn't mind; I even liked the fact you were out of the way, because I could get on with the decorating. But then I realised you were going to be away about half the year. There would always be conferences and meetings and you were now an important person who had to be there talking to politicians and community leaders and whoever.

I was unhappy for a while, as if I'd lost you; you'd decided your work was more important than me. Then I realised that it wasn't a case of your work or me. You needed both. If you'd been the kind of person who stayed at home you wouldn't have been Andy McIllray and maybe I wouldn't have loved you as much as I did or I wouldn't have loved you at all. So though part of me didn't like the fact you were away so often, part of me was proud of what you were doing. And everything was always all right again when you came home.

Now sitting here writing and thinking makes me realise how different things will be when you come back. You won't recognise the farm. You won't know James. Even I'm different. Physically stronger, more self-confident, although I still miss and need you. You'll have changed too. God knows how.

* * *

Tuesday 29th. Another warm day. Some of the plants need watering. Willy and Wally need feeding. Like the cats, I can see personality differences in them — Willy's slightly fatter, more curious; Wally hangs back a bit more. Guy says I'm getting too attached to them and I won't want to have them killed. He's wrong; I look at them and all I see is pork chops.

There's someone interested in the new field. His name's Beeton; he has the farm on the other side of Doris's cottage. It's only good enough for sheep, he says, and not many at that. He says he's putting an offer in to the lawyer next week. I'm going to buy six more hens. Guy's been on at me to do so for months. Any more and I'll have to build another henhouse.

Brian's trip to Lima has been postponed. It's been over a month and he hasn't heard back from the people who are supposed to be holding you. I wonder if it was all a hoax. He doesn't want to go out if there's no one to talk to. I think he should go out and start talking to everyone. Guy says there's no point.

The Committee carries on. Money keeps coming in. There are postcards being printed to send to the government, the Peruvians, Shining Path offices in Brussels, all asking for help in setting you free. I don't know how much use it all is. Look how long the hostages were held in Lebanon. I talk with Guy sometimes about whether you'll be there that long. He doesn't know. At least Shining Path aren't religious fanatics, he said. But when I asked what difference that made, he said not much. If you're being held by psychopaths, it doesn't matter what motivates them.

That depresses me sometimes. But not in the way it did last year. It makes me more angry now. I think they should just let you go. You're no use to them. You're no use to anyone but me. Okay, I know that's not true, but it's all I care about. It's all that matters.

* * *

Wednesday. Your Dad called. I'm going to Edinburgh at the end of next week. I would never have believed it a couple of years ago, being accepted by the in-laws. A pity it had to happen this way. Anne and George will look after the farm for a couple of days. I feel bad about it considering I hardly ever see them these days. Maybe Guy can come down.

Eric's lost his job. He knew it was coming. At the end of August with a handsome redundancy. He didn't sound too depressed. He doesn't think it'll be difficult to find another. He might even take time off to consider a career change.

I love you. I worry about you. I miss you.

* * *

Thursday 1st July..Do you know how fast I am on this machine? I just timed myself. Sixty words a minute! I could get a job with that speed. Mind you, the spellcheck programme helps. I tried using the grammar as well, but that picked up so many points I gave up on it. When I read it it makes sense — well, most of it does — and that's all that matters. I'm doing better with the spreadsheet as well. I still don't know if I'm getting it right, because I was hopeless at maths at school, but Guy's looked at it a couple of times and says it seems okay. I've been trying to work out how much profit I'll make from the stall. It looks like a lot, but that's because I'm not paying myself or Guy.

Summer is well and truly here. Some rain forecast for tomorrow, which is good. It won't last, which is also good. I know it's winter there. I hope you're warm.

* * *

Monday 5th. I was in the attic when I came across your diaries again. I brought them down here, but I'm not sure if I should read them. On the other hand, why shouldn't I? I don't have any secrets from you. I can't believe you have any from me.

All right, I admit it; I opened one. It's from India, about ten years ago. There's a paragraph about how you got caught in a downpour and everything in your luggage got soaked and you hated the monsoon. I could just see you standing there in the middle of a dirt track, soaked and fuming.

I probably shouldn't read them. But then I think it's a way of remembering and keeping in touch with you. If you never came home, it's all I would have.

That's just an excuse; you are coming home, I know.

* * *

Tuesday 6th. Nothing new. Sun, work, phone calls. But I feel really good at the end of the day.

I never thought it would happen. After I left John, things just got worse. I went into work that morning and was lucky I didn't get fired. I had my black and whites in my locker and cleaned myself up a bit in the toilet, but I still must have stank. Straight after work I went back to get my stuff and discovered John had changed the lock already. I hammered on the door but he wasn't in and there was no way I could get up to climb in a window. I was really upset. I had a little money that I'd borrowed at work, but no clothes or belongings and nowhere to go. In the end I spent all my money in the same hotel in Earls Court, so I could get a shower and try and wash my clothes. It didn't work. I looked so scruffy the next day the manager fired me. So I was out on the streets again. I walked back to Clapham and John was there, but he wouldn't let me in. He said he'd thrown everything of mine out. He looked really angry and I kept thinking he was going to push me down the stairs. All I could do was leave.

I didn't know what to do. I had less than a quid. I thought about begging but the only people who did it then were dossers on the booze and I wasn't one of them. Then I thought about hitchhiking back to Runcorn but I couldn't. Even if I could persuade Mum to put me up, Jeff would kick me out.

I suppose I was lucky, although I didn't feel it at the time. I walked back to Soho; it was the middle of the evening and the shelter I'd found the other night was open and had a spare bed. God knows there'd be no room now if I tried to get in. I told the woman who ran it about being kicked out of my flat and losing my job. She let me stay for a fortnight and lent me £20 to buy some clothes. I got a job in McDonalds round the corner. The pay was terrible but I could work double shifts and even save a little. There was a young guy in the hostel on the game. He said I should do it too, but therewas no way I could. I didn't want to have sex with anyone at all, not for money, not for anything. The woman was going to find me a place in a long-term hostel, but I didn't like the idea of that — it sounded a bit like a prison. I kept ringing all the rooms to let in the gay papers and finally I found one where I only had to put down a week in advance. It was the place in Stepney Green I told you about. There were three or four of us young guys and Harry, the landlord. He was old, ugly and never properly dressed and always hanging around as if he wanted to sleep with us but never dared ask. If he had, I would have walked straight out, but I think he was more frightened of us than I was of him. Not that I wanted to leave. My room was tiny, at the back of the house and had a window that looked onto a brick wall. But it was mine, my very own and no one else could come in unless I wanted them to.

I stayed there for over a year. I had a job and a little money and I began to make friends. Not really friends, but people I could say hello to. I didn't have much sex; I didn't really want it. It was like back home — the guys I wanted didn't look at me and the guys who did look at me I didn't want. And when someone did pick me up I was all nervous; even if I liked them, I didn't think I could trust them. I'd see them once or twice and then not see them again. That was what everyone I knew did. You were friendly with a guy, went out with him a couple of times, had sex and then you forgot about him or he forgot about you. That's what I thought for a long time. In many ways I still do.

* * *

Thursday. You were lucky. Everything in life seems to have gone right for you. Your parents brought you up in a nice house and gave you plenty of money. You went to university and got a good job and moved into a nice flat in Hampstead. You get to travel round the world. You've always had a lover and they've always been handsome or rich or intelligent or all three — you picked the short straw with me. None of them ever hit you or used you or lied to you. And you've got a nice house and someone to come home to; someone who'll be here for the rest of your life.

I'm not jealous. I can't be; not with you stuck out there. No matter how good it's been for you, this must be hell. But I wonder if you really understand how I felt for most of my life. Maybe you do; maybe that's why you do the job you do. I hope so; I hope it isn't the way the *Sun* says it is — because you like travelling first class, staying in five-star hotels and picking up boys.

I always got it wrong. I was born to the wrong family in the wrong town and when I came to London I met the wrong man. Then for years I didn't meet any man and I lived in grotty flats and worked in grotty jobs. It just went on and on and I didn't know what to do. Sometimes I thought the easiest thing would be to end it all. Looking back on it now, it doesn't seem so bad, especially with so many young people sleeping on the streets, but at the time it felt like hell. I didn't tell you all about it. I didn't want you to know how weak I was. I didn't want to give you a reason not to love me. For a long time after we met I was afraid that one day you'd look at me and decide you didn't want to see me any more. I wasn't worth it. It had happened before. It was only when we moved in here that I began to believe you really loved me.

I told you, I didn't mind Stepney Green; I even got used to Harry. But we all had to leave when he decided to sell up and go and live in Spain. I found a place in Archway, miles from the tube, sharing with four others. I hated it. Apart from Roger the Young Conservative there was a guy who sat in the kitchen all day drinking coffee and spouting crap about not being able to get a job because he was gay and a communist. The real reason he couldn't get a job was he didn't want one. He and Roger were always shouting at each other. The shower hardly worked and there was a squat next door to us with junkies playing music at all hours of the day and night.

Things didn't get better. Any time I got a job, it never seemed to last. I'd have to leave because the pay wasn't good enough or the chef was a maniac or the manager didn't like me and always gave me the worst shifts. Or business would be slack and a couple of us would be fired, or the whole place closed down. It wasn't always easy to get another job, not even when yuppie cafes were opening all over the place. There are always foreigners who'll work for nothing — Arabs or South Americans are the worst. And you can't get a job in the ethnic restaurants — who wants a waiter from Merseyside in a restaurant in Chinatown? I always did find something in the end, but every time I was out of work I was spending whatever little money I'd saved and wondering if I'd ever see a pay packet again.

Even when I was in work I could never save. I'd have thirty or fifty quid put by and one day I'd be depressed and go out and buy myself a shirt or a pair of jeans. Or I'd go out with a couple of friends and we'd spend a fortune in a night on drink and a disco. So every time I thought about moving somewhere better I never had enough money. I just had to stay there and lie in bed staring at the lines of flowers on the wallpaper.

All that's over now. It's in the past, unimportant. It was a waste of eight years of my life. It should have been different. I should have arrived in London that day, stepped out of the tube at Piccadilly Circus and walked straight into you. You're all that has ever mattered in my life. I love you.

* * *

Tuesday 13th. Brian's finally off to Peru next week.

I got back from Edinburgh yesterday. It was weird. The last time I was there it was with you and your parents were very distant. This time I was alone and they were very kind. It's like I was a substitute for you. I told you before, your dad seems to cope, but your Mum is lost without you. More lost than I am, because she's old and there's nothing left in her life, while at least I'm still young and have got the farm and friends.

Your Dad met me at the bus station and drove me home. Your Mum had prepared dinner. It was all a bit stiff at first. We talked about the Committee and Brian's visit and the people that Guy and your Dad have been meeting. I said I hadn't been doing much but they didn't seem to mind. After dinner they showed me the scrapbook they'd kept. It's much fuller than mine. I've just been putting cuttings in a box, but your Mum pastes them into a book. A lot I hadn't seen — whenever I'm in Guy's office there's never time to look at everything. There were clippings from all sorts of papers and magazines. The photo of you we give out in the press pack was everywhere. Even I was mentioned a lot more times than I knew.

I was getting tired and had been drinking wine and I sort of forgot to be polite. We were looking at one of the clippings and something your Mum said made me realise how much I missed you and suddenly I couldn't stop crying. I sat there between your parents with the tears streaming down my face and your Mum held my hand and your Dad patted me on the back and said, "It's all right, son, it's all right". For a second I thought, I'm not his son, I'm thirty-one years old, but that was stupid, they were being kind and because I was your lover that made me their son-in-law.

Everything was much easier after that. There was nothing between us any more, nothing to keep back, nothing to hide. We spent the next two days just talking and doing some sight-seeing. I realised I actually like them both. Until you disappeared I hadn't liked either of them because they were never anything but cold to me. It was only when you got kidnapped that I began to see them differently. Seeing your Dad at Committee meetings in London, I began to respect him — he's sincere and trustworthy. And talking to your Mum on the phone and meeting her again made me see that she's kind and friendly.

They told me what you were like when you were a boy. They said you were quiet, always independent, spent a lot of time on your own. I heard all the stories that would have made you embarrassed, like losing the egg-and-spoon race when you were six and your first day at school. I got the feeling that they wanted to be closer to you than they are. And I wondered why they never had another child. I couldn't ask and you never told me.

Your Mum said how difficult it was for them to accept your being gay. She said you had told her years ago, but she'd never been able to talk about it with anyone else, not even your Dad. None of her friends knew till it came out in the newspapers. That made it a little easier, because there was nothing to hide any more, but she's still not used to it. She wishes you had kids, but that isn't going to happen, and she's frightened you're going to catch AIDS. I thought about telling her you wouldn't get it from me, but then I wondered, what if you'd already got it from somebody else? I can't offer her any guarantees. All through this your Dad just sat there listening and not saying anything; I don't know what he thinks, except I'm sure that in his way he loves you.

I told them a lot about myself, where I grew up, the jobs I've done, that kind of thing. Your Mum seemed really upset that I'd lost touch with my family and that Mum had died. She was surprised I didn't miss them, but it's like being poor — if you've never had money, you don't know what it's like. I'd never been close to my family so there was no one to miss. Sometimes I miss the family I never had — a Dad who wasn't always somewhere else, brothers and sisters my own age — but there's nothing I can do about it, so I don't really think about it.

* * *

Thursday. It was hot today. I've just come back from the Lamb, having a drink with Anne and George. It's the first time I'd been there since the last time you and I went. I thought the woman behind the bar would recognise me — seeing as how I'm a local celebrity — but she didn't. The three of us sat outside and chatted. Ada was with a neighbour and George and Anne were in a really good mood; they sat teasing each other and Anne spent half the time cuddling against him. You don't expect people in their forties with hair turning grey to act that way. I felt jealous because it was something that you and I wouldn't do, not even in a gay bar. Maybe we should.

I walked home about ten. The sun had set but the sky was still light. I came round by the copse and saw the house. The kitchen light was on. It was home and — maybe I shouldn't tell you this — it was still home without you. Don't take that in a bad way. What I mean was when we were living here together, even though my name was on the title deeds and I did all the decorating, I never quite believed it was my home as much as yours. If anything went wrong, I would be the one who had to leave. Now it feels like my home, completely. Perhaps too much; as I said before, when you come back, you'll find so much has changed.

* * *

Friday. I've been looking through your photos — the albums before you met me. You with your parents and your dog — all blond hair and toothy grin. That one of you at twenty in your flares; your clothes look daft but there's a look in your eyes that says there's something special about you. All your ex-lovers — a real United Nations. It's strange looking at them, wondering what they're doing now, what you think of them, whether you'd want to get back with any of them. None of them have contacted the AMC — unless they've done so and hadn't said who they were. Our tastes really are quite different. You go for the pretty boy type. Boy's the wrong word; young man. Is that how you see me? If it is, will I soon be too old for you? I'm kidding. I know perfectly well that it's who we are and not what we look like that keeps us together. Still, sometimes I wonder how much I have in common with all your ex-lovers. Although you've talked about them, I can't imagine what any of them are really like. I don't know if I would get on with them. I can only guess from the pictures.

The only one I find attractive is Luis, but he's far too young for me. How old was he? Twenty-two? Twenty-three? All I know is that he was an actor who didn't get much work and was always very jealous. Yucky — Yuki — does nothing for me; I can't see what you see in Japanese. Blank faces and narrow eyes; they're like something from another planet. I could never imagine having sex with one. And what did you talk about all the time you were together? Sushi? Karate? How to make motor-cars?

You look happiest with Chuck. Such an all-American name. You look good together, both grinning and arms around each other. He wasn't handsome, but he looks older, reliable. Why did you let him go? You could have gone to the States with him; you would have found a job easily enough.

Then there are the lesser fry — the ones you had a fling with, nothing more. There seem to be an awful lot of them. I don't know who they are; you write the date on the back, but not the place or name. Some of them you told me before, but I forgot. Looking at them is like watching a film with the sound turned down; you try to work out what's happening, but you really don't know. I suppose if I looked in your diaries I could find out. But not tonight; I'm far too tired.

* * *

Sunday 18th. You bastard. So the *Sun* was right; you do fuck around when you're away. Your code was pretty easy to spot — asterisks by the guy's name. I'll eat a week of dinners from Willy and Wally's trough if I'm wrong. Enrique in Colombia, Rang in Bangkok, Ashok in India; how many others have there been? I've just skipped through a couple of the notebooks. It seems that every time you go abroad you pick up someone. You bastard. You slut.

I've calmed down. I've deleted some of the worst comments. But I still think you're a bastard. I've counted eight so far. Why do you do it? Is it like your souvenirs — you've got to have at least one pick-up every trip? What are you thinking when you do it? Do you think about me? Do you tell them about me? What do they mean to you? Do you fall in love with them? What do you tell them? What do they give you that I can't?

I got mad again and had to stop. To be honest, I'm not surprised. Most gay men fuck around — some a lot more than you do. And though I never talked about it, I always suspected you did too. To tell the truth, that's why I didn't talk about it. If I'd made you tell me about it, it would have made me unhappy, and if I'd wanted you to stop, I don't know how you would have reacted. Maybe you would have refused and that might have made us split up. At least there doesn't seem to have been anyone in England, not since you met me.

I'd just hoped that because I didn't fuck around you didn't either. I hoped I meant as much to you as you mean to me. Now, I don't know. I know I mean something to you. You bought this house with me; you come home to me. But obviously I'm not giving you everything you need. Or you wouldn't want these boys. I'm confused; I shouldn't have looked at any of your stuff. It tells me things I don't want to know; it asks questions I can't answer.

It's three o'clock in the morning and I can't get to sleep. I don't think I'm jealous but I don't know what I feel. I lie in bed with the light off and all I see is you — now and in the past, with others and with me. You're a different man and I'm not sure how. I wish you'd come home, so I could forget all this. Just let me pick you up at the station as I always did, and maybe everything will be all right. Come home, Andy, please, now. I need you.

* * *

Monday 19th. Brian has finally left. He's taking a letter from me to you in case there's any way he can get it to you. It tells you I love you, I miss you; we're doing all we can to help you. I sent it before I read your diaries, but I still feel the same about you.

That's not quite true. What I mean is, I love you as I always did, but in some ways you're a different person. I don't — I'm not sure I should write this; maybe I'll delete it later — I don't know if I still trust you. It's like John and Alex — you think you know someone, until suddenly you see they're quite different from what you thought they were. What do you think about when you're not with me, Andy? What goes through your mind? Do you think about me as much as I think about you? Do you miss me as much as I miss you? My life is the house and the farm, the animals and you and friends. That's all. Your life is totally different. It's every country in the world. It's people in South America and Africa and Asia, people who are poor or illiterate or oppressed and need help. That's your world. I'm part of it, aren't I? I must be, or you wouldn't come home to me. But what part of it?

I keep thinking I should put the diaries away, forget about them, maybe not even talk to you about them when you get back. Then I think I ought to read them, year by year from the beginning; I really ought to know everything about you. They're sitting on the floor by the desk, a pile of schoolbooks from all the different countries you bought them in. I pick one up and start reading it and then feel bad and put it away. It's not just what you write about your pick-ups, it's the way you write. It's boring. "Pompous," Guy would say.

Anyway, the important thing is that Brian is on his way to Peru. I don't know if I believe in God but I've started praying. Anything to get you out.

* * *

Tuesday. No news. It rained. I took the afternoon off and watched an old film on television. Eric called, needing cheering up. Ben, the guy he lived with before he met Dave, has died of AIDS. I said he and Dave should come down for the weekend; I haven't seen them since Christmas.

* * *

Wednesday 21st. My birthday. No card from you for the second year running. Sorry, that's a bad joke. Anne and George had me over and there was cake. A nice little family gathering; just the three of them and me. Last year I had them over here; Anne was still pregnant, waddling around.

I got half-a-dozen cards. The best was from Kathy and Frank; it was a Far Side card of a dog tempting a cat into a washing machine. It was the opposite of our cats and James. They think he's a bit simple.

Brian phoned Guy. He's arrived and met the ambassador and some people in the government. No news, of course. Tomorrow he's meeting his Demotica contacts. I don't think he should waste time there; he should fly straight out to Cuzco; that's what I would do.

I was hoping this morning when I woke up that I would hear something from you as a birthday present. Wrong again, Tom, wrong again.

* * *

Thursday. Nothing on tv. I thought maybe Martin Bell or Kate Adie would have flown out to do a special report. Guy says he's been keeping all the press informed, but they won't do anything until there's some solid news.

I've been reading your diaries and thinking about what's in them. About what you do when you're not with me. I used to think that when you got on that plane you were counting the days until you got back to me. I was. Remember that calendar in the kitchen with the blue circles for your departures and the red circles for your coming back? I'd look at it ten times a day. I'd count the hours sometimes. Why do you think half the time I drove all the way over to Heathrow when I could have picked you up at Reading or Midgham? I wanted to see you again as soon as possible, even if that meant getting up at three to meet the four-thirty from Delhi.

It wasn't the same for you, was it? It's not just you didn't think about me, but you're a different person when you're away from home. It's not just the sex. You do things abroad that you haven't done for years in England. Go out to bars and nightclubs, get drunk, stay up late. Meet people, talk to them, fuck with them. Always someone new, not like here, where it's always the same old friends. Then there's all sorts of things about your work you never tell me. I always ask you how it went, and you say good or bad, this person turned up or didn't, that person made a good or bad speech. But you never go into detail, not like your diaries.

There's a couple of pages from your last trip to India about some woman you met who organises a sewing circle. You go on and on about how important she is and how the sewing circle is the only place for women to meet and talk and educate themselves. She's a real hero. If only there were lots more like her, there wouldn't be any problems in India because all the women would learn to sew and read and vote. Or something like that. You never told me about her.

Maybe it's my fault. When we first met, you'd talk about a lot of things like that. But I didn't listen much. I knew the things you were telling me were important to you, but there was too much detail. They didn't mean anything to me. I should have listened more, tried to understand. Then maybe you wouldn't need to put so much in your diaries.

I don't mind so much about the sex. The more I think about it, the more it seems that the sex you have with these boys is different from the sex you have with me. For a start, you don't seem to do it in England. I had my suspicions about you and the YMCA, but they soon passed. I don't think you ever lied to me about working late or missing a train. And after we moved down here, you spent less and less time in London, not more. I get the impression that your pick-ups abroad pass the time, that's all. You seem to forget them when you leave, because you never mention them again.

Then I wonder if it's fair on them. You wining and dining them, making love on big double beds. It doesn't matter if they are just call-boys out for what they can get, but what if they want something more? What if they fall in love with you? What if with you they're like me with Alex, what then? Aren't you responsible for them?

You really are different from what I thought you were. No, that's not true. There's just so much more to you than I'd known. I still love you, though. I can't help it. You've given me so much. You're a part of me, whatever you do.

* * *

Sunday 25th. Andy, Andy, Andy, Andy, Andy. It's all gone wrong. Will you ever understand? Will you believe me?

I don't know what to do. Even Guy is worried. I don't know if you'll hear about it. But here the whole country knows. And I'm sure they believe it, whatever we say. There's no smoke without fire. So there goes all our good will.

It's hit your parents worst. When Guy called them, your Dad was so angry and cold. When I spoke to your Mum, she was crying. They believe us, I think, but the damage is done. I don't know if they'll ever trust me again.

And if you hear about it, what are you going to think? That we don't give a damn? That we're letting you rot? That the Committee is just an excuse to get money? You'll hear what the papers say; you'll never hear our side of the story.

I love you, Andy, I love you, I love you, I love you. If you ever read this, believe me that it's true, whatever the newspapers or other people say. It's always been true; it always will be true. I love you so much.

It started yesterday at half-past six. I heard the geese and before I was properly awake, someone was knocking at the door. They wouldn't stop. I pulled on my dressing-gown and rushed downstairs thinking it was the police or someone from Demotica with some kind of news. Of course if I'd been properly awake I'd have realised they would have used the telephone. For a second I even thought it might be you, somehow got back here without anyone knowing and having left your key in Peru. Instead there was this woman in a red suit who said good morning Tom, could she speak to Guy. Of course he'd followed me down and was standing right behind me in nothing but boxer shorts. "My name's Mary Henderson," she went on. "I'm from the *People*. I understand that the two of you have been sleeping together for some time."

It was like she had hit me across the face. I couldn't say anything, but my face went all red. "That isn't true," Guy said sharply. "I'm afraid it is," she said, "we have photographs." And she held out half a dozen pictures. They were all of our bedroom window at night; you could see right in and there was Guy and me undressing. You could even see the two of us in bed.

Everything stopped. I just stood there looking at these pictures and thinking it can't be true and knowing it was. They must have been taken with a telephoto lens from that rise on the other side of the stream. And of course the curtains were open; I never close them when you're away, not even in summer. There's no one to look in — or so I'd always thought.

"Well?" she said. I felt as if I'd just been caught committing the worst possible crime in the world and I was desperately trying to think of something I could do to stop anyone else finding out. I thought of taking the photos from her, ripping them up, pleading with her, bribing her, even killing her, but I knew nothing would work. If I took the photos, there would be other copies that would get out and everyone would see.

"These pictures don't prove anything," Guy said. His voice was calm but I knew he was angry.

"They prove you're sleeping together."

"Sleeping," Guy said, "that's all."

"You don't expect us to believe that, do you?" she said. "There are two spare bedrooms in the house. You're both adults. If you're not having an affair, why are you 'sleeping' together?" She had this horrible voice that made it sound perverted.

Then I saw a man taking photos of the three of us. He was standing by the sty, the same spot as the man from the *Sun* the first time this happened. "Stop that!" I called out. "Get off our land!" I wanted to rush over and grab his camera but Guy pulled me back. "You're wearing your dressing-gown," he said, "it wouldn't look good on film."

I didn't give a damn what I looked like, but it made me stop and realise that if I wasn't careful, I would just make things a hell of a lot worse.

Meanwhile this woman stood there with a smug smile on her face, so happy with what she was doing. "When did you start having sex together," she asked, "before or after Andy was kidnapped?" I was about to let blast at her but Guy got in first. "Listen very carefully, Ms Henderson," he said. "I'm going to give you a statement. You're going to write it down, word for word, if you're not already recording it. And if your paper doesn't print it in full or if it makes any suggestion that Tom and I are anything other than friends and colleagues, both it and you are going to be hit with by the heaviest of libel suits first thing on Monday morning."

She didn't change her expression, simply said that she presented facts and it was up to the readers to decide the truth. "Fine," said Guy, "as long as you stick to the facts. And the facts are that Tom and I are no more than friends. It's true that we sometimes share a bed, but we're both under a lot of stress and sleeping together — just sleeping together, no sex — is one way of relieving tension. It's a gesture of affection, nothing more."

She wrote it all down, but I could see that she didn't believe it. Meanwhile the photographer was still taking photos. He came closer and I was very uptight but Guy said to keep cool, we had nothing to hide. So with a great deal of difficulty I stood there, praying they would both go away as soon possible.

"That's all very well," the woman said when she had finished writing, "but it's true, Guy, isn't it, that you're not in a relationship with anyone else? Is that why you come to see Tom every weekend? And he sometimes comes up to London to stay with you?" "I only go when I have to," I said, "when there are Andrew McIllray Committee meetings." "How often are these meetings?" she asked.

"Once a fortnight? That's very convenient, isn't it?" Guy shook his head and sighed. "We've got nothing more to say," he said. "Now will you please leave?"

"Do you have anything to say, Tom?" she asked. "I mean, Andy's been away for a year and a half; you must be feeling lonely. Does Guy make up for it?" "He's a friend," I said, "nothing more." "But friends can become lovers too, can't they?" she asked. "I mean, you spend all this time together. You're a good-looking young man. I'm sure you have a normal sex drive. All my gay friends tell me how easy it is to sleep around."

"I can't imagine you've got any friends, gay or not," I said before Guy shut me up. "The only thing I want to say is Andy's the only person I'm in love with, now and forever. And if you print anything that hurts him I'll break your fucking neck." She just carried on smiling and said, "There's no need to get upset. You should have thought of the consequences before you started, shouldn't you?" "Started what?" I asked, but Guy pulled me in and shut the door.

It didn't stop her. She raised her voice, not really shouting, but loud enough so that we could hear. "How close are you to Guy, Tom? Are you in love with him? What do you think Andy will feel when he finds out?" I stood there in the hall wanting to lash out, to open the door and punch her ugly face in, but Guy said, "It's all right, don't worry," and gently pulled me into the kitchen. There was James, who hadn't even barked, looking at me as if he knew there was something wrong and he wasn't sure if he was the one who'd done it.

"I want to kill them all," I said. "Every single journalist that's ever lived. That's the second time they've done this to us. Why can't they help instead of hurting people like this? What right have they got to destroy people's lives?" Guy said I was right, but there was nothing we could do. We just had to make the best of it. In the end I calmed down and we made breakfast. The woman seemed to have gone. I looked out of the window thinking one of them was going to be staring in, but there was no one there. I went through to the front room to check and saw them sitting in a car just outside the gate. She was talking into her mobile phone.

Guy said the best method of defence was attack. He sat down and wrote a press release denying the story. He repeated that we occasionally slept together but we were not having an affair. It was irresponsible of the *People* to publish the story, because it meant that there might be less public support for you and that could delay your release. "It's the best we can do," Guy said, and I could tell he was worried. That was when we phoned your parents to warn them what was going to happen.

Guy drove up to London to get the statement to all the newspapers and tv and radio. Before he left, he phoned a few of the journalists he had been dealing with, to see if he could get them to write a sympathetic story. He asked if I wanted to go with him because he knew all the hassle with journalists visiting would start again, but I wasn't going to leave the farm for anyone to wander over it. The two of them were still sitting in their car when he left.

When I went out to feed the animals the woman came down the driveway to ask if we could talk. I said I had nothing to talk about. I was going to clean out the sty and I wasn't going to be responsible for where all the pigshit went. I was quite calm; I'd let all the anger out and nothing I could do was going to stop the story appearing. She followed me over to the sty and asked me if Guy was a good lover. I looked up and asked if she was proud of what she was doing. She went on about how it was her job to get at the truth. I just said very calmly and quietly that she wouldn't know the truth if it hit her in the face and if she didn't get off my land in five seconds a bucket of pigshit would.

She didn't believe me until I had it in my hand, then she rushed back up the driveway. The man was standing at the gate taking pictures again. I kept walking with the bucket in my hand. The man started to say something and I said that I didn't care what happened to his expensive camera and at that they both got into the car. They didn't drive away or anything, but I just went up to the car and started pouring the shit all over the roof and windscreen. Then I turned back and walked back home. When I looked back, the man was taking photos again, of me and the car, and I didn't give a damn.

I got hardly any work done that day and there was no way I could have run the stall. The phone calls started within the hour. I just handled them as best I could. Sometimes I got confused and sometimes I got angry and when that happened I had to leave the phone off the hook until I had calmed down. Some of the journalists were quite hostile and some were friendly. It was only when I read the papers today that I realised that it was the friendly ones who wrote the nasty articles. A couple wanted me to do radio interviews there and then, but I told them to contact Guy. I was lucky that no one else came down. Guy said that there were a couple on his tail and outside his house and as long as he was in London, he didn't think anyone would bother coming down here.

Guy spent the rest of the day getting as many interviews as possible and spent the night in London. He managed to get on both radio and television. It made me depressed watching the one on ITV; he was telling the truth that we weren't having an affair, but I knew that people wouldn't believe him.

As the day went on I thought more and more about what effect all this would have on you. The story was bound to get to Peru. Shining Path would use it as an excuse not to release you. That reminded me of Brian and I called Guy and he said he'd already called. He wasn't happy, Guy said, and that really depressed me.

When I went to bed, I lay there for ages thinking how I'd destroyed the chances of getting you free. I wondered if you'd hear the story, if you'd understand that I hadn't done anything wrong. I'd just been lonely, that was all. I'd wanted someone to hold. But because I'd been that selfish, it might mean you were going to be held a prisoner forever. In the end I took a pill to get to sleep. It worked, although I woke up with a headache and still worrying. I was at the newsagent's before he opened up.

The story was everywhere. The *People* headlined it: "Gay Hostage Lover Storm; Tom Dayton Finds Consolation in Another Man's Arms". There were photos of Guy and me and the woman at the front door, and of pigshit all over the car. The *Sunday Mirror* had "Gay Hostage Lover in Share-a-Bed Scandal". The *News of the World* said "Gay Tom Denies Affair" and then spent most of the article suggesting that Guy and I had been lovers for months. By the time I'd read all the papers I felt sick. I felt like one of the most perverted people I knew. It didn't matter whether the article said Guy and I were lovers or the victims of a cruel trick, we came out as two randy, selfish, untrustworthy perverts. And because it was in the papers — every paper — it had to be true. And because it was true of us, it was somehow also true of you and without doing a thing I could feel all the support and sympathy for you drying up.

Guy called and tried to tell me things weren't as bad as they looked. I called your Dad and he told me things were much worse than he had expected. Your Mum didn't even want to talk to me.

Anne came over and picked me up and I spent the day with her and George. They didn't ask whether the story was true or not. I didn't want to talk or do anything but stay there and let them look after me until it had all died down. George brought me back in the evening and I fed the animals and went to bed. I couldn't get to sleep and didn't want to take any pills, so I started to write it all down. Now it's three in the morning and my head aches and my back and arms hurt and I'm wider awake than I've ever been.

Do you understand, Andy? Why I did it? I didn't mean to. The first few times he came down he slept in the back room. But one night I told him how lonely I felt and how much I missed you and when we went up to bed he asked if it would help if he slept with me. We both knew that's all it would be. I just needed someone to hold and to hold me. We got into the habit. It was friendlier and it saved sheets. It didn't mean anything except affection. We've never made love. Not really. Sometimes it's a bit more than holding each other, but it doesn't mean anything. It's not like with you, Andy; it's nothing like with you. I never forget you; sometimes I even wake up holding Guy and for a moment I think it's you. It isn't, but at least with him, I'm not alone.

I didn't write it down because I didn't want you to know. There was no point, like you never told me about the boys you sleep with when you're away. It's got nothing to do with you and me. At least that's what I thought. But I was wrong. Now it might mean I'll never see you again. Guy says it depends what the daily papers say. If most of them accept the denial it might be all right, but I don't believe they will. People always think the worst, whatever you tell them.

I don't love Guy. I like him a lot and things have gone much better since he started coming down for the weekends, but I'm not in love with him. It's you I love, Andy; it's you I always love.

It's dawn. Everything looks different. Everything feels different. I'm staring out of the window and I can see the barn and greenhouse. I've just let the hens out; one them is pecking the ground and Billy Joe is strutting around. The geese have woken up too. It's the same every morning, but it's different today. It's as if it doesn't belong to me any more. Or it belongs to me, but I don't give a damn. All that matters is you. Somewhere out there, thousands of miles away, up a mountain on the other side of the ocean, you're locked up and blindfolded and afraid for your life. And I've made it worse. No matter what you've heard, Andy, it isn't true. I love you. I love you. Please, please forgive me.

* * *

Tuesday. Guy has spoken to Brian again. The story was on CNN and in all the Lima papers. Only one carried our denial; the rest say that we're lovers. Brian has put out the statement that Guy faxed over, but it's hardly been mentioned. The embassy is embarrassed and the Peruvians have cancelled a meeting. He's going to Cuzco tomorrow, but all his contacts say this new scandal on top of your being gay makes things very difficult.

What are you thinking, Andy? Please, God, make him know it's not true. Make him love me still.

The papers here were more sympathetic yesterday, but it's too late now. Guy says the AMC has had a few hate calls. He says it'll be a few days before we know how much public support we've lost, but that doesn't matter any more. The real damage has been done in Peru.

I'm so sorry, Andy.

* * *

Friday. Brian's flying back tomorrow. He spent three days in Cuzco getting nowhere. Eric and Dave are coming for the weekend. I asked Guy not to; I think he was disappointed and I wasn't sure if I'd said the right thing.

* * *

Sunday 1st August. One year, four months and nine days after you disappeared. Another month has gone by. Your second winter. Are they looking after you? How's your health? I've read that people can lose their teeth, fall ill and get all sorts of diseases when they're locked up for a long time. I'm so frightened for you. And I've made it so much worse.

Thank God for Eric and Dave. They got here about eleven on Friday night and the first thing Eric did was give me a great big hug. "Well, tell me all about it," he said. "Get it out of your system." "Get what out of my system?" I asked. "Everything — after you've given us a drink. By the way, where do we put these?" They'd brought down with them bags of shopping, like Guy on his first visit. As well as food there were magazines and videos and several bottles of wine. "Just so you don't think we're here to drink you out of house and home," Dave said. "It's the weekend. We have to relax," Eric said. "We were so desperate, we had to stop for a drink on the way down." Which meant, Dave explained, that he stopped and Eric drank.

We talked into the night. They knew it all already — I talk to Eric about twice a week, but you can never say as much in phone calls as you can tell each other face to face. And because they drink, I drank, and I began to relax. It had been a bad week. I hadn't wanted to do anything. I'd kept feeling I wasn't going to see you again, so there was no point in keeping the farm going. All I'd done was feed the animals and potter about and spent most of my time watching tv. And even though Anne and Guy had called almost every day, it hadn't made me feel any better. I just wanted them to go away.

With Eric and Dave it all came out. How I felt about you, the farm, Guy, what I'd been doing. I told them things I couldn't tell Guy, because he had enough problems of his own, doing his job and keeping the AMC going. Things like feeling guilty because I wasn't doing enough for you and not being sure if I should be doing all I was doing with the farm without discussing it with you. It was good to get it all of my chest and to hear them give their opinions. You tell Guy something and, no matter what it is, he treats it very seriously, goes through all the ins and outs before giving his opinion. Dave's a little like that, but Eric has this "What the heck" attitude. No matter how serious the problem is, Eric makes it seem much less so. So the newspapers claim Guy and I are randier than bunnies? Who cares? If straight people are so hung up on two friends sharing a bed, that's their problem. You'll know it doesn't meant anything. So you'll come home and see a pigsty where we once thought of putting a fountain? If you don't like it, we'll get rid of it and put in a fountain after all.

We got to bed about four in the morning. Eric said I could sleep with them if I needed company. It was a nice gesture but I didn't need it and anyway I was thinking there was someone out there with a long-lens camera and some kind of film which could see in even if we pulled the curtains.

I got up late on Saturday and had the livestock fed before they came down. I didn't want to do the stall, because I was sure there would just be a lot of sightseers staring and making comments, but they said we could do it together. As it happened, there was no one difficult, although I'm sure there were a couple who recognised me. It wasn't very busy and we made less than £20. On Saturday evening Anne and George and Ada came over. Eric and Dave did the cooking and we had a great time, the best time I'd had since you were taken. We got up earlier today. We did the stall for about four hours, reading the papers and chatting. There was nothing in the tabloids, just a long boring piece in the *Independent on Sunday*. Guy told me on the phone that he thought it was helpful; I couldn't see how.

They left about five, promising to come back soon. Eric said he might come down for a week after he'd left his job. I thought he'd be desperate to find another, but he says he isn't. He can survive for half a year on his redundancy and he wants a couple of months break before he starts job-hunting again. It would be good; I could do with his company again.

It's true. I do feel much better for their visit. Even though we talk on the phone, I'd forgotten how much they mean to me, how much they helped me before I met you.

* * *

Tuesday evening. Brian's back. No news. I'll hear all about it when I'm up in London at the end of the week. Your Mum called. "You mustn't blame yourself for what the papers say," she said. It was nice of her, but I don't know if she meant it. I wonder what she would have thought if I'd been her daughter-in-law caught sleeping with another man?

Guy insisted on coming down next weekend. He said we might as well carry on as normal. If he stopped coming down, the press would say we had something to hide. If he did come down, they would still say it was true. He's right, and anyway, after Dave and Eric's visit I no longer care.

* * *

Wednesday 4th. I've started drinking herbal tea. It helps me sleep at night.

I was remembering the last Christmas we had together. Of course you had to be in Senegal the week before and coming back on flights that got delayed. I'd decided to meet you at Heathrow and ended up spending the whole day there. Each time there was another delay it was only for a couple of hours, so it wasn't worth coming home; it wasn't till almost midnight that you got in.

You think an airport is a big place because there are all these airline desks and destinations and shops and so on, but it isn't. Terminal Two is mind-bogglingly small. I was bored to tears. I'd sit for quarter of an hour and then walk up and down outside the arrivals point. I'm surprised the police didn't arrest me as a terrorist or for loitering. I watched the other people and tried to guess who they were waiting for. I got it right about half the time. There was a little Indian or Arab girl who got lost. The security woman was very kind, but they couldn't speak to each other and the kid was bawling her head off. Finally the mother came running up and started shouting at the kid for screaming and at the security woman for trying to kidnap her. When I got bored with all that, I inspected all the airline desks and the shops. By the end of the day I could tell you the arrival and departure times of every single plane from Poland to Portugal. I spent hours looking at the covers of every magazine and every paperback in the bookstall — I never realised that women's books had so many hunky half-naked men on them.

By the time you arrived I was almost spare, but I didn't really mind. I wanted to be there to meet you. Your flight came up on the board and I stood there with half a dozen others who had been waiting all day. Then you appeared, tired, carrying more souvenirs in that brown case. You weren't looking for me. You thought the last bus had gone and you were either going to have spend a fortune on a taxi or get the tube into London and get the train. You thought I'd gone out, because you'd called from Paris and I wasn't in. Then you looked up and saw me and this great big smile spread all over your face and I knew how happy you were to see me. Not just because I was there with the car and you'd get home quicker, but because it was me, because you loved me, you were glad to get home and be with me.

It was a good Christmas. The second we'd spent in the farmhouse, but the first where everything was decorated and in its proper place. I'd got a tree and decorated it and put it in the hall. Eric and Dave came down and we all went over to Anne and George's. We both relaxed. We were both on holiday so we just lay around, eating or drinking or talking or watching television. Or making love.

It was only ten days, but I never wanted that holiday to end. I thought this is what it should be like every time. He can go away as often as he likes as long as it's always like this when he comes back.

We'd got it right, hadn't we? We had this nice house in the country. You were getting on with your work and I was happy looking after the house and land. I had my job at the school so I wasn't dependent on you. We had friends, each other, everything we wanted.

You went away once more, back to India — the time you wrote about the woman with the sewing circle — and everything was still

101

fine. I knew that Peru was coming up, but it didn't seem different from any of your other trips. You were always going off to places where half the country was in rebel hands or everyone had malaria or mugging was the number one industry and you'd always come back. I'd always thought you had some kind of diplomatic status; nobody could touch you. It wasn't like other, dangerous, jobs you could have had — war correspondent or mountain rescue or something.

So the day you went off to Peru was just like any other. You worked in the morning, had a flight to Miami in the afternoon and a connection to arrive in Lima in the middle of the night. I drove you to Reading, kissed you goodbye and drove off again. I didn't even get out of the car. The last I saw of you was your back as you walked away, case in hand, shoulder bag over your arm. You were wearing your brown jacket and beige trousers. You never did have a sense of style.

Just your back; that's all I saw and I hardly noticed it. I'd be seeing you again in a couple of weeks... Now it's getting on for a couple of years.

We can't change anything, can we? I can't go back and stop you getting on that plane. I can't change what the newspapers printed. I can't fob off 'Jack Burns' or insist that Guy sleeps in the back room. All I can do is pray for you.

* * *

Sunday 8th August. Guy's just gone. I was running around London on Friday and we drove down that night. My mood hasn't been particularly good. The only good news is that Willy and Wally are getting bigger and bigger. It's odd, looking at them and working out which bit's bacon, which bit's ham and which bit's pork. I wonder if they know what's going to happen to them. Some people say pigs are very intelligent. They don't look it to me. Guy gets mad at me and refuses to have anything to do with them unless I agree to keep them for life as pets. Which I won't do.

Everyone came to the meeting to hear about Brian's trip. He didn't have much to say. Everyone says Shining Path is a spent force. No one's afraid of them any more. Only one person claimed to be in touch with them and he had said that they didn't want to talk. It wasn't so much because of me and Guy, although they knew about that. It was more that Brian didn't have anything to offer in return for getting you free. He'd wanted them to let you go on humanitarian grounds, but Shining Path aren't known for being humanitarian. They wanted to speak to the Peruvian government, but the government didn't want to speak to them. Or if they did, they didn't want to do it through Brian. Brian got the impression that whoever was left in Shining Path didn't know what to do with you. He wasn't sure who'd authorised your kidnapping or why. He'd asked for proof that you were still alive and didn't get it, but he trusts the guy he met and thinks you are okay. Everyone at the meeting tried to be cheerful but it didn't work. I just sat there thinking how long it had taken to get the hostages out of Lebanon and how long Salman Rushdie had been in hiding. Your Dad asked a few questions but your Mum just sat silent. I spoke to them afterwards, but there was nothing I could say. They weren't angry with me, not even cold; it was like I didn't matter to them any more. All they want is you and they can't get you.

The weekend was almost like before. We did some gardening and set up the stall. Only one person asked if we were the couple in the papers. Guy said yes. She said it was terrible what papers printed these days and she hoped you would soon be set free. That cheered me up a little and I thought that despite everything Brian had said maybe there are people in Peru who think the same.

Guy and I talk a lot about you. I think Guy was in love with you at university, even though he thought he was straight. Were you ever in love with him? He can't have been so bald then, but I can't imagine he was ever good-looking. He's tall and thin and got that earnest kind of face. He's a big brother rather than a lover. Perhaps that's why he's never had a relationship with a man. It's a pity, because he's almost forty and it's unlikely to happen now.

You were different. You never stopped having love affairs before you met me. Or after. You must have broken a lot of hearts. All these foreigners you pick up and then drop. Is it fair? On them? On me?

I'm confused again, Andy. Everything used to be so clear. We were lovers. You travelled abroad a lot and I stayed here. You got taken hostage and I waited for you to return. But it's not like that. We were lovers, but you had lovers in other countries. And maybe because of me, you're being held longer than you might have been. Then there's Guy and though I'm not in love with him, I am fond of him and I'm not sure what he feels about me.

Even if none of that matters, things will never be the same. I can't help hearing and reading all these stories about other people who've been held hostage. Your mind changes, your health changes. You come back a very different person. I may have to look after you. You may not want me around. Guy and Brian tried to warn me and I didn't believe them, but now I do. You'll be different, but I don't know how. I know I'm different. I've made mistakes — boy, have I made mistakes — but I carry on. I never did that before. It's made me older but it's also made me stronger. I don't need you as much as I used to. I can live without you. That doesn't mean I don't want you. I do, desperately.

But something has to happen, Andy, soon, to bring us together again. Or maybe it'll be too late.

* * *

Wednesday 11th. I never was very successful with men. There were a couple after John that I really fancied, but I never got far with them. Like Lewis. I was about twenty-two and he was thirty. He was tall, dark and handsome and took me away for a long weekend to Torquay. We drove around Devon and ate in good restaurants and spent hours in bed. I thought that was it; I was planning our whole life together. But I was wrong. I don't know what I did or said, because it didn't make any difference at the time, but after we came back to London, he never got in touch again. I called him again and again and he kept putting me off until I finally got the message. I never understood why. For me, everything had been perfect, but for him I had been nothing.

That's what made me so careful about Alex. I didn't allow myself to fall for him so easily. I'd moved out of Archway, found a room with a couple of New Zealand girls from one of the restaurants I was working in. It was a mistake. They wanted to party all the time and they kept bringing back these men who knew I was queer and didn't like it. I'd started going to Heaven on a Saturday night, sometimes with friends, usually alone. I hardly ever picked anyone up. It wasn't a one-night stand I was looking for, but a lover. I was twenty-four years old and it was five years since I'd been with John and I was sick of being on my own. Sometimes I thought a one-night stand was better than nothing, so I hung around to the end. If you wait long enough either you pick someone up or you go home so tired that you don't give a damn. I would walk up and down and hang around watching everyone go in and out of the toilets, but it was always the same old story — the guys I fancied didn't look at me and the ones who did look were too old or too ugly or just not my type. That night I stayed till they played the last few songs and the lights went on. Everyone started collecting their coats; half of them were still wide awake — whatever drug they got the energy from I couldn't afford to buy it.

I was waiting by the cloakroom for the queue to die down when this guy came up and started talking. He said I'd smiled at him earlier, although I didn't remember. I wasn't interested. He was much too old — about forty — and he wasn't very good-looking and his accent was much too posh. But I didn't have anything else to do, so I stood and let him talk. He was making comments about the people around us, but not in a nasty way. It was quite funny and I looked at him a bit more and thought he wasn't that bad; he was my height, strong dark eyes, tanned and he looked fit. By the time we got our coats I'd agreed to go back to his place, partly because I didn't want to be on my own and partly because I was beginning to like him.

He had a Range Rover. I'd never been in one before. It was great sitting up there listening to classical music. We drove back to his house in Fulham; it wasn't big, but it was beautifully decorated. We sat in his living-room and he offered me a joint. I hardly smoked the stuff because I couldn't afford it, so it really had an effect on me. I lay back and before I'd noticed, he'd started to make love to me. No one had ever done it like that before; they'd never been so gentle. They'd never wanted to give me all the pleasure. They'd always expected me to do things for them, but Alex just wanted me to lie back and enjoy it. And all the time he was making love, there was this soft music like I'd never heard before, distant bells and things. It was so wonderful, I never wanted it to stop.

We must have got to bed about six and slept till one. I woke up and he was looking at me. I thought he was going to ask me to leave, as the others usually did, but he didn't. He just put his arm round me and started to make love again. It was wonderful. I was lying there in this enormous bed being fucked by a guy who really cared that I was enjoying it as much as he was. It was as intense as the night before and when I came it felt almost as if I was exploding.

I had to work that evening and when I left I didn't think I was going to see him again. But he called the next day and I saw him again on the Tuesday or the Wednesday and after that I began seeing him once or twice a week. He'd call me up and take me out for dinner or we'd go away for the weekend. He never came to my flat or the restaurant and he never wanted to meet any of my friends. But I met a lot of his friends — we used to cook for dinner parties together in his kitchen. They were all his age or older. Some of them had boyfriends my age. At first I used to think they were just kept boys and then I'd wonder if I was a kept boy too. But I was still working. The only thing that made me see myself as a kept boy was the fact that Alex paid for me every time we went out. The first few times I tried to pay my own way but he stopped me. He could afford it, he said, and I couldn't, so that was an end to it.

He gave me all sorts of things I'd never had before and never had since. Weekends on his yacht. I never did learn what all the ropes were for and I was sometimes seasick, but I could at least cook a meal in the galley and entertain his friends when they came aboard. Then there were the trips to Paris and Amsterdam. I'd never been abroad before — never been able to afford it. Now he was taking me up the Eiffel Tower and on the Dutch canals. I loved it. And there was the sex. It seemed that all he wanted to do was to turn me on. Sometimes we'd try out new things — new for me, I'm not sure about him — and once or twice we picked someone else up. We often had sex with a joint — sometimes with other drugs, but I was afraid of them, afraid of losing control and becoming hooked. It didn't bother him; he wasn't hooked on anything. It went on for almost a year. I never moved in with him; we never talked about it. I should have realised what that meant, but I just closed my eyes to it. I was in love with him and couldn't admit that he wasn't in love with me. Looking back, it was obvious. He never told me he loved me. I was just one compartment in his life and it wasn't going to interfere with anything else he did.

When he started seeing less of me, I got worried and didn't know what to say or do. We didn't have so much sex and it wasn't so good. It was like he couldn't be bothered any more and nothing I could do could bring back the feeling of the first few months. I was afraid to say anything in case it didn't bring us together but made us split up. I was frightened to lose him. I didn't want another five years on my own again. I would be thirty by then and over the hill. Nobody would want me.

The end came one night when we were out for dinner in some expensive Italian place in Soho. He said he thought we should stop seeing each other. I couldn't believe it, even though I'd been half-expecting it. For a year he'd given me everything I thought I had ever wanted and now he was telling me I couldn't have it any more. I didn't say anything. He didn't either. We just sat silent for about five minutes. I carried on eating, thinking he'll change his mind or I'll think of something to make him change his mind, but it didn't happen. When he spoke again it was about something else. And I realised that was it. It was all over.

I thought I was going back home with him that night for one last time, but instead he took me home. He dropped me at the door and said he'd be in touch. A couple of days later he sent me a note saying thanks for all the good times and a cheque for five hundred pounds. I tore it up. I should have kept it but I was too proud. I suppose I could have called him and said it had fallen in the washing machine and been ripped to shreds and could he send me another one. But I didn't.

I never spoke to him again. I saw him once, a few months later. I was in the King's Road and he was on the other side of the street. I looked away, started staring in some shop window. I didn't want to avoid him; I just wanted to think carefully what I was going to say to him. But by the time I'd calmed down and turned round he was gone. I didn't know whether I was pleased I'd missed him or upset because I hadn't said all the things I wanted to say.

Splitting up with him made me so depressed. I thought it was all my fault. I used to lie in bed and think of all the nice restaurants we'd gone to and the weekends we'd spent on the coast. Eric saw something was wrong, but I was still more of a lodger than a friend; I told him what had happened but didn't go into details. I couldn't work out what I'd done wrong, why I'd lost Alex. Now I can see I'd been lucky to have had the year. I don't know what he'd seen in me. If I'd had his money, I wouldn't have picked me up — I'd have gone for someone more attractive, with more personality and class.

It was with you, Andy, that I realised I'd never really been in love with Alex. I'd loved being with him — being in his house, in his car, at his parties and on his yacht. But I'd never loved him. I'd never been close to him. I'd tried. But he'd never been close to me. I'd ask him what he was feeling and he wouldn't say anything or he'd say he was all right or he'd change the subject. He didn't trust me, or maybe he didn't trust himself. I don't know. Living with you was the first time I realised what love could be, that we could trust each other, accept all the good things and the bad. Especially the bad.

* * *

Thursday. 'Jack Burns' has just telephoned. Bretherton, the man from the *Sun*; the bastard who started all this. Out of the blue. I didn't recognise his voice at first, and when I did I almost slammed the phone down. I told him what I thought of him, that ever since he wrote that article everything had gone wrong. He said that wasn't true; it was the articles about me and Guy that had caused the problem. I said none of the rest would have happened if he hadn't written about you being gay in the first place. He claimed that wasn't the point; his article had brought nothing but good. The AMC had started as a result of all the publicity and lots of money had come in. The way he put it, it sounded as if he was almost right.

He said he'd called for a chat and to see if there was any news. He wanted to come down to see me. He knew he'd been underhand with me, but promised not to write anything more about me or you without letting me check it first. Or I could have Guy check it over if I wanted. I told him I still didn't trust him. He offered to tape the conversation and to leave a copy with me and then there was no way he could put words into my mouth. Anyway, it wasn't an interview he wanted, but to help get you out. He didn't just work for the *Sun*, he had other irons in the fire.

I was confused. I didn't want to speak to him, but he sounded genuine. And what he said about the publicity helping you was true in a way. Until his article appeared, none of us had done much to help you, apart from Brian. So I told him I'd speak to Guy first and call him back, but when I phoned Guy there was only his answering machine. Bretherton called back to say why didn't he come down anyway. If I didn't want to see him, I could turn him away with no hard feelings. I don't trust him, but we'll see.

* * *

Friday. Bretherton has been and gone. He was very polite, very careful not to say anything to upset me. He said I had to realise he was only doing his job. Sometimes people didn't like it, but on the whole it got good results. Like when they exposed government ministers who'd been lying. He'd been reading all about you and me ever since his story got published. He felt a personal interest and wanted to help. That was all.

It was strange, because he wasn't aggressive, didn't try and make me say anything I didn't want to. He even apologised for upsetting me before. I asked him why he had lied to me the first time — the whole story about being a friend of yours. He said it was easier to get the truth that way than to say he was a reporter. People are wary about talking to reporters. I said he should feel guilty about what he was doing, but he said he didn't. The people who should feel guilty are the ones who commit crimes — like kidnapping you.

I didn't say much. I talked about the farm a bit, but kept off the question of how much money I was making. I showed him all the vegetables and the pigsty and everything else. It felt a bit strange at first, but it got easier. He left in the middle of the afternoon. First he made a copy of the tapes he'd been recording and gave them to me. He said he'd come down again next week some time, if that was all right with me. I said I'd think about it.

I've been listening to one of the tapes, although there's not much point. There's a lot of silences and I can hear James barking at the pigs. I hate the sound of my voice but at least I sound as if I know what I'm talking about. And there's nothing on it I shouldn't have said.

* * *

Monday. We're pigless, and the freezer is full of meat. It wasn't easy. I'd hired a van and at six in the morning I was trying to get them one at a time up the plank and into the back. Guy refused to help and drove back to London in a bad mood. I had to drag them up with a rope; it almost broke my back. One of them kicked me hard in the shin. There's a really bad bruise. When I got over to the abattoir they started panicking and squealing — that horrible high-pitched sound. It's not surprising; the place stank and I'm sure they knew what was going to happen. A couple of the men came out to help me unload. They must have thought I was an idiot; the fact that I'd used a hired van and hadn't a clue where to go or what to do. The inside of the van is damaged as well; luckily the company didn't notice it when I took it back.

I felt really guilty on the way back, like I'd betrayed them somehow. Then I got angry with myself. People have always eaten meat. Why should we stop now? You kill plants to stay alive; why not kill animals? God knows we kill enough human beings.

When I got back I looked at the sty and couldn't make up my mind whether I'd done the right thing or not. I sort of miss them, coming out to feed them and say hello. It's like a bit of my childhood gone for ever. My first pigs reared and slaughtered. I haven't decided if I'll do it again.

* * *

Tuesday. Jack — Bretherton — was here again, as friendly as before. Now that I know what's going on, I almost trust him. He gave me a copy of the article he was writing for some magazine about me living alone, my daily routine. It seems all right. I'll show it to Guy.

We sat out in the back and talked. The tape recorder was there, like before. It reassured me. He asked a lot of questions about how I felt, how much I missed you, that kind of thing. I didn't say very much at first, but then I thought there was no harm in talking if I thought carefully about what I was saying. Not the kind of stuff I write here, that comes straight off the top of my head. I've put my copy of the tapes in the box if you ever want to listen to them.

I told him what I'd been thinking recently. That I should go out to Peru. Either to look for you or to offer myself to Shining Path in your place. I didn't think they would want me, but it would show them, show the world, how important it was to get you back. Whatever happened, I'd stay out there trying to find you. I'd learn the language and find out everything about where you'd been and who you'd been with when you were kidnapped.

I know it's just a dream. I don't have the money; I don't have anyone to look after the farm; I wouldn't know where to start. But Jack took me seriously, not like Guy, who always says it wouldn't work. He even made a couple of suggestions about getting help in Lima. Maybe we can do something from here. It would be better than nothing.

* * *

Wednesday. I've been thinking a lot more in the last few days. About how I feel about you and how I felt about Alex. After we split up, I didn't give a damn about anything; nothing was important. I just got up every day and went to work and came back home again. I didn't think there was going to be anyone after Alex. He was proof that I was never going to have any success with lovers. John had beaten me, Alex had lost interest and there had never been anyone else who was serious. I didn't have anything to offer people. I had no money, no looks, no personality. I could stand in a pub and see all these guys my age who had so much more than me. They were all with lovers or could find lovers easily enough. I had nothing.

It was like living in a tunnel, with no light ahead of me, just blackness. There was nothing I could do about it, I didn't see how things could be any different. I'd go for a drink with a couple of friends after work and they'd be laughing and gossiping and I'd smile, because I had to, not because I felt anything. And sometimes I'd go out on my own, to the pub or the cinema and it wasn't any better. I'd sit watching a comedy and I'd realise I was on my own and everyone else was with friends or partners and I'd start crying and crying while everyone else around me was laughing their heads off.

I didn't wake up that day and decide what I was going to do. I was just lying in the bath that afternoon and every time the water got cold, I'd top it up a bit. Eric and Dave were out; the house was quiet. It was nice and warm lying there and my mind began floating away. I was in a completely different world, all bright and peaceful, with no work, no worries and no need for other people. I remembered I'd once read that was the easiest way to do it; you just cut your wrists in a warm bath and fall slowly asleep. There wouldn't be any more darkness or unhappiness. It was so easy and just what I wanted.

I wouldn't have got that far if Dave hadn't used old-fashioned razors. There was a packet of blades in the cabinet beside the bath. I just had to reach up and pull one out. I thought it was going to hurt, but I realised if I did it under water and the water was quite hot, I'd hardly feel it. And I wouldn't have to look. I could do it in two or three places, up and down the arm. One of them would hit the spot. I did my right arm first, carefully, because I wanted the cut to be straight and clean. It was a funny feeling. It hurt, but at the same time it didn't hurt. There wasn't as much blood as I thought, so I tried cutting again, deeper. That was better; the water was really turning pink. I was feeling tired, but it was a pleasant, warm, tiredness, as if I was just falling asleep.

Then I realised that Eric was hammering at the door. They'd been shopping and he was desperate to piss. I lay there, not sure what to do, as I heard his voice changing. First, he was joking, then he was angry and then he sounded really worried. Then I heard Dave asking what was going on. But it was Eric saying he'd break the door down if I didn't open it that got through to me. Somehow I managed to get up and unlock it, and then I fainted and didn't wake up properly until I was in the hospital.

They saved me. I don't mean they got me to hospital. I mean they didn't kick me out afterwards. That's what most people would have done. You don't want someone that unstable around. But they had me back and didn't tell anyone what I'd tried to do. They were worried and wanted to know why I did it. I tried to tell them, but it didn't sound right, so I shut up. It was good just to be with them and know that they cared and in the end I began to feel better. I decided I might as well live, start again. But if I hadn't met you, I don't know how long I could have kept it up. A year? Two? Three? If I'd hit thirty and still been alone, I think I would have done it again, with pills, or in the bath at a time when I knew I'd be alone.

Don't worry. I would never do it now. I've got you. And the farm. And friends. More than I ever expected.

* * *

Friday. The end of another week. Guy's coming down tonight and we're going over to have supper with Anne and George. He says he's working on a few projects. But nothing's really happening. Everyone's forgotten about you again. It's like a famine or a war that you see on television; there are headlines for a few days and for a while you think so many people are concerned that something's getting done. But nothing's getting done. People keep dying of hunger and killing each other and television and the newspapers have found something else to talk about. One of the *Eastenders* stars is pregnant and the father's not her husband — and that's far more important than any famine, any war, any chance of freeing you.

* * *

Sunday 22nd. Guy's gone home. We had a fight last night — the first time it's happened. I said we weren't doing enough to help you. He said he was working his butt off and couldn't do anything more. I said maybe we were doing the wrong things. We should go out there, talk to people, spend as long as we needed and not come home till we'd found you. He said we'd been through it all before and it wouldn't work. Imagine if the IRA had kidnapped a Peruvian and was holding him somewhere in London and two of his friends landed at Heathrow and didn't speak a word of English. How would they get on? How would they find him? I said they would find someone to translate for them and start going to Irish pubs and talking to people. They could put adverts on the paper, appear on television, offer to pay a ransom. They'd find out where he was being held in the end. Guy said I was talking rubbish; you couldn't do that sort of thing.

I said it was better than whatever Brian had done. He hadn't got anywhere. I was the only person who cared and I wasn't doing anything. Guy said Brian did care and so did he — he was spending every evening and a lot of his days working for the AMC. "And it hasn't done a fat bit of good," I said. At that point he just turned and walked out of the room and went upstairs to bed. I felt guilty, but not so guilty I wanted to apologise. I mean I knew he was working hard, but why couldn't he see that none of it was any good? You were still there and we didn't even have any contact with the people who were holding you. I was still mad, and I threw the nearest thing I could find onto the floor. It was one of your wooden statues from Africa. I'm sorry; I'll glue it back as good as new.

Everything was all right this morning. I said I was sorry and Guy said he knew just how I felt. Despite all the work we were putting in, we didn't seem to be getting anywhere. There were monthly meetings at the Foreign Office and fortnightly meetings of the Committee and we'd raised thousands of pounds from people all over the country and nothing seemed to be happening. Guy was as upset about it as I was. We gave each other a hug — I looked out of the window to see if any photographer was hanging around — and things were almost the same as before. They won't really be right, though, until you get back.

Don't get jealous, Andy, but I'm really fond of Guy. He does so much for you, for me, and he gets no thanks for it. He needs a lover, someone to look after him, someone to care. Sometimes I think he sees me as his lover. Maybe if you weren't around, I would be. Don't worry, it's not going to happen. But I think the way we feel is beginning to make things between us difficult, especially when it seems that everyone is watching us.

You have to come home soon, Andy, before we get into more of a mess. We can't go on like this; you, me or Guy. We have to bring you home.

* * *

Monday 23rd August. Jack called. He's coming down again tomorrow. I told Guy — although he's seen the article and heard some of the tapes, he's still suspicious of him. I cleaned out the sty at the weekend. I still haven't decided whether I'm buying more pigs.

I've just come in from watching the sunset again. I love these summer evenings when there's hardly any wind and the only sounds are the birds and the occasional car. I sit out at the back with James or one of the cats on my lap — sometimes both James and a cat — and a can of beer in my hand and watch the sky. It's beautiful. The only thing that's missing is you.

* * *

Tuesday 24th. I can hardly believe it, but I think it's about to happen. I'm coming to Peru after all.

It's Jack's idea. He says he's got the money from the *Sun* to fly the two of us out there to look for you. They'll lay on an interpreter and transport. They'll even put up some reward money.

I didn't believe him at first. I still don't think I do. The *Sun*'s so homophobic that they're not going to pay for one gay man to go and look for another. But Jack says they're not anti-gay, they're anti-militant queer. And you're a British citizen; they want to get you back. If they can, it'll be great publicity for them.

That's the catch. I can't tell anyone we're going. Because if we don't get you out or if anything goes wrong, the *Sun* wants nothing to do with us. They'll bring us back all right, that's guaranteed, but if I breathe a word to anyone before you get out, the whole deal's off.

I said I couldn't. I couldn't fly off to Peru without telling Guy and your parents and Anne and George and half a dozen other people. If I just left without telling anyone, everyone would panic. And I couldn't leave the farm. He'd thought about all that. I'd say I was going on holiday to Greece or somewhere, with an old friend. Then I could get someone to look after the farm, and the *Sun* would arrange for someone to send postcards from Greece as if they came from me.

It sounded like a con at first. But Jack was so convincing and every objection I made, he had a solution for. I began thinking maybe it was possible, and if I didn't find you, at least I would have tried, instead of sitting on my arse.

He told me to think about it, but not to tell anyone, not even Guy. If I did, he and the *Sun* would deny everything. He said he'd call back in a couple of days, and gave me his phone number in case I wanted to talk about it any more with him.

I don't know what to do. Half the time I think he's having me on. The other half I think he's serious. But even if I do go, what'll I do when I get out there? Guy's right. I can just see Jack and me in the middle of Cuzco stopping passers-by and asking if they know of anyone who's kidnapped a blond, blue-eyed Scotsman. It's not going to work.

But I can't not go. No one else will. And you'd never forgive me if I left you there for a day longer than I could. Maybe I'll find you but the kidnappers will want to keep me too, like what happened to Terry Waite. But I'm sure they wouldn't. They don't need two faggots. I don't know what to do. I'm desperate to help you and I can't decide if Jack's idea is stupid or not.

Why did this have to happen? Why did I have to get stuck here alone not knowing what to do? Why do people do this to each other? Why can't someone tell me what to do?

I talked to Eric. I made him promise not to tell anyone. He says I should go for it. He thinks it's a gimmick the *Sun*'s thought up, but I have nothing to lose by taking them up on it. He doesn't think we'll find you, but it's no skin off my nose. And Jack'll look after me; the paper can't risk being held responsible for a second hostage being taken.

He made it sound so simple. And he said that now he's not working, he can come and look after the farm. So there's nothing to stop me.

* * *

Wednesday. I hardly slept last night, thinking about Peru. Eric's right; I have to go. I couldn't face myself if I didn't.

I called Jack but his phone had been switched off. I started looking out clothes to take with me. I've no idea what the temperature's like there. I'll have to get a book from the library to see.

Guy phoned; he heard something funny in my voice and asked if I was all right. I said I had a bit of a cough. Odd thing to get in summer. I don't like lying to him after he's helped me so much. Maybe there's some way I can tell him without Jack finding out.

After supper I began thinking that even if Jack or the *Sun* call the whole thing off, I'll still go. I've got enough money to buy my own ticket. There's no going back now.

* * *

Thursday 26th August. No word from Jack. I'm getting impatient. I phoned the Peruvian embassy — not telling them who I was, of course — to see if I needed a visa. British citizens don't. Tomorrow I'm getting a book from the library to tell me what clothes I should take and if I need injections. *Rehen.* That's what you are — a hostage. I looked it up in your Spanish dictionary. There are some funny marks after it that tell you how to pronounce it, but it looks simple enough. *Tu rehen — yo salvador.* You're a hostage and I'm a saviour. Simple, isn't it? Okay, I know it's not, but it's better than nothing. I love you, in any language. In every language.

* * *

Friday. Jack called. We're going a week tomorrow. He was worried I'd changed my mind or I'd told someone. I told him about Eric and he almost blew his top, until he saw that it was Eric who had persuaded me to go and Eric'd be the one to look after the farm. Then he calmed down and made me promise not to tell anyone else. He was going to come down tomorrow to go over details. I said he couldn't because Guy would be here and it's the long weekend. So he spent a long time telling me about the invitation I was going to receive from Greece and the 'friend' I was supposed to be going out to see. It really was like a spy story; the invitation had been sent earlier in the week and I should get it any day now. Anyway, the friend is called Mark, and I used to work with him, and he's heard about you and he's got this house on a tiny island called Kimolos and he wants me to go out and stay with him. There are all sorts of other things I have to remember for when Guy and others start asking questions. I'm not sure it's going to work, but as Eric says, if it doesn't, I won't have lost anything. I just have to try.

I got a guidebook from the library. It told me about temperatures and other things. All the diseases they get out there. I'd never thought about that before. When you were travelling you were never in one place long enough to catch anything. And you told me you always stayed in hotels where the water could be trusted. But you've been a year and half in the back of beyond where they have all sorts of things like malaria and hepatitis and yellow fever. You could have caught anything. I don't even know if you were vaccinated before you went off and if you were how long it lasts. Maybe you're ill now, but I don't want to think about that.

* * *

Monday. Guy has gone. He wanted to stay and drive up early tomorrow, but I asked him to leave tonight. I need to get ready for Peru. He's noticed something wrong, but doesn't know what it is. Mark's invitation came on Saturday. A long letter, which I showed Guy. It said that a ticket to Athens was waiting for me; we phoned Olympic and it was true. Friday morning from Heathrow. 'Mark' will meet me off the plane, we'll spend the night in Athens and we get the boat to Kimolos on Saturday. Neither Guy nor I had heard of Kimolos, but we looked up your atlas and there it was. Luckily, 'Mark' doesn't have a telephone to call him back; I couldn't have kept up the pretence with Guy in the room. Instead, I had to send a telegram care of the post office. God knows who'll pick it up.

The whole weekend was weird. There was me sending a telegram to Greece, to someone who doesn't exist, in order to get on a flight to Peru, without telling the guy who's helped me most of all in the last six months. I'm sure Guy thinks I've flipped. Going on about you so much and then suddenly saying, fuck this, I'm off to Greece for a fortnight's holiday. I feel really bad about it, but I have to do it to get you back. All weekend, I felt kind of torn between him and you. First I'd let you down, and now I was letting him down. I couldn't get to sleep last night for thinking about it. It wasn't just Guy. It was the fact that this was the last weekend before I came to Peru. That when I came back, everything will be different. It might be in a fortnight, it might not be for a year, but it'll be with you. So I've been doing everything extra carefully — making sure that all the hens got an equal amount of feed instead of just scattering it, watering each plant instead of splashing it everywhere, being extra polite to everyone who stopped at the stall. We made £43 today; not bad.

I have to stop, sometimes, to remember what it was like living with you. Three and a half years together, then one and half years without you. I've written down a lot of it in the last few months and I still feel I've said almost nothing. There are so many things you wouldn't remember, but I do. A few months after we met, at a party in Maida Vale — I can't remember whose — we were standing talking and you just put your arm around me. You didn't seem to be aware of what you were doing, and that's why it meant so much to me. The fact that it was so natural, so easy, making me a part of you. The first postcard you sent me from abroad: the Washington Monument. I've still got it somewhere. The way you smile and relax when I want to make love. Not like John, who'd just push me away, or Alex, who only had me over when it was convenient for him.

It's not just the little things. It's everything. Everything I feel for you and everything you feel for me. And I can't express it. All I can say is I love you, but everyone says that. I want there to be a word that expresses everything that I feel for you. And there isn't. Or it's all the words. It's happiness and desire and want and fear and hunger and wish and admire and longing and...

I should go to bed. It's getting late again and I have so much to do. I'll look at this in the morning and if I have any sense, delete it.

* * *

Tuesday 31st. Jack spent half the day here going over the arrangements. He's got the tickets and money and everything. We called Eric. He's coming down on Thursday and driving me to Heathrow on Saturday.

I told Jack that I was having second thoughts. Guy had said there were over twenty million people in Peru. We hadn't a clue where to start. And even if we did get to Shining Path, what were the chances that we would get kidnapped too? He said he wasn't that stupid; he'd been doing some spadework already. He'd already arranged a number of people for us to meet in Lima.

Part of me's frightened. After all, you went out there knowing the people and speaking the language and you still got kidnapped. But maybe Jack's right. Maybe it's so simple as just to go and ask.

I'm still not sure why he's helping us. Eric says it's for the kudos — when he brings you back to London he'll be famous and the *Sun* will make a packet. Sure, he's using you, Eric told me, but I'm using him just as much. More — for him, it's just money; for me, it's you. So I guess we are using him, Andy, both of us. I've committed you to an exclusive before you've even landed at Heathrow.

I was so busy the rest of the day I hardly had time to think. I've been checking feedstocks and writing down all the things I have to tell Eric. Probably the most important is to give him Anne and George's number to ring when things go wrong.

The nights are already drawing in. It's less than a month to the equinox. I was doing my exercises out the back and watching the sun go down. It was beautiful. But like everything else, it was like looking at it for the last time. As I said before, when I get back, it'll be with you and everything will be very different.

That's not it. It's like I know I'm going to get on that plane on Saturday, but I can't imagine what's going to happen after I get off in Lima. Where we'll go, what we'll see, who we'll talk to. Maybe we'll go straight to Cuzco. I feel like I'm entering a tunnel and I've no idea what's on the other side. I keep telling myself that I'm going to find you, Andy, but what if I don't? What if something goes wrong? What if we never see each other again?

Maybe something'll happen to me and you'll get back and I won't. You'll walk in the door and find Eric and this diary and wonder what happened to me. And no one will know. I have to stop thinking like this. I just have to get by, day by day.

* * *

Wednesday 1st September. So many things to remember, so many things to do. I've called your parents, told them about Greece. I'm sure I sounded guilty, but I think they believe me. It felt like I was betraying them — again; the first time with Guy. But everything will change if I bring you back. And if I don't, they'll know I tried.

Guy called. He kept asking if I was all right. I said I was upset about you; it was as near the truth as I could get. Then he sounded funny. He told me how much he respected me for what I felt for you and what I was doing for you. I said that wasn't much and he said it was. He said he was sorry about what had happened when the newspapers had taken pictures of the two of us together. I said it was my fault; I'd started the thing of our sleeping together. He said it was his fault we'd got into the habit and hadn't stopped it. I kept getting the feeling he was hiding something from me, but I didn't know what or how to make him tell me. Besides, I was hiding a lot from him.

I've bought enough feed to last a couple of months and I've signed the final papers leasing the extra land. I told the lawyer I'd be away for a fortnight, but there's nothing more I have to do. I got back just after six, took James for his evening walk, exercised, ate and sat down here. Down by the stream I had the same feeling again, that everything's coming to an end, to some kind of transformation. At the same time nothing was important any more; if I just walked away from the farm, it wouldn't matter. Someone would look after it, feed the animals, give James and the cats a home. It didn't have to be my responsibility any more. You were my responsibility. Only you.

Sitting in the evening sun, I couldn't help thinking about you, as a man, as my lover. I've never told you, but I still make love to you. I lie back and kiss you, hold you, make myself come, thinking of all the things we used to do, all the times we made love — here and in your old flat. And I imagine what it's going to be like when you come back. When everyone's gone and there's just you and me standing in the hall. And we start kissing, because at first that's all we'll want to do. We won't want to make love. We'll just hold each other so tight, to make up for all the time you were away. But then we'll move a little and I'll start kissing your ear and your neck and I'll see the mole under the collar of your shirt and I'll want you to open your shirt so I can kiss more of you. It still won't be sex; it'll be love, showing you how much I care. And you'll want to do the same to me. You'll pull off my sweater and open my shirt and for once I won't smell of sweat or manure.

We'll want to kiss each other all over — to remind ourselves how much we love each other, to see how much we've changed. I expect you'll be thinner and I'll worry about you, but I'll love you more than ever. And we'll begin to feel cold, standing there with no clothes on, so we'll go up to bed. It'll be warm under the blankets and we'll huddle there for a while. And we'll feel each other's body again and remember what it's like to be together again. When we're warm again, we'll kiss a little more and our hands will start to move. And I'll feel your prick and it will be hard and I'll hold it gently and stroke it and it'll still be love, not sex. And then I'll want to kiss it and your balls and your arse, to show how much I love all of you — as I've always loved all of you. And at some point we'll start making love — slowly, gently. And when we come, it'll be such a relief, because then we can just carry on holding each other and kissing and falling asleep together, because we'll know you're back and we'll never be separated again.

That's what I dream about. That's what I need. That's what keeps me going.

* * *

Thursday 2nd September. Forty-eight hours from now I'll be in Miami or Lima. I'm not sure about the time difference. I've rushed around all day packing and getting ready to go. In the evening I went over to Anne and George's. The first time in over a month. There was no problem. They're convinced I'm off to Greece and they're happy to give Eric advice or a hand. They fed me, in their kitchen, with Ada on Anne's lap pounding the table with a spoon. Anne's vegetarian lasagna with broccoli, followed by one of George's cakes for dessert. With all the time he spends at the office, I don't know how he finds time to cook. I had a couple of drinks, but was careful driving home.

Even when I don't see them for weeks, just being there makes me feel at home. Even though their house is always a mess, with Ada's toys and George's books all over the place. I can talk to Anne about almost anything. Once Ada was put to bed we talked about what we'd been doing, how I'd been coping. They think I've done really well. A year ago there was nothing but the hens and half-a-dozen rows of vegetables. Now it's almost a fully fledged business.

Leaving them was like everything else this week; it felt as if I was doing it for the last time. They stood at the door as I reversed out and waved as I drove off. I wondered when I would see them again.

On the way home, I was thinking about what it's going to be like when we meet again. When we're sitting in that plane coming home. How easy or difficult it'll be to talk to you. How much older you'll look. How much you'll have changed. Whether you'll want to talk to me. I'm frightened we'll be complete strangers to each other and we'll have to start all over again. And I have no idea whether you'll want to, or whether we can.

Eric was here when I got back, so I had to push all these ideas to the back of my mind; they're still sitting there. He'd let himself in with the key in the henhouse and was sitting back with a cup of cocoa and a drink. He's having a bath now and then we're both turning in. Separate beds, of course.

* * *

Saturday 4th September. I'm all packed and ready.

James is here, looking up at me. He can tell something's happening. I hope he'll be all right. The cats can look after themselves, but Eric'll be third owner he'll have had in almost as many months.

I'm not tired. I've got all this energy that I don't know what to do with. I'll sleep tomorrow on the plane. Two planes. I wonder if we have time to see Miami or if we're stuck in the airport.

I called Brian and Richardson to see if there was any news before I went 'on holiday'. I'd tried to pump them before for the names of people they'd been in contact with, but I wasn't very good at it. Jack says he knows some of them anyway.

I spoke to Guy again in the evening. It was easier. He thinks I'm all excited because of Greece. I promised I'd be back in a fortnight. I think he's going to miss me. If I were going anywhere else, I might miss him. I almost felt guilty about leaving him alone. He shouldn't be alone. None of us should be ever alone.

That's it, lover. I'm on my way. I'm leaving everything behind me to come and get you. A knight on a white charger. Somewhere in Peru, a week or a month from now, I'm going to open a door and there you'll be. You won't be expecting me. You'll just look at me in surprise and won't be able to say a word. I'll just hug you and say I've come to take you home. And we'll never be apart again. Never.

Lima, Cuzco, Andy; here I come.

II
Andy: Near Cuzco

Yo, Andrew Cameron McIllray, ciudadano británico e empleado de la organización internacional Demotica, confiso mis crímenes y los de la dicha organización contra el pueblo peruano y la clase trabajadora en los países en desarrollo. Confiso que vine a Perú como agente del imperialismo estado-unidense-europeano para destabilizar el Partido Comunista Peruano, único representativo auténtico del pueblo trabajador peruano, para semear confusión en las mentes de los paesanos andeanos y para sostenir la opresión del pueblo quechua por la regime ilegal de Lima y por las fuerzas políticas, económicas e armadas de los Estados Unidos y sus aliados europeanos. Confiso que

* * *

I, Andrew Cameron McIllray, British citizen and employee of the international organisation Demotica, confess my crimes and those of the above-named organisation against the Peruvian people and the working class in every country of the developing world. I confess that I came to Peru as an agent of US and European imperialism to destabilise the Peruvian Communist Party, sole authentic representative of the Peruvian working class, to sow confusion in the minds of Andean peasants and to support the oppression of the Quechua people by the illegal regime in Lima and by the political, economic and armed forces of the United States and its European allies. I confess that whatever I write here is untrue, written under duress and under protest. I confess that I am tired, cold and angry at spending my twelfth month in confinement.

* * *

Two days ago Rosa gave me a dozen notebooks and pencils. I was confused as she held them out to me, the first time I had been brought anything other than water or food. "For you," she said, gesturing me to take them. "For your confession."

It was only after she left that I remembered the 'trial' with which I was threatened the first weeks they held me here. Day after day, I listened to Fernando accuse me of every conceivable sin of Western imperialism. Each time the door opened I expected to be hauled to my feet and marched downstairs, out into the yard and the mockery of a tribunal. Fernando, a self-appointed judge, would sit behind a rickety wooden table, one of the others would read out spurious charges, I would be allowed a futile statement in my own defence, then I would be tied to the nearest tree and shot.

Instead of which, Fernando disappeared and for months afterwards my only human contact was the occasional creak of the stairs, the door pushed open by one of my silent jailers, food and water set down on the floor, the bucket removed and later returned. There were three of them: El Gordo, El Magro and El Surdo — Fat, Thin and Deaf — typical Andeans with impassive faces, oriental eyes and Roman noses, their only words gruff commands in a Spanish I hardly understood. In time I gave up trying to communicate with them, interpreting their silence as contempt for a gringo who allowed himself to be captured and chained like an animal. So I retreated into my own silence, watched them enter and leave, allowed myself the luxury of imagining our positions reversed and listened in frustration to the undertones of their Quechua as they talked outside in the afternoon sun.

In that year my sanity faded. I fought to retain it, until despair overwhelmed me with images of others who had been held and abandoned for years. I tried to keep my mind alert with mental exercises and the plots of films or books, but I became more, rather than less, confused by square roots and irregular verbs, by the same scenarios recalled again and again. I thought of Tom and friends and parents, but their memory disturbed as much as it reassured, as if there were some misunderstanding between us or as if I had somehow let them down. As time passed, my life shrank to the emptiness of this room and the emptiness of my mind. Only Rosa's arrival brought me back from the madness that I still occasionally glimpse and fear.

She sleeps, I believe, in the room next to me and takes her turn with the others to bring me food and water. A short, almost dumpy, young woman in jeans and t-shirts and sweaters that are too old and tight, her features are as Andean as the others but younger and softer. Above all, she talks to me, in rare rudimentary conversations. Thus I have learnt that she has replaced Jacobo — El Surdo. I know her age — twenty-eight — the origin of her nom de guerre — Rosa Luxemburg — and her provenance — Huánuco. In return, I comment on the food or the weather and ask questions about why I am being held that she politely refuses to answer.

Nothing else has changed. One-point-four-three percent of my life has been stolen. Three hundred and sixty-five days have been spent gulping down burnt meat and tasteless vegetables. For eight thousand seven hundred and sixty hours I have listened to the voices of my jailers and wondered whether they intend to kill me or set me free. For five hundred and twenty-five thousand, six hundred minutes I have peered at the ancient copies of *El Diario* that are piled against the wall. For thirty-one million, five hundred and thirty-six thousand seconds I have survived in a room nine feet by fifteen feet, with nothing but a bucket, a rotting mattress, a wooden chair and a window I cannot look out of because my chain does not reach that far.

In that year I have seen nothing but two distant snow-covered mountains. Today they jut into the clear sky as beautiful as the scene from a postcard; on other days and at other times they fade into mist and darkness. Unable to see what lies beyond, I imagine a wilderness, a paradise. I understand why the Incas believed that the mountains were the homes of the gods; if I sought a faith, I might find it there. Meanwhile my body has become thin and unhealthily pale. A scab that never quite heals rings my ankle. A ragged beard irritates my chin. Despite the weekly wash grime lies thick on my skin. A year ago, I was one of the many firm bodies and short haircuts at the YMCA; now I am undistinguishable from the homeless and mentally deficient who sleep in its doorway.

* * *

Occasionally anger returns as I think over what they have done to me. They have let me slip towards insanity, ignored my needs for freedom, for company, for explanation. I lie here hour after hour, day after day, month after month, measuring time by the beat of my heart, by day and night. They are stealing my life from me — the lives of all who are close to me. They have placed burdens of pain and loss on Tom, on my friends, family and colleagues.

They have no right to do this. They have no right to call themselves civilised. They are hypocrites who preach freedom and deny others the right to be free. They should be chained in my place, without blankets, without food, without water for the rest of their lives. They should be locked with Guzmán, their beloved leader, in his cell, condemned for eternity to rant slogans at each other, to tear at shackles that scrape and bleed their ankles, to eat rotting food, drink polluted water and smell day in day out the stink of their shit lying in unemptied buckets. One day I will get out of here. One day I will get my revenge.

* * *

There was no warning. One moment we were driving along a deserted road, the next there was a man standing by a lorry waving for us to stop. The driver asked what we should do. It did not cross my mind to drive on. It was the middle of the afternoon, a part of the country that had seen little activity even when the guerrillas were active. A man sought our help; we could not refuse. We stopped; I stepped out. Even when the others suddenly appeared and we were surrounded by rifles, I did not feel afraid. If we handed over our money and valuables, if necessary the car, we would not be killed. At worst we would have a long and difficult walk.

I became apprehensive when I realised that I, not my money, was the objective. Yet I continued to be the typical Brit who asked what was wrong and offered to help as my hands were tied, the blindfold was bound so tightly that it pressed against my eyeballs and my mouth was taped with bandage. Only when I heard the incomprehensible threats in Quechua and the scared and receding voice of my driver, did I accept that I was being kidnapped. Then, without warning, I was picked up and heaved into the back of the truck. It moved and my head hit the floor, again and again, no matter how I tensed.

By the time we arrived and they pulled me out, I was exhausted, disorientated and in pain. My legs almost gave way as they marched me into the house, up the stairs and into this room. Then I was dropped onto the mattress and left until someone came to lock my leg into the shackle. Perhaps I should have kicked out at that point, shown some resistance, but it always seemed better to cooperate in the illogical hope that they might cooperate in return.

Then my blindfold, gag and handcuffs were taken off and I looked up at Fernando. He was taller than the average Andean, about my age, and stared at me with an expression of disdain. "What the hell are you trying to do?" I asked in English, as if that language would impose some authority. "Let me go." He said nothing. "Let me go," I repeated in Spanish. "You are under arrest," he replied. For what, I asked, the trigger for an hour or more of abuse. I was a lackey, an imperialist, an oppressor, a reactionary. Demotica was an instrument of oppression, of capitalism, of anticommunism, of the highest evil. Sendero Luminoso, the Communist Party of Peru, was the instrument of liberation and salvation, the only true representative of the people, the only power in the land. My time, the time of all oppressors, was coming to an end. Peru was being liberated and criminals of every type were being put on trial. As an enemy of the New Republic I too would be sentenced.

At first I tried to interrupt, to focus his rhetoric on the here and now. There was a mistake; I was no enemy but an impartial observer. Besides, everyone knew Sendero had been defeated; surely all he and his gang-members really wanted was money. Something could be arranged. I was ignored. With El Gordo standing silent beside him, Fernando ranted on as if the revolution itself depended on one bound and shackled European being made the scapegoat for every ill that had befallen Peru. I fell silent, tried to shift into a more comfortable position to relieve my aching body. At last he came to end, looked at me in disgust, spat on the floor and turned to go. "You can't leave me like this," I complained, gesturing at the chain. "Why not?" he asked. "It is the way we have been treated for years." Before I could protest, the two of them had gone.

Day after day, he came in to lecture me and pose rhetorical questions which I was only occasionally allowed to answer. Why did I think I could oppose the people's war? What does history teach us about the fate of tyrants? Each question was the opening line in a Castro-long speech of mind-numbing jargon. The first few days I tried to debate with him, to analyse his statements and offer interpretations of my own; later I simply ignored him, lying back with my eyes closed as his words thundered above me. Then he would shake me awake until I pretended to pay attention. Then one day, after I had adjusted to my role as prisoner and his as tormentor, he did not appear and my repeated questions to the others as to why and where he had gone brought no reply. Apart from the daily delivery of food and clean bucket I was alone and remained so until Rosa came.

* * *

I never believed Sendero threatened me. I knew more about the organisation than most Peruvians, had spoken to those who supported it and expatriates who had worked or travelled here. I knew that both the New Republic it planned to establish and the means by which it would achieve its goal were anathema to every principle Demotica stood for. I knew that when they were active they had murdered and destroyed without compunction, controlling whole villages and swathes of land through protection rackets and terror.

Yet despite this knowledge I dismisssed them as easily as I dismissed the hysterical slogans of British Maoists. At the heart of my insouciance lay typical Brit prejudice: the inability to take seriously the followers of a man who called himself Chairman Gonzalo. Even in Spanish, it was a clown's name and it was a clown the world had seen ranting in a cage the day he was captured. Proof of his failure had come with his recantation. "Without Guzman they are nothing," a colleague had said; "a bunch of incompetent misfits."

It seemed to be true. The bombings ceased and the army began to regain control. I pronounced the lion comatose and walked into its den; the lion, not unreasonably, pounced. Even then my folly continued. I expected strings to be pulled so fast and effectively that my jailers would realise within days they were holding a friend, not a foe. After all, as Demotica's representative I had scrupulously invited sympathisers to every meeting we arranged. Besides, long-term hostage-keeping was out of fashion. Instead, a year has taught me that I have no privileges; I am merely one of millions following a path trod down the centuries. The Portuguese under the Inquisition, the Chinese during the Cultural Revolution, a hundred nations under one or other dictatorship: since history began, heretics, enemies and counter-revolutionaries have been abandoned for years in prison or forced to confess crimes they never committed, their broken or dead bodies serving as paving-stones for someone else's Brave New World.

I wonder what, if anything, is being done to set me free. Has Sendero approached Demotica or vice versa? I suppose it is up to Brian, who has no experience of Peru. He will have had to start from scratch, trying to interpret my database and the usefulness of each name. Or perhaps it is some minion in the Foreign Office who has more important things on his mind, like the balance of trade with Chile or the price of Bolivian tin. Whatever Brian is doing to help me, I am sure it is not causing him to lose sleep. We were never friends; our ages, backgrounds, sexual interests and above all, temperaments kept us apart. He is probably more concerned by the need to find my replacement — preferably an Oriental woman to complete our ethnic mix. The lesson will have been learnt. If I had been female, or African or Chinese, I would not have been kidnapped. Being a white male may confer power, but, as this prison shows, with that power comes vulnerability.

Sunil will be even less concerned. He is too much the old-fashioned Brahmin to care about me. As long as I brought money into the organisation, he was happy, but my being kidnapped will merely confirm my unreliability. Kathy will miss me but she is burdened by too much — the whole of Africa — to be able to turn her attention to help me. Accidents and catastrophes are inevitable: planes crash, children die, friends disappear and life goes on. I will be in her past, not her present. I am even more remote from the others; no matter how liberal the sentiments, the lives of gay men based in Berkshire and married couples with children in Clapham or Islington rarely overlap. Berkshire. How homely it sounds, and how far away.

* * *

Rosa contemptuously dropped my 'confession' onto the mattress. What I had written was worthless, she said. My sarcasm indicated that I did not realise the seriousness of my situation. What do you expect, I asked.

"Insight," she said. "You might at least have learnt that."

"Insight into what?"

"Why you are here."

"How much 'insight' would you gain if you were locked up alone for a year?" I asked. I still speak slowly, remembering not only forgotten Spanish but the art of conversation. "Perhaps all you would feel is resentment."

She shrugged, her commonest gesture, a slight movement of the shoulders that acknowledges and usually ignores what I have said. "You have no right to feel resentment," she said. "We should resent your arrogance and interference."

"I did not come here to interfere." I insisted. "I came here to help your people. I was invited."

"You were invited by fools and traitors."

"By elected representatives."

"In this country no one elected represents the people. They only represent the ruling class."

I was about to deny it, though there was a kernel of truth in her simplification which lay behind much of my work for Demotica. But I had lost the ability to argue and persuade her to my point of view. She waited for a response that I did not give.

"What would you do with my confession?" I asked eventually. "Publish it? Why not make one up for me, have it say whatever you want?"

"What would be the point of that? We need you to understand fully why you are here. Not the rationale that someone 'invited' you. Your whole philosophy and how it developed." She looked at me with an expression of both conviction and condescension. I stared back, again speechless, almost angry. What would she know of philosophy? I had ten years' more experience than she did, in more countries than she could ever imagine. I knew what I was doing; she was the one who had been seduced by slogans.

"Oh, go to hell," I said in English. "Leave me alone."

Whether she understood or not, she shrugged and left me to an empty room.

* * *

An orange and more unidentified meat. As usual it is tough and stringy and half fat or tendon. However hungry I am — and I am always hungry — I am still the fastidious middle-class Brit longing for a three-course meal properly cooked and served. Staring at the greasy, brown-black mass, I try not to remember the flies that buzz thick round the slabs of meat on every market stall in this part of the world. It is better to swallow it fast and let it rot in the stomach than to chew it and feel the bile rise.

I have been trying to find a better position to exercise my legs. To keep the chain still, my right foot has to stay in the same position, which limits my movements to stretches and squats. I thought I could move my foot if I held the chain, but it still rubs against the skin. I know too well how easily it injures and how long it takes to heal.

It is turning cold again. I asked Rosa for another blanket but she made no promises. She sat by the window for half an hour or so, staring out without speaking. From the back she looked small and vulnerable, a lonely girl at boarding-school, a child without friends. When she turned, she was my jailer again, a young woman in faded clothes with an authority impervious to all my hostility and arguments. Another day. Another empty, meaningless day.

* * *

Last night I dreamt of, or perhaps remembered, Tom. We were having dinner at home. There was wine on the table and music in the background. He asked about my next trip; I said it was to Washington. He told me he wished I would not go away so often. I said I had to, but as I spoke I knew I did not want to leave. There was the warmth of the kitchen, the comfort of his presence, the darkness outside, Sheba in her basket, one of the cats on a chair. I wanted to believe that my work was over, that the rest of my life was my own, to spend with Tom, to spend at home, never wanting, never having to leave. That feeling has remained all day. Ironic, isn't it, that after a year here all I want to do is exchange this prison for another. I hate to think what this is doing to him. At least he has the security of the house and land. But he will be miserable alone. Although I never promised to be with him forever, I have let him down, betrayed him.

* * *

Rosa tells me it is March 8th. I was two days out. At the beginning I refused to mark the wall — it was too melodramatic a gesture. By the time I started, I had lost count of the days.

I am huddled under my third blanket, almost warm. I shivered so much last night that I started coughing and could not sleep. This morning when El Gordo came in with my food he threw me the blanket in a gesture thick with contempt.

* * *

I am cold and ill, impotent and angry. I lie here coughing as my mind paces between anger and despair. I want to be out of here. I want to be a thousand miles away. I want to be curled up in my own bed. I want to be home.

Rosa felt my forehead, saw my clothes sodden with sweat. "Are you ill?" she asked, apparently concerned. "Of course, I am," I snapped. At least the diarrhoea I had last year has not returned. Then it took me two days to persuade El Gordo to get enough water to drink. Although the evidence was before his eyes and in his nose, he did not believe I was ill. Fuck him. Fuck them all.

* * *

I feel better. Rosa stayed and we talked about Peru. She appeared impressed by my knowledge; I have seen as much of the country as she has, and more of Lima. On her only visit she found the city too big, although, of course, she welcomed the revolutionary spirit and activity in the shanty-towns. I know how she feels; there is an air of desperation about Lima, of millions of people on the brink of homelessness and starvation. If I had a family squatting on its outskirts, scrabbling less than a living from day to day, I too would be drawn to Sendero and its promise of wealth, dignity and salvation for all.

* * *

Mother and Father; what are they thinking? Perhaps my kidnapping is simply one more disappointment, the consequence of a lifestyle and career that they have never understood. As their son I should have found a job in insurance or banking and married a quiet respectable girl from Newington or Corstorphine. They would have watched my gradual progress up the corporate ladder and been proud of the two or three grandchildren they could see every week. Instead, all I can offer them is fortnightly telephone calls, a man that I live with four hundred miles away, a job best classified as "worthy" and yearly visits of stilted conversation and silence.

Others share intimacies with their parents, laugh and talk together. Mine were always too old, too rigid, too formal. They kept me warm and sheltered but never drowned me in their love. In return I have never known how to love them. I have no idea how to make them happy, how to bring them closer to me. Instead we have drifted apart until this final blow. Nothing I can do or say will ever repair this last year.

* * *

Rosa opened this notebook and read a few words in an incomprehensible accent. "What does it say?" she asked.

"Nothing much. This room. How I feel. You."

She nodded slowly. "That's all?"

"That's all."

"It doesn't explain what brought you here?"

"To Peru? I've told you before: I was invited." There was another silence.

"What really brought you here?" she asked.

"What do you mean?" Her insistence confused me, made me suspect that her Spanish held a meaning deeper than my understanding.

"I will tell you what brought me here," she said finally, "why I fight for freedom." She was pacing the room slowly. "I grew up on my parents' farm. They grew maize and kept some animals and chickens. I had three sisters and one brother. I was the fourth child. When I was young, the economic situation was very bad. Inflation was rising fifty, a hundred per cent or more a year. But the price for our crops never rose by the same amount. We became poorer. When I was five or six, we had enough food to eat and clothes on our backs. By the time I was twelve, I was hungry. It was about then that my father decided to grow coca. We had always grown a little for ourselves, but the price had started to go up with the cocaine boom in the United States. By the time I was eighteen my father had made enough money to send my brother and me to college. He was a proud and independent man, who wanted all his children to be educated, but the money had come too late for my older sisters. So I went to Ayacucho and studied to be a teacher.

"In my second year of college," she went on, "the army came and burnt all the crops on my father's land. It was easy for them; we lived near the main road. If we had been up on the mountains, it would have taken longer, until the Yanquis started bringing in helicopters. My father's livelihood was destroyed. The people who bought his crop did not help. He did not know what to do. He didn't have enough money to bribe the army not to burn his land — he had spent it all on our education and building a better house. He tried to grow maize again, but the price was low and he did not make enough to cover his debts. He had to sell half his land to a man who has enough money to grow coca and bribe the army to look the other way. Since then my father has got poorer and now he is ill and I think he will die. He is not the only one. Many others in Huánuco have suffered the same way.

"It is the Yanquis who buy our coca and heroin and the Yanquis who force our government to burn it. It is a civil war in the United States between those who want to use drugs and those who want to ban them, fought with Peruvian lives and on Peruvian land. We did not invite them here, but they came. We have never invaded them or ordered their government to do what we say, but they have invaded us and they dictate to the regime in Lima how they will spend their money and what laws they will pass.

"It is not only the Yanquis. All of you, Europeans and Canadians and Australians, you come here with your fair skin and your garbled Spanish and tell us how to live our lives. You work for the World Bank or for your government or your charities, and you spend a day or a week or a year here, telling us that if we only do this or that our poverty will end. So because you have education and money and we don't, we listen to you. We forget our past and our pride and do what you tell us and a year later nothing has changed — except you have gone back to your nice comfortable houses in London or Berlin and we are left even poorer than before.

"I have read that there are many problems in England, many homeless people and people without work. Why aren't you there, solving your own problems, instead of coming here? What happened to you that made it so important for you to come to Peru? Tell me what right you have to be here. Tell me how Peruvians told you what you could and could not do with your land. Tell me how our soldiers came to London and 'advised' your prime minister. Tell me about the coups we plotted to overthrow your government and the years of poverty and repression that your people suffered. Tell me how your family starved because of what the people of the Andes did to them. If you can tell me what we have done to you, I will understand why you came here."

She looked down at me, an earnest teacher, a lecturer, as I stared up, a chastened student. A year ago I would have responded, agreed where she was right and corrected her where she was wrong. But I was confused by her words, unused to debate, unable to find the words to contradict her. Her conviction, her freedom to move and think, gave her the authority I had lost; after twelve months of imprisonment and isolation, I was no longer certain what I knew or what I believed.

"If you can't tell us what we have done to you," she said, gesturing at the notebook, "then at least be honest. Tell us by what right you came to Peru. Justify yourself, but don't use the excuse that someone invited you." She stared at me, still waiting for an answer that did not come. Finally she turned and left the room. In the emptiness my mind cleared and familiar arguments returned. That with its stick and carrot of violence and false promises, Sendero oppresses the people even more than the US or Peruvian governments have done. That the world is too small for communities to live in isolation. That democracy creates and does not destroy. Yet even as I rehearsed my defence for the next time we speak I was aware that these were not the words she wanted to hear. The words that would persuade her to free me would be quite different and I do not know what they are.

* * *

I have not seen Rosa for two or three days, although I have heard her with the others outside. When the window is open, I hear their voices clearly; I try to make out words and syllables but still do not know more than two or three words in Quechua. All I can say is the pronunciation bears some resemblance to Arabic, but, as they speak it, it lacks that language's strength and clarity.

I would write more, but it is an effort requiring more energy than I have. My hand aches and I long for a word-processor. Sometimes I sit against the wall, the notebook on my right knee. That feels comfortable at first, but I write less evenly and my shoulders and legs soon begin to ache. Then I stretch out across the mattress and support my neck in my left hand. That is easier, although it hurts my elbows. I asked Rosa for a table, but it was simply another request from a European too accustomed to getting anything he wants in life. A table is a luxury, too good for a prisoner. He has a mattress and shitbucket already; what more does he want?

* * *

Still no Rosa. I am haunted by our last conversation, the longest we have had. I rehearse different answers to her question, but know that they would not satisfy her. "To help people" is glib. "To see justice done," is only half the story when I do not know why justice concerns me so much. Besides, I could stay at home, as Rosa suggests; heaven knows there is enough poverty and injustice in Britain. "Because I like to travel," is the closest I can come to honesty.

Rosa ascribes her presence here to a single event — the burning of her parents' land. I cannot identify that same point in my life; I am not even sure it exists. Yet the idea rings true. Perhaps the chaos theory should be applied to human psychology — as the notorious beat of a butterfly's wing in Beijing can raise a tornado in Chicago, a single event in childhood may determine the pattern of each person's life.

Looking back, I suppose I can see the first tentative beat of the butterfly's wing: not when I chose my career, but when I wanted to travel. I was eight or nine, my grandfather had died and I was with my parents as they cleared out his house — a cold, dark building in Trinity. Bored with the emptying of wardrobes and the packing of old clothes, I wandered into the living-room. Rows of books waited there: dark, heavy, leather-bound novels, natural histories, dictionaries and other reference books, none of which intrinsically appealed to a child. Nevertheless I pulled out and leafed through one or two. An old atlas fascinated me. I lay on the floor and turned its pastel-coloured plates, picking out Italy and its neighbour Greece. To the right of Greece I found Turkey and, further down, Palestine. I wanted to know what came next and tried to follow the map onto the next page, but was confused by the differences of scale. When Father came in I pestered him to show me what lay further east and he pointed out Persia and the red triangle of India. It was a revelation. I already knew that roads and ferries could take me through England and across Europe; now I was beckoned further, to the Near and Middle East and beyond. Lands that had been as enticing but as fictitious as Wonderland and Narnia leapt into life, complete with fezzes and loincloths, elephants and rope-tricks, endless deserts and blazing sun.

My father saw my enthusiasm and gave me the atlas. It was not all I inherited that day. As we were leaving, I saw waiting to be thrown out a thick semi-transparent, greasy-looking garment, an oilskin cycling cape. My mother opened it to demonstrate how it covered both body and bicycle and, when I insisted, let me try it on. It was much too big and cumbersome, yet I wanted it desperately. It would wait for my adulthood, for the day when, the atlas stuffed into panniers beside clothing and food, I would take leave of my parents, mount my bicycle, don the cape and ride out of Edinburgh on the long journey south, to England, to Europe, to India and beyond.

I never made that journey. I came closest to it in my hitch-hiking days but they were overshadowed by the knowledge that I could not travel forever, that, always sooner than I would have wished, I would have to come home. Since then my wanderlust has had to be satisfied by countless Airbuses and 747s, bloody mary or gin and tonic in hand, mindless film on the screen and headphones shielding me from neighbours' conversations and the nightlong squawls of unhappy infants. Even the promise of arrival in Bangkok or Delhi, Nairobi or Kingston, which once would have thrilled me, has withered in the knowledge that I have a strict timetable of conferences and meetings and the inevitability of the flight home.

Nor could I make that journey now. Tom would not come with me and I could not leave him behind. If there were no Tom, my progress would be hampered by the wars and suspicions that block every stretch of the road between Switzerland and Singapore. But even they are not the deciding factor. What would hold me back now would be neither Tom nor wars, but myself and my middle age — the fear that I have seen it all and have nothing more to learn, the belief that I have come to the end, not the beginning, of a road.

* * *

Weeks ago I asked El Magro for a change of clothes, pointing to the months of dirt and grime. He ignored me. I repeated the request to Rosa. Today she brought a pile of clothing taken from some tourist — French by the labels on two of the shirts. There is a thick woollen sweater in red and green — colours I hate — and a pair of jeans too loose at the waist and too long at the ankle. There are even three pairs of underpants — also loose, but incredibly clean. For a second I considered refusing them as stolen property, but the gesture, I knew, would be pointless.

I thought of the dirt that covered me; Rosa misunderstood my hesitation and offered to leave. "I'd rather be clean when I put them on," I explained. To my surprise she brought me water. When I was alone again, I stripped completely, forcing my filthy trousers through the narrow gap between my ankle and the chain. Washing was a slow, careful process, using my old shirt to wipe the grime from my body. Clean, naked, cold, I felt both vulnerable and free. I inspected myself and was pleased to see that, apart from my ankle, my skin was only raw at the groin.

I pulled on briefs, the jeans — which were even more difficult to manoeuvre through the shackle — a t-shirt that declares I have visited La Paz, a blue cotton shirt and the hideous jumper. I felt good and even Rosa was impressed when she returned. My underwear is white, not grey and brown; the t-shirt feels smooth against my skin; even the sweater is bright and cheerful. For the first time in months I am properly clean. I sit here with half a smile on my face and, although I have no cause, I cannot stop feeling upbeat and optimistic.

* * *

Another long conversation, with Rosa sitting by the window and me reclining, a parody of a Roman emperor, on my mattress. She traces the origins of Gonzalist thought to the Incas, repeating Mariátegui's claim that their empire was the first communist state. I reminded her it was both a theocracy and one of the most hierarchical societies the world had ever seen. That, for her, was irrelevant. Every citizen was fed and sheltered and therefore happy. Everyone had a role to play in society and everyone supported the existence of the state. It sounded about as fair as the caste system in India, I said, but I had lost her by referring to a world she did not know.

I changed tack, argued that the subjugation of the Aymara by the Quechua had been a brutal act of colonialism worthy of any Spaniard. She protested it was not subjugation but liberation, implied that the Aymara were lazy and needed the discipline of the Quechua. As the Quechua needed the discipline of the Spanish, I suggested, but she ignored or did not understand me. Then came the Spanish, their armies suppressing the natives while their viceroys plundered the land. In the nineteenth century, nominal independence brought the economic domination of the British. Now the country is burdened by the United States, its Monroe Doctrine justifying every interference in internal affairs. For four and half centuries, wealth has flown to the men of Madrid and Lima, London and Washington, while the Andeans have been strangled by poverty and hunger, illness and death.

Of course there were rebellions which always ended in bloody defeat. Rosa does not blame her ancestors for their failures; before the prophet Mariátegui and the saviour Gonzalo, they blundered in ignorance, with no more understanding of their salvation than pre-Christian pagans. Only now can the revolution succeed. The history of every European colony is scattered with rebellions headed by leaders whom the natives idolised and the invaders reviled. In Peru, as elsewhere, both sides committed mass torture, murder and rape. The execution of the second Túpac Amaru in Cuzco's central square was typically bloody, as he was torn apart by four horses and decapitated. For a second I tried to convince myself that such actions were the product of an ignorant and barbarian past, but I knew they were simply expressions of universal human brutality — the precursors of concentration camps, electric torture and ethnic cleansing.

I did not dispute that the Spanish exploited their colonies, nor that the British only encouraged independence in order to create new markets and find new sources of raw materials. Where Rosa and I part company is in our different interpretations of historical forces. Like all Marxists, she sees the past as a relentless process which allows no scope for human initiative or folly; the poor will always struggle to free themselves from poverty while the rich will use any means to keep them in their place. Each event in history is either a victory or defeat on the path to the utopia where the workers forever lose their chains. Thus every ruler, from Pizarro to Fujimori, is a dictator and every resister from Atahualpa to Guzmán a hero.

To me, history has always made more sense as a series of random acts. In place of the eternal struggle between rulers and the ruled, all I see are individuals teetering between chance and circumstance. If Harold had lived, William might not have conquered; if Mao had died on the Long March, the Nationalists might have remained in control; in both cases the history of the world would have been very different. The past cannot be judged by the values of the present; an eighteenth-century liberal who favoured freedom of worship and greater democracy would be condemned as a bigot two hundred years later for his view that slavery was sanctioned by God and a woman's place was at her husband's beck and call. Ideas and attitudes change; Marx is already fading into history, Mao's influence would be shorter-lived and progressive thought a hundred years from now would see Rosa's ideology as limited and exploitative.

She agreed with the last point; revolution should be permanent and in the new century Marxist-Leninist-Maoist-Gonzalist thought would take further strides under the leadership of a new

Guzmán. I silenced the opinion that if this new messiah's only contribution to political discourse is to curb further hyphenisation he or she will do the human race a major service.

I pointed out that revolutionaries were no better than the rest of us. Stalin had millions murdered, while Mao's temperament was gross, his language coarse and his taste for young girls demeaning. Worse, he was a brilliant leader who degenerated into a petty schemer who half-destroyed the paradise he wanted to create.

I was wasting my breath. She will always ignore the inconvenient. Furthermore, no longer certain of my own beliefs, I was not interested in demolishing hers. It was the contact I relished, the fact that as we spoke we were partners in debate. My adrenalin had risen, my brain creaked into action for the first time in over a year. As her voice maintained its quiet monotone and she sat, almost motionless on her chair, my words rose and fell and my gestures regained a forgotten animation. In the end, however, unable to dent her self-confidence, I fell silent. We watched each other for a few minutes as the sun began to set, until she stood up, and with a nod and "*Hasta mañana*" that saw me almost as an equal, left the room. For a while I enjoyed being alone again, but as I lay there and night approached, I shivered to feel the room fill with the ghosts of men whose centuries-old wars and deaths had brought and trapped me here.

* * *

Another long conversation, which began as soon as Rosa walked into the room. If her aim is to convince me of her analysis before setting me free, I ought to agree with her more often, but I am incapable of doing so. Before I can think, I have spoken, pointing out defects in her argument. She appears to listen, but if I contradict her basic assumptions, I am ignored and, no doubt, my intransigence is noted.

Today was sociology — the unofficial apartheid between the country's Andeans and the Spanish-speaking *criollos*. For a few years during the war of independence the two forged an alliance, but liberty for the *criollos* was accompanied by virtual enslavement of the Andeans until the mid 1970s.

Rosa hates *criollos* with a passion. *Criollos* are the *pishtacos* of myth: blood-suckers and strippers of flesh. *Criollos* are the politicians, the army officers, the landlords, the businessmen, the writers and artists, the rich who live behind barbed wire and send their children to school in the United States. *Criollos* are the drug-traffickers, traitors and liars who pretend to be proud of their country's heritage while spitting on true Incas. *Criollos* are parasites who deserve no more than the enslavement and death that they have meted out for centuries. Luckily I am not a *criollo*, merely a gringo, a hapless European.

As a gringo, I acknowledged that over the centuries we have tortured, murdered, raped, enslaved and expropriated land. Yet we did not do so because we are white, merely because power was in our hands. Violence is not confined to those of lighter skins. Indeed, similar excesses have been committed by all the revolutionaries she admires. Of course she denied such an analysis; in her eyes, Russian and Chinese collectivisation were essential acts of revolution, the Khmer Rouge genocide was an acceptable, if exaggerated, solution to the problem of the ruling class, and Sendero's assassinations are necessary warnings to all those who would betray the people.

I should have stopped there, but I was intent on exonerating my ancestors. I argued that not all imperialism had been equally evil, that the British had been less prone than others to torture and murder. I compared the colonisation of North America with that of the South, the Calvinists in New England seeking to create a moral society with the renegade Catholics in Lima and Rio who revelled in their distance from the heavy hand of church and state. The more I spoke, however, the less certain I became. The English colonisers may have been more principled, but their principles still condoned atrocities in the name of the Lord — the theft of continents and the enslavement of millions. Faced with Rosa's scepticism, I tripped over my own arguments, contradicted myself and eventually fell silent. She listened to me without comment, no doubt smiling inwardly at my ineptness. Finally she spoke, but the impetus for discussion had gone and shortly afterwards she left me once again confused and uncertain.

* * *

When she does not come, I sulk. When I hear her outside, I want to call for her company, but dare not reveal my weakness. Instead I imagine her here, in her dark brown cardigan and tight jeans, clothing which somehow emphasises rather than diminishes her authority. I talk to her silently, repeat the conversations we have had with better responses, rehearse the conversations that I imagine are to come. At other times I search my past for the beat of the butterfly's wing. I tried to unravel the influences of my childhood — parents, school, friends, Edinburgh — but found that like the ingredients of a cake, each interacted with the rest. My parents chose my school and from school came my friends. Edinburgh, as Presbyterian as Rome was Catholic, moulded all our lives yet was no more than the sum of its inhabitants. With such a background, I could not help being a typical middle-class Scottish schoolboy of the fifties and sixties.

My sense of justice and honesty, the former much stronger than the latter, come from my parents. Of a much earlier generation — both were in their forties before I was ten — their values were rooted in the certainties of their own childhoods, in the stern but secure world where good and evil were clearly defined and violence was as distant as the Great War battlefields of France and Germany. Yet these same values which shielded me from uncertainty also frustrated me. The older I grew the more I longed to find the excitement, the essence, of life that I was sure existed elsewhere.

From classmates and friends I gained little but a sense of alienation. I did not understand them and therefore did not trust them. I liked a boy if he had something I wanted — a bigger garden or a better model railway set — or if his parents and mine were acquaintances. As far as I could tell, other boys liked me for the same reasons. Friendship signified no more than the absence of dislike; never expecting closeness, I did not find it.

School was home writ large — a place of routine and strict authority. Year after year we studied obediently because no alternative to obedience could be conceived. School gave me the depth and breadth of my education, but it was never anything other than a waiting-room, a place to pass time until my adulthood arrived. Perhaps Edinburgh had the greatest influence. The houses and gardens of Morningside, the cobbled streets of the Old Town and the wide avenues of the New Town, had as strong a personality as any adult of my acquaintance. The city was an austere parent, busy during the day, silent at night, at rest on Sundays and Saturday afternoons. Its dark stone buildings watched over me, alert for misbehaviour as I walked from house to bus stop, from bus stop to school. A cold city, with bright but distant sun, grey clouds and cruel winds, its welcome lay in its familiarity rather than its warmth.

Somewhere there may be the butterfly's wing. I have no idea how different my life and attitudes would have been if I had grown up elsewhere. If I had been Sudanese and escaped the civil war for the safety and wealth of London or Los Angeles, would I have still gone on to work for World Aid and Demotica? If I had been Chinese, would I have ended up in Tienanmen Square? Or would I have ignored the ideals of others and made my fortune manufacturing televisions or shoes? And Rosa — how important was the burning of her father's land? Thousands of peasants grow up as impoverished as she did but few rebel. Remove Rosa from her environment and how much does she change? Brought up on some council estate in Newcastle or Birmingham, would she have devoted her life to the Socialist Workers Party or the IRA? Would she have ended up a single mother, on the dole, drugs or petty crime, or would she have educated herself into the middle class?

What made me what I am; what brought me here? The old pointless question of nature or nurture. The only certainties in the darkening light and falling temperature are my presence in this room, the hunger in my stomach, the chain round my ankle and my jailers talking in the yard.

* * *

I told Rosa a little about my childhood. It was remote to her, the six-year-old boy in short trousers, red blazer and cap boarding a double-decker in a grey North European city. My home was large, warm and comfortable. My father herded no animals, grew no crops; my mother did not work in the fields. Instead he attended patients while she kept house and visited neighbours in daily coffee mornings. I had no duties but my homework; my room had drawers full of clothes and cupboards stuffed with toys and books. As if her mind had been elsewhere, she asked if as a child I had ever stolen. A couple of times, I told her, taking sweets from counters with sweating hands and pounding heart. A dare to myself more than to others, the agony it caused was far greater than the meagre reward.

My confession was merely a preamble to hers. "When I was about eight," she said, "my mother was very ill and my brother and I went to stay with my uncle's family in Juliaca, a long way away. They were poorer than us, had only a small shop selling groceries. In the afternoons my cousins took us to the station to meet the train for tourists. They were always in the last coach. I had never seen so many gringos before. At first I just looked at them, their pink faces and big bodies and strange clothes. I was frightened of them; they seemed very special and important in that big train. They kept staring and pointing at us and taking photographs.

"When the train stopped, a lot of women would get on to sell the foreigners ponchos and sweaters. They filled the aisle and bargained with the gringos, who would be very proud when they managed to beat the women down by a dollar or two. While their attention was taken, my cousins and other children of five or six were crawling under the seats and stealing whatever they could — money, travellers' cheques, sometimes even a camera. The gringos thought they were being clever keeping their valuables well away from potential thieves in the aisle, but they did not realise that we Andeans were cleverer.

"I was too big to join them. José — my brother — was much smaller, so he went along. He got caught once. He had found a leather bag and was dragging it behind him as he crawled out of the last seat when a gringo saw him. It was obvious that the bag didn't belong to an indio," her voice harshened with the insult. "He grabbed José by the collar and pulled the bag out of his hands. José hit out as hard as he could but he was too small to do any harm. The gringo called out for the owner, who turned out to be some German or North American. To throw him the bag, the man had to let José go. The second he did so he jumped down and ran into town as fast as he could. We thought he was being chased and got ready to trip over whoever followed him, but no one did."

I remembered Juliaca, pictured the train standing in the midday sun, the peasants clambering in and out, the crowds in the tourist coach. I saw the gringos through Rosa's eyes, heard their arrogance and petulance as they haggled. I was not sure why she had told me the story and was reluctant to ask.

"Would you teach your children to do the same?"

"Perhaps," she said, "but only from gringos."

"Why?"

"We only rob those who rob us. Each time a tourist pays a dollar for something that would cost him five or ten dollars at home, he is stealing from us. He is stealing our dignity, our opportunity to escape from poverty, to invest in our children, our future. But because we cannot refuse him, we have to sell whatever we have for whatever he will offer. It is not true selling; it is extortion, theft.

"It is not only the money," she went on. "It is the contempt that foreigners have for us. The worst are those who are old and fat, who demand that we speak your English or your French or German; they insist on the best hotels and the most comfortable means of travel and they are always complaining because something they want is not available or not as good or as new or as clean as in New York or Paris. The young are different but almost as bad. They claim to be poor but they come here with more money in their pockets than we earn in a lifetime. They haggle and haggle and still complain we overcharge them. They devalue our culture by turning it into souvenirs. They think because they know a few words of Spanish and they have read their guidebooks — always written by gringos, never by a Peruvian — that grants them some kind of status. Yet they show no respect for our history or land. They dress indecently, crowd onto our buses, try to seduce our young women and push our old aside."

The picture was exaggerated but true. I had seen it in a dozen countries, committed the same crimes a hundred times. "In the New Republic we will ban all but a few tourists," she went on. "Restrict foreigners to travel in escorted groups, charge them high prices, make them stay in special hotels."

"Like Saudi Arabia or North Korea," I said. She agreed, as I wondered whether the irony had been misplaced; banning foreigners would help maintain the purity of the revolution. I tried to imagine Cuzco without tourists, the plaza empty of hotels and bars and souvenir shops, a duller, but more Andean place. I would appreciate it more, I realised, assuming, of course, that I was one of the chosen who still had the right to visit.

* * *

More than once she has accused me of knowing nothing of her world. Yet I have visited this country enough to have glimpsed and sometimes shared her life. I have travelled the roads of the Altiplano, clinging with freezing hands to the rails of lorries as they bounced over potholes and threw dust in my eyes; I have listened to countless men in dusty, tired Sunday suits and round-faced women in bowler hats and layers of cardigans and skirts; I have filed out of buses with peasants and shown my papers to young soldiers whose ignorance and fear lay beneath their mask of arrogance. I have eaten Rosa's food — the flavourless rice, the chicken broth with the claw still lying in the bowl, the tough and stringy kebabs. I have been breathless with altitude sickness, chewed coca to give me energy and strength. I have sailed Titicaca, walked mountain roads and stood dumbfounded amongst the ruins of her ancestors.

Most of all, I have seen first-hand that life for so many here, as for so many throughout the world, is little more than a flickering candle of existence — the monotony of labour from dawn to dusk, hours in the fields broken by inadequate meals, occasional visits to market and rare festivals. The five-year old child by his mother's side staring vacantly into space wakes for a few years of boisterous energy, then sinks into a lifetime of coca-induced lethargy. I know, much more than Rosa realises, that here, as in so much of the world, birth is not opportunity but a sentence of squalor, discomfort, disease and early death. But if I cannot make her see this, I cannot make her understand that I sympathise. I cannot get it across to her that I am her friend, not her enemy. I want for her people the same things that she wants — food, education, health, self-determination and self-sufficiency. Our goals are the same, only our means are different.

Perhaps the fact that she is willing to listen is a hopeful sign. She may ignore the arguments she dislikes, but she cannot help but hear them. One day, perhaps, they will sink in. One day we will understand each other. One day she will set me free.

* * *

If I hoped that Rosa was here on my account, an interrogator come to see if I should be set free. I was wrong. She is in hiding, as imprisoned as I am. She was one of a group that ambushed a general in his car. His bodyguards killed two of her companions. She was the one who stepped forward and fired the bullet into his brain.

She told me when I asked about her involvement with the party. Naively, I expected something safe or abstract — writing leaflets or daubing walls with slogans. Even here, even now, part of me tries to keep reality at bay. I do not know whether I feel detachment, disgust or fear. I asked a few questions — who, where, why — that she barely answered before, apparently annoyed at having told me, she left the room. Alone, I found myself squatting in the corner under my blanket, staring at the wall. My mind was rebelling, offering pictures of her dumpy, ungainly body suddenly moving fast, smoothly, a gun in her hand — pictures that I tried to reject. She was almost my friend; I could not conceive of her taking life. If I could not trust her, I could trust no one. Hours later, I fell asleep and dreamt of her finger on the trigger, my forehead beneath the gun.

* * *

There is no closeness between us — we are kept apart by half a millennium of history and a year of my imprisonment — but there is understanding. We offer each other what El Gordo and El Magro lack: intelligence and the willingness to debate. It is routine now, her sitting at the window, half in shadow, looking out when thinking hard or bored, my shifting position on the mattress, never finding comfort. I am still sometimes deceived into thinking that she is no more than an adolescent girl briefly infatuated by a religion she calls Gonzalism. Then I see her posture, intent, motionless, devoid of gesture, listen to her words and look at her dark eyes and realise that in many ways she is more adult than I will ever be.

We swing back and forth between the motives of the different organisations we work for. She is impressed by what I know of Sendero, my previous knowledge supplemented by the copies of *El Diario*, damp yellowing pages in mind-numbing jargon designed to repel all but the most zealous of converts. They are years old, from the time when García was president, Guzmán was free and each year brought Sendero greater success. Nevertheless they inform our discussions, although I quote the paper's wilder assertions with little reverence. She ignores the sarcasm; the Revolution is, after all, inevitable, even after Guzmán's arrest and recantation.

"Come on," I said. "Without Gonzalo you have nothing."

"Gonzalo's thought lives on, like the thought of Chairman Mao."

"Mao was free to lead his people to victory."

"Chairman Gonzalo's spirit is free. He has given us the strategy. Now we must choose the tactics. The strategy," she went on, when I asked, "is to extend operation zones through guerrilla warfare and to accumulate political power through the establishment of People's Committees." Mao's strategy of taking control of the countryside in order to strangle the cities.

"Meaningless words," I said.

"Meaningful words — rule by the people."

"Rule by the people: democracy. For every adult a vote. Demotica's objective."

She shook her head. "You believe in manipulation of the people. You claim that your committees and political parties give them power. But all these committees and parties do is fight each other, not the system. You claim to set the people free, but by approving the system you continue to exploit them. The Party ignores your false goals and seeks to liberate the people from all tyranny."

"To impose a tyranny of its own."

"The tyranny of the proletariat."

"Still a tyranny."

"But a beneficial one."

"The thoughts of Chairman Gonzalo."

"The thoughts of all revolutionary leaders: Marx, Lenin and Mao."

"None of them infallible. Millions died in China during the Great Leap Forward. Most were innocent."

She shrugged. "The innocent have been dying for centuries. Ever since the Spanish arrived, the innocent have died. Sometimes they have to die for the benefit of those who live."

"Tell that to the young soldier who dies because he was in the wrong place at the wrong time. A life is not like a house or money or a llama. It can't be replaced. Tell his mother that her only son died for the revolution. Don't you realise the responsibility you have?"

She shrugged again, uninterested in my middle-class European outrage. I persisted. "Who decides who has to die? Who orders these assassinations and massacres?"

"The people."

"All the people? All at once? In a vote? Private Fulano has to be blown up by a mine tomorrow. All those in favour raise their hands?"

"If you oppose the people you deserve to die. The man who takes up arms against the people surrenders his right to life."

I did not have the courage to ask whether I too deserved to die. Instead I asked if everyone was equal. "Or is the man with more land less equal than his neighbour? What about the man with two llamas instead of one? The woman with higher education? Are they heroes of the revolution or its traitors? Do you want to emulate the Khmer Rouge and bring everyone down to the level of pigs wallowing in the muck? Or Kerala in India, where peace and education have raised everyone's living standards?"

I had strayed too far from familiar ground. "Theories, theories," she said. "The death of a few is not important if everyone else becomes free."

"Free from what? Free to do what?"

"Free from capitalism. Free from the domination of the West. Free to live our own lives in dignity."

"In poverty. You can't live without the outside world. You need a government in Lima that will represent your interests fairly. You need the West to buy your exports. You need tourists to bring you income. Without the outside world you will remain poor and die poor."

"We do not need you, your money or your aid. We want nothing from you."

"Then why watch our television? Why buy our machinery? Why speak our language?"

"Because you will not speak our language and we must understand the word and deed of the oppressor. Besides, we will ban your television and build the machinery we need."

"Tear down the satellite dishes? Build machines out of mud and wood? What about decent houses, sewerage and hot water? You don't have the resources and expertise. Half the country's middle class — the ones with knowledge and skills — have fled and the other half are desperate to go."

"We do not need the middle class," she said, "or their so-called skills. We survived for generations without concrete, iron or the wheel. We can survive for generations more."

"You survived in poverty. You're sentencing your people to slave on the land."

"They have always worked on the land for others. Now they will work for themselves."

"The tyranny of poverty," I said.

"Freedom from tyranny," she replied. Back at the same argument, the same meaningless phrases. We were silent for a while.

"It won't happen. The Revolution failed," I said.

She smiled. "How would you know? You've been here for over a year."

"Has Guzmán been freed? Fujimori toppled or is he still in control?"

"In control of what? Lima and a few towns? The people welcome us everywhere," she said. She may have believed it, but I did not.

"If even that were true, they do so because they have no option. You kill them otherwise."

"There is no option to freedom."

Our arguments circled each other again. When she left there was no hostility between us, but in its place I felt a growing inadequacy. Rosa speaks with frightening conviction, as a free and healthy young woman, in clear, fluent Spanish even though it is her second language. I can only respond as a prisoner, a man approaching middle age who is cold, half-sick and soul-tired, in a Spanish which says less than I mean and with arguments whose premises I have often forgotten. For a year I imagined that when I met a guard who was capable of listening to reason, I would be able to persuade him — or her — of the injustice of holding me. Now she has appeared, my ability to persuade has gone.

* * *

Sunny, almost warm in this corner of the room that receives little light. Even the food — chicken broth and relatively fresh bread — was palatable today. We talked about Demotica. She wanted to know where our money came from and how we could claim to be independent if we were funded by governments. I told her that all funding, whatever its source, had to come without strings. Besides, only the good guys gave us money: the Canadians, the Dutch and the Scandinavians.

To her the justification was as irrelevant as obscure points of theology to an atheist; it proved the absurdity of my cause. She wanted to know why, if we claimed to represent the South, we were based in London. I cited lack of censorship, ease of communication and the fact that, like it or loathe it, English was the international language. I pointed out that half our staff and most of our executive board came from the developing world. I ran her through our decision-making procedures, our neutrality towards every shade of political opinion. She listened, but only in order to reject each justification, claiming that problems can only be solved by those they directly affect. Whatever their colour or nationality, our board members come from the moneyed middle classes, whose experiences and theories are irrelevant to the poor. Only when the rich and the gringos say "We are ignorant, tell us what to do," can assistance be genuinely offered and accepted.

From Demotica in general to my work in specific. She remains convinced that I came to Peru with a hidden agenda to swamp the

Andes with unwanted advisors and aid. She is certain that at each meeting I attend, I choose delegates, influence debates and manipulate votes and decisions. Our Peruvian partners she sees as quislings deserving even greater contempt than myself. I remembered the papers I had with me when I was kidnapped, the names of those invited to a meeting that I presume never took place. She shrugged with disinterest when I asked if my contacts had come to harm. It angered me to think that their association with me may have led to their injury or death. I insisted that my role was to advise, that I did little more than make opening or closing speeches. The examples I gave of Demotica's lack of power — our failure to bring opposing sides together in Sri Lanka and Liberia, our being banned from the UAE — she saw as irrelevant.

I repeated again that I had come for a meeting on funding that had no motions to pass or conclusions to be drawn. She shook her head, unable to see the point of having people travel so far for so little. "See me as a catalyst," I said, "responding to local needs."

"If you had responded to local needs, you wouldn't have come. Whatever you say, your presence influences others. I've seen it before. You're the gringo expert. You represent money and power. They defer to you, they listen to you. You get what you want."

"We don't want anything. They only defer to foreign governments or development agencies. Demotica is different; we have no money; we have no power."

"People are naive. They're not aware of subtle differences between foreigners. Whether you want to or not, you intimidate them."

"We don't," I said, although I was sensitive to the charge. "You don't have much faith in your own people."

"I know them better than you."

"Do you?" I asked.

"And you? You hardly know this country and you have the right to tell me what we think?"

"Yes," I said, suddenly angry, "I do. It isn't just this country. It's all the countries I have visited, all the poverty I have seen. People across the world want a roof over their heads, a job, food for themselves and their family and the chance for their children to have a happier and healthier life than they have had. I have been doing my best to help these people for the past fifteen years. The older I get the more I realise that to get that security, that promise of a better future, they need to have control over their lives. That's why I moved to Demotica. That's what I was trying to do when your comrades held me up and threw me in here. I have seen more poverty and suffering than you can ever imagine. I know a damn sight better than you ever will the problems that face the world we live in. I may not speak your Quechua, but I know your country, I know your people, I know as well as you do what they want and need."

She was silenced, although not taken aback, by my outburst. "All I have ever done is offer advice and information," I repeated when I had calmed down. "On how to strengthen democracy. On different systems of government. On effective political organisation. I have never, ever tried to persuade anyone to change their political views." Neither of us spoke for a while. I watched her thinking over what I had said and felt more pride than at any time since I had been kidnapped.

She sat up, stretched her legs, brushed some hair from her eyes. "You've done this in a lot of countries?" she asked.

"Personally?" I asked. "About fifteen. Demotica as a whole works in over fifty."

"You say you're neutral, but what if your partners, as you call them, are fascists or military dictators?"

"If they're fascists or dictators, they're unlikely to want to work with us."

"And if they see you as legitimising their rule?"

"Then I doubt we'd work with them."

"So you're not neutral."

"We only reject extremists."

"All revolutionaries were extremists once." A truism to which I had no answer. "What you call democracy is a fraud. It pretends to give power to the people but in reality it deprives them of power. It has never worked, not even in England or the United States." I protested and she reminded me that US presidents are routinely elected by a quarter of the adult population, that British elections give huge majorities to parties with a minority of the vote. I admitted there were defects and that no system could be perfect. She insisted that democracy had done nothing for Peru. The army always took power when it wanted and Fujimori had led his own *autogolpe*. And all the time the people became poorer and poorer.

"Because democracy has always been weak here," I said. "It needs to be strengthened, in each village, in each town, in each community. Take away the corruption, increase participation."

"Democracy doesn't put more food on people's plates."

"Nor do guns and bombs."

"Guns and bombs destroy those who steal from the people."

"Guns and bombs only destroy. They do not create wealth or grow food. You have been fighting for twenty years and have achieved absolutely nothing."

"After twenty years Mao was still in the mountains. He won in the end." Again I was silenced. I felt like a rat in a maze he had once known intimately but had now forgotten. I had once believed in my deepest gut that democracy should be firmly established in every nation for the good of every human on this planet. Now I had begun to lose faith in my own arguments. Rosa watched me, waiting for answers that I could not provide. I shrugged, in conscious imitation of her gesture. I had lost my way and felt cold, in every sense of the word.

* * *

Another dream that I had returned home. Tom was shouting at me in the bedroom. Gradually I understood what he was saying — "You left me, you left me" again and again. I reached out to comfort him and half-woke, became aware of the early morning, the roughness of the blankets, the hard mattress, the raw skin on my ankle. Before I was fully conscious I knew that no matter how uncertain the welcome, home was far preferable to here. I tried to slip back into the dream, to see Tom and reach out for him. For a moment I succeeded, but then I was awake again.

I have thought about Tom more today than I have for weeks. Usually I push him to the side of my mind, unwilling to be reminded that I cannot be with him. Today, however, I wanted to remember him. I saw him in a hundred different situations, up the ladder painting the front window, feeding the hens, watching television and making love. Above all, I remembered the first day he invited me to Eric and Dave's flat, the day when, watching the intensity with which he tried to please me, I realised I loved him, his honesty, his vulnerability and his capability of responding to affection.

I still cling to that memory. The table littered with uncleared dishes, cups of coffee and half-empty glasses of wine. The small dining-room, pale yellow walls and dark ceiling; the table and chairs better than junk shop and not as good as antique. Eric to my right, Dave to my left, arguing about some common friend while Tom and I caught each other's eye. I smiled and he smiled back, blushing slightly under the hair that he still wore long. Open-necked shirt, blue I think; black jeans which hugged his crotch and backside. I could not help but fall in love, though I had not expected to. That first night in the bar he was merely a handsome face in a bar offering sex with no complications. Later he became the attraction of opposites: unsophisticated, working-class, home-bound, almost as exotic as the affairs I had on my travels. For a time I pitied him, the years working in second-rate cafés and restaurants, living in one rented room after another, alone or with an unsuitable lover. I only fell in love with him when I fully understood him. Above all, he was the first and only lover to understand and respect the work I do, the only one who recognised its importance to me and, however dimly, the key it held to my character.

I tell myself I still love him, but I am no longer sure if that is true. My love for him never dominated my life as his love for me dominated his. I do not know how I will feel when I get out of here and I have no idea how he will feel after being left alone for so long. In the first few days I worried how he would respond. I pictured myself a hero returning to comfort a man who had been shattered with worry. Now, the longer I have been held, the more I have lost touch with him. Sometimes I think I will find he has abandoned me for a lover who offers the reassurance of coming home each night. At other times I imagine him paralysed without me, sitting at home day after day, night after night, unable to do anything but wait for my return.

I know I will want to see him when I return home. I will want to hold him and have him hold me. But I do not know how close to him I will want to be, whether I will want to cling to him for a lifetime or soon push him away, whether a year and more of solitude will have made me desperate for his company or eager to be alone.

When Tom faded, other memories returned. The untidiness of my desk at Demotica, being stranded in the tube by a security alert, waiting in the rain at Reading station, my credit card being refused at Geneva airport, a power cut in the hotel in Kathmandu, a tedious interview with a government minister in Bangladesh. No matter how mundane, each image was so sharp, so infused with nostalgia, that it left me trembling with an emotion halfway between sorrow and anger. Now, at the end of the day, I sit with my back against the wall, notebook on my knee, my body tired, my hand aching, my guts heavy and my foot in a chain. I do not want to be disturbed by memories. I cannot cope with them. The longer I stay here, the less

I want to think about my past, my home, Tom, the people I knew and worked with. Perhaps it is self-protection — a refusal to be distressed by events I cannot control. Perhaps I am trying to project an image of self-sufficiency. Perhaps it is simply that my reality has shrunk to this room, my daily meal, the meanderings of my mind.

* * *

Rosa was away, came back wearing a denim jacket I had not seen before. "You went to the village?" I asked; she gave no reply. I have never been able to work out how close this house is to others, whether there is indeed a village nearby. I never hear voices other than those of my guards, nor is there traffic near or in the distance. There must be a road here, because a lorry brought me here, but I heard no engine to accompany Fernando's departure or Rosa's arrival.

Wherever she went, she had access to news: some scandal in the ruling party. Rosa was pleased. "It means *el Japonés* will be replaced before long."

"Someone worse could take his place," I pointed out.

"Even better. The people will see the true face of the dictatorship."

"And if the new man is more honest or liberal?"

"That will also help. He may release some of our sympathisers."

"So they can carry on killing?"

She shrugged. "If necessary. It is more important to organise the people. "It's funny," she said suddenly, "that you and I claim to be doing the same thing."

"Doing what?"

"Empowering the people." I felt and suppressed a glimmer of hope. "At least you recognise my good intentions."

"We always have," she said.

"So what do you intend to do with me?" She seemed about to answer, but said nothing.

"Let me go."

"Don't throw out a tool until you know what is used for." A proverb I did not recognise. She sat down again. I picked up a copy of *El Diario*, with a headline celebrating some Sendero action, and made a cynical comment about how difficult it was to mobilise the masses. That led to a lecture about Sendero's strategy. I listened reluctantly to her explanation that Sendero's setbacks are merely illusory. As Mao explained, once the rural masses are aroused, defeat is impossible. Mao's analysis, however, was incomplete. He had argued that the peasantry must build strongholds to besiege and take over urban areas, while Guzmán proved that these stages were unnecessary. The New Republic can be established immediately in areas that have been liberated; as these areas grow, the armed struggle will eventually win.

We had returned to the only ground I felt sure of: the random brutality of the 'armed struggle'. Again I insisted that many of those who Sendero killed — local mayors, low-ranking soldiers, peasants turned informer — were natural supporters forced by circumstance and often against their will, into opposing the *senderistas*. Murdering them was surely counter-productive. Rosa shrugged off my complaints. She had no sympathy for those I defended, only anger that they saw their own lives as more important than the masses from which they came. I argued that Sendero's actions were excessive: villagers executed without trial, cities bombed without warning. She responded that the armed forces committed atrocities a hundred times worse. "In many ways, the army do our job for us," she said. "They bring thousands to our cause. They kill and steal from the peasants. They uproot whole villages and move them miles away. The army claims it is 'protecting' the people from the revolution, but they forget that the revolution is everywhere."

"The people are the water in which the fish of the people's army swim." One of the few Maoist sayings I remembered.

"The soldiers force villagers to set up 'Civil Defence Committees' and 'Peasant Patrols', to 'protect' themselves from us," she went on, "We have to destroy these tools of oppression and show the villagers that true power lies with Sendero and not the armed forces."

"But these 'tools of oppression' were set up because you terrorised whole communities," I said. "You destroyed the civil structure. Of course the army — and the peasants — want to replace it."

She shook her head. "The New Republic is already operating. We have our own People's Committees. These Patrols and Defence Committees are a laughing-stock. They collapse within days. The peasants only join them because the army forces them to."

"Are you sure?" I asked, suspecting that her rhetoric bore little relation to reality. "Anyway," I went on, "you do exactly the same. You force people to cooperate with you. If they don't, you kill them yourselves or tell the police they are *senderista* — knowing they will be arrested and probably tortured."

"We do not force people. We invite them. We educate them."

"Why can't people lead their own lives without swearing allegiance to either you or the state?"

"Because the egoist is the enemy of the community."

"The egoist contributes to the community in his own way. Let a thousand flowers bloom, as Mao said," I added, without reminding her it was a phrase that he soon disowned.

"Diversity within the revolution, not against it."

"No room for the individual?"

"The cult of the individual only leads to capitalism and poverty. Look at England," she said. "In the fifties and sixties you were moving towards a socialist state. Thatcher destroyed it in the eighties. Now the rich are getting richer and the poor are getting poorer." I was tempted to tell her she was right, that homeless youths once again begged in Britain's streets, but I was not willing to concede that her alternative was better. We carried on quibbling over points that advanced neither argument, until the sun began to set. She left me thinking over the fundamental differences between us, the fact that we cannot agree on the value we place on human life. She is an evolutionist who sees the masses, the species, as paramount, the individual as expendable. I am the psychologist who sees the individual as supreme. Yet I recognise the roots of her argument. There has never been room for the individual in this society. It has always been the community that matters, the community that has to prosper, the community that looks after its members in times of trouble. And it is the community that has been oppressed by the Spanish, the *criollos* and the North Americans. It even begins to make sense to me that those who organise within the system — priests, aid workers, union leaders, liberal politicians — oppress the people by supporting it. Perhaps Rosa is right and the apathy, corruption and racism is so entrenched that only a revolution can destroy it.

* * *

El Gordo brought my food this morning. Once more I tried to talk to him, to make contact with the person beneath the shambling form, but all I got was silence. He has been here as long as I have, must feel as trapped as I do, yet he never reacts, never shows any emotion. When I hear his voice, it is deep, almost aggressive, yet the phrases are short and I am sure his intelligence is low. El Magro is the one I fear. He comes in perhaps once a week, equally silent, his expression a cold sneer. I suspect that if the choice were his, he would have slit my throat long ago.

I long for some form of distraction. For months I have been desperate for something other than *El Diario* to read. If allowed one book on this desert island, it would be Conrad. I came across him at thirteen, when I had exhausted the children's library and found no pleasure in the Muriel Sparks and Iris Murdochs that my mother read. I read *Youth* first, intrigued by the title, and was immediately addicted. With every book of his I opened, he confirmed my belief that the world was too vast and varied for any individual to exhaust. He reassured me that beyond the horizon Chinese farmers in coolie hats laboured in sodden paddy-fields, Africans danced naked in the bush and Pacific Islanders in log canoes pulled exotic fish from a transparent sea. Their hot, humid homelands could only be reached after weeks traversing oceans in battered ships crewed by men who daily faced danger and death and thereby glimpsed and understood the mystery of life. The few who travelled with them were solitary Europeans as scarred by adversity as the sailors who abandoned them on distant shores. Survival was precarious, dependent on luck and the wit to integrate into alien cultures.

I longed to enter Conrad's world. I knew that time had passed, that airplanes linked continents and colonies had become independent states, but in my mid-teens I believed that little else had changed. I was convinced that there were still beaches no European had ever seen, Himalayan villages where the esoteric was commonplace, whole countries where my language was unknown. It was not until my early twenties that I learnt I had been born too late and wherever I went, white men had been before; the dollar was the world's currency, English its creole, hamburgers and Coca-Cola its meat and drink.

Beware of wishes that might be granted.

This hell is indeed Conrad's world. Abandoned by my compatriots thousands of miles from home, surrounded by hostile and uncomprehending natives, with no prospect of salvation, perhaps I will only survive if I shake off my past and become one of them.

* * *

Perhaps I should have left Edinburgh when I left school. If I had gone to Oxbridge or London, explored a new city and made new friends, my wanderlust might have been stillborn. Instead I stayed to study anthropology and linguistics, convinced that these subjects were the academic equivalents of Conrad. I was wrong. I expected to be transported to Ugandan villages and Burmese temples, but found myself mired in geometries of kinship and lineage. I looked for instant access to the world's tongues, and tripped over Swedish vowel shifts and Polynesian colour concepts.

As my enthusiasm waned, I paid less attention to my studies and more to the peripheral benefits of my education. My parents had begun to treat me as an adult, allowing me to go where and when I wished and to return in my own time. If I did not abuse the freedom it was because my imagination did not stretch further than the few excesses I could see. I got drunk infrequently, unwilling to tolerate the accompanying nausea and headaches, and smoked cannabis rarely, inhibited by the difficulty of inhaling when I had never taken up cigarettes. I made new friends, the novelty of their opinions and accents compensating for any lack of deeper empathy, and lost my virginity almost by accident.

The greatest freedom came each summer when, with some money from my parents and the rest earned in bars and neighbours' gardens, I travelled abroad and alone. Hitch-hiking through England to the continent beyond, I discovered the exotica of trams and late-night bars, of French and Italian swear-words, of open markets and inner courtyards, of heat and light. In comparison to grey Scotland, Europe exploded with colour and life. Although there were times when I was tired, depressed or afraid — drenched with rain and no car in sight, threatened by thieves, or lost in a silent town at three in the morning — I never wanted to return home. I wanted only to move on to the next day and next experience, to sharpen my vocabulary and accent cruising down the autobahn with an autocratic German or walk home after midnight with a stranger in the middle of Florence. This, ignorance and youth told me, was freedom; this was how I always wanted to live.

* * *

I know what brought me here. I know the beat of the butterfly's wing.

That second summer, twenty years old, some money in my pocket and a rucksack on my back. A month in Greece, the days spent wandering through ruins and lying on beaches, the nights in cheap hotels and bars. Full of life, energy, and the exhilaration of youth. After ten days in the Peloponnese, I was returning to Athens before sailing to the islands. It was late afternoon, the train ambled through the heat and dry landscape. I practised my limited Greek with a mother and daughter, disdaining the phrasebooks used by other tourists. We pulled into the city, the day still warm and the light gradually darkening from yellow to orange. I hauled on my rucksack and stepped down to the platform and the melee of garishly garbed foreigners and soberly dressed natives. Once out of the station, I would head for the Plaka, treat myself to a single room, have dinner, go to a bar, drink, dance and, with luck, find someone to make love with. This was Life, this was Freedom; to go where I wanted, to do what I wanted, to be what I wanted, on my own or with another as I chose.

She stood to one side of the exit. She was small, old, wrinkled, dressed in black. She stood motionless, her hands outstretched, offering plastic necklaces and toys for sale. Her eyes were focused in the middle of the crowd, seeing us all but unaware of each individual. None who passed in search of friends, family, a taxi or bus, returned her look or stopped to buy. The second I saw her I knew she had been there all day, unmoving, unblinking, unhoping. I knew that she had sold nothing. I knew that on the days she did not come to the station she could be found at one of the markets in the same half-crucified position, from dawn to dusk, silent, motionless except for the rare moments when someone paid twenty drachmae for a trinket. I knew that she lived alone. I knew that her husband was dead, her children gone. I knew she had no money. I knew that her body was stiff and ached in every bone. I knew that life for her was no more than this hopeless stance and the bare room in which she curled up each night. I knew that all she knew was pain, pain of the body and pain of the heart, a pain deadened, but never obliterated, by the monotony of her days. I lost sight of her almost immediately as the crowd swept me on. I wanted to stop but she had nothing I wanted to buy. I had no words in English, far less Greek, that would relieve the pain of her age and her existence. I could not make her happy. I could not share the exuberance that until a moment ago had bubbled within me. I could only walk on through the station, shaken, trembling with the deepest pity.

In that moment I had seen not one old woman but, standing behind her, equally silent and motionless, all those I had known about but had never taken to heart — the ill, the starving, the homeless. Man, woman and child, European, African and Asian, each stared at me through her eyes and asked what right I had to life, to pleasure, as long as they lived in hunger and misery and pain. As I came out into the street, the light, which moments ago had bathed the world in warmth and beauty, was dying and dull. The evening of celebration I had planned lay shattered. I could no longer rejoice in life, if life for others was the misery I had just seen.

I found a hotel, left my rucksack and sought a restaurant away from the crowds where I could sit undisturbed. Afterwards I wandered through the city, tracing the triangle between Syntagma, Omonia and the Plaka, leaving the light and talk and movement in the cafes and squares to walk along dark deserted streets. My thoughts were calm but unclear, looking for the solution to a problem that I had barely begun to comprehend. The poverty I had witnessed until then — the few alcoholic tramps in the Grassmarket, the occasional beggars in various European towns — I could attribute to minor defects in the welfare state; whatever the cause, it could surely be put right. The sight of one old woman had shattered my illusion; her pain and the pain of all others had become my pain. As I strolled through the summer warmth I was overwhelmed by images of suffering I had seen over the years. I recognised for the first time how harsh and cruel was the world. More than that, I knew that my own life was to have meaning, if I could take pleasure in my existence, it could only be if I were to somehow mitigate that harshness and cruelty.

If that old woman had not been there, or if I had arrived in Athens one day later, would my life have been any different? Would there have been another incident at another time that affected me so deeply? Or was that evening the last moment that I was still impressionable and a week, a month, a year later, would I have seen her or a starving child, a distraught mother, as merely picturesque, unfortunate, but no concern of mine? Until that summer I had not decided on a career. The salaries and opportunities of the UN and EC beckoned, although I suspected I did not have the patience to wear a suit and tie and deal with the minutiae of agricultural or trading policy. Translation was possible, although it meant a year or more of further study. Tourism was the most likely choice. Whatever decision I made, I am sure I would have been successful, but an old woman intervened, awoke within me a deep sense of responsibility, a sense — yes, Rosa, I admit it — of community.

An old woman in Athens on a summer evening. Without her there would have been a different Andrew McIllray, a more selfish individual, one who lived in Fulham and had a partner in the City, one who made money and holidayed in Key West, one who talked too much and laughed too loud and got drunk and didn't give a damn. And who did not spend his fortieth year chained to a wall high in the Andes wondering if he will ever be free again.

* * *

Back in Edinburgh, the old woman still in mind, I joined the International Society, attracted by its name more than a clear understanding of its aims. I found an organisation that was moribund, its activities restricted to occasional talks by foreign correspondents and theme evenings of faded posters and cheap wine.

I would have lost interest if it had not been for Guy. We met one evening when a meeting ended early and spent two or three hours talking in a bar in Forrest Row. It was he who made me see the potential of the Society and the part we could both play in it. He sat there, undrunk pint in hand, more a lecturer than a student, a lanky intellectual with greasy dark hair falling over his glasses, arguing passionately that here was an opportunity we could not pass up. Scotland had always looked beyond its own horizons and contributed more to the world — the steam age, the telephone, television — than it had ever received. We had a heritage to maintain, a duty to be informed and to influence international developments, from Rhodesia and the Common Market to Cuba and Vietnam.

I recognised and ignored the hyperbole. I was listening partly to Guy and partly to myself, to the voice that told me that I was capable of taking initiatives that others ignored. I heard myself propose a strategy that would achieve Guy's vision. We would take a theme a term — a war here, a dictatorship there, starvation wherever. We would hold high-powered debates, raise money and question Members of Parliament. Guy listened, contributed, argued, agreed. I corrected, repeated, searched for paper to take notes. By the end of the evening we had committed ourselves to two years of hard and probably thankless work.

Of course we achieved much less than we planned. The Society committee was politely unenthusiastic about our proposals. We had neither the time nor the money to do all we proposed. Invitations to cabinet ministers were politely refused; press releases were lucky to be reprinted half-length in the *Evening News*. Occasionally, in one or other bar, Guy and I and the two or three others who shared our enthusiasm bemoaned the insularity of Scottish and English students until our mood could only mellow. Yet we had some successes, if only demonstrating outside the US consulate and barracking Heath on a rare visit to the city. Most of all, the International Society, more than any class on phonemes or morphology, encouraged me to learn, to become adult, to recognise my capabilities and potential, the power to influence and change that was almost in my grasp. It also gave me Guy — the first person that I genuinely liked, the first whose qualities of honesty, kindness and intelligence I fully recognised, the first who accepted who I was without comment or curiosity.

* * *

Too much writing in the last few days has made my hand and forearm hurt again. Oh, for a laptop and printer! Or is it rheumatism? Despite the exercises, different parts of my body ache almost all the time. At least my cough has gone, although I have constipation again today. There are never enough vegetables and the meat lies heavy in my gut.

* * *

"*Tu eres maricón.*" Rosa had never looked at me so intently before. The hesitation before I replied was as good as a confession.

"What makes you think so?" I asked, cold with fear.

"It's in the newspaper. Your friend's name is Tom Dayton." She pronounced it Digh-ton, as if it were Spanish. I had a sudden image of Tom, dark hair and suspicious eyes.

"Which newspaper?"

"Two or three."

"Show me." A vain plea. "What do they say?" I went on, trying to remain calm.

She shrugged. "Very little. Simply that you are 'gay'" — she hesitated before the unfamiliarity of the English word — "and that your friend wants you to be set free." She watched as emotions collided in my mind. I was afraid of what the news meant, how much it changed her attitude towards me, yet even greater was the relief that Tom still cared for me, that he wanted me to come home.

"When was this published?" I asked.

"Yesterday."

"The first report there's been about me?"

"No."

"There have been others?" She nodded. I felt a surge of joy at this first acknowledgement since I had been taken that I had not been forgotten by the world. "What have they said?"

She shrugged. "What you would expect. The fact that you were missing. Statements from the government and your embassy. From Demotica."

"Why did no one tell me?" I asked.

"Why should they?" Of course there was no reason; in this room I had no rights, not even to news about myself. I almost dared not ask the next question.

"People have approached you to negotiate my release?"

"Yes," she said, dismissing the matter as of little importance.

I was almost bursting with emotion. "When?"

"At various times."

"You told me before you didn't know." She shrugged. "I need to know," I went on. "Who contacted you? What's been discussed? What are the terms?"

"There are no terms. Nothing has been agreed."

"Nothing?" My mood died as swiftly as a punctured balloon. "Why not?" Again she ignored me. "What about now?"

"Now?" She was staring out of the window. "Are you going to let me go?"

She turned back. "Why should we? Because this Tom asks us to? What do you think? A man should be released from jail simply because his wife — or his friend," the irony was heavy, "wants him back?"

"A man in jail has committed a crime. I haven't." Again she did not respond. "When are you going to decide?"

"I don't know." The words carried neither threat nor promise.

"It's unfair." Another shrug. I stared up at her, enraged by her complacency and my impotence. She sat there, half-teenage girl, half-maiden aunt, an plain-featured, plainly-dressed woman like any other, with a power over me that I could neither deny nor reject.

"I was surprised to learn that you are *maricón*," she said at last, looking out of the window again. "We knew you weren't married, but I thought it was for other reasons."

"Lots of men are *maricón*."

She turned back. "How can you be?"

It was my turn to shrug. I did not want this conversation. It was enough to be imprisoned; I did not want the additional burden of being seen as even more of an outsider than I was. "How can you be *maricón*?" she repeated.

"Why not? Don't you know anyone gay?"

She thought. "One or two. There was a hairdresser in Ayacucho. A boy I knew at school. But you could tell at once they were *marica.*"

"*Marica*," I repeated. "Feminine, effeminate. *Maricón*; masculine, macho. Perhaps there are more *maricones* in Peru than you realise." It was a stupid comment, as likely to confirm prejudice as to disperse it. Luckily, she ignored it.

"I don't understand. What makes you *maricón*?"

"I don't know. What makes you heterosexual?"

"It's natural."

"So is homosexuality."

"It's natural for men to love women, not other men."

"It's natural for some men to love women and for others to love men."

"That's a perversion."

"Perversion is a meaningless word. There are homosexuals in every society."

"There are very few in Peru."

"You haven't been to the Plaza San Martín in Lima. You would have seen a lot of young men hanging around waiting for pick-ups."

"Paid by tourists?"

"Not all paid. And most of the men who pick them up are Peruvian."

She shrugged it off. "Western influence, the legacy of colonisation." *Criollos*, in other words.

"And the hairdresser in Ayacucho? Or the boy you knew at school?"

Thus we went on, the conversation bouncing between assertion and denial, she curious, I a reluctant spokesman for gay rights. Eventually the topic ran dry and we sat silent. I knew that she was unconvinced by my arguments, that every defence I offered she saw as sophistry, words to confuse the ignorant. Once again there was an abyss between us. She was a woman who could not understand a man's sexuality, an Andean who rejected European tradition, a Marxist with no understanding of Freud. She looked at me curiously when she left, both of us wondering how much my status had changed. I lay here reflecting that *maricones* are the parasites of society. We are the hairdressers, the shiftless youngsters in San Martín, the men in drag in back-street dives hauled away by police raids. We are amoral, effeminate cowards and petty thieves. We are the brutalised corpses abandoned by the roadside. We are the garbage to be disposed of by Gonzalo's revolution.

* * *

Rosa did not stay. Neither of us mentioned yesterday. She perhaps because she had nothing to say, I because I want the subject forgotten. But I cannot stop thinking about Tom. He wants me back. He has waited. He still loves me. As I cannot help but love him.

* * *

The bastards. The bastards. THE BASTARDS. THE FUCKING BASTARDS.

* * *

Whoever next comes into this room I want to slit his throat and rip open his belly and cut off his prick. I want to slam my fist so hard into his face that his nose and jaw break. I want him down on his knees begging for mercy as I kick his balls into jelly and face into pulp. I want him to suffer and scream and suffer for hour after hour until I grow tired or bored. Then the next one will come in and I will do the same, and the next and the next and the next. Bastards. Bastards. Bastards.

* * *

I should have expected it. I lie here hour after hour wondering whether they will come back, then fall asleep and dream that they have. I wake up sweating, alone, in pain, angry and afraid.

* * *

I want you, Tom. Tom Tom Tom Tom Tom. TOM.

* * *

He does not look at me. Like before, he comes in, drops the plate and leaves without a word. I shout at him all the swear words and curses I know, in English and in Spanish, but it isn't enough. They don't affect him, they don't hurt him.

* * *

I hear Rosa outside. I would scream at her if I knew what to say, if I knew what I wanted. She is a cunt, a fucking cunt. She knew. She let it happen. She pretends she stopped it, but she knew. She probably told them to come in, to see what would happen. An experiment in the name of Gonzalism. She's the one who's keeping me here. She's the one who doesn't want to let me go. It should have been her. I would have chained her up, pinned her down, kicked her legs apart and driven my prick into her as fast and as hard and as deep as I could. She would have screamed and screamed and I would have pushed and pushed and thrust and stabbed until blood streamed out of her. She would have lain there and cried and I would have laughed and done it again and again and again. "It's for Gonzalo," I would have told her. "For the revolution. For the victory of the masses. Now lie there and take it."

* * *

I would not have believed the pain or the tension could last so long. Only now, days later, is the headache beginning to go. My body is less stiff and the bleeding has long stopped, but between my legs and on my ankle there is still pain and deep bruising. The scar on my cheek is long and deep.

* * *

I must not try to forget it. I must force myself to accept it, to make it part of me.

It was dark. I had fallen asleep but must have woken with the sounds on the stairs. I looked up and saw the deeper shadow of the door and the man coming in. El Gordo. El Magro behind him and a third, short, stocky figure, a man I have never seen. I sat up, alarmed, certain that this was the moment they had chosen for the execution. Suddenly there was a hand on my mouth, others grabbing my wrists. "*Siléncio*," a voice whispered in a thick accent, "*o te pasará mal.*"

There was a moment in which I did not understand, then a moment of relief, almost laughter, when I thought this was an invitation I could refuse. Then the realisation that I had no choice.

I struggled to pull my hands free, to shout, to shake them off. My whole body shook and for a second they fell back, until I was hit by a blow on the side of the head so powerful that I collapsed.

So much, so quickly. My face squashed into the mattress, a weight on my back, a voice in my ear, whispering, deep, evil, violent, warning me not to move, not to speak, not to make a sound.

My hands wrenched forward, held together. Pain in my head, my neck, my back, my shin. Blood in my mouth, blood where the shackle had ripped the scab off my ankle. A fog of bad breath, old clothes, dirt and sweat.

My own sweat sudden and cold. My neck twisted, my throat compressed. From the corner of my eye silhouettes against the night.

Dazed, frightened, I could not think; an animal in terror, paralysed prey.

Hands ripped my jeans down, fingernails tore my skin. I bucked and shifted the man on my spine, hurting myself more than him. He pulled my head back by the hair; I heard a voice in anger, felt a knife slicing across my cheek and the blood begin to flow. "*¿Quieres esto?*"

No, I did not want it. I froze, tried to think. Relax, I told myself, relax, but the words were meaningless in the mist of darkness and pain and fear.

My legs pulled apart. Words — a comment, a suggestion, an order — that I did not understand. Someone kneeling behind me, pulling open his clothes.

I moaned in protest, not knowing what I was saying. I doubt they heard. There was flesh against my buttocks, pressure and pain against my

* * *

I never understood how women were raped. A knee in the balls will free you, I always thought, a punch in the face, the nose broken, fingers stabbed into the eyes. Your attacker has weak points; you can always win.

Not when there are three. Not when you are chained to a wall. Not when you are thousands of miles from home.

* * *

I did not hear her come in. The second man was inside me when suddenly all movement stopped. In the darkness there was her voice, quiet and clear.

It surprises me now that they obeyed her. One was already standing; the weight of the others left me. In words I did not understand, I heard the excuses: "A gringo, a *maricón*, a prisoner. He wanted it, he'll live, it doesn't matter, no one cares". I lay there, paralysed by uncertainty and pain, wondering what would happen next, sharing their sense of shame.

She waited until they had gone. I moved slowly, aching everywhere, wondering if anything was broken, afraid of the ache in every muscle and bone, afraid of where I could feel pain and where I could not.

"Thank you," I said, straightening my shirt and jumper, pulling up my jeans. I expected her to ask if I was all right, to do something to relieve the fear and pain, but she said nothing, perhaps stared at me for a moment before slamming the door as she left the room.

For a few moments I tried to wipe away the blood, the sweat, the... Then I lay in the darkness and trembled and screamed.

* * *

A year ago I was strong, physically and mentally. Now I have nothing; everything has gone.

* * *

This is hell. This is the hell I have seen others suffer, but I have always escaped. This is the hell of solitude and poverty and illness and pain. This is the hell of torture and famine and death. This is the hell of no hope, no fucking hope.

I used to be angry if someone was late, upset if someone did not call. The worst I ever suffered was a flight delay, the loss of a suitcase, an accident in the car. But this... But this...

* * *

If I ever return home, I will never leave again. I will curl up on the sofa with Tom for the rest of my life.

* * *

El Gordo and El Magro come in as before. Rosa avoids me. It was three days before they brought me water to wash; three days in which I rotted and stank.

* * *

Rosa came in again today for the first time in a week. My anger, which had exhausted itself, returned. "Why did you do it?" I asked. "Why did you let it happen? You sat there next door and listened, didn't you? You could have stopped them at any time, but you didn't want to."

She shook her head. "I wasn't here. I'd been away."

"Where? Where is the nearest village? How far is this house? At least tell me that."

"A few kilometres."

"Is that where the third man came from?" She shook her head again. "He's a *senderista*." She had moved to the chair, sat down as before.

"Still here?"

"No."

"No doubt wherever he's gone, he's telling them there's a gringo to be fucked. Just ask Rosa, the brothel-keeper. She'll tell you where to go."

She was about to say something but changed her mind. "I told you, I would have stopped it, but I wasn't here."

"I don't believe you." She shrugged. "You told them to do it. He's a *maricón*, you said. Do what you like with him."

Another shake of the head. "It was in the newspapers. They saw it."

"They can hardly speak Spanish, far less read it. You told them." Another shrug. Her complacency angered me. It was dishonest — patronising and dishonest.

"I hate you," I said. "I used to like you, but now I hate you."

"Do you want me to leave?"

"Yes. No. I want to understand why the fuck you keep me here." She said nothing and in the silence I realised that my anger had gone and been replaced once again by fear. Perhaps her story was true. Perhaps she had stopped it as soon as she could. And if she were to go away or if I were to anger her, I would have no one to protect me. That night could be repeated, or even worse.

I sat against the wall, she on her chair. We half-faced each other, half-stared into the distance. In time my eyes closed and I began to doze, found myself at home, wandering along the stream with Tom and Sheba. When I looked up, Rosa was still there, looking out of the window. An hour, perhaps two, passed, then I was alone again.

* * *

We communicate as on the first days she was here. A few words, like strangers on a train establishing polite contact then letting the shutters fall. I sit here and try to write again, remembering a past without pain or isolation.

This is not what I expected almost twenty years ago, on my first visit to South America, my first trip out of Europe. It was the year I graduated. I hired the gown, received the scroll and posed with my parents for the photograph in front of the MacEwan Hall. I think they were moved, although neither would admit it. Perhaps they were simply relieved that I had proved my intelligence.

I was in no hurry to look for work while money from my grandparents allowed me to consider the future at leisure. A year or so abroad would be a useful addition to my cv. I rejected Asia as too popular; South America was equally far yet more remote. I boarded the Pan Am flight that July, seeing myself as no longer a teenager making forays into Europe, but an adult on a journey to the extremes of the globe and my own ingenuity. Each detail of my surroundings fascinated me: the accents, the unsought familiarity of the air crew, the lifestyle of wealth in the inflight magazine. At Miami, Edinburgh was twenty-four hours and a lifetime behind me. Waiting for my connection, I wandered from terminal to terminal, fascinated by garish souvenirs, the *New York Times* and *Miami Herald*, black and hispanic voices. I had not expected the States to be at once so foreign and so true to the images of television and film. I was tempted to stay, to walk through the glass doors, out into the heat and one of the long, low taxis that waited in line. I could spend a year or more exploring this land; I could find a job, make some money and then travel South. All that held me back was the fact that my luggage had been checked and my visa allowed me to stay only twenty-four hours. By the time I arrived in Bogota, shortly before midnight, jet-lag had set in and my confidence was waning. Yet the minute I stepped out of the plane to be greeted by a warm breeze wafting the scent I would come to recognise as burning oil, my sense of excitement grew. I walked across the tarmac to a shabby but modern terminal building, was confronted by signs in Spanish and interrogated by short, dark-skinned men in over-elaborate uniforms. All around me couples, families and friends jabbered in a language I recognised but hardly understood. I cleared customs and stood for a moment in the arrivals hall, half-expecting a stranger to recognise me. It would not happen, of course. This was Conrad country. I was alone in a strange land, dependent only on myself.

Three weeks in Colombia, a few days in Ecuador and then Peru. The country was quieter then, Sendero unknown. By the time I arrived in Cuzco, my sense of excitement had given way to quiet pride in my ability to speak Spanish, to haggle, to find cheap hotels and enjoy long, dusty bus-rides. I had developed a routine of one day travelling followed by three or four wandering through side streets or loitering in provincial museums, straining to read through dusty glass the inscriptions accompanying ancient artefacts or primitive paintings. Tall, fair-haired, fair-skinned, in shorts, I was the archetype of Rosa's despised tourist, despite my belief that my knowledge of the language and interest in local history and ethnography made me a Traveller, an honorary Andean.

I saw and regretted the poverty that surrounded me, yet was curiously untouched; no scene, no individual, cut through my complacency as had the old woman in Athens two years before. Indeed, for a time I became less sympathetic, irritated by the mercenary tones of the owners of shops and hotels. My patience came to an end in Cuzco, when a youth with a conspiratorial smile talked of "*el amor entre chicos*" before abandoning me on the realisation I would not pay for such love. I left the town for the ruins of Ollantaitambo, where I rested in the sun before waiting with a small group of Europeans for the train to Machu Picchu. Hours late, it arrived after midnight and trundled through the darkness, winding between the river and mountainside. One of the group suggested getting off at the station before our destination, where his guidebook indicated a hotel that might offer us a bed for the rest of the night. Thus in the darkness before dawn half a dozen of us found ourselves in a village where all that could be seen were the whitewashed silhouettes of houses fading into the mountainside and the lights of the train disappearing into the night.

No hotel. No restaurant. No sound. Only cold moonlight as we picked our way up an unpaved street. "Let's ask," a German said, a tall man in his early thirties with long hair and a beard, destroying the silence as he pounded on the nearest door. We had no right to do this, I thought, disturbing people's sleep, but did not protest. Eventually the door creaked open. "*¿Hay hotel?*" our leader asked in a loud voice. I could not hear the reply. A short conversation followed. "It's all right, come in," he said. We shuffled into the warmth of a large room dimly lit by an oil lamp. "This is fine, yes?" he asked as we sat round a large table watching a middle-aged woman light the fire under a kettle. There was a low ceiling, rough whitewashed walls. Thick sheets of plastic hanging from the ceiling divided the house into rooms. I heard the faint noises of others asleep. As glasses were put in front of us and filled with tea, one of the sheets parted and a youth emerged, wiping the sleep from his eyes. "*Buenos días*", he smiled blearily and stepped outside to urinate.

The woman watched as we drank; her son returned to prepare his breakfast. My companions discussed our options, agreed that we had no choice but to walk along the railway line through the darkness to Machu Picchu. I sat silent, wondering what the woman and her son thought of this intrusion into their lives. If at that moment she had flung the contents of the pot all over us, I would have sympathised. Instead, she waited patiently, even smiled as we placed money on the table and took our leave.

I can imagine my parents' response if a group of Peruvians knocked at their door in the middle of the night, demanding accommodation or food. Bewilderment would be followed by polite rejection and the threat of the police; while the poor need the wealthy to survive, the wealthy have always had the luxury of rejecting the poor.

* * *

That first trip remains in greater clarity than many of those which followed. From Cuzco to Bolivia — a colder land and a quieter people. From Bolivia to Brazil. I took buses from town to town in Mato Grosso, looking for the exotic and finding only dusty streets of bare one-roomed bars and overstocked shops selling groceries, agricultural implements and fashionless clothes. In Diamantino I met an Englishman in his late twenties in a half-empty restaurant. He had spent the previous night in a convent, having knocked on its door in the darkness thinking it might be a hotel. The sisters ran a girls' school but had no one to teach English. There was a job for someone there; he, meanwhile, was heading for brighter lights and bigger opportunities.

I had been looking for an excuse to neither go home nor travel on. I had not found Conrad country but I was in Greene land — a solitary Brit in the middle of a jungle, hundreds of miles from home. I wanted to see if I could survive in a community where I knew no one, where I scarcely spoke the language, where the days were featureless and the heat never-ending. This was life beckoning me from the other side, offering to reveal its secrets and my own weaknesses and strengths. I could not refuse. With directions from my compatriot, I headed for the outskirts of town.

I was young enough not to realise what I was letting myself in for, and young enough that if I had known I would not have cared. I walked into the courtyard in shorts and a crumpled shirt open almost to the waist, a battered rucksack on my shoulders. My Portuguese was rudimentary and heavily influenced by Spanish; it took time for the two young nuns I met to understand why I wanted to see the Mother Superior. I was finally shown into a cool dark room lined with dusty books and old icons, where I waited for a quarter of an hour, doubting the wisdom of my decision. A short elderly woman entered and addressed me in a French whose accent I found difficult to follow. Slowly, we managed to communicate. I had heard she might need an English teacher; perhaps I could take the job.

She looked at me warily, asked questions and listened sceptically to my answers. My qualifications were poor, she pointed out. Speaking a language was not the same as teaching it; grammar had to be explained and curricula followed. The pupils came from deprived backgrounds; some were deficient in their native tongue. Nor was she sure about a young man teaching adolescent girls. If she was to take me on, the timetable would have to be changed, which she did not want to do if I were to leave after a week. I only half-heard these objections. The longer I sat in the old-fashioned office, aware of the heat, the dust, distant voices, the more I wanted to stay. There would be no salary, the Mother Superior added, her final defence, only room and board, although I might earn money giving tuition in town. Fine, I said, determined to stay, and she nodded her reluctant agreement.

My room was one of the whitewashed cells on the far side of the yard allocated to men attached to the convent — gardeners, a handyman and visiting priests. There I prepared lessons, read the devotional books that I found in the small library and wrote letters and a brief and uneventful diary. Three or four times a day I entered one of the long classrooms where thirty or more shy and well-disciplined girls sat in rows of blue uniforms and white collars. Most were of the mixed race scattered across the Brazilian hinterland, two or three were pure Indian. Despite my inexperience and their lack of interest in English, as the only male teacher, little older than they were and with near-Scandinavian looks, I easily held their attention. My first lessons depended on repetition, rote, spelling and arcane grammar; through trial and error and advice from my fellow teachers, I began to elicit answers rather than supply them, to encourage rather than suppress spontaneity. I began to enjoy teaching, until it dawned on me that English would be of little use to the farm labourers, factory workers, shop assistants and mothers that most of them would become.

It was only at lunchtimes, when nuns, pupils and hangers-on sat down together, that I entered the life of the convent. Breakfast and supper were taken in a side room with the other men. I attended mass, the devotion of the congregation occasionally tempting me away from my atheism. In the evenings I walked into town to eat or drink in one of the handful of bars and restaurants or see a faded kung-fu film or witless sex comedy in a fleapit cinema. I spoke with few of the nuns, becoming friendly only with one in her thirties who helped me with my Portuguese, and the elderly mathematics teacher from Milan whose accent I always found difficult to understand. With the men I did little more than exchange greetings. They were labourers with limited vocabulary and impenetrable accents; I was too young to understand that they were also individuals whose experience I might welcome and whose company I might enjoy. What they thought of the tall foreigner who barely acknowledged their presence, I could not imagine.

Time passed. My walks into town became less frequent as I realised that whatever I sought there I would not find. A few locals were curious and friendly, but no easier to get on with than the convent gardeners. It was to be several years until I grew out of the unease with strangers that Edinburgh had bred into me. I half-heartedly looked for sex, but was too naive to recognise other men's signals and too uncertain to offer signals in return. All that was left was the jungle, that mythical place of giant trees and creepers, jaguars and parakeets, snakes and monkeys, through which Indians stalked their prey. More than once I stood at the edge of town, gazing at the road and the razed land that stretched to the horizon. Wherever the jungle was, it could not be reached on a Sunday trek by a European in walking shoes. I asked others how to find it, but for them the *selva* was no more than an abstraction, beyond their interest or reach.

After three months term ended and my visa was about to expire. On leaving I was surprised to hear from the Mother Superior how much my company and dedication had been welcomed. She would have liked me to stay, but understood I could not. The only thanks she could give was a letter of introduction to the other convents of her order. It was in Portuguese, but if I translated it into English, she would sign it. In addition, she held out a Bible, a present from all the nuns. The book in my hand, I looked down at the old woman and realised that I would miss this quiet life, the perpetual heat and humidity, the rumour of voices from the classrooms, the clatter of lunch and even her stern expression. I thanked her, aware for the first time that I was growing old, that a portion of my life had passed and would never return.

* * *

She was away that day. She came in too late to stop them. I have to believe it; I have no choice.

We are almost at ease with each other again but we will never be close. I cannot imagine what goes through her mind during the hours she spends with me. She should despise me, yet she does not waste her emotions on individuals. It is capitalism she hates, the world of commerce, the military, all the institutions that deprive her people of their freedom, while her devotion to Mao and Guzmán is to symbols, not to men.

I should hate her and at times I do. I look at her and wonder how someone so intelligent can keep a man chained up like this and how much of the account that she gave me of that night is true. I do not, however, remain hostile for long. My real anger is directed at the others, the men who captured me, who hold me, who raped me. Fernando, who brought me here, threatened me for weeks then disappeared. El Gordo, who lurches in like Quasimodo, the monster freed feeding its shackled master. El Magro's cold contempt and hostility.

In more generous moments I see Rosa as imprisoned as I am, a fugitive, an idealist condemned by the force of her own logic. Circumstance rather than enmity has brought us together. I sometimes imagine that she would release me if the decision to do so was in her hands; at such moments I find myself liking her — her quiet manner, her thoughtfulness, her dedication to her cause.

Others might say my view was distorted; I should be wary of the syndrome that brings hostages to sympathise with their guards. Yet to be hostile to the one person who talks to me, who keeps the others at bay, would be futile; to reject Rosa would be to reject all contact with the world. Indeed the outer world and all its definitions are meaningless here; people are people, one man's terrorist is another woman's freedom-fighter, Rosa is simply a human being doing what she thinks is right. The fact that she is holding me against my will does not mean that her every other action and word is wrong. And whether my release depends on a decision that she or others make, it does no harm to treat her as an equal.

* * *

I have learnt a little of Rosa's past. After leaving university, she became a teacher, wishing to give children what she had not received. Her teachers had been ignorant, taught by rote. The questions she asked were beyond them — why had this happened, what was to be gained from that knowledge, how could she be certain that what they told her was true? As children there were perhaps similarities between us; we both suspected that the world was full of secrets. The difference was that for me the secrets lay far beyond my horizons, while for her the secrets were all around.

"The only value of teaching is to explain why," she said, "and if you cannot explain why, you have to teach how to find out why." I imagined her in a classroom facing rows of quiet, dark-eyed, red-cheeked children. The walls would be whitewashed, bare except for a blackboard and map of Peru. She would listen to them recite multiplication tables and walk up and down as they copied verbs from the board. There would be periods of animation when she asked questions they could not answer or gave answers that her predecessors had not known. She would hope that the animation became enthusiasm, that the curiosity she nurtured would strengthen, that independence and pride would emerge. I am not sure, however, that she succeeded. Children here are naturally passive; most seem to do little but stand open-mouthed, as if what little energy they have were needed to trap the rare oxygen in the air.

She gave up teaching for Sendero, spending a month in a guerrilla training camp. More than that she will not tell me, in case, perhaps, I am released and pass on information to others. I was disappointed. I wanted to know more to satisfy my curiosity, to understand better the transition from teacher to soldier.

In turn I told her of my first visit to South America, the empathy I have always felt for her country. She listened politely and did not, as I expected, interrupt to draw a Marxist parable from my experiences. Perhaps she too is learning, is beginning to see me as more than an enemy of the people, as more than a *maricón*.

* * *

She can sit for hours on the chair staring out of the window or watching me. I ask her what she sees outside; she tells me a few trees, fields and the mountains in the distance. I lie here studying her, her upright posture, her calm expression, the few gestures she makes, her clothes as old as mine but better kept. A week or two ago, I wanted to hurt her, to rape her; now sometimes I imagine myself making love to her, here on this mattress, under these blankets. We would be warm, naked, holding each other. I would enter her so gently and we would lie there all night, holding, reassuring each other. Only in the morning would I begin to move, would I give us both the orgasm that would release us, and with that proof of our common humanity, might persuade her to release me.

She always looks younger than her years, a student, not a teacher, a teenager rather than adult. Yet it would be easy for me to misjudge. In the last year I have only seen three people. Perhaps my ability to interpret human features has weakened since my capture, as the speech of the man who goes deaf becomes more artificial when his voice no longer reflects the sounds that others produce.

Nor do I have photographs to remind me what others look like. I have only my memory and the closer I examine it the more it fails me. I see Tom at Reading the last morning I left, and each time I try to look closer, to remember the clothes he wore, the angle of his head, his expression, whether or not he had shaved, the picture fades. All that remains is an impression — black curls, a broad forehead, a small nose, rough cheeks, a round chin. In place of an image I have an emotion and even that is sometimes uncertain.

My parents are no clearer. The image I formed of them as a child obscures the picture I have of them now. The last time I saw Mother I was saddened by how much older she looked. I had always remembered her tall and upright, a severe expression behind her glasses, but when I went home that Christmas she appeared to have shrunk, her back had bent, she looked tired and not quite focused on the world. I had known her as a mother and suddenly she was a grandmother; from the prime of life she had slipped into old age. Father too was older, but he had simply gone grey and more thin. To me he has always been old. I dread to think what the last fifteen months must have done to them.

And myself? I was always so proud of my appearance. I was lucky enough to have some looks, although I always worried that they were never as attractive as others sometimes told me. It was only in the right light and at certain angles that I could not see the over-generous nose, the too thick lips and dull eyes. I was never overweight and if I took up weight-lifting with every other gay man as soon as it became fashionable, I at least had the sense not to take it to extremes. Now my skin is thin and rough, I have a scar across my cheek, scabs and infection on my ankle, long hair and a ragged beard. I know without a mirror that my looks have faded with my muscles, that if I were shorn and shaved, the dirt showered away and clean clothes donned, I would be tired and gaunt, an old man of fifty rather than one under forty who can still call himself young.

* * *

It is over a month since Tom made his appeal. When I asked what progress had been made on my release, Rosa was surprised by the naivety of my question. None, she said. "We are not ready to respond."

The disappointment was a physical blow. "You have held me for over a year. When will you be ready? What do you need?"

"I don't know. The Party will decide."

"Who in the Party?"

"It doesn't concern you."

"Of course it concerns me. Who? You? The other two? Someone else? The man who was here that night?"

She said nothing.

"You know what I think? You've held me for over a year and you haven't the foggiest idea what to do with me. Nobody dares make decisions because whoever does so will be criticised by the others. And you can't get together to decide because most of you are in jail or on the other side of the country. You have all these grandiose words about the inevitability of the revolution. But the revolution has failed. You're wasting time and energy by keeping me. I won't betray you; I can't. I have no idea who you are or where we are. Just blindfold me, drive me to Cuzco or some other town and let me go."

She looked at me; in the shadow in which she always sat, I almost saw sympathy in her expression. "We have to make use of you."

I said nothing for a while. Eventually I asked who had approached them, what had been discussed.

"I don't know."

"You don't know? You don't know what they said, what they offered?"

She shook her head.

"Why not? Because you, Rosa, aren't important enough to know? I don't believe that. You're too intelligent not to know what's going on." She said nothing, looked back out of the window. "But whatever they say," I went on, "you never give them an answer." Another silence. I do not know which frustrated me more — her refusal to speak or my inability to get through to her, to have her understand the futility of holding me. Somewhere, somehow, I was sure there were the right words, the right intonation or mood which would pierce her indifference and persuade her to set me free. But whatever they were, I was incapable of finding them; my Spanish was too poor, my understanding of her motives too limited.

"Why do you keep me?" I asked, for the tenth or hundredth time.

Before, she had ignored the question as if it were not important or she were not sure of the answer. Today she was more thoughtful. "Because you are different from the rest. If we take or kill a tourist, it means nothing. We would need to kill a thousand to make our point and the more we killed, the more repression there would be from the army and the more the people would suffer. Nor are you an aid worker. You don't come here with a little money and a lot of promises to open a school or to plant a new crop before going home after two or three years and leaving our people as poor as before and even more confused. Nor are you a government official or a military advisor; if you had been, you would have been killed as you stepped out of the car.

"You are different. You claim to be our servant. You speak fluent Spanish and you encourage the use of Quechua and Aymara. You know more of our history and culture than most Peruvians. You have the support of many community leaders who think you are helping them. You are persuasive. Our people do not realise that under the pretence of bringing power to the masses, what you are doing is imposing your own power by subtle means. First you will set up your little democracy in Puno and Juliaca and Ayacucho and then you will set up your greater democracy in Lima. The proletariat will support you because Fujimori is as corrupt as all who preceded him and they think you will clean out the whole political class. You might even succeed and put an honest man in the presidency. But even he would be no more than another puppet and you would use him as you have been using puppets for years. Our people would continue to starve and die and if they protested loudly enough for the world to hear, the United States would invade as they invaded Grenada and Panama.

"You are innocent enough to believe that what I am saying is not true," she went on as I tried to interrupt. "You think you are independent of the imperialists because you criticise them almost as much as we do, but you are not. You are simply another means of distracting the people from the real oppression in their lives. That makes you dangerous. We have to stop you, but we are not sure what to do with you. Chairman Gonzalo would have had you killed, but he is no longer with us. We think perhaps we can use you, but we are not sure how. So we are waiting until we find a solution, and we can wait a long, long time."

There was a silence as I absorbed what she had said. Her description had been a distortion, both critical and flattering. Again I was caught between the impression that she was right and the belief that she was wrong, and I could not resolve whether the impression or belief was correct.

"A long time?" I asked at last. "How long? And if at the end of it all, you decide you cannot use me, what happens then?"

She looked at me. "I don't know," she said, and for the first time I felt she sympathised with me.

Like an old machine creaking into motion, I began to argue what I had argued before. That Sendero would gain more sympathy by releasing me, that I was not an enemy of the people, that she was wrong to believe I had influence and power. I disguised my desperation as bargaining — I would never return to Peru; I would publish a statement of Sendero's demands; I would go into hiding for a month or more before I pretended to be freed. She listened, or appeared to do so, waiting until I had exhausted every possibility before standing up to stretch and stroll around the room.

"You don't know how much I would give to be able to walk around like that."

She stopped and looked at me. "You still don't know how much our people would give to be free."

I was not sure if her words carried sympathy or hostility, but she had turned away. Neither of us had anything more to say. Shortly afterwards she left. Alone, I imagined meeting her in other circumstances, at a conference abroad, in someone's office, in a cafe or bar in Lima, somewhere we could debate on equal terms. She would have put forward her beliefs and I would have gently corrected them, overwhelming her with my knowledge and years of experience.

When at last we parted, I would been convinced that I had sown the seeds of doubt, that in time she would gradually come round to my point of view. How wrong, how very wrong I would have been.

* * *

I wonder whether Tom is still at home, driving to school each morning, coming back in the early afternoon to walk Sheba and potter in the garden, or whether he has gone back to London, to stay with Eric and Dave. He could sell the birds or give them to Anne and George. The cats, too, although they are already half wild. In London it shouldn't be difficult to get a job. He has plenty of experience and knows enough people in the trade.

At least he still wants me. The fear that he might desert me has gone. I just hope he can hang on until I return.

Whenever that is. So much will have happened while I was away. Anne and George will have had their baby. After fifteen years of protesting about Indian and British politics, Sunil may actually have gone back to Delhi. God forbid that Kathy should return to Uganda. Brian will still be there, but others at Demotica will have come and gone.

London will have changed in little ways that will emphasise how long I've been away. New one-way streets, higher prices, new cars, perhaps a different government. The Queen dead, a military dictatorship or aliens from Jupiter in charge. Or perhaps everything will be exactly the same as I left it and somehow that would be equally depressing.

I have to get out of here.

* * *

For the first time since that night, Rosa brought up the subject of my being gay. I was naive enough to hope the subject had been forgotten, buried under the weightier matters of Maoist thought and permanent revolution. I should have known that she is incapable of leaving a problem unresolved — a problem that will haunt her as long as she is confined by the view that human behaviour is determined solely by economic status.

Like all who are hostile to homosexuality, she holds the contradictory position that heterosexual desire is determined by nature and homosexuality is a matter of choice. In her opinion I need only a gentle kick in the intellect for my eyes to open and the attraction of women to become obvious and overwhelming. She cannot accept that if her sexuality is beyond her conscious control, then so is mine.

I could not convince her. None of my arguments enabled her to step beyond two principles: that homosexuality is as deviant and regrettable as a hare-lip or an extra limb, and that homosexual desire is no more than irresponsible hedonism. Perhaps eventually she will understand that the last two words conflict — once all injustice and poverty are eradicated, hedonism will be humanity's natural aim.

I have seen her incomprehension before. I learnt my lesson years ago in Bombay. The middle-aged, middle-class woman I had been introduced to was eager to have me watch her literacy classes for women sex workers. I sat on a bench in the small room on the first floor of a brothel, surrounded by giggling girls and older, tired women. It was the late morning, the beginning of their day, too early for customers. Two or three wandered in during the middle of the lesson, yawning, tying their hair and adjusting their saris. Children ran in and out, seeking comfort from their mothers or satisfying their curiosity as to my presence. A shrine sat in the corner with incense and fruit; a boy came in with a tray of tea. Although Marathi and the nuances of its alphabet were beyond me, I watched, intrigued for an hour as my pedantic host gently encouraged her hesitant pupils.

At last the lesson came to an end and I became the focus of attention. Where did I come from, why was I in Bombay, did I like it, what did I think of Indian women? The seventeen-year-old in the blue sari sitting beside me, with thick black hair, beautiful eyes and youthful smile, giggled a question to our interpreter. Did I have a girlfriend? No, I said, I preferred men. My host stared at me, not sure whether she had understood. I did not make it a joke; I did not deny it. I said that it was common for European men to be homosexual and I was one. The more I spoke the more I stumbled. I saw from her incomprehension, her fear and her disgust that my insistence on this aspect of my private life was causing her bewilderment and pain. The other women looked on, curious and disturbed, until I gave in. "Tell them whatever you like," I said. Whatever explanation she gave, the atmosphere was only partly relieved. As we stood up to leave, I was conscious of their curiosity and my embarrassment. I forced a smile of thanks for their hospitality and made my way down the steep narrow stairs, angry that by insisting that these strangers know every detail of my life, I had lost the opportunity to become part of theirs.

Since then, when asked, I have always invented a girlfriend, with Kathy in mind if the questioner asks more. That my fiancee should be African silences most people, who seem to feel that to ask more would be unpardonable intrusion. No, that is a misinterpretation. Those who ask if I am married or have a girlfriend are not interested in my private life. It is simply a means of establishing contact, maintaining common ground, like commenting on the weather or confirming the name of my hotel. To respond with the truth rather than platitude would be to create discord rather than harmony.

* * *

My being gay has never been a secret to my London colleagues. Abroad I have been open to those who could understand — those who were gay themselves or who had lived in Europe or North America. In the past few years AIDS and the gay organisations emerging in the South have made openness more easy. Yet wherever I am, if I tell others about myself or Tom, it has always been my choice to do so. I resent that choice being taken from me, making me weak and the victim I should never have been.

If I was never an ardent gay liberationist, it was, I suppose, because I seldom found being gay a problem. My parents, to their credit, never interfered in my private life. I was never racked by guilt, nor did I persuade myself into marriage. Coming out was a slow, natural process that began at nine or ten, when I became aware of boys who were handsome and of the boy heroes in the books I read. In both reality and fiction I saw the brother or close friend I'd never had — the boy who was devoted to me and who accepted my devotion. In my dreams we wandered through forests together, confronted enemies and explored deserted houses, his presence so intense that it always forced me awake.

As I grew older, the desire became more physical; I noticed, without understanding why, lengthening limbs and emerging muscles. I wanted to reach out for these bodies, found myself doing so in horseplay and sports, but soon realised there was a limit to such contact that could not be crossed. In my mid-teens, while half the class boasted girlfriends, work and exams took my energy and concentration. During summer holidays I spent time with a few girls, but never felt pressure from friends or parents to establish more formal relations.

I was lucky in that I lost my virginity with both sexes at roughly the same time, the summer between school and university. The girl's name I have forgotten. She had long blond hair, an attractive body and a round, pleasant face. Part of a group that had driven to Gullane in borrowed parents' cars, we lay on the beach in the watery sun. She offered me sun lotion as I lay back to digest the late picnic lunch. My eyes closed, I felt her hand massage first my arms, then my chest. Her movements, at first gentle, became stronger as they approached my belly and swimming-trunks. There was a reaction I could not hide; when she did not stop, I looked up and saw her smile. She lay beside me and I pulled her gently against my erection. It was a question that expected the answer no, but she pushed her hips forward and kissed me. Three hours later in a friend's flat, I realised I was not the first she had seduced and was grateful for her experience. In the narrow north-facing room, on a single bed, I stared down at my first naked woman, entered her cautiously, glad of her guidance, and thrust my way to the pride of an orgasm which it seemed that she shared.

Three days later I had sex with my first man. I already knew Ewan, who was openly gay. Several years older, he must have known me better than I knew myself, but he did not contradict my assertion that my interest in his lifestyle was merely intellectual. I had decided I was not gay, on the dubious grounds that I was attracted by none of the men I knew to be homosexual. They were, however, more interesting than my contemporaries, and when Ewan gave a party I was always willing to attend. That Saturday evening in his crowded New Town flat I met Felix, a Canadian on his European tour, twenty-one, handsome and intelligent, with long golden hair and eyes that never left mine. I fell for him immediately, as only an eighteen-year-old can, mistaking physical desire for the complex emotion of love. We sat at the window overlooking Dundas Street and talked all evening, hardly aware of the other guests until they had gone and Ewan was offering us the use of his spare room.

Three days before, with a woman's body below me, I was a rutting animal; standing beside Felix, feeling his fingers gently caress me, trying awkwardly to respond, I was a young man discovering the delicacy and power of the sexual act. Her body had been soft and yielding, ultimately disappointing; his was strong and hard, ultimately reassuring. Before, I had panted, grunted and sweated; that night I was relaxed, leisurely and calm. With my first woman my orgasm had been dull and gross; with my first man it sparkled and uplifted.

Felix left the next morning. I saw the girl three or four more times. She must have grown tired of my lack of adventure, my kisses moving methodically from mouth to neck and breasts while I fumbled between her legs. Although I did not miss her, I did not reject all women on her account. A few months later I met Irene and for several weeks enjoyed her sense of humour and her energetic lovemaking. Eventually, however, I realised that no matter how much I liked her or others of her sex, I would never find in women the excitement that men offered. Women were strangers offering the security and claustrophobia of a suburban home; men were more familiar yet offered the challenge of the exotic and forbidden. I occasionally thought of myself married and with children, but with the same lack of interest that I considered a career in business or banking. More and more of my time was spent with gay men and by the time I left university, all pretensions of bisexuality had dropped away.

* * *

Nothing changes. The temperature falls. Rosa comes and goes. I wake at night at each animal cry, each creaking timber. I bury myself in these notebooks, hoping that time will pass and one day I will look up to see that El Gordo and El Magro have gone, Rosa has knelt to unlock my chain and I am free.

It will not happen. It is beyond her power. She does not have the authority to let me go and those who have the authority have forgotten me. Worse, the whole organisation has crumbled, no one is in charge, no decisions can be made. Rosa and the others are as condemned as I am to stay here, condemned to grow old together, to debate a world and politics that have long passed us by.

* * *

The story of my life... When I returned from Brazil those many years ago I moved to London in search of work. My parents, always generous, gave me money to find a bedsit and survive for a couple of months. Finding a job was easier than I expected and much easier than it would be now. World Aid was looking for a dogsbody; my experience in the International Society and knowledge of Portuguese, at a time when they were expanding in Brazil, gave me the edge.

I was fortunate. I walked into a job that was enjoyable and reasonably well paid, working with colleagues who were pleasant and helpful. We were a small organisation, with no more than forty London-based workers and a hundred projects abroad, proud of our uniqueness that the public contributed only to the projects that they wished to support. I never expected to stay as long as I did. Most people moved on after two or three years, higher up the ladder in another charity. Instead World Aid offered me two years in London, four in Brazil, then half a dozen travelling the world inspecting projects.

Kathy was another long-timer, the only one with whom close friendship grew. At first she made me nervous. I had never spent time with an African woman before, far less one of her type — tall, overweight, intelligent, aggressive and with a barely concealed hostility towards men and Europeans. Head of our African department, she ran it well, but like a fiefdom, tolerating no intrusion from others. If she and I got on, it was partly because neither was a threat to the other, partly because I was willing to learn from her, and partly, I suspect, because the elder sister—younger brother relationship masked the deeply buried possibility that in other circumstances the attraction might not be platonic.

Of all my friends, it is Kathy that I miss most. I sometimes wish I could nestle into her, be comforted by her. I want to rest my head on her breasts and feel her arms around me. I want her to tease me and insult me and tell me the fact that I am imprisoned proves that I am as useless as any other white man. I want her to protect me, to guard me from El Gordo and El Magro, to prove, in one brief gesture, with one word from her booming voice, that all Rosa's arguments are false; I want her to sweep aside this whole room, the debris of my life and take me home.

* * *

They do not teach you such situations in Development Studies. The part-time course I took at the LSE was concerned with global issues, population size and structure, health indicators and transfers of income. Poverty was the absence of wealth, easily measured and easily put right. It was the tail-end of optimism, when the realities of commodity prices meant less than the exhilaration of African independence and Structural Adjustment was a solution not a nightmare. The statistics that were our icons were slow to reflect reality and, with few dissenting voices, we all believed in the power of Development to overcome the disparities between North and South.

There was no emotion in our classes, no sense of frustration, depression or rage. I read Fanon, but was convinced the end of old-style colonialism had made him redundant. I tried Debray, but he was too French, too oratorical and too theoretical, while the circumstances of Guevara's death revealed him as nothing more than a romantic. If I had been intelligent or more perceptive, I might have understood better the task that faced us. My time in South America had shown me the ubiquity of poverty, but I had not understood its weight, the relentless drudgery that gradually extinguishes hope. It had stared me in the face — in Santa Cruz, for example, where I had watched the laughter and energy of the shoe-shine boys and the lethargy of the elderly street photographers and wondered how long it took for one to become the other — yet the implications had passed me by.

I was even further from the anger and outrage that half humanity could be condemned to death, disease and misery while the other half neither knew nor cared. All I saw in that year of evening classes was a breakdown in economics; a breakdown that could be repaired by tinkering and rebuilding. The MA I earned was a mechanic's certificate equipping me with the knowledge that would set the world to rights. My ego inflated, I continued working for World Aid, over-confident with youth and without the shield of wisdom.

This imprisonment is what that course should have taught. This is reality. This is true poverty, where the horizons are narrowed to one bare room, where consciousness is no more than waking, eating — or permanent hunger — shivering, excreting and sleeping. Here there is no future, no hope, no release except death. This is what every Northerner should feel, every stockbroker in Wall Street, every fashion designer in Milan, every lager lout vomiting up his dinner in some Mediterranean nightclub; if each of them felt another's pain there would be no poverty, no disease, no crime. But none of us can ever see beyond our own reality and it is that blindness which brought me here.

* * *

I suppose I have no cause to complain of others' indifference when I remember my first years in London. By day I was engrossed in other people's affairs, in the desire to help them — a literacy project in Nepal, copper prices in Zambia, Chagas' Disease in Brazil — but at night and at weekends I had no time for anything but my own amusement. I explored London, visited its parks and museums, its cinemas and theatres, its nightclubs and bars. I found friends and a social life and moved from the Notting Hill bedsit to a pleasant flatshare in Crouch End. Yet, however much I believed I had matured in my year abroad, I was still young and naive, mistaking my intelligence and limited experience for insight into the human condition.

In time my horizons broadened, less at work and college, than in bars and nightclubs and strangers' homes. The more I sought and found sex, the more insights I gained into people's lives. I learnt that others could lie and steal and feel no remorse, could spend days in bed and nights on the streets, could be self-confident to the point of egomania or delusion, could find pleasure in the weight of moustaches and black leather or the flippancy of drag and camp. In short, I discovered that others were not like myself, that their view of the world could be very different from my own.

The search for love justified my sexual drive, for I still had not learnt that reciprocated love was a proof of maturity rather than an imperative of youth. I was twenty-four when I met Chuck at a dinner party; he was a year younger, studying politics and law. Tall, blond, with the looks, body, name and accent of the North American jock, he was a second Felix, only now I was not the virgin but the adult ready for a serious relationship. We shared a sense of humour and an interest in contemporary affairs and offered each other the attraction of the foreign — twentieth-century Baltimore and ancient Scotland. The novelty of the situation — being one of a couple — blinded me to the reality. I had a handsome, intelligent partner who could make me laugh and was good in bed; what more did I need? I did not see the yawning gap underlying the apparent compatibility. Essentially, Chuck was cold and though I am not the most emotional of people, I came to resent his lack of affection. Superficially, I grew tired of his obsessive tidiness, his obsession with wearing the right clothes, making the right impression. On a deeper level, I was rejecting the system; he was impatient to enter it, to return home to Washington and the day when his name would be as familiar inside the Beltway as the president's. We drifted apart with more apathy than acrimony.

Chuck must know that I am here. Whatever his work now, I am sure it gives him the ear of shakers and movers. I doubt, however, that he has done anything, has simply read the article in the *Post*, told himself "I know that guy" and moved on to George Will and the editorial. If I were younger, I would resent his indifference; now I recognise that resentment would be pointless. I have no place in his life, as he has none in mine.

* * *

Rosa told me there has been a massacre in Brazil — an Indian village burnt down in retaliation for the murder of a gold-miner. I could see that she was not sure where her sympathies should lie. At first sight the natives are the Brazilian equivalent of her Quechua, the miners the middle class in Lima. Yet her philosophy is ill at ease with indigenous culture — the nakedness, the hunting for fish and game with blow-pipe and spear, the wish to conserve the forest rather exploit it. Her instinct is to support the miners, poor migrants from other parts of Brazil who flood into Amazonia in search of a means of survival.

"What would Chairman Gonzalo say?" I asked.

"I don't know," she admitted.

"I suspect Mao would be on the side of the gold-miners."

"Why?"

"Tibet. Inner Mongolia. The Chinese have always repressed ethnic minorities."

"We do not have this problem in Peru."

"That's not true," I said. "You have the descendants of the Spanish, the descendants of African slaves, Chinese immigrants, your own native tribes in the Amazon and a president whose parents were Japanese, not to mention the millions of Quechua and Aymara you claim to represent. This country is as ethnically diverse as any other. The only difference between you and the Brazilian natives is that you are the majority."

"So the *indigenes* are vulnerable and should work with the miners against the Brazilian government, form a common front."

"It's not that simple. Too much divides them. The natives can only maintain their culture by complete isolation from the outside world. The miners, searching for security and wealth, threaten that by invading the natives' territory.

"You have a similar problem in Peru," I continued the lecture. "As you said yourself, if you want your people to maintain their culture, you have to cut them off from the outside world. On the other hand, if you want to improve their standard of living, you have to open them up to all the influences you hate — the middle class, foreigners, tourists."

"We have to destroy the middle class in order to survive."

"You said that before. Who are the middle class? Peruvians like yourselves. In some countries your father with his land would be considered middle class. The middle class are as much victims as the *andeanos*. Instead of making them your enemy you could try to cooperate with them."

"Cooperate with people who steal from us and kill us?"

"Cooperate for your own sake, to help empower your community. All you are doing is destroy it."

"You have to destroy in order to build anew."

"We've been here before. By that logic we should blow up the whole world and let some other species start again."

She ignored the point. There was a brief silence before she returned to the Brazilian natives. "Perhaps they should give up their land."

"That means giving up their identity."

"For the greater good of other Brazilians."

"They aren't interested in other Brazilians."

"They must be."

"Why? When those other Brazilians steal their land and destroy their culture — as you claim your land and culture have been stolen."

"It's not the same," she said, but it was and we both knew it was.

The conversation died. I thought of pictures I had seen, stories I had heard. The native tribes, Brazilian or Peruvian, Colombian or Venezuelan, struck me as pathetic, a few thousand individuals trying to stem the tide of progress before their communities collapsed, their women became prostitutes, their men alcoholics and their children the debris of the twenty-first century. Yet the gold-miners were not to blame. Why scratch a living in Rio or São Paulo if the government promises you land and the chance of making money two or three thousand miles away? Hope is better than despair and no naked savage has the right to stop you feeding your wife and children.

I saw the illogicality in Rosa's argument — fight for what you believe in while denying others the right to do the same — but, to my surprise, accepted it. For years I had tried to unravel the Gordian knot of conflicting demands — a knot which changed shape as each year passed, as knowledge grew and different factors came to the foreground. A dam designed in the 1970s to provide water and electricity in the 1990s destroys lives and the environment; a crop with better yields lies unharvested because labour has migrated; giving men work increases the dependence of women; and so on and so on and so on. For years I had left such problems unresolved. Now it seems simpler to cut the knot and accept that sacrifices have to be made. Build the dam and displace communities; bring in outsiders to grow the crop. So why not lose the Brazilian natives and save the miners; on razed jungle land a sustainable economy might emerge, with children vaccinated, schools, clinics and factories opened. Harsh decisions have to be made, sides taken, and I begin to understand why Sendero and Rosa act as they do.

* * *

Plus ça reste la même chose, plus rien ne change. Health the same; weather the same; room the same; food the same; mood indifferent.

There are cracks in the monolith of Rosa's ideology. She speaks of a Peru liberated from capitalism, but her true vision is narrower, an Altiplano free of foreigners and *criollos*. She resents the fact that the country's oil is to be found in the jungle, its copper in the coastal regions and its manufacturing on the outskirts of Lima. As a result, when she talks of the New Republic, it is never clear whether she means the country as a whole or only her people and their homeland.

Because she attributes the weakness of the economy to the influence of foreign banks and multilaterals, her solution is simple — nationalise the means of production and renege on the foreign debt. A period of retrenchment would limit oil consumption to the output of the country's wells, while, properly cultivated, the land could feed the whole population. The income from exports — legal or illegal — would be used to import only essentials. I argued that she was still at the mercy of foreigners who set the price for produce, whether drugs or guano. She shrugged. "We can grow some other crop."

"It sounds like paradise," I said but she missed my sarcasm. "It's unrealistic," I went on. "People want to be richer and you want to make them poorer. You want to deprive them of the few imported luxuries they can afford. You'll even stop the buses running if you cut down on oil."

I was wrong, she said. Her people lived for thousands of years without luxuries, without buses and oil; they could do so again. She speaks with such conviction that it is difficult to contradict her. All my experience and knowledge of the powerlessness of individuals and communities in the maelstrom of the international economy fades before such certainty. The only argument I can muster is human nature and greed. "No one wants to be equal," I told her. "Everyone wants to hoard and be richer than their neighbour."

She shook her head. "That is not the Andean way. Here we are so poor we have to support each other. And those who do not do so will be punished."

The rhetoric of Maoism that even the Chinese have abandoned. I shifted tack, pointed out that equality is a mirage; some people are more skilled, others more energetic and others still more honest and altruistic. Even if you could suppress such differences, a society of equal contribution and gain would be a society of ants, not humans. She shrugged, unwilling to hear or unable to understand.

The society Rosa longs for is unreal and unattainable, founded on the false memory of the Inca empire and the false promise of Maoism. Its walls are the illusion of a strong and selfless peasantry. Its roof is a people's army, keeping out foreigners and capitalism. She is doomed to failure and frustration. Even if by some miracle she were to achieve her goal, it would not be long before Peru followed the examples of Russia, China and Albania: dictatorship by the proletariat become no more than dictatorship.

A hundred years ago she might have been more successful. Today the world has become too small and vulnerable; no society is isolated and no individual stands alone. Once, flying from Northern Quebec to Montreal, I saw 20,000 feet below thousands of trees dying from the acid rain that drifts north from the USA. The radiation from Chernobyl swept across a continent. The Alps are a picture postcard crossed in twenty minutes, the desert islands of the Pacific can be reached in a day. Rosa may keep individual foreigners at bay, but she cannot protect the Altiplano from pollution, ozone depletion, global warming. She is equally vulnerable to ideas, to invasion by telephone and fax, by satellite and radio. As Romania showed, the tighter the ideological cordon, the more powerful the rebellion when it comes. An economic miracle is no guarantee of security, for it inevitably leads to the political revolt of Tienanmen Square or the political indifference of Canton.

Yet despite my reservations and experience, I sympathise. All Rosa wants is justice, wealth and peace. All her problems stem from the interference of outsiders, from conquistadores to Western bankers and the War On Drugs. They have left a land and people poor and exploited, their misery masked by the myth that this is a Western country, free and democratic. Had I been brought up on the Altiplano, I would respond the way Rosa does. I would have had no choice.

* * *

Brazil, Brazil... Back to Brazil...

Twenty-six years old, World Aid sent me out as assistant country director. I lived in Rio, in a small but comfortable flat between Copacabana and Ipanema. I arrived with trepidation and enthusiasm, eager to learn and eager to teach. I monitored education programmes and health schemes, inspected accounts, agreed budgets, hired and sometimes fired. I was back in a country I loved, where the heat was overwhelming and reassuring, where the people were open and articulate, where life was immediate and poverty, however widespread, never suppressed the national *alegria*. I sat in a tiny room half-way up a *morro*, enraptured by the drawl of a project leader explaining the success of her money-spinning scheme; I watched homeless children chant multiplication tables with beaming smiles; I listened without boredom to lectures from the politically correct. The work took time and energy but all I had to do was channel the enthusiasms of others. Even the routine of writing reports and amending budgets was welcome, translating the successes and enthusiasm of Brazilian colleagues into pedestrian British prose.

"A waste of time," Rosa commented. "Bandages for a dying man." If I had heard such arguments then, I would have dismissed them by pointing to our achievements and the potential for further change. I would have compared our success with the failure of her revolution — Brazil's middle-class urban guerrillas had merely generated greater repression while leaving the average Brazilian as poor as ever. As others played with guns, I helped children to learn, mothers to feed their babies, families to improve their standard of living. True, we reached only hundreds while millions struggled to survive, but this was merely the first stage; in five or ten years' time, my successor would be supervising projects that had multiplied ten- or a hundred-fold.

Yet the longer I stayed in Brazil, the greater was the culture shock. My work confronted me with poverty — shanty-towns and street children, disease and early death — while my background and salary made me rich. It was some time before I fully understood the hostility and indifference of the wealthy in their islands of luxury to the mass of poverty that surrounded them. I learnt that one could witness misery and have no urge to alleviate it, could flaunt wealth and blame the starving for wishing to steal it. The elegance and smiles of expatriates and middle-class acquaintances turned sour and I began to despise myself for cultivating them.

Alienated from the rich, but never one of the poor, I sought a niche in *carioca* society. At least I could kid myself that the contradictions between wealth and poverty in Brazil softened in the gay world, although they never entirely faded. I could sit at the pavement tables of the Galeria Alaska with half a dozen friends, half of whom lived at least as comfortably as I, while the other half squatted in squalid rooms in Lapa or the Zona Norte. Together we would talk and laugh, with no distinction between us except the occasional deference of youth to experience. When the bill came, those with money paid and although for some sex might follow, that was a separate transaction where any currency — cruzeiros, affection, beauty — was valid. In time I would get up and leave, alone or with a partner, to return home or to dance in the Sótão, coming out at three or four in the morning to the majestic sweep of Copacabana — its lights and apartment buildings looking over the dark beach and black Atlantic. This was paradise, I told myself. This was home.

* * *

In Rio it was inevitable that I met Luís; if not him, it would have been a João or Nilson or Renato. Where Chuck had been cold, Luís was hot, in every sense of the word. Swearing eternal devotion, he made love with an energy and imagination unimaginable in Brits and North Americans. A year younger than my twenty-seven, tall, dark-haired, with the skin and complexion of an Italian and the slim body that was sexy before muscles came into vogue, I could not resist. I especially could not resist a man who threw himself at me, who loved to be seen and make love with me, who was proud to call me Leão, lion, and himself Leinho, lion-cub. Here was no Chuck, no calculating mind planning a future and lifestyle five years ahead; here was no self-absorbed Londoner commuting between bedroom mirror and nightclub dance-floor; here was no impoverished *carioca* cadging a bed, a meal, a lifetime security. Here was an intelligent actor from a middle-class background who could only be an equal to myself.

I was too absorbed by my work and his infatuation to be disturbed by remarks or events that at other times would have made me stop and question. For the first year, I was happy to have someone to spend evenings and weekends with, to wine and dine and dance with. When he was free, I could be too; when he was busy, I had other friends and commitments. After several months he moved in with me, and for a time everything went well. Then I met him by chance in the city centre, on a day when he had told me he would be in São Paulo. His excuse was unconvincing, reminded me of other times when something he had told me had not quite rung true. I said nothing, but became suspicious and it was then that our arguments began — not the sarcastic and tight-lipped disagreements of British couples, but violent rows in which he dashed plates to the floor and I found my arm occasionally raised and ready to strike. I could not tell him to leave; since both of us were fighting, half the fault was surely mine. I tried to change my own behaviour to stop such rows before they began. Only when I learnt that he had taken another lover, an older, richer Brazilian who lived in Tijuca, did I realise how blind I had been.

He begged forgiveness. Reluctantly, I gave it. It did not prevent us from breaking up several weeks later, one hot humid night in Carnival, after hours of drinking and dancing in the streets. I wanted to go home, he wanted to stay out; he screamed that I had always been impossible, that I had never considered what he wanted to do. I threw back at him his lies and deception, the Brit in me hating the scene we were causing. It was, however, the comment of a passer-by — *"Calma, bicha"* — that silenced me, the idea that I was behaving like any camp queen. *"Faz o que quiser"*, I told Luís — do what you want — and turned to take the bus home. One of half a dozen tired revellers — a battered feathered headdress on my brow, my face covered in gold paint, and wearing only a sodden white loin-cloth — I came to the inevitable conclusion that I was tired of Brazil and when my contract ended I would return home.

* * *

A decision taken in the heat of the moment can be overturned. The temptation was strong to stay on in Brazil. I could have found a more reliable partner. I was well-paid and, despite my misgivings, integrated in both *carioca* and expatriate society. As a career, however, it would have been a cul-de-sac. I would have held a succession of similar posts, eventually losing interest in my work and drifting apart from both my European employers and the communities I was supposed to help. I would have reached fifty, an opinionated Anglo-Brazilian, believing myself the epitome of both cultures while in touch with neither. It was wiser to leave while I was still ahead, while there were other countries to visit, other work to be done.

Six months in São Tomé on sabbatical, gaining Africa experience by visiting project after project, spending long evenings with the country's few expatriates and intellectuals. There at least, the contrast between rich and poor was muted — everyone was poor apart from the few foreign diplomats and a handful of businessmen. It was a relief to be in a society where life was slow and simple, where my only responsibilities were to observe and listen. It was almost paradise — indeed it would have been if I had not been aware that there was a world beyond these islands, a world where millions shared what Tomeans lacked — health, wealth, comfort and longevity.

Back in London I returned without too much hesitation to World Aid. I found myself a step up the ladder and in the job of project development officer, initiating new projects and finding new income. A series of automatic salary increases began; my savings began to accumulate and, just before the property boom, I acquired a mortgage in Hampstead. Not surprisingly, it took several more years before cynicism set in.

* * *

After a week or more Rosa returned to the subject occupying her mind. It was less my sexuality, however, than Tom, as if she could develop a whole matrix from one couple's relationship. She asked about him in a surprisingly delicate manner. She wanted to know what kind of person he was. I tried, despite lack of familiarity with the subtleties of Spanish adjectives. He was, I said, *amistoso, irascible, leal* and *serio* — friendly, short-tempered, loyal and serious. There was a silence in which she waited for me to say more and I struggled to find the words, even in English, that described him best. What came to mind was not so much his personality as what he meant to me, as if he did not exist outside our relationship.

I told her about our first meeting, no doubt confirming the image of a dive in which debauched glances met across a darkened room. As I spoke, I remembered forgotten details — the friends I was with, Tom standing alone, a desire that was almost overpowering. "You fell in love?" Rosa asked, and I could not tell if it was contempt or curiosity uppermost in her voice.

I fell in lust, I wanted to say, but could not translate it. "More or less," I said. "He was very handsome; he looked moody...."

"You like that?" she interrupted, as I wondered whether *caviloso* had the right connotations.

"It's a challenge," I said. "It suggests a strong personality."

"And is he *caviloso*?"

"No. He loses his temper sometimes, but he's soft and generous. He's not effeminate," I added, suddenly aware that *dulce* might have given the wrong impression.

"No? So which one of you is the man?" she asked.

I had wondered when the question would come. I talked about social roles, the attraction of masculinity rather than pseudo-femininity, the desire to be equal partners rather than dominant and submissive. She interrupted what she saw as evasion to ask who played the active role. I still did not want to answer the question without giving it context; I argued that if masculinity was strength and strength bred self-confidence, the ultimate masculinity was to have the self-confidence to allow oneself to be penetrated. She was not impressed by such sophistry; I gave in and admitted that we took turns to *joder* and *ser jodido*.

She asked if I missed him. "Of course," I said, then wondered if it was true. I sometimes wonder if it is Tom that I love or the security he represents. He was — is — the man I returned to, the man I slept with, the man who waited for me. It was once Chuck, Luís or Yuki. Would I have felt the same for them if they had been my lover when I was kidnapped? How much do I love Tom and how much is he only a housemate? Am I incapable of any emotional goal higher than some Victorian ideal of compatibility, where the husband works, the wife keeps house and mutual respect takes the place of love?

We talked on, Rosa trying to understand our relationship, but only able to do so within the model of husband and wife. Eventually I tired of the discussion, disturbed by the questions of emotion and separation it was raising. "And you?" I asked. "Do you have a boyfriend — or a girlfriend?"

"No boyfriend," she said. "I have the revolution." I was not alert enough to ask if it kept her warm at night.

"And boyfriends in the past?"

"Never," she said.

"Have you never wanted one?"

"Later, perhaps."

"What kind of man would you like?"

"It doesn't matter."

"Come on, tell me."

"It doesn't matter," she repeated.

"I told you about Tom."

She shook her head, stood up to go.

"Come on," I said, aware of the wheedling in my voice. "What kind of man do you like? You must have had a relationship with someone. Tell me about it. What was he like? What did he do?"

The door closed behind her and I was left lying here, suddenly — and still — angry and afraid. Why had I thought that an hour of conversation could sweep away thirty years of prejudice and centuries of cultural belief? Why had I opened myself up so much? In talking about Tom I betrayed both him and myself. He gave me no permission to introduce him here, to discuss his life and our shortcomings. Rosa gained no flash of understanding, no awareness of the damage she was doing to both of us. All I have done is confirm her prejudices and leave myself even more naked and vulnerable than before. I reminded her I am *maricón*. I reminded her I am the hairdresser, the rent-boy, the victim. I am lucky only to have been raped, where others have been beaten, castrated and left to die.

* * *

Tom accused me in my dream of leaving him, and I woke in guilt and sweat. It is not true, I said, I simply do not know when I will return.

Yet it is true that the longer I am apart from him, the more uncertain my feelings become. The longer I am here, the less I believe I will return home, and the less I believe I will return home, the less real Tom and the rest of my life becomes. If I love Tom less, it is because I believe in him less.

It is the wrong reaction, I know. If they have kept me this long they do not mean to kill me, and if they do not mean to kill me, they must one day set me free. I tell myself that every day and yet every day I find it more and more difficult to believe.

I have every reason to love and stay with Tom. I once thought that I settled with him as much because I was seeking a home as because he was the person I wanted to create that home with, but such an interpretation is too critical. He has always been much more than a flatmate to me. I have always relaxed with him, had fun with him. I have been glad to fall asleep and wake up with him. Those first months in Hampstead, when we arrived home at two or three in the morning and slept until noon, were as intense as a teenager's first affair. Little things — his being locked out that first December, having brunch in Chelsea, watching old videos after making love — told me how much he meant to me. House-hunting, the upheaval of the move and settling in taught me how reliable he was, how enthusiastic and willing. By the time I came to Peru we had reached the perfect equilibrium, close but not suffocating, in love but not obsessed. Of course there were difficult times — his occasional tantrums, my absences, the adjustment of moving out of London — but they were no worse than every couple goes through.

Certainly life with Tom has always been more stable and profound than with any of his predecessors. Chuck and I were too naive to see that we had nothing in common but our youth and the romance of being in love; with Luís there was too much drama and passion; Yuki was too self-centred. Tom is the only one who has loved me and who I have loved with such depth. If I ever get out of here, without a doubt it is to him I would return.

* * *

If Luís was inevitable, so was Yuki. Back in London, thirty years old, work under control, I looked again for a partner; the Y, with its eligible young males, was the inevitable mating ground.

It was Yuki who approached me. I had seen and ignored him before. My tastes were still focused on Caucasian features, although the skin colour might be Indian or Scandinavian or South American. I found oriental faces too expressionless and bland. Besides, the Chinese and Thais I saw in gay bars were too small, too young and too effeminate — children to tolerate rather than men to respect. But when Yuki asked me for change for the hair-drier, I could not help noticing that he was almost my height, almost my age, and had a body as hard as my usual fantasies. Fishing in my pocket for the right coins, I realised that I had been blinded by my own preconceptions.

The sex was efficient. His English was perfect, the result of six years of studying and working in London. He was intelligent, slightly dismissive and had a dry sense of humour that took time to recognise. We met again for a drink and more sex, then again for a meal and a visit to the theatre. I learnt that he worked for a Japanese bank, discerned a European outlook underlain by a slight coldness that I took to be typically Nipponese. By the fourth or fifth meeting it was obvious that each of us had found something he sought in the other.

We were not a typical East-West couple. We were contemptuous of those we saw, middle-aged Englishmen with florid faces and spreading waistlines accompanied by simpering dolls. I was insulted by the expression "rice queen" as if all that attracted me in Yuki was the colour of his skin and the slant of his eyes, as if I could only respond to a lover who was younger and submissive. Yuki shared my distaste, although he expressed it less often, more concerned with his reputation at the bank than with the opinions of other gay men.

We were together for three years, at one point sharing lives so much that we left each other's telephone numbers on our answering machines and I would forget in which wardrobe I had left a favourite shirt. Our lifestyles slotted into each other with ease. My trips abroad complemented his long hours at the bank, so that the time we spent together was never too much, never threatened boredom with over-exposure. We were like every middle-class childless couple; with flats in Hampstead and Holland Park, separate cars and overlapping circles of friends. We entertained others and were entertained, got up late at weekends, paid weekly visits to the cinema and theatre and took holidays together — Paris in spring and Florida or the Mediterranean in summer. Like any gay couple, our eyes wandered — and we gave each other permission for hands to wander further — but, at least while I was in London, neither felt any need to do so.

We seldom used the word love — it sounded wrong, adolescent. I am not sure now how I would describe my feelings for him. He was the first man who made me feel emotionally mature. Chuck had made me uncertain of my own feelings, Luís had made me uncertain of his. Yuki was completely reliable, as smooth, stylish and dependable as a Sony or Hitachi. Yet he never fully allowed me into his life. He received letters without telling me who they were from, descended into moods without explaining their cause or how I might alleviate them. I was prepared to open myself to him, but he would not, could not, open himself to me. Typical was his lack of interest in my learning Japanese; his English was all we needed to communicate, he claimed, unimpressed by my desire to gain insights into his background and national character.

In the end we drifted apart, both more dedicated to work than to each other. I had become frustrated by World Aid and was beginning to look for solutions to irresolvable problems. Yuki was frustrated by the ceiling he had encountered in the London office; too European to return to Kyoto, he looked for work elsewhere. Eventually he found a job in Paris that offered a significant rise in responsibility and salary. If he had asked me to go with him or hesitated on my behalf, we might have saved the relationship, but it was clear that he had not considered such a move. I joked about it once, one evening in the cheap sushi bar we often dined in, and saw from his expression that he did not understand.

I accompanied him to the airport, half regretting his departure and half looking forward to my freedom. We hugged each other and promised to telephone and write, but I knew it was a promise he would find difficult to keep. I stayed with him once, a year later, while attending a conference. Over dinner we talked with enthusiasm of his new job and my plans for Demotica, but neither of us regretted the fact that we slept in separate beds. Now I have no idea where he is. Like Chuck, he might read about me in the papers, but news only interested him for the impact it might have on the money markets. Like Chuck, his reaction would be little more than a flicker of recognition before his attention turned to other things.

I wonder what Rosa and Yuki would make of each other. I half-understand each of them, but neither would understand each other. Thirty thousand years ago, their ancestors wandered the plains of Mongolia together; today their thoughts and attitudes to life have nothing in common. Rosa would be repelled by a man whose only goal in life was the pursuit of money and the comfort it brings; Yuki would have only contempt for a woman who had refused the opportunity of education to escape the poverty she grew up in. I can see them facing each other in this room, staring at each other in silence; even if they shared a common language, they would have nothing to say.

* * *

Today I heard more about the assassination which brought Rosa here, her first, although she has assisted at others and planted bombs that she has not seen explode. It was in the early morning as the general drove to the airport. Four *senderistas* waited not far from the barracks; one drove a van into the road to stop the approaching car. He died, killed by the general's bodyguard. The other two guerrillas stepped forward to kill the driver and bodyguard; one was himself wounded. The general, a man in his fifties with grey hair and a sour expression, sat in the back, hardly moving. It was only when he was shot in the chest that he reacted, bringing a hand to the wound as his face creased in pain. Rosa's role was to offer the coup de grace, to step up slowly, see the blood ooze over his hand and his uniform, to study the blank expression in his eyes. She aimed for his forehead but the bullet crashed through his nose. His head fell forward as she shot again and blood spattered over the back of the car.

She was not afraid, she said, nor did she feel remorse. It was a job that had to be done; she had to kill, he had to die. I asked about his wife and family, the pain they will have suffered from his death. Rosa's anger was as great as my insensitivity; what about the pain and suffering of the peasants that the general had ordered killed or tortured or imprisoned? What does it matter to an over-painted widow that a husband she probably never liked is dead? What does it matter to his children, who are probably themselves soldiers carrying on his butchery?

The passion in her voice matched the reason in her words. Once I would not have understood her coldbloodedness, the ability to take life without regret or hesitation. I would have argued that no one was beyond redemption, that reasoned argument can lead to compromise and cooperation. In other words I would have responded as an armchair critic, as a man who believes he knows everything and in reality has experienced nothing.

I find it strange to be so close to terrorism and yet so distant. All my life I avoided war and violence in my belief that those who indulged in it were less human than myself. A year of imprisonment and three months with Rosa have taught me what I have always known but would not admit — that a man or woman with a gun is no different from any other. It is a disappointment. I wanted my prejudices confirmed; I wanted proof that those who resorted to violence were somehow deficient — madmen, emotional cripples and social failures, aberrations who could be excluded from the rational world. Then I could claim that peace and equality could only come from negotiation and fair political process. Instead I have learnt that the fanatic can be as ordinary as Rosa, as ordinary as myself.

The only difference between us is that the fanatic has no doubt, no shades of understanding. Those who are not friends are enemies; the individual must be sacrificed for the community; the means justify the end. There is no scope for change of heart. It would not occur to Rosa to talk to her general, to convince rather than kill him, to negotiate rather than confront. It is the simplistic approach I have always resisted — the righteousness of the extremist, the inability to understand others' pain, others' point of view.

Yet I too failed to understand and that failure brought me here. I thought my fair skin and blue eyes were irrelevant, that each time I stepped out of the plane I became a native of whichever country I entered. I had come not to impose solutions but to enable others to find them; I was an emissary of a great wisdom to be shared with those of narrower horizons. I never recognised that those who did not welcome me might be right to prefer their own analysis of their problems than the one I brought.

Consciously or not, I set myself up against Sendero. Implicit in my coming to Peru was the claim that I could rescue the people from the corruption of their government, the brutality of their army and the oppression of their terrorists. Sendero had to respond as it did and prove that my words, my beliefs, all Demotica's experience, meant nothing the moment my car stopped and five guns pointed at me.

* * *

So much unites us and so much divides us. We are both angered by injustice, although we believe in different means to overcome it. Her anger comes from an abstract ideal — that all are born equal and none has the right to dominate others. My anger, although dulled by time, has its roots in emotion, in sympathy for others' pain. Rosa wants a just world because the present one offends her sense of order. I want a just world because others hurt.

She claims to be closer to achieving her goal than I am mine. All I can claim is to have increasingly seen the inadequacy of my approach. Each step upward in my career has given me a wider perspective of the work that needs to be done. What I saw as local difficulties in my twenties I realised were global issues by the time I turned thirty. In my fortieth year I can see improvements only by closing my eyes to failures — look at Berlin and forget Yugoslavia, remember Zimbabwe and forget Angola. Democracy might return to half of Africa, but the whole continent has been impoverished by forces beyond its control.

However harsh its methods, where Sendero operates freely it may replace a corrupt authority with one that verges on honesty. Whatever his failings, Mao succeeded in dragging China into the twentieth century and giving its people a dignity and self-respect they had never known under the emperors or warlords. It and other countries in Asia have succeeded economically precisely because democracy was no more than cosmetic.

It is not surprising that in Sendero's eyes I am dangerous. With my talk of democracy and cooperation, I distract the people's attention from the real problems of hunger and oppression, I indeed encourage them to work with and not against their enemy. I am simply another Northerner who meddles in other people's lives before returning to my comfortable home, leaving others to struggle against the poverty and repression. I do not face prison, torture or threats of assassination.

For years I have known that Rosa was right, although I buried such knowledge under rationale and self-justification. Whether it was education or democracy, I only planted the seed; I never stayed to nourish and protect the plant. I persuaded myself that I followed a nobler path than most of the human race; my goal was not selfish money or pleasure, but the bringing of food and sustenance to the world's poor and the bringing of democracy to the world's disenfranchised. With Demotica I saw myself as an elite within an elite. With their literacy and agriculture and family planning projects, other agencies duplicated each others' work, but like Amnesty or Panos, we were unique. We were the only ones to work for self-determination — for the ballot box to be effective and universal. I believed that the ballot box brought power. I was wrong; I had forgotten true power only comes from the barrel of a gun.

* * *

There is another contradiction that I always avoided. I wanted people to have the same benefits that I had — food, shelter, clothing, freedom to live they way they choose. At the same time I wanted them to maintain their cultures and languages and lifestyles. Yet the more I tried to contribute to their well-being, the more I destroyed their culture and language. I came to Peru and forced Andeans to speak the language of their oppressors. I stayed in hotels from Nepal to Namibia, only to drink Coca-Cola and watch MTV. I overthrew centuries of tradition by insisting that Western democracy was their only salvation. When they adopted it, they followed personalities not policies — the US model but ten times worse.

The mess the world is in is the mess that we democrats created. Each time we try to repair the damage we have inflicted, we only succeed in destroying more. We substituted our intolerant myth of Christianity for their often more benevolent gods. We destroyed their independence and when we nominally set them free substituted economic domination for colonisation. We armed them and created the monsters of Mobutu, Amin and Noriega, and the monstrosities of Cambodia, Somalia and Mozambique.

World Aid taught me that I am not innocent. The longer I worked for them, the more uncertain I became about the morality of decisions taken in London or Washington as to how to spend money in the Sahel or Dar es Salaam. We claimed to listen to the South, to respect their right to determine their own lives, and still went ahead and set up our own organisations to hand out our wealth. The inevitable result is that the developing world is littered with hundreds of competing agencies offering condoms and training and emergency relief, each justifying headquarters and executive salaries and a thousand duplicated projects.

I moved to Demotica because I wanted to strike at the heart of the problem, to say to the poor, you take control, you create your own wealth. I was convinced that the ballot box was the magic bullet and too naive to recognise my argument as rationalisation, sleight of hand to give me a better job and allow me to pretend I had risen above the mundane world of development aid. If I had been honest, I would have recognised even then that true democracy was a goal that will never be achieved. Even if it were, alone it could not bring economic independence from the North.

Rosa is right; there is no middle way.

* * *

Meanwhile my life goes on. Food — so little of it — and excretion. Cold and discomfort. Rosa's presence and absence. Bored with writing, with thinking, with talking, I have begun to doodle, to try to draw. I cover the pages with endless windows, darkened corners, the battered shoes on my feet, even Rosa. I tried to draw Tom from memory but tore the result up in disgust.

What do I have to do to retain my sanity? What do I have to do to get free?

* * *

Rosa comes in less often and seems less inclined to talk. I hear all three of them outside and I want to scream. Why are you punishing me for a crime I have not committed? Why don't you try to help me? I lose my temper with Rosa and she tells me my petulance is a luxury that others cannot afford.

* * *

I remember the beat, the butterfly's wing that took me from World Aid to Demotica. In Tanzania, one afternoon near Lake Victoria, I was the only *msungu* in a bus that had broken down on its way to the Rwandan border. We passengers loitered in the sun while the driver and his mate lifted the bonnet and sweated over whatever component had broken. Locals from a nearby village walked past, glancing at the group of strangers and the white man at its centre. I drank occasionally from a warm can of mango juice, watching a group of boys in the shade of a nearby tree. Their attention swung between whatever game they were playing and the spectacle of a dishevelled European who travelled by bus rather than roar past in the comfort of a private jeep. One in particular stared intently. Ten years old, shoeless like the rest, his maroon shirt and blue shorts had darkened with dirt while his eyes remained bright and hesitant. As he watched, I gradually understood that what held his attention was not the colour of my skin but the can I was absently twirling between my fingers. He wanted it, desperately, apparently more than anything he had ever wanted in his life.

I had been working in development for a decade and thought I had become inured to poverty. What I saw before me was by no means the worst I had known — he looked healthy and carefree, had, presumably, a family to care for him. Yet the wall that I had built around me, that separated the pain of poverty from the means to overcome it, that could block out expectations where none could be fulfilled, suddenly collapsed. I thought of a British child of his age, of the new clothes he would wear and the school he would attend, of the mountain bike and computer games he would receive, of cinema and television and trips in the family car, and I almost wept for the boy in front of me and the lost opportunities he represented. All he could aspire to was a drudgery that would gradually extinguish his smile. He would grow into adulthood, take a wife and leave her farming their land while he sought employment in some distant town; there would be too many children, disease, hunger and death. Life had no higher goal than work, getting drunk, the occasional purchase of shoes or a new shirt. Until he died his meals would be cooked on an open fire, his meat and vegetables would rot without a refrigerator, his wife and children would carry water from the lake or the village's solitary tap.

In an hour or two my bus would be repaired and on its way; a day later I would be relaxing with a drink in a luxury hotel; in a fortnight I would be home again, feet on the sofa, flicking through the channels on television. I had wealth, but, more importantly, that wealth gave me choice; at any moment I could change my plans, change my job, alter the direction of my life. I would leave this dry, dusty place; this boy before me could only stay. If he could fully understand the difference between us, I wondered, would he still shyly smile?

All that I could offer him was all that he wanted. I drained the can and held it out. With a beam of happiness, he reached for it, but one of his companions was faster, grabbed it and ran off. The boy's face fell while I was angry that my gesture of reconciliation had failed. I signalled him to wait, climbed back into the bus and searched amongst the bag of waste that, eco-conscious European that I was, I had been collecting in anticipation of some non-existent litter bin. I pulled out an identical can that I had finished earlier and wiped it clean. Outside the bus again, the boy was watching his companions play a ruleless combination of football and rugby. I handed over the second can, both of us aware it was no more than consolation. Nevertheless he smiled his thanks and proudly held it out of the reach of another boy who was already trying to grab it. Then I turned and walked back to the bus, hoping that it would get me quickly out of there.

It was then I decided to leave World Aid, convinced its work was not enough. We did what a thousand other charities did, but no matter how many we worked with, we only dealt with the smallest percentage of those affected. For every street-child we gave shelter to, a hundred more slept or were murdered under flyovers or in shop doorways; for every village woman who benefited from our credit unions, a hundred more had no access to funds for the cheapest fertiliser or hoe; for every case of river blindness we prevented, a hundred more developed.

Even if I could persuade myself that these odds could be overcome, that individuals and institutions and governments could multiply their donations a hundredfold, I no longer wanted to arrange transfers of money from North to South, from wealthy to poor. I was losing the confidence to explain to donors why they should support World Aid's projects rather than those of Oxfam, Care or a hundred other charities. There had to be another, a better solution.

I considered emergency work — driving convoys into the Sudan or setting up refugee camps in Cambodia. I would give up the pretence that any long-term solution could be found and simply rush food and medicines to where they were most needed. The results of my labour would be immediately apparent, the job was well-paid and there would be the warm glow of the hero making his way through the grimmest of conditions. But I did not have the stomach to face unrelenting human misery at its most extreme — those dying of starvation or maimed and blinded by warfare.

I returned to the need for long-term solutions, the awareness that much of the misery in the South was the result of weak or corrupt governments. Democracy had to be strengthened at every level, from the village up to national government. Increase the power of the voter and the accountability of the elected representative, and the nation as a whole can only benefit.

Such analysis was always too simple; it skates over too many differences and nuances, the recognition that democracy differs in Sweden and Singapore, in Tanzania and Taiwan. Nor does it take into account the failure of democracy in Russia or the economic success of the mainland Chinese. Nonetheless, the four of us who came together to discuss these ideas shared the common belief that while greater democracy was not the panacea for every ill, it certainly smoothed the path to greater responsibility and wealth.

I was closest to Kathy. We shared a frustration with World Aid, hers stronger since her attachment to Africa was greater. Her contempt for the men who, post-independence, ruled and plundered the continent would have been the deepest racism if expressed in my voice. Only a few merited respect — Museveni, not merely because she herself was Ugandan, and Senghor, the latter more, I suspect, because of what she had read than because of what she knew.

She had no time for the niceties of democracy — which voting system, whether presidential or prime ministerial — was concerned only with the imperatives of open government and the limitation of power. "We have to stop the bastards," she would say, with a controlled anger, each time another general assumed or clung to power.

Brian was a more recent acquaintance whose pedantic approach irritated me until I saw the radical opinions underneath. He introduced us to Sunil, who had arrived in London during the worst of Indira Ghandi's excesses. Over dinner one evening the idea of Demotica was born. For the men it was a pipedream; for Kathy a brainwave. Unknown to others, she took each of us for lunch, drew from each our ideas, strengths and weaknesses. Two or three months later, she brought us back together and presented us with a fait accompli — half think-tank and half pressure group.

It was two years before we all worked together. Tired of fundraising, I had time to quit World Aid and spend a year taking a master's in politics and international law. By the time I formally joined Demotica, Kathy and Brian had persuaded half a dozen agencies to fund us. On my first day I sat in our Camden office, as excited as when I had started working for World Aid. I would no longer enable individuals but nations. I would be the spark that lit the flame of democracy across the world. Perhaps my name and contribution would be forgotten, but a generation from now genuine democracy would have taken root in every country on the globe.

It was hubris, I knew. Despite my ambition, I was likely to make little impact. With Demotica I would be working on a larger scale than before but in many ways I would have less influence. Most governments were either welcoming or indifferent to World Aid; they were more likely to be suspicious or hostile to an organisation threatening the very basis of their power. Yet I needed that hubris; I needed to believe that I could sow the seeds of genuine democracy and accountability. Without it, I would have had no motivation.

Without it, I would not have ended up here.

* * *

It was Tom who rescued me from becoming too involved in my work. Sometimes it had seemed that Yuki and I had seen each other as accessories — the professional lover to match the Filofax and mobile phone. Tom was too real, too demanding, too different from

Yuki to slip easily into my life. I had to care about him, think about him, recognise that he was both more vulnerable and, in ways I did not always understand, stronger than me. Sometimes I wondered why I was seeing him; at other times I would spend the day thinking about him, desperate to return home. The year after we met, when I was jobless and studying, made me realise how close we were, for none of the others — Chuck, Luís or Yuki — would have tolerated someone who had so little free money or time.

And it was Tom who cemented the relationship with his suggestion that we move out of London. With lack of imagination, I had been considering Putney and Fulham. The idea of living neighbourless in the country appealed, although the thought of a daily commute did not. Tom pointed out that it made little difference: I spent half my working life abroad and, with technology, most of the other half I could work at home. There would be disadvantages — rarer visits to the gym and cinema, fewer meals and drinks with friends — but with planning a decent social life could be maintained.

I had not expected the house-hunting to bring as much pleasure as it did. Weekend after weekend we threw snacks and a change of clothes into the car and set out to look at half a dozen properties within an hour's train ride of London. Tom's map-reading skills improved as I came to know the roadworks and traffic jams of the M25 as intimately as Shaftesbury Avenue or Piccadilly Circus. We drove for miles to discover that a charming eighteenth-century house faced a soul-destroying twentieth-century estate, or that 'requiring modernisation' meant 'requiring rebuilding'. We met elderly widows afraid of life, young couples divorcing and middle-aged couples hostile to two men so comfortable in each other's presence. Frequently too lazy to return home, we overnighted in the anonymity of a modern hotel or a cobwebbed room in a 'period' inn where floral curtains, a double bed, an oversized television and a trouser-press jostled for space in what had once been a scullery or laundry.

We had been together for almost two years, but those weekends brought us even closer together. I relaxed with Tom, looked forward to being with him — sitting in the car together, inspecting drains and cupboards, tracing our route through darkness, wind and rain. I understood emotionally what I had always known intellectually — that he was dependable and honest, that I had been lucky to find him. All the negative traits that I had once seen, the pessimism and undertones of hostility, faded with the realisation that I needed him as much as he needed me.

If I had had any remaining doubts, they would have come once we made an offer on the house. On the one hand I was having problems convincing a building society to give me a mortgage; on the other I had begun to travel again and found myself calling the solicitor and estate agent late at night from a hotel in Indonesia. Meanwhile Tom, aware of the significance of the expense and the move, was uncertain as to how much he was really involved. It was, after all, my money, but the home was to be ours. I only hesitated before making him joint owner because I did not trust myself. Tom, I knew, would stay with me for ever; I was not sure that I could stay with him. Yet if I was not ready to settle with Tom, I would never be ready to settle with anyone. I had to make him the gift of half the house; I had to make myself the promise to stay with him.

As I now have to make the promise to return.

* * *

Rosa is not here. El Magro deigned to tell me she had gone away. He claimed he did not know if she would return.

I wonder if her absence means something. Recently, it seemed, we had become tired with each other. She has come in less and while she has been here, we have hardly talked. I sat here writing or drawing, while she read a dog-eared edition of Mao that I glanced at and returned without interest. It seemed that we had come to the end of our communication. She had learnt all that she wanted to know, and I had given up trying to convince her to set me free.

But I need her. I need her to be here. I need her to talk to.

I need her to protect me.

How frightening that is. All that keeps me from harm is a woman six inches shorter and ten years younger than me, a woman who despises all that I am and all that I stand for.

* * *

I slept badly last night. I cannot concentrate. I cannot do anything except wait.

Perhaps I am over-reacting. I keep listening for creaks on the stair but have heard none except for the delivery of my morning meal. Perhaps she is coming back and they dare not touch me. Perhaps there is no thrill in raping for the second time a skinny gringo who trembles with fear.

* * *

Rosa has returned.
>Brian came to Cuzco and has already gone home.
>Rosa refused to meet him to negotiate my release.
>Tom is living with Guy.

* * *

"We did not meet," she said. "We were not ready and he would not wait."

"Wait for what?"

"Many things. We had to be sure it wasn't a trap. We had to have a clear understanding of what he was offering."

"I know Brian. It wasn't a trap." I spoke calmly, but inside I was shrieking. "Why didn't you try harder?"

She shrugged.

"Why do you need to meet him? Why can't you set me free anyway? I've told you before, blindfold me. Dump me miles from here. I can't identify you or this place. I don't know where I've been."

"The time is not right."

"The time for what? When will it be right? What do you want? What use am I to you?" I had to stop myself becoming hysterical.

"Gold is useless but one day you may need it." Another bland proverb.

"Tell me again what happened."

"Your colleague spent a few days in Lima. He met one of our contacts and came to Cuzco and wanted to meet us."

"Why didn't you meet him?"

"He had nothing to offer. All he said was he wanted to talk. It wouldn't be worth our time."

"What could he offer? Didn't you ask him?"

Another shrug. "The release of political prisoners. Fujimori's resignation."

"You won't get that."

"I know. But we wouldn't get our prisoners released either. For all your grand words, Demotica has no influence. Your colleague met only one minister, a formality. He should have met the US ambassador. He pulls all the strings." I thought of Brian in Lima, uncomfortable in his suit and bow tie, at the mercy of interpreters in a country he did not know. He was the wrong person to come, an old-fashioned radical with views that owed more to existential philosophy than guerrilla warfare. His contacts would be retired politicians, academics and trade unionists, all old men, old guard despised by Sendero. I felt my heart sink.

"Besides," Rosa went on, "Fujimori is not interested in you. He prefers to have two thousand *senderistas* in his prisons than release them in return for one interfering Englishman."

"Interfering Briton," I corrected her automatically. "So what happens now?"

"Now? Nothing. As before, we wait."

"For what? Orders from Gonzalo?"

She shrugged. I watched her in her usual position by the window, a small, round figure with an implacable small, round face.

"Tell me the truth," I said. "Do you think I will ever get out of here?"

"I don't know," she said after a moment. "Perhaps you are not very important."

"That's not what you said before. So let me go. You and the others can get back to more important things." Killing more generals.

"Releasing you for nothing would be an admission of failure, a step backwards."

"Then create a reason."

"What?"

"Let me take a message to the world from you."

"Every action we undertake is a message."

"The revolution is not going well, is it?"

She made no response, but I thought I could see resignation in her eyes.

"I'm in the way," I said. "I'm using up your time and resources. In the end they'll find me, and you'll be in danger. Just let me go." Again I heard and could not suppress the desperation in my voice. Again I sought the magic word, the irresistible tone or phrase that would have her give in, give me back my freedom. "You can't keep me forever. What will you do with me? Kill me?" My voice threatened to tremble out of control.

She looked at me. "We might have to." I searched for humour or insincerity in her eyes and saw none. Afraid, I did not know whether I should plead for my life or feign indifference.

"How?" I asked.

She shook her head in exasperation. There was a silence. I sought more details about Brian, how he had made contact, where he had stayed. Through a local journalist, at a hotel whose name I did not recognise; pointless questions that she answered absently.

After she had gone, I lay back, half in despair and half disgusted by my despair, convinced that with Brian's departure I had been dragged unwittingly across some Rubicon. Now I sit straining my eyes to write in a room that is as dark as my mood. Yet, despite my pessimism and the talk of death, I do not believe they will kill me. It seems more likely they will keep me here indefinitely, until the revolution is won; I will be a trophy, some kind of symbol, proof of the failure of the Western ideal.

* * *

Guy and Tom? I still cannot believe it. Tom would never fall for Guy. He never liked him, found him boring and unattractive. I was sure it was another Guy, someone Tom had met in London, but Rosa assured me it was indeed Guy Spesson. It is absurd, but so is everything else in this situation. And so I find myself accepting it.

She said the story, complete with photographs, was in all the Lima papers. Of course she refused to let me see a copy. I asked for details she could or would not give. Instead she wanted to know who Guy was. "A friend," I said, "an old friend."

"Not so much a friend," she commented.

In the end I asked her to leave. I wanted to be alone, to try to understand what was going on, but in the empty room I became more, not less, frantic. Images of Guy and Tom circled in my mind. My lover and my friend. My friend and my lover. Two people I trusted betraying me, laughing at me.

In the whirlpool of doubt I clutched at straws. They were living together but not lovers. Tom was still faithful but Guy was somehow using him or he was somehow using Guy. The newspapers were wrong; the photographs were a mistake. Eventually I calmed down, decided that some kind of friendship could emerge between Tom and Guy which did not reject me. Guy, after all, had been one of my closest friends. There must be other information that Rosa had withheld or had not known, something to explain this apparent affair. Tom might abandon me, seeking security wherever he might find it, but surely Guy is too honest to betray me.

* * *

I cannot stay calm. I imagine Tom with Guy, with someone else, a stranger, making love, and I am jealous, jealous, jealous. Not of the sex, but the emotion, the transfer of loyalty to someone else.

He is the anchor in my life, the only thing of value I have in the world. Now he has gone. He waited seventeen, eighteen months, then gave up. I am not sure if I blame him. We never promised each other a lifetime, never exchanged marriage vows. He mentioned it once and I shrugged it off; we shouldn't need to tie each other down, I said, idiot that I was. If we had made that vow, I know he would have kept it whatever happened.

Perhaps a Guy in the hand is worth more than an Andy five thousand miles away. Guy will keep him warm, Guy will provide the security he needs, Guy will come home to him every night and hold his hand and watch television with him; Guy will be there for him. And Andy will lie and rot on the other side of the world and Tom will not give a damn about him.

Brian goes home without trying. Doesn't leave the safety of his hotel room. Doesn't make the slightest effort to try to find me. Doesn't do a thing, not one fucking thing. "Difficult situation. Did what I could. Can't be helped. You understand. Life goes on." For him, perhaps, for everyone else except for me.

As for the British government, according to Rosa not a word. *Nihil facio* — I do nothing — is the Foreign Office motto, or *verbis bellis solum* — by fine words only. Forget McIllray. He's unreliable, a pervert; we can't trust Demotica. No need to sweat over him. Can't have amateurs getting above their station. It is the Lebanon all over again: "We're working behind the scenes," they said as year after year went by and still the hostages rotted as I am rotting now. They won't do anything. Heaven forbid that the United Kingdom should use what's left of its tattered prestige to help one of its subjects, especially a gay man held by a bunch of second-rate guerrillas in the middle of the Andes. This isn't the Falklands. This isn't an easy fight that they can pick and win.

* * *

I am dispensable, forgettable, like Rosa's peasants. So a few die from hunger or bombs; what does Sendero care as long as the revolution is won? What does Fujimori care as long as he remains in power? What do the traffickers care as long as they can fly out their heroin and cocaine? What does anyone care? Thousands starve or are killed in famines and wars; last year Angola, this year Afghanistan, next year who cares? People die, so fucking what. No one gives a damn about anyone else. Tom wants someone to keep his bed warm, so he gets it. Brian dislikes Peru so he goes home. No British commercial interests are served in Peru, so I get filed at the back of a drawer. No one wants me. No one gives a damn.

* * *

I recognised his face the minute he came in with my plate in his hand. My expression must have been one of stupor.

"*¿Qué tal, amigo?*" he asked with a smile that was almost pleasant. "Long time no see."

"Fernando."

"The same."

He stood over me, as he had stood over me day after day all those months ago. He appeared much stronger than I had remembered, while I was much weaker. He was free and I was still imprisoned. Above all, he must know what happened that night.

"What are you doing here?" I asked, in as strong a voice as possible.

"I've returned to be your *compañero*." The sarcasm was underlined with a smile.

"Where's Rosa?"

"Ah," he sighed. "*Pobrecito*, wants his mother. Don't worry. She's still here."

His mood alarmed me. "I don't want my mother," I said. "I want my freedom."

"What you want isn't important."

"I'm important enough to be kept here for a year and a half."

"Perhaps," he said, looking round the room as if to see if anything had changed. "How have you been?" he went on conversationally.

"What do you think? I haven't moved from this room in over a year. I haven't been able to move, I haven't been fed properly. I can't wash properly. A dog shouldn't be treated in this way."

"You look okay."

I wanted to say something withering but my Spanish failed me. "When are you going to release me?"

"When we're ready." He had moved to the window, stood watching me. He looked younger than I remembered; in his mid-thirties, thinner, slightly taller than El Gordo and much better dressed.

"How is the revolution? I haven't had much news. Gonzalo is still in his cage?"

"You seem to know a lot about Chairman Gonzalo."

"How would you know how much I know?"

"I hear things."

"I try to understand," I said. "What motivates you all. Why I'm here."

"And do you understand?" He took a match or toothpick from a pocket and began absently scraping one of his teeth.

I shrugged, the gesture borrowed from Rosa. "Probably more than you realise. Do you understand what motivates me?"

"We don't need to," he said, moving the pick to the other side of his mouth.

"You used to shout at me," I said after a moment's silence.

"Perhaps I'll shout at you again," he smiled. I imagined him suddenly angry and violent. If he were to attack me, there would be none of El Gordo's clumsiness.

"Are the others still here?"

"The others?"

"El Gordo and El Magro. Rubén and César."

He smiled at their nicknames. "They're still here. And what do you call me?"

I shook my head. "Nothing, yet."

"Rosa likes you," he said suddenly; I was not sure whether his voice carried comment or threat.

"We talk," I said. "I told you: I try to understand the revolution."

"There's no need."

"I might be able to help you."

He snorted. "How?" he asked, opening the window and tossing the toothpick outside.

"I could publicise your cause."

He smiled patronisingly. "By making a speech? By writing to the United Nations? And because of you, the world would rush to support us and Fujimori would fall? How influential you must be. Don't insult us. The revolution can only come from the people." Now he had started, he would not stop. "You are nothing. You don't mean anything. We could set you free tomorrow and it would not make any difference. Nothing you can do can help us or hinder us. You are irrelevant, a stupid gringo who has got caught up in something he does not understand. You could go back to England and preach the revolution as much as you liked and no one would listen to you. They would think we had brainwashed you. Certainly the proletariat would never believe you, because all you are is a pen-pusher who has never suffered, who has never understood in the depth of his heart why the revolution must come."

The old Fernando; the same words, the same thoughts, the same hostility as before. Only this time calmer, gesturing less. Sitting back against the wall, depressed at this return to the past, I stared at him, trying to show that his words had no impact. When he fell silent, I heard myself speak, all the arguments I had rehearsed over the past months. He was the one who did not understand, who could not see that the masses were not so monolithic that they would all support the Party without question. His revolution had failed, leaving the people poorer than before. There were alternatives — the rule of law and the ballot box were stronger and fairer than the bullet, poverty and corruption could be eradicated through other means.

He appeared to listen, but it was a knee-jerk response, and as I spoke I realised I believed his words more than my own. I faltered and my energy and my Spanish began to fail. When I had finished, he made no response other than to say I should eat before my food became cold. With that, he left the room and I stared at the congealed mess on my plate, wondering what his presence means, whether anything has changed.

* * *

I hardly slept. Late last night I heard noises on the stairs. The door opened and Fernando and El Gordo stood there in shadow as I cowered in the corner, trying to mask my fear. Fernando laughed as he said something in Quechua. They left and I waited all night for them to return. Only after dawn did I begin to sleep.

I had thought I was adjusted to this life, that I had kept my sanity and equilibrium. I was a fool. I cannot concentrate on anything, I cannot trust anyone. All I can think is three men outside hold my life in my hands and all efforts to set me free have failed.

I had imagined that if Rosa were here I would be safe. It is not true. I have no protection. I have nothing, I am nothing, simply a collection of bones and memories and fear.

* * *

A second night in which I was kept awake by anger and fever. As soon as I closed my eyes visions of Tom and Guy and Brian and Rosa and Fernando came to me. My head burst with the words they spoke which I could not hear and with the rage I could not express. The blankets trapped me. I kicked out at the figures that surrounded me and the weight of the chain woke me with its pain as it scraped more skin from my ankle. In my nightmare I even saw Gonzalo, his stupid, fat, bearded, bespectacled face ranting behind his bars. Rosa laughed at me. Tom had his arms round Guy as I shouted at them. Fernando grinned and Brian stood there, silent and unhearing.

Each time I opened my eyes the figures receded. I straightened the blankets, lay down carefully and calmly, closed my eyes and tried to meditate myself into sleep, but each time they returned and again and again I awoke sweating.

In the morning it was Fernando who brought me my food. He asked what I felt now that my *amigo* had left me. I shouted at him not to say another word; just to get out.

It's what they expect, a *maricón*, a hysterical screaming queen. It's what they'll get. I don't care any more.

* * *

A better night. In the morning again Fernando came in. "Here's more bread," he said, throwing me half a loaf. "You're too thin." Fattening the turkey for the slaughter. He added something in Quechua that I did not understand. "Don't worry about the other night," he said in Spanish, "I'm not going to touch you."

"I would kill you if you did."

He laughed. "How?"

I had no reply.

"When are you going to release me?" I asked, hoping for the answer that Rosa could not give.

"Perhaps tomorrow. Perhaps never."

"What do you need to set me free?"

"Nothing," he said, "or everything." I gave up the game.

"You don't like me," I said.

"You're gringo, *maricón*."

"I'm human." Another snort and then he left.

My last defence. I am human. Empathise with me, protect me, because I am human, because like you I think and feel, I love and laugh, I fear and cry. Destroy me and you destroy a part of yourself.

Except it is no defence. I am human and therefore I am your enemy. I stand in the way of what you want. I represent all that you hate. I am human and so I must be destroyed.

I am human and so I am nothing, nothing at all.

* * *

Hell, I wrote the other day. Hell is where I and hundreds of millions live.

Sometimes hell is only in the eye of the beholder. The small children laughing as they play on landfills are unaware of their poverty. A couple living in a mud hut with nothing but a change of clothes can be more content with life than I have ever been. But that is not the point. Hundreds of millions suffer and see no end to their suffering. They suffer because they are starving, because they are old or sick, because they are African in a white man's world, *andeanos* in Peru, Muslims in Serbian Bosnia. They suffer because they live in a world where the pleasure of the rich is of greater import than the pain of the poor. They suffer because others let them suffer, because as individuals we spend money on the toys of new cars and stereos and as nations we spend it on the toys of mortars and bombs.

I tried to stop it. In my own little way I tried to redress the balance. An education project here, a conference there. I should have laughed at myself: Sisyphus barely able to push the stone, Canute with the waves up to his ankles.

I wanted to haul others up to my level. I wanted to throw them a lifeline so they could pull themselves out of the mire. Instead the line jerked and I toppled in, became one of the people I had spent my life trying to save.

* * *

I have not written for several days. There seemed no point. The routine continues of Fernando, Rosa and Rubén — El Gordo — bringing my food. El Magro, it appears, has gone. Sometimes I have even received a second meal, of bread and soup, in the afternoon. Rosa said that they were cooking more. I suspect Fernando was as dissatisfied as me with the food we were getting.

Rosa comes in less often. She sits by the window as always, but we seldom talk. Fernando looks in every day. I suspect he wants to rant at me as before, but I do not give him the opportunity. I acknowledge his presence, then sit silently drawing, inviting neither discussion nor disapproval. Soon he leaves, and I am happy to be left alone.

I am creating my own world of imaginary landscapes and grotesque faces, swiftly running out of notebooks and pencils. Rosa says she will get more. I complain about the light and the fact that the view never changes, but I know that they will never move me. So I make do.

* * *

I do not know what the relationship between the three of them is. In this room they always appear separately, Rubén the taciturn jailer and Rosa the good cop to Fernando's bad. I suspect that Fernando is of higher rank but when I tried to determine his position in the organisation, it merely gave him the excuse for another of his diatribes. Nevertheless I am sure he is the reason that Rosa comes in less frequently. Either he forbade her being too friendly or she decided that she had gone too far. I ought to miss our discussions, but they are becoming as distant to me as my life before I was brought here.

I frequently hear the two of them, and occasionally Rubén, talking outside. They always speak Quechua, with the occasional Spanish word. It sounds as if they are discussing policy or strategy, each trying to convince the other of a decision they have to make. It has to be me they are discussing, but I listen in vain for my name or Demotica or *inglés*. Of course, I could be wrong, so different is the intonation of other languages. Fernando could be wooing Rosa or they might be discussing the best land on which to rear vicuña or whether it will be cold tomorrow. Sometimes I ask what they talk about but "nothing important" is always the answer.

* * *

This morning I watched the sunrise on the mountains opposite. I have seen it hundreds of times before, the pink light on the grey rock and white snow, and the dark blue of the sky gradually dissolving, yet today it was very different, majestic and somehow empty. It made me a child again, a child who finds the world mystery and promise.

All day I have felt strange, as if, as the cliché has it, it were truly the first day of the rest of my life. Rosa was here but has left, respecting my silence. Rubén brought food which, for once, I did not eat. Later he brought a bucket for me to wash in and I sponged myself carefully with one of the filthy t-shirts I once celebrated as clean and new. In the middle of the day, when the light was at its strongest, I picked up these notebooks and read entries at random. What comes across is a weak, whining personality, obsessed with myself, my past, my opinions. Not someone I would be happy to know. Now I lie here, half-aware of the shadows in the room and the voices in the yard, wondering who I am, who I will be if I ever leave here.

* * *

If I had not ended up here, how long would it have taken me to realise the futility of my work? Would I have carried on until retirement or death, convinced by my own momentum that I was achieving something, bringing the world food, wealth and happiness? The truth is, twenty years on, children still defecate in the streets, fourteen-year-old girls still sell themselves, families still starve. Whatever success I might claim should be weighed against a hundred failures. Even the successes are meaningless. I can claim no credit for greater democracy any more than priests who chant each dawn can claim responsibility for the sun rising. Other forces were always at work and any changes that took place while I was active were merely a coincidence.

Perhaps the disillusion is inevitable. Every young man and woman believes that the world is gradually improving, that our technological advances are dragging us out of the primaeval slime. In my twenties it seemed certain that we had the resources to feed the world, negotiation was better than conflagration and the petty conflicts around the globe would eventually end. It took me another twenty years to learn that feeding the world depends not on the availability of resources, but on the will to distribute them, to learn that violence is so deeply rooted in the human psyche that wars will never end.

We kid ourselves if we think we care for those who live across oceans or national boundaries. Altruism is illogical. As Rosa and Fernando know, but I was too blind to see, you can only make a stand on your own ground; you can only defend yourselves. My liberal, middle-class, multicultural European viewpoint, all my theorising, every conference paper I drafted, every speech I wrote, everything was irrelevant idealism, whistling against the wind. I not only failed to save the world, I failed to save myself.

* * *

Rosa once told me about an ambush. An army vehicle blown up somewhere, a dozen killed. Thinking about it again I realised I had no reaction. I no longer objected to the loss of lives; I no longer had compassion for the families of those who died. The bodies and blood were unfortunate but of no greater importance than a pawn lost in chess.

It does not matter if a few die for the sake of the many. It would not matter to others if I died. Only the blinkered and pampered Westerner insists that life is precious, pretends that it can be protected by medicine or law. Since the dawn of history human beings have been dying unpleasantly before their time.

The life of a politician or general is no more sacrosanct than that of a farmer or market trader. Indeed, it is worth less because the politician and general know what they do, the suffering they cause. They may blind themselves and others with ideology, but the state they support is the state that starves and kills. It is politicians and generals who agree to economic policies that cripple the nation and its people, to military policies that kill and maim. Nor is there reason to fret over teenage conscripts who die. They had a choice; a difficult one, perhaps, but nevertheless a choice. They chose their own welfare over that of their people. It was a gamble which they lost.

I could not endure a lifetime chained to the land, mired in poverty, at the mercy of men in Lima and Washington; nor do I have the right to insist that others live that way. I would laugh at any foreigner who wagged his finger and told me to place my faith in democracy, in abstract institutions. In another country I might come to a different conclusion, but I am in Peru, on the Altiplano, and here the picture is simple. I would take up arms and fight.

* * *

For the first time in months Rosa picked up a couple of notebooks and glanced through them. Seeing her name, she asked what I had written. It was the time she had told me about her teaching. She asked me to translate it. When I stopped, she asked how much of each day I wrote down. I said it depended on the mood I was in.

"And this?" she asked, pointing to another page.

"Something that happened to me in Africa."

"Tell me."

I told her about the bus, the boy and the tin can.

"Is that what brought you here?"

"It's part of it. I've told you it all. There's nothing new."

"Your life story. What do think you've achieved?"

"In Peru, nothing. Elsewhere? I'm not sure. Family planning and education projects here and there. Voter registration drives, judicial protection, wider debate, less corruption."

As I was talking, Fernando came in. "Again?" he said. "Will you never give up?"

Rosa said it was she who had asked the question. He half-listened as he dropped to the floor and sat back against the wall opposite me, radiating energy across the room. "Gringo," he said, "I'm tired of all this."

"Surprisingly," I said, "so am I."

"You don't understand. I'm tired of rationale and explanations. Not only from you, from everyone. I want action. I want to take Lima, perhaps this year, no later than next. Nobody believes it, but we're strong enough to do so; the whole rotten structure is ready to fall. I want to execute Fujimori and all his gang, line up the generals and shoot them one by one. I've had enough wasting time with a bomb here, an assassination there. We have to take power, sooner not later."

"So?"

"So you're a cockroach in our path, and we've all stopped in case we trip over you. We're standing around debating what to do with you. Why shouldn't we just stamp on you and carry on?"

It was only later that I began to feel afraid. At that moment, my fear was buried under the vigour of debate. "I'm the only thing between you and Lima?" I asked. "Come on. I'm stopping the three of you doing anything, perhaps, but that's all. Let me go and the problem's solved."

I looked at Rosa, but she was looking out of the window. I turned back to Fernando concentrating on the dirt he was cleaning from under his fingernails.

"That would be pointless," he said. "We have to use you."

"I've already told Rosa. I can do something for you."

"'Publicise our cause'?" He looked up with a mocking smile. "How naive do you think we are?"

"I don't," I said. "I'm saying it because I agree with you."

"You agree with the revolution? The armed struggle?" His eyebrows were raised. Rosa's expression had not changed.

"I would do the same in your position," I said. Another Rubicon.

"Do what?"

"Take up arms."

"You, a *maricón*? You'd be too scared."

"It has nothing to do with being *maricón*," my voice rose in anger. "Can't you get that into your head?"

"He's right," Rosa suddenly said. Fernando snorted.

Let's get back to the point," I said. "I don't believe the revolution is at hand. I think you've failed and don't know what to do next." Fernando said nothing but glared; Rosa looked at me almost in sympathy. "But whatever the situation is, I have been telling Rosa for months that keeping me is a waste of time and resources. We can work out some statement that will keep everyone happy. You're releasing me for reasons of compassion, I am fully converted to your cause, the revolution is so far advanced that your strategy has changed. Something like that. Anything."

"You'd take up arms?" Fernando returned to my earlier point. "And your principles? The ballot box and the rule of law? Justice through democracy? Flexibility seems to be your strongest principle." I welcomed his sarcasm; it was somehow hopeful.

"Can't people change their minds?" I asked. "I didn't have the background you have. I had a nice easy life. Perhaps if I'd been Andean I would have thought like you much sooner."

"You're just frightened. You're saying whatever comes into your head just to please us."

"That's not true."

"He's offered to support us before," Rosa said.

"For the same reasons." Fernando leapt up, brushed the dust off his jeans.

"Listen," I said. "You might be right. I could be saying anything in the hope you'd set me free. But so what? It doesn't matter what I say or think. You said yourself I was in your way. Just let me go, then you can be free to go on with the revolution and I'll return to London and that's the end of it."

"Are you crazy? Whatever you say, if we let you go here, the military will be after us. You'll help them find this house, you'll describe us to them. If they don't find us, other comrades will get arrested and killed in retaliation. You aren't going to keep quiet; even if you wanted to, they'd persuade you to talk sooner or later. For revenge, for democracy, for your *amigo*. Whatever you say now, you'll end up betraying us one way or another."

"How can I? I don't know where I am, I don't know who you are. I can't identify you."

"There are only two ways you'll leave here," he went on. "In a coffin, or as part of a deal with someone we can trust. And so far there has been no deal. Fujimori won't talk to us, your government won't talk to us, and your colleague flew off home before we could meet. And nothing you've said has been of the slightest interest."

There was an emptiness in the pit of my stomach. Fernando stood at the window. Rosa sat watching me without emotion.

"What do you think?" I asked her.

"Me? Fernando's right. We have to make use of you somehow."

There was a pause. "So what was the point of these notebooks? Why did you ask for my 'confession'?"

She shrugged. "I thought it would help you pass the time. I was curious. I thought I might learn something. Then I saw you wouldn't write in Spanish and I couldn't read your English."

"You didn't bloody ask me to write in Spanish!"

"It doesn't matter."

"And if I give you something in Spanish now?"

She dismissed the idea with another shrug.

"What are you talking about?" Fernando turned from the window.

"When Rosa first came here, she asked me to make a confession of my 'crimes'. She wanted to know what motivated me, what brought me here."

"And that's what you write in this notebooks." He picked one up, glanced through it and let it fall. "A waste of time," he said.

"You once talked about a trial," I said. "This could be your evidence. The Chinese use such 'confessions' in their re-education."

"It's too late for a trial."

I raised my voice. "Don't you understand that what I want and what you want are so very similar?"

"I don't care," he said. "I don't give a damn what you think or why you do what you do."

"But you care, Rosa?" I turned to her, a sister, a protector.
She gave a half-nod.

"And you believe that a person can change, that I could actually agree with some of your aims?"

The same gesture.

"Well, doesn't that mean that I am right? That logic and the revolution demand you release me, let me help you?"

Fernando snorted. Rosa kept staring at me. I kept talking, but nothing I could say would make either of them grasp the importance of the question, the reality that my freedom, my life was at stake.

Fernando said something in Quechua. I asked for a translation but was given none. Rosa stood up and together they left the room. "Hey," I said, "let's finish this discussion. Let's get somewhere for a change," but all I heard was the sound of their steps on the stairs and frustration bouncing between the walls of my mind.

* * *

I do not know what to believe about Tom, whether he has indeed left me. Torn between the warmth of memories and cold suspicion, I no longer know what I feel.

Sometimes I think that if he has abandoned me, he has freed me. He has released me from the obligation to return to a past where I fear I no longer belong. I would have walked into the house and found the kitchen warm, the lights on, Tom, Sheba and the cats where they had always been. It should have been welcome, yet it would have made me uncomfortable; the Andrew McIllray who returned home would be very different from the one who had left. The foundations of his life destroyed, he would no longer be sure of who he was, what he wanted, why he was there. With no Tom, I would have no obligations. I would truly have a new beginning.

I am fooling myself. I desperately want Tom to be there. He is too much a part of me for me to be able to abandon him so easily. I have to see him, I have to talk to him, I have to return to him, even if after a year or two we go our own ways.

I feel so empty. I feel so lonely. I want to cry and can't because there is no point. I want Tom with me, his arms around me. I want him to hold me and tell me everything is all right, it was a mistake, a nightmare that's over, I'm home again, I'm with him, we'll never leave each other again.

* * *

Perhaps this story of Tom and Guy is poetic justice. I am sure Tom was faithful all the time we were together, while I had pick-ups every time I left the country. Yet they were never more than brief affairs, perks of the job, like duty-free drinks and hotel swimming-pools. I sometimes pretended they helped me understand the local culture, although cheap bars, camp gestures and sexual drive are the same, whatever the local language and customs.

They were never lovers; they never replaced Tom. I never told him, because I did not think he would understand. All he needed to know was that each time I left home I was returning to him. Wherever I was, I called him, sent him postcards, bought him souvenirs.

I keep telling myself that this story with Guy is the same, some innocent remark that the newspapers have picked up. If Tom knew about it, he would deny it, and of course the newspapers wouldn't bother to reprint it.

Four years together, the house, the fact that I love him; he can't have thrown all that away.

* * *

As I accept that my life is beyond my control, my moods swing from tranquil acceptance to deep despair.

I have been looking back over the last twenty years in search of moments to celebrate. Ten years ago, sailing with Alan and Daniel in Chesapeake Bay, lying in the sunshine next to a twinkie in Speedos and a suntan as we skimmed across the water with no destination or timetable. Relaxed with Sarah and Leonora in Dakar overlooking the ocean and, years later, with half a dozen friends in a similar restaurant outside Madras, the food, the open air, the intelligent conversation. The wit and confidence of the second and third drink in any of a hundred bars. The joy of sex when the awe was still greater than the dryness of the technique.

And yes, at times I have achieved something. In Diamantino the girls learnt, their fluency and knowledge improved. Through World Aid I helped women learn to read, children go to school, adolescents keep healthy. Through Demotica I produced papers and organised conferences which caused governments to change their policy.

Much rarer has been a sense of peace. That first visit to Greece, on the top of a hill on some island, lying with my eyes closed in the afternoon sun and a light breeze. The present dissolved into an eternity where the world and its problems disappeared and my consciousness was dissolving in the wind. Years later, in Thailand, in some temple in Chiang Mai, miraculously empty of tourists and keepers, I walked slowly round, drawn back again and again to the central statue of the Buddha, so smooth that his face was almost featureless. In the garish yellow paint, the black pencilled features and red dot on the forehead, I glimpsed all the wisdom and knowledge that he represented. And there was always peace at home with Tom on long Sunday afternoons.

Now it is all memory. My life is reduced to this room, to filth and discomfort and cold, to obsessions with food, my health and my cleanliness. I listen for each sound, magnify its significance into impending humiliation, pain or death. I sleep uneasily. I eat greedily and excrete in discomfort. I exercise as stubbornly and pointlessly as an animal in a cage. I wait and wait and feel myself disintegrate.

* * *

Another night of vivid and unsettled dreams. I opened my eyes uncertain where I was but convinced I was free, only to be confused by the weight round my ankle and the same lifeless view of the window set into the darkness of the wall.

God knows what I will do if I ever get out of here. I could not return to Demotica as if nothing had happened or move into the UN system as I had once thought. The political route has gone. There will be the book, I suppose, a round of television and magazine interviews, before I descend into oblivion.

Irony of ironies; the book will make me money, while Rosa and Fernando and Rubén remain as poor as before.

My imagination is running away with me. Freedom, home, fame and fortune. All I can be sure of is the here and now, the candle flickering in the wind.

* * *

Today I told Rosa I wanted to walk out of here. She shrugged, thinking I was referring to my freedom. I meant something simpler, just to look round this house, to sit in the sun, to walk a little down the road.

"I don't mean return to London," I went on. "I just want a few hours outside in the sunshine."

"I don't think Fernando would permit it."

"Fuck Fernando."

She smiled.

"I'm not your enemy," I said.

"Perhaps not."

But he who is not with us... "I want to help you."

"You've said that before."

"I mean it still."

"This is not your struggle." She was beginning to lose patience.

"I can make it mine." I tried once more to explain my thoughts: the recognition that in twenty years I had attempted too much and achieved too little, that it was time for me to narrow my sights, to reject the abstract and to make a stand.

"What would you do?" she finally asked.

I imagined myself blowing up bridges, mining roads, assassinating generals, and recognised it as a fantasy; I had neither the courage nor conviction to kill. I tried to see myself — a fair-haired, blue-eyed foreigner with pedantic Spanish — organising strike committees in a shanty-town and knew that I would never receive the respect such work needed. "I don't know," I admitted.

"Your only use to us is as a hostage."

"You keep saying that," I said. "So use me, but don't leave me here."

"If your colleague had stayed..." She fell silent.

I wondered what she was thinking, whether my continuing rejection of the principles that had brought me here had gained her contempt or respect. I wanted to keep talking, but months of talking have got me nowhere, so in the end I said nothing, for there was nothing more to say.

* * *

"So you still want to be a *senderista*." Fernando mocked.

"Why not? I've been trying to tell you for days that people can change."

He did not respond.

"Listen to me," I said. "I'll prove I mean what I say."

He shook himself as if suddenly waking. "We've listened enough. We've heard first an apologist, then a class traitor. Tomorrow, what will you be?"

"What can I do to make you believe me?"

"It doesn't matter whether or not I believe you. There is no place for you in the revolution." He fell silent as he paced the room. "What," he asked, stopping by the window, "what if we told you that the greatest service you could do for the revolution was to die?"

His voice was cold, quiet, serious. I hesitated. "There must be other ways."

He laughed and shook his head. "I knew it," he said. "You will never be a revolutionary. Every action we undertake we are prepared for death."

"You don't understand," I said, trying to keep the desperation from my voice. "I want to help."

"You want to save your skin."

"Of course. But I can do more than that."

"What can you do?"

"Translate, write."

"Do you think you are the only person who can do that? Everything Chairman Gonzalo has written has been translated into a dozen languages. And what can you write? What do you know? It's all been said before."

"So let me go."

"Do you know any other song?" he asked. "That one is driving us crazy. Listen, gringo, stop worrying. Stop thinking. You can't do anything. We're in charge and we'll come to a decision. Something will happen soon."

"What?"

"Something."

"But.."

"No buts. No more words. Just silence, okay?"

"But..."

"I SAID SILENCE!" The anger exploded from nothing. His arm was raised and I flinched. When I looked up, he had gone.

* * *

Day after day after day. Rubén brings me my food, takes away my bucket. The others do not appear. I shouted at them in the yard yesterday. There was sudden silence. I thought for a moment Fernando might come up, half in curiosity and half in anger, but no one moved. Eventually they started talking again.

I do not know what to do, I do not know what to say. I stare at my chain and recognise that I am, quite literally, at the end of my tether.

This room is driving me mad. Its dark walls and ceiling, its emptiness, its cold, its window, its mattress. It never changes. Nothing ever ever ever changes.

I stink. I am filthy and thin and weak and stink. My ankle is bleeding again; it is covered in blood and dirt. I took off my t-shirt to wipe it, but it still looks just the same. It hurts like hell. I have a pain in my teeth and an itch in my groin; the skin is even rawer where I have rubbed it. I can understand animals caught in traps that gnaw off their own legs in order to be free.

I have had enough, enough, enough.

* * *

I call for Rosa but she does not appear. I even called for Fernando but he did not respond. They have abandoned me in this stinking cell.

I threw my plate at Rubén. The food fell all over the floor. A lump of meat and dirty rice. I could not reach it. I had to use my shirt as a lasso, dragging the meat across the dirt on the floor. I tried to clean it but it was covered with filth and I couldn't eat it.

I thought Rosa understood. I thought she was willing to help. I was wrong. I am never going to get out of here.

* * *

I think of living with Tom, growing old with him. I think of his concern, his love. I think of his snore, the warmth of his body, his arm around me in bed.

Tall, dark curly hair, a square handsome face, an expression of concentration, slight concern. A body whose thinness was giving way to age. Rough skin, hairy legs, a faint smell of sweat.

Making love.

The last time I saw him. It was just another departure, getting up early, driving to Reading. I can't remember what he was wearing, what mood he was in, whether he had already eaten or shaved.

A quick kiss in the car by the bus stand, I dragged my bag out and walked away. I didn't even watch him drive off. Perhaps he waved; I suspect he did, every time.

His voice the last time I called, happy to hear from me and happy to talk. Nine o'clock in the morning in Lima, after lunch. Neither had any news. He was tidying the house, wondering whether to visit Anne and George. I told him what I had been doing, who I had met. I'll try and phone from Cuzco, I said, and never did.

Perhaps I did not deserve him. Perhaps I assumed too much, assumed he would always be there. If I had told him more often that I loved him, if I had shown him how much he meant to me, he would not have left me.

I love you, Tom.

* * *

I have been thinking about my 'confession'. Perhaps it will work if I write it again and think more carefully about what it should say. Fernando might be impressed. If nothing else, it will pass the time.

Confiso que
I confess that
I confess

* * *

"How much are you worth, gringo?" I don't know whether he is serious or joking.

III
Tom: Lima and Cuzco

Sunday 5th. I'm sitting in the dining-room at half-past eight in the morning. Jack's gone to make some phone calls. This is the most expensive hotel I have ever stayed in. There is an enormous buffet of fruit and cereal and every type of cooked breakfast. Every so often the waiter comes up and offers me coffee. So is this how you live when you leave home? No wonder you like to travel. We're here. In Lima. We arrived at midnight, five in the morning London time. I thought I would be exhausted, but I was wide awake. I kept thinking I was coming closer to you. The airport was small and grotty, nothing like Heathrow, full of Germans with backpacks and soldiers standing around with guns. They're all small, the Peruvians, got big faces like Red Indians. I thought we'd have problems when they saw my passport, but nothing happened. Obviously I'm not as famous as I thought. There was a car to drive us to the hotel. It was miles away. Jack tried talking to the driver, but he didn't speak English. I just looked out of the window. Dark broad streets with houses and trees. But you know all this. You've been here before.

* * *

Sunday evening. We spent all day meeting people. First Jose Maria and Renata. He's Jack's contact, a 'stringer' for some paper in the States; she's our interpreter. He's about forty, loud, speaks with a terrible American accent. She's about thirty, dresses very fashionably, made Jack and me both look tacky. Mind you, everyone here in the hotel dresses better than I do. Jack told them he wanted to contact Shining Path for a story he was writing. He said I was his cousin here for a holiday. I don't know if they believed him. Jose Maria wasn't very optimistic about getting in touch with the guerrillas. He said it's no longer fashionable to support them. Some fashion! The only activists who aren't in prison are in hiding in the countryside. Either that or pretending they were never involved.

He gave Jack a list of people he'd contacted. After he'd gone, we got on the phone, or Renata did, and started calling all these lawyers and politicians and writers. Some of them we're meeting tomorrow, some weren't there or wouldn't talk. Four of them came over today. Everyone was very formal, shaking hands and being very polite, and I sat there like a dummy while Renata translated Jack's questions. They all understood some English but didn't speak it very well, so at times all three of them were talking at once, trying to understand what each other was saying.

They all denied having any connection with Shining Path but they all claimed to know someone else who did. They'd ask a few questions and get back to us. A couple gave us phone numbers we already had. Of course they'd heard about you, but they had no idea where you were or whether you were still alive. Some rumours said you were and others said you weren't. It was like they didn't care. I sat there listening to it all, getting uptight and almost giving the game away, but I stopped myself in time.

The last one left about five. Renata went off shortly afterwards. That left the two of us sitting in the bar, where we'd been most of the day. Jack was cheerful; I was depressed. We didn't seem to have got anywhere. Jack said it was early days, these things take time. "You've got to get to know people. They've got to get to know you. Then they'll tell you what they know. It'll all work out, I swear." I hope he's right.

I'm exhausted. My hand's tired from writing so much. I miss the computer. I miss you.

But I'm nearer you now than I've been for a year and a half. And if I've come this far, I can only keep going. We'll find you, lover. Just hang in there.

* * *

Monday evening. We've been all over Lima, Renata, Jack and me, in these Beetle taxis. It's a strange city, all flat and spread out. There's all the traffic and pollution and noise and coloured tin buses rushing by. They even have VW campers as minibuses. We went from one office to the next, first a Victorian building in the centre, then a two-storey concrete block over a pizzeria in the suburbs. The first guy was a lawyer about your age, long thick hair and moustache. He kept trying to impress us with his English, which was awful, and got annoyed with Renata when she tried to correct him. He'd represented some of the guerrillas at a trial, but had no contact with anyone still free. I thought about going to see some of them in prison, but that was out. They wouldn't talk, not with the police listening to every word. "They're idealists," he said, "even with their revolution falling apart. They won't say anything to betray their comrades." "But don't you know where their comrades are?" Jack kept asking. "No, they come to me. I cannot go to them." He's lying, Jack said when we left, but there's no way we can prove it.

The rest were just the same. There was a journalist who'd interviewed their leader in the 1980s. He seemed to expect us to help him track the guerrillas down rather than the opposite.

We met Jose Maria again at the end of the day. He'd been doing a bit of research on his own. He'd found out who I was and guessed why we were here. He promised not to tell anyone, but he still couldn't help. Even Jack seemed down at the end of the day. "Taking time, isn't it?" he said. "Not like England." He told me he'd tracked me down in a day. He had taken a fancy to your story and gone to Demotica and started talking to the new receptionist. He'd said he was doing a story on all sorts of charities, and wasn't Demotica the one with the hostage? Oh yes, she said, she'd heard all about you. Jack asked what kind of guy you were and in five minutes she'd told him you were gay. Half an hour later he'd gone through every telephone book in the country and found your name. A quick check of the voters' list gave him my name and there was his story.

I almost like the guy now. I still think what he did was wrong, but no real harm came of it, I suppose. Besides, he brought me here. He's trying harder than anyone else has to get you back. I need him. You need him too. If the price of your freedom is your pretty blue eyes on the front page of the *Sun*, it's worth it.

* * *

Tuesday. We're getting somewhere! Jack had a phone call from some guy who wouldn't give his name. If he wanted information on Shining Path, he had to come to a certain address alone. No Renata.

"Could be a trap," Jack said, making fun of it. "You coming along?" I thought of Terry Waite again, then I thought they might take one new hostage, but two would be too much trouble. So we left a message for Renata and got a cab. It drove for almost an hour and ended up miles from the centre, some kind of suburb of one-storey terraced housing, except some of them were shops, some were workshops and only a few were houses. The address Jack had was a bar. Everyone stared at us when we got out of the cab. We stuck out like sore thumbs. I'm taller than most Peruvians while Jack looks half like a brickie, half like a politician and one hundred percent British. "Watch your wallet," he whispered to me. I felt in my back pocket to check it was still there. Of course that was stupid, showing everyone who was watching where I kept my money.

This guy came out of the bar and walked up to us. Quite tall, bearded, heavily built, in his thirties. He knew Jack's name. He wanted to know who I was. Jack said I was a colleague, Philip Jenkins. Mario, the man said. His English was not bad. He took us round the corner to where a car and driver were waiting and told us to get in. "Where are you taking us?" Jack asked. Mario smiled and shook his head. "You get in?" he asked. Jack looked at me. "Sure," he said. All the time I was thinking, maybe this guy's got nothing to do with Shining Path; he's going to rob and murder us. But we had to take the risk, in case he could lead us to you.

We must have driven for another half an hour, and I'm sure we doubled back on ourselves more than once. Jack tried asking a few questions, but Mario just said, "Later, later." At last we got out in some slum even worse than one we'd just left, full of dirty kids with torn shirts and no shoes. They crowded round us but Mario pushed them away. My arse kept twitching as I thought about my wallet but no one laid a hand on it.

We ended up in this room in a scruffy house overlooking a courtyard. There was a table and some chairs and piles of old books and newspapers on the shelves and along the wall. It looked like Communist Party stuff; the covers of some of the books had pictures of Marx or Lenin. There were a couple of others already there, same age as Mario, dressed as casually as me. Jack held out his hand and introduced us. They didn't take it and didn't give us their names. It turned out neither of them spoke English.

"Well, now you've got us here," Jack said when we'd sat down, "tell us what you know."

"About what?" Mario asked.

"About Shining Path."

"What makes you think we know anything about Shining Path?"

"You called, didn't you? It's pretty obvious, isn't it?"

"What do you want to know?"

"How it's going. The revolution."

"It is going."

It went on like that for about quarter of an hour, like trying to pull teeth. Jack wanted to know how many guerrillas there were, where they were strongest, who was in charge since their leader was in jail, whether they thought they'd lost support. I must admit he seemed to know his stuff. All the time Mario kept giving him non-answers. Sometimes he'd talk to one of the others but they didn't give us any more information. I just sat there looking round, staring out of the window or at the books on the wall.

Then Jack asked if there was any possibility of something to drink, like a cup of tea. Mario spoke to one of the others, who left the room. He and the other Peruvian exchanged a few words, then he suddenly turned to me. "Give me your passport," he said. "Why?" I asked. "I want to see it." "I left it in the hotel in case it got stolen." He shook his head. "Give me your passport." "I don't have it." "Here's mine," Jack said, pulling it out. "I want to see his." "Why?" "To see his name." "Philip Jenkins," Jack said. Mario shook his head. "Tom Dayton," he said, pronouncing the name funny. "Who's he?" I asked, feeling my face going red. "You're Tom Dayton," he repeated.

"What if he is?" asked Jack.

"It explains why you're here."

Mario turned back to the other guy. Jack looked at me with a big grin on his face. Then the third guy came back in with the tea. It was awful, lukewarm and no taste. I didn't really pay attention to it. I kept thinking, they know about me; that means they know about you, you must be alive. I wanted to ask all these questions, but the three of them were talking and Jack whispered me to wait.

When they turned back, Mario said to both of us, "Let's start again." Jack said that yes I was Tom Dayton. We were in Peru to negotiate your release. We wanted to meet the people responsible for holding you. If it wasn't Mario, could he put us in touch with whoever it was. Prompted by the others, Mario asked a whole lot of questions; who did Jack work for, who he knew in the British and Peruvian governments, who had authorised the trip. It took him a long time to believe that only the two of us and a couple of others at the *Sun* knew about it. Then he said it would take a couple of weeks to get in touch with those responsible for you. Jack shook his head and said that wasn't on.

There was another pause while the three of them talked together. I was getting excited because we were getting somewhere, and mad because these were the people who'd kept us apart for so long. They were just sitting there talking like it was nothing to do with them or it was just a business deal that we could take or leave.

"If we could contact these people," Mario turned back to us, "what would we say?"

"Tell them we want them to release Andy. We will pay a fee, or a ransom."

"How much?" Mario asked.

"I don't have a figure in mind."

"How much?" he repeated.

"Ten thousand pounds. Fift.. twenty thousand dollars."

Mario laughed. "I do not think they would be interested."

"How much would interest them?"

"A million dollars, perhaps." My heart sank.

"Where would we get that kind of money from?"

"That is not my problem. Your newspaper, your government."

"Let us think about it." Jack said. Mario shrugged. "And we want proof that he's still alive."

"I don't know about that," Mario said.

"Is he alive?" I suddenly shouted, fed up with keeping quiet.

"Maybe."

Jack put out his hand to stop me getting even more mad. "It's okay," he said. "We wouldn't be here if he wasn't. What do we do now?" he went on.

Mario spoke to the others. "First give us some money. A thousand dollars."

"What for?"

"Our expenses. Proof that you are serious."

"Then what?"

"Then we call you in a couple of days if we have any information."

"And if you don't, I get my money back?"

Mario smiled but did not reply.

"How do we know you are not just taking our money and you won't do anything?" I asked. "How do we know Andy's still alive?"

"You trust us," he said.

"I don't," I said, but again Jack made me keep quiet.

"We don't have the money with us," he said. "I have to get it from the hotel. Do you want to come back with me?"

Mario turned to the others. One of them, a short, overweight guy with a permanent frown, didn't look happy. As they talked I asked Jack if he trusted them. He said we had no choice. I was worried by the million dollars, but he said that was just their opening price. Then I heard them mention your name a couple of times. That's when it hit me that you were still alive, that I was going to see you again, that everything was going to be all right. I wanted to leap up and down and shout, stop all this talk, just take him to me now.

At last Mario turned back to us. "I will come with you for the money," he said. "Someone else will contact you in two or three days." "Who?" Jack asked. "I don't know." "How do we contact you?" "You don't." "Give us proof that he's still alive?" I asked. Mario shook his head. One of the others, the one with glasses, looked at me with a cold expression and said something. Mario translated. "You're his lover?" "Yes," I said. He carried on looking at me as if I was some kind of strange animal. "Is there a problem?" I asked. Mario was about to translate, but Jack gestured him to drop it. "That's irrelevant," he said, "all we're talking about is getting Andy free." It kind of worried me, that look, because I felt scared for you, surrounded by these men who didn't give a damn about you. I'm sure they wouldn't care one way or another whether you lived or whether you died.

* * *

Wednesday. Sitting by the pool. There's nothing else to do but wait. Mario came back with us yesterday and waited in a taxi outside until Jack brought him the money. Jack's off in town today seeing more contacts. He doesn't think they'll give us any more than what we've already got, but it does no harm to keep trying. I'm staying here in case Mario's friend tries to contact us.

I am so nervous. I'm frightened something will go wrong. I'm worried in case Mario's lying and you're not alive or they're nothing to do with Shining Path. They just want the money and they'll keep coming up with stories about what they have to do to put us in touch with the people holding you, and we'll keep handing over hundred-dollar bills and get nowhere. I suppose I should be worrying about whether they're going to kidnap us too. But that doesn't bother me. I keep thinking it won't happen, or if it does, I'll at least be with you.

The only thing that keeps me calm is drink. Not that I'm getting drunk. Just enough to relax. I sit here thinking about you and how nice this place would be if I was here with you on holiday, like in Brazil. We could sunbathe for an hour or so — if the sun came out; it always seems to be cloudy — then have a meal and go out sightseeing. At night we could go to some disco, assuming there's a gay one here. Then we could go and see the Inca ruins. A real holiday, just the two of us.

I phoned Eric this morning. Everything seems okay. I didn't tell him about Mario. I didn't want him getting his hopes up. Or he might tell Anne and George, and Guy would get to hear of it and things would start to go wrong. It's better this way, but I hate having to wait, having to keep it a secret.

* * *

Thursday. Nothing. Jack has run out of people to meet. We just have to wait.

Jack says one of the journalists he met thinks the whole organisation has collapsed. The leaders are in prison, a lot of the followers gave themselves up during the amnesty and no one's in charge any more. The economy is improving which means that the people are less dissatisfied and though the army still has a bad reputation, Shining Path has an even worse one. So Jack's contact thinks most of the guerrillas who are left in the field are just bandits.

That should make things easier for us. If it's true, they'll only want money. Jack says the *Sun* can offer a hundred thousand at most. More than that and they have to go to Murdoch, and God knows what he would say.

I'm on tenterhooks. I'll have to take sleeping pills again or I'll be awake all night.

* * *

Friday evening. There was a phone call for Jack. A different voice, poor English. We have to go to Cuzco tomorrow, just the two of us, stay in the Grand Hotel and wait. Cuzco! That's where you were. We are on the right track. Jack spent the afternoon at the airline office. All the flights were fully booked, but he managed to get us seats by paying a 'supplement'. Life is so easy when you have money.

* * *

Cuzco, Saturday evening. Another big hotel, full of tourists. There was only one room vacant so we have to share. Jack said the *Sun*'s accountants would be pleased, after all the money he's spent.

I've been for a walk. I've never been in such a weird place. I think we're ten thousand feet up and it's cold. Half the town is narrow streets and one-storey houses painted white; the other half is these massive buildings of big heavy black stone that the guidebook says the Incas built, cut perfectly straight and slotted together like Lego bricks. Nobody knows how they did it. Some people think spacemen came and helped them. The streets are full of backpackers and Indian women in brown bowler hats and thick woollen jerseys. They've all got Chinese eyes and they're all carrying bundles on their backs, either a sleeping kid or stuff you sell at market.

I kept passing these houses and thinking, what if Andy's just on the other side of that wall? What if he could hear me if I called out? Then I thought the guerrillas might have rung while I was out, so I rushed back to the hotel, but of course they hadn't. All that happened was that Jack had called London to tell them where he was and to confirm how much money he could offer. Maybe I could get more, I said. From Guy or Andy's parents. As a last resort, he said; but there was no point in getting others involved at this stage.

We spent the evening in the bar, trying to keep our mind off you by talking about other things. We got joined by this old American who'd just been to Machu Picchu and wanted to tell us all about it. I got bored, but Jack seemed interested. Maybe that's why he can do the job he does; he can speak to anyone and get them to talk, like he did me. Certainly it's thanks to him that we've got this far.

* * *

Sunday. It's working. Someone called but he hardly speaks English. He said he'd call back. Oh, Andy, Andy, please let it be true.

* * *

Sunday evening. Your passport! They showed us your passport. Two of them, a man and woman, in another grotty house in the middle of nowhere. She was young and short, with big breasts. He was older; he looked mean.

First we had to go to a restaurant. Then we were driven out of town. Then, even though it was dark and we had no idea where we were, we were masked and driven over a rough road to some kind of barn. The two of them were inside while the driver waited in the car.

"It doesn't prove he's alive," Jack said when he saw the passport.

"He is alive," the man said. He spoke a strange, slow English. Jack and I kept having to repeat ourselves to make sure he understood. She didn't seem to speak any English at all, and they kept stopping to talk to each other.

"Near here?" Jack asked, but they refused to answer. "So what do you want?" he went on.

"In change for McIllray?" He pronounced it funny: MacAylrey. "The release of Comrade Gonzalo."

"Who?" I asked. Their leader, Jack explained.

"We can't arrange that. We've got no connections, we're just ordinary people. We thought you wanted money."

"We do not need money," he said.

"But that's all we have."

The woman asked something and the two of them spoke for a little. She kept looking at me, but it wasn't the same way as the man in Lima; it was more curious than hostile.

"How much money?" he asked.

"Thirty thousand dollars."

He translated. There was another discussion. I was sure she was saying take the money, but he just repeated, "We do not want money."

"Well," Jack said, "maybe we should go. I have no contacts with either the British or the Peruvian government. I can't influence them. Haven't they already tried and you wouldn't even speak to them? But I think the fact that we've got this far tells me that you really do want the money. If I'm wrong, tell me, make another proposal."

Jack sounded quite reasonable about the whole business. I was going crazy. These were the people who were holding you. The very people; I was sure of it. All we had to was convince them and it wasn't working. Or maybe we just had to point a gun to their heads. Then I thought maybe they had one and if I just leap over the table and grabbed it from them...

Meanwhile the two of them had begun to argue. It was like in Lima, only much more aggressive. He had raised his voice, but she was quiet. I couldn't understand them. I wasn't even sure they were speaking Spanish, it sounded so strange. I began to shiver because it was so cold.

"What are you talking about?" Jack asked after about ten minutes.

"Nothing," the man said.

"It doesn't sound like it."

There was a pause in which we all looked at each other. Everything seemed to be going terribly wrong. "We will talk tomorrow," the man said.

"Why not now?" Jack asked.

The man shook his head. "Tomorrow."

"How can we trust you?"

"How can we trust you?" the man asked, suddenly angry. "You come from nowhere. How do we know you do not bring the police or the army? How do we know you have the money? Show us. Where is it? You have thirty thousand dollars in your jacket? Is that all you have? Perhaps you are being followed. Perhaps you have a radio that tells people where you are," he reached over and grabbed Jack's jacket. The woman pulled him back.

"We don't have anything," Jack said. "You can check if you like."

The man sat back but didn't say anything.

"What do you want to talk about tomorrow?" Jack asked. "Money?"

"We will speak to you tomorrow." He stood up, followed by the woman. He looked angry, but I was sure she was sympathetic.

"Is he all right?" I asked, looking at her. She didn't understand. I spoke to him. "Is he all right?"

"Go," he said.

I stood up, but Jack didn't. "Is he all right?" he asked. "You're right. You have no reason to trust us and we have no reason to trust you. I want proof that he's alive. A photo or a letter or something."

"We cannot do that."

"Is he all right?" I repeated, louder. The woman said something; he replied.

"We are more concerned with our people than with your..." he tried to find the word, "your friend. Believe us. He is all right. Now go."

"Tell Andy..." I wanted to tell them to tell you I loved you, but I couldn't. I thought they would just laugh at me. "Tell him we're here," I said. "Tell him we've come to bring him home." I wanted to say more but Jack had stood up and was pulling me out. "Leave it," he said. "He'll know." We walked back out to the car and let ourselves be blindfolded again. It seemed to be ages before we were back in the hotel.

I've taken two pills, but I still can't sleep. I'm so near to you, Andy, but I can't get to you. I'm frightened it's going to go wrong. Then I think they've got to let you go. Otherwise they'll have to keep you forever. They might as well get some money for you. Only maybe Jack isn't offering enough. I told him to say much more than thirty thousand, but he says they'll get round to it. I hope so. You're worth whatever it takes, whatever they want.

* * *

Monday afternoon. We still haven't heard. Jack's gone sightseeing.

* * *

Monday evening. We have to go to a different address. The car will pick us up there.

* * *

Monday night. One hundred thousand dollars. They agreed. They agreed! I knew we should have done this months ago. Now all we have to do is get the money here. Jack says it will take a day or two.

* * *

Tuesday. If we get you out tomorrow, we can fly to Lima on Thursday and get you home by Saturday. If you're okay, that is. Jack says we could get you to a doctor here, but if you've survived this long, it would be better back in England.

He's paranoid that someone's going to find out about you before we get you back into the country. He won't even tell the embassy. He's hoping if we fly back on a US airline they won't recognise your name. There'll just be the *Sun* photographer at Heathrow and then we'll have a couple of weeks at a health farm with the best doctors and no one will know. Jack says you can give him the first part of the story on the way back, and then the rest of it over the fortnight.

I can't stand the wait. I've been shopping. I've bought you sweaters — they're so cheap here — and jeans. I also bought a belt in case you've lost weight and can't keep them up. It's a good thing we're the same shoe size; you can borrow a pair of mine.

I wanted to call Eric, but Jack wouldn't let me. It hasn't happened yet, he said, besides he doesn't want anyone to know. But I can't stop thinking about getting you home. We don't need a health farm or wherever hostages go when they're released. We just need to be at home. You need to see everything again, say hi to the cats, get to know James, meet Ada, say hello to Doris. I need to show you all the clippings, everything we did to get you out. And then there's the pigsty, the land we rented out, the stall...

And then I can stop writing this diary. I'll be able to talk to you. I'll be able to see you, to hold you, to kiss you.

I need you so much, so much.

IV
Tom: Berkshire

15th October. One month. Guy says I should write it down. It will help.

It won't. It won't bring you back.

The doctor said it was straight to the heart. You wouldn't have felt anything. You may not even have known.

If I only I could blame someone. But I can't.

Jack had asked Jose Maria to make sure we were followed, in case we got into trouble. So there was a private detective from Lima that I knew nothing about, on the same flight, but staying at another hotel. On these empty roads they must have seen him. And they caught him and shot him. And then they shot you. And that morning, while Jack and I were having breakfast and waiting to call the bank to see if the money had come in, they'd taken you from the square in Cuzco where you had been dumped, along with all your notebooks, to the police station. And we sat there drinking our coffee and wondering how soon we would hear and I kept looking at my watch and thinking when I would see you, maybe by two o'clock, maybe by three o'clock. And while I was working that out, the police were calling the embassy. And the money came and while Jack made arrangements to withdraw it, I went for a walk and looked at the cathedral and bought you some souvenirs. And there we were in the hotel bedroom watching CNN while we were getting ready for lunch and they announced that your body had been found. And I didn't believe it and then I did and I broke down and cried and cried and just couldn't stop. Jack got through to the embassy and they told him it was true. And they asked me to go and identify you.

You were so thin, Andy, and so strange with that beard. But it was you. It was you. I wanted to hold you. I wanted to get on that slab and cuddle you and warm you up and bring you back to life and they wouldn't let me. I couldn't even kiss you. I couldn't even fucking kiss you. And you looked a mess, but at least you looked calm, as if you hadn't known what was happening. But I didn't want you to be dead. I wanted you to be alive and come home with me and live with me. I needed you, Andy, I needed you so much.

And then there were all the reporters and the man from the embassy and the problems of bringing you home. And it all started again with the press and everyone was mad at me for going off without telling them and sometimes it seemed everyone was blaming me for what happened — not just your parents and Guy but every single newspaper and magazine.

But it wasn't my fault, Andy, believe me, it wasn't.

* * *

In the end they sent me all your notebooks and I read them. I don't know what to make of them. You sound so confused, especially towards the end. And there's so little of me in them. All these months I was writing to you and you'd hardly mention me. At least you say you were thinking of me, but at times, especially after what happened with me and Guy, it seems that you didn't trust me. Then you say you didn't tell me enough you loved me. You didn't need to; I knew.

Guy says it's not surprising you didn't write about me much. The most important thing in your life was to persuade them to let you go. That's what was on your mind all the time. I suppose he's right.

Then there are all the drawings. I don't like them. I don't think they're very good. But they're yours, so I've framed some of them and put the rest in a collage and it's hanging here above the computer. Sometimes I think I'll take them down, because they're not what I want to remember you by.

I don't even want to read the notebooks again. I think about what they did to you that night. I think about Rosa and how she must have been the one who killed you. And I get so angry. Even more so, because they were never captured. Nobody knows where they are. But I hate them. I hate them so much.

* * *

14th December. Your fortieth birthday.

Not much has changed. I'm still on the farm. I still think of you all the time. I've got no money. Jack suggested writing a book, but I don't want to. It would be like making money out of you.

Guy still comes down sometimes. I think he wants us to be lovers, although he hasn't said anything. I couldn't; it would be a kind of betrayal. Sometimes when he's here I get angry with him, because he reminds me of you. Then I get angry with myself, because he's only trying to help; he was the person who did the most for you and me.

Anne says I have to let you go, get on with life. The farm needs me. In a way she and George and Guy, even Eric and Dave, need me. God knows, I need them.

She's right, I know. But I'll never forget you. Your picture will always be here, that one of you and me in Rio sitting on the wall. It means I love you, Andy. I always have. I always will.

THE END

Recent literary fiction from The Gay Men's Press

Rudi van Dantzig
FOR A LOST SOLDIER

During the winter of 1944 in occupied Amsterdam, eleven-year-old Jeroen is evacuated to a tiny fishing community on the desolate coast of Friesland, where he meets Walt, a young Canadian soldier with the liberating forces. Their relationship immerses the young boy in a tumultuous world of emotional and sexual experience, suddenly curtailed when the Allies move on and Walt goes away. Back home in Amsterdam, a city in the throes of liberation fever, Jeoren searches for the soldier he has lost. A child's fears and confused emotions have rarely been described with such penetration and openness, and seen as it is from the child's viewpoint it invites total empathy.

Rudi van Dantzig is artistic director of the Dutch National Ballet and a leading international choreographer. Published in Dutch in 1986, *For a Lost Soldier* received the Geertgan Lubberhuizen prize for best literary debut. The film of the book won the Best Film and Audience Prize at Turin in 1993.

"A literary happening not soon to be forgotten"
— *NRC Handelsblad*, Amsterdam

"A beautifully chronicled document of wartime life"
— *Gay Times*, London

"I was filled with admiration for the way in which Rudi van Dantzig has transformed a difficult and unusual autobiographical theme into a compelling literary work"
— *Times Literary Supplement*, London

ISBN 0 85449 237 2
UK £9.95/ US $14.95/ AUS $19.95

Noel Currer-Briggs
YOUNG MEN AT WAR

Anthony Arthur Kildwick, born in 1919 to a well-to-do Yorkshire family, finds the love of his life in a German exchange student at his public school. Both boys are passionate to avoid another war between their countries, but when Manfred returns to Germany he is seduced by Hitler's nationalist rhetoric, while Tony meets the outbreak of war as a conscientious objector. Yet as the Nazi regime shows itself ever more demonic, Tony reluctantly decides he must fight, is recruited into the Intelligence Corps, and is eventually parachuted into southern France, to work with the Resistance. There he discovers Manfred is now an officer with the occupying forces, and their paths cross again in dramatic circumstances.

Noel Currer-Briggs, well known as a writer on history and genealogy, has based this novel in part on his own experience. As well as a fascinating story, it conveys a vivid sense of the conflicts of the 1930s, and the interplay between friendship and internationalism, homosexuality and pacifism, patriotism and democracy, that was characteristic of those years.

ISBN 0 85449 236 4
UK £9.95/US$14.95/AUS$19.95

Richard Zimler
UNHOLY GHOSTS

A classical guitar teacher from New York seeks a new life in Portugal after the death of so many friends. But the *viral eclipse over sexuality* pursues him even there, when Antonio, his talented and beloved student, tests HIV-positive and threatens to give up on life. Desperate to show the young man that he still has a future, 'the Professor' arranges a car trip to Paris, hoping to be able to convince a leading virtuoso there to begin preparing his protege for a concert caareer. Antonio's father Miguel, a stonemason by trade, insists in coming along with them, and en route the three fall into a triangle of adventure, personal disclosure, violence, and at last a strange redemption.

Wittily funny and deeply moving, *Unholy Ghosts* was written with the support of the National Endowment for the Arts. Richard Zimler won the 1994 Panurge prize for his short fiction, which has been widely published in Britain and the US, and has lived in Portugal since 1990.

ISBN 0 85449 233 X
UK £9.95/US $14.95/ AUS $19.95

Gay Men's Press books can be ordered from any bookshop in the UK, North America and Australia, and from specialised bookshops elsewhere.

If you prefer to order by mail, please send cheque or postal order payable to *Book Works* for the full retail price plus £2.00 postage and packing to:

Book Works (Dept. B), PO Box 3821, London N5 1UY
phone/fax: (0171) 609 3427

For payment by Access/Eurocard/Mastercard/American Express/Visa, please give number, expiry date and signature.

Name and address in block letters please:

Name
_____

Address
_____

_____

_____